The Workhouse Girl

Dilly Court grew up in North-east London and began her career in television, writing scripts for commercials. She is married with two grown-up children and four grandchildren, and now lives in Dorset on the beautiful Jurassic Coast with her husband. She is the bestselling author of seventeen novels. She also writes under the name of Lily Baxter.

A Mother's Courage

When Eloise Cribb receives the news that her husband's ship has been lost at sea she wonders how she and her children are ever going to manage.

The Constant Heart

Despite living by the side of the Thames, eighteen-year-old Rosina May has wanted for little in life. Until her father's feud with a fellow bargeman threatens to destroy everything.

A Mother's Promise

When Hetty Huggins made a promise to her dying mother that she would look after her younger sister and brothers, little did she know how difficult this would be.

The Cockney Angel

Eighteen-year-old Irene Angel lives with her parents in a tiny room above the shop where her mother ekes out a living selling pickles and sauces, whilst her father gambles away what little money they do manage to earn.

A Mother's Wish

Since the untimely death of her husband, young mother Effie Grey has been forced to live on a narrowboat owned by her tyrannical father-in-law Jacob.

The Ragged Heiress

On a bitter winter's day, an unnamed girl lies dangerously ill in hospital. When two coarse, rough-speaking
individuals come to claim her, she can remember nothing.

A Mother's Secret

When seventeen-year-old Belinda Phillips discovers that
she is pregnant, she has no option other than to accept
an arranged marriage, and give up her child forever.

Cinderella Sister

With their father dead and their mother a stranger to
them, Lily Larkin must stay at home and keep house
whilst her brothers and sisters go out to work.

A Mother's Trust

When her feckless mother falls dangerously ill, Phoebe
Giamatti is forced to turn to the man she holds responsible for all her family's troubles.

The Lady's Maid

Despite the differences in their circumstances, Kate and
Josie have been friends since childhood. But their past
binds them together in ways they must never know.

The Best of Daughters

Daisy Lennox is drawn to the suffragette movement,
but when her father faces ruin they are forced to move
to the country and Daisy's first duty is to her family.

Dilly Court
The Workhouse Girl

arrow books

Published by Arrow Books 2013

2 4 6 8 10 9 7 5 3

Copyright © Dilly Court 2013

First published in Great Britain in 2013 by
Arrow Books
Random House, 20 Vauxhall Bridge Road,
London SW1V 2SA

www.randomhouse.co.uk

Addresses for companies within The Random House Group Limited can be found at:
www.randomhouse.co.uk/offices.htm

The Random House Group Limited Reg. No. 954009

A CIP catalogue record for this book
is available from the British Library

Typeset in Palatino by Palimpsest Book Production Limited,
Falkirk, Stirlingshire

Penguin Random House is committed to a sustainable future for
our business, our readers and our planet. This book is made from
Forest Stewardship Council® certified paper.

Printed and bound in Great Britain by Clays Ltd, Elcograf S.p.A.

For all the hardworking staff at Dorset County Hospital and a special mention for the operating department team

Chapter One

St Giles and St George Workhouse, London, 1859

'My name is Sarah Scrase, and I don't belong here.' White-faced and terrified, but defiant, Sarah clasped her small hands tightly behind her back, digging her fingernails into her palms in an attempt to control the tears that welled into her blue eyes.

'What?' Matron Trigg bellowed like a cow in calf, causing the other children in the schoolroom to huddle together in fear. 'What did you say, girl?'

'My name is Sarah Scrase and I want my ma.'

Matron Trigg turned to her husband, the workhouse master. 'Did you ever, Mr Trigg? No you did not, nor I neither. What is the world coming to when a young child speaks back to her elders and betters?'

'Shocking, Mrs Trigg. Deal with her as you see fit.' Mr Trigg beat the air with the cane he was holding, and the swishing sound sent a ripple of terrified murmurs around the classroom. 'Another peep from any of you girls and you will all feel a taste of the Tickler's anger.'

Sarah was trembling violently and a feeling of faintness almost overcame her, but she struggled to keep calm. She had already experienced the Tickler, Mr Trigg's much used method of corporal punishment, twice, and she had only been an inmate at the

1

workhouse for a few hours. The Tickler had punished her for clinging to her mother's skirts when they were first separated, and had beaten her soundly for refusing to abandon her own clothes for the grey grogram workhouse uniform, coarse calico petticoat and blue check apron, and now she was likely to endure another assault with the fearsome instrument of torture. She glanced nervously at Matron's bulldog jaw, set in a harsh line despite her flabby jowls, but she was not going to give in. 'I'm Sarah Scrase,' she whispered, 'and I want my ma.'

'Your mother is a whore,' Matron said in a voice that reverberated like a clap of thunder. 'She is no better than she should be and at this moment is giving birth to another spawn of the devil.'

'You take that back.' Forgetting everything other than the need to stand up for her beloved mother, Sarah put her head down and charged at Matron's corpulent body, butting her in the stomach and sending her staggering backwards into her husband's arms. Sarah fell to her knees, bowing her head as if waiting for the axeman's deadly stroke.

There was a moment of horrified silence and then someone giggled.

Mr Trigg thrust his wife aside and flailed the air with his cane as he grabbed Sarah by the white cap she had been forced to wear. It came off in his hand, exposing her spiky hair, which to her horror had been cropped short when she was admitted to the workhouse. Seizing her by the scruff of her neck, he dragged her to her feet. 'You are indeed the devil's daughter,' he said, bringing the cane down across her back. 'Spawn of Old Nick. Offspring of Old Scratch.'

Sarah cried out as he beat her again and again until she crumpled in a heap at his feet. He released her with a growl. 'Let that be a lesson to you.' He turned to his wife who was leaning against the teacher's desk, clutching her large bosom and groaning. 'I'll leave this brat to you, my dear. Treat her harshly. Teach her manners in any way you see fit.' He stormed out of the classroom, slamming the door behind him.

Matron Trigg raised herself, aiming a savage kick at Sarah. 'Get up.'

With difficulty, Sarah scrambled to her feet. She faced her tormentor with a defiant toss of her head. 'I'm not the devil's daughter,' she said in a low voice. 'I used to go to Sunday school regular, and he's got no right to say things about Ma. It ain't her fault that Pa got drownded in the Thames when his wherry was run down in the fog.'

'What is your name?' Matron Trigg leaned over so that her face was close to Sarah's.

'I'm Sarah Scrase.'

'Not now you ain't.' Matron's bloodshot eyes opened wide and her nostrils flared. 'I'll tell you what it is, girl. You'll bear your demon father's name for the rest of your time in this institution. From now on you will be known as Sal Scratch.' She beckoned to one of the older girls. 'Nettie Bean. Come here.'

Sarah looked round and saw an older girl making her way between the regimented lines of wooden desks. Freckle-faced and with hair the colour of gingerbread, Nettie Bean looked as though she might know how to stand up for herself. Sarah met her green-eyed gaze with a mute plea for help.

'Hurry up,' Matron Trigg said crossly. 'I haven't got all day.' Taking a sheet of paper from her desk, she dipped a pen in the inkwell. 'Can you read, Sal Scratch?'

'Yes, and I can write me name.'

Matron thrust the pen into her hand. 'Then write this – I am the devil's daughter.'

Sarah's instinct was to refuse, but her backside was still smarting from the Tickler's harsh punishment, and her ribs were sore where they had come into contact with Matron's boot.

Without waiting for the ink to dry Matron snatched the paper from her and gave it to Nettie. 'Pin it on her back. She'll wear this until she has learned her lesson.' She took a pin from her collar and put it in Nettie's outstretched hand. 'Hurry up, girl. I haven't got all day to waste on stupid and ungrateful children.'

'Sorry,' Nettie whispered as she fastened the placard to the back of Sarah's bodice.

It was barely more audible than a sigh, but the single word came as the first hint of human kindness that Sarah had encountered since she entered the fearsome building in Shorts Gardens. 'Ta,' she whispered, lifting her hand, and for a fleeting second their fingers touched. In that moment Sarah knew that she had made a friend for life.

'Get back to your seat,' Matron said, pointing to Nettie. 'And all of you write on your slates – I must not speak to Sal Scratch.' She pushed Sarah off the podium with a vicious prod in the ribs. 'Go and stand in the corner. You'll remain there until the end of the lesson.'

Sarah stumbled and only just saved herself from falling on her face, but no one laughed. Heads were bent over slates and the scrape of the girls' slate pencils and laboured breathing filled the air. Sarah stood in the corner, hands clasped firmly in front of her, willing herself not to cry. She closed her eyes, praying silently for her mother, who had been in labour for two days before desperation drove her to the workhouse door. Sarah had been present on two occasions when her mother went into premature labour, and the tiny infants had barely taken their first breaths when they had given up the struggle for life. No doubt they were in heaven with Pa, but he was buried in a pauper's grave. There had been no money to buy him a plot or even a headstone.

Sarah had loved her pa, but she had also been a bit frightened of him. Big, muscular and inclined to fits of temper, Jed Scrase had been a force to be reckoned with, but he had also been a gambling man. Drink had not been his major vice, but he would bet on anything from a bare knuckle fight to dog ratting, and the money he earned as a wherryman was often gone before he arrived home at night. They had lived mainly off her mother's earnings as a cleaner in the Theatre Royal, Drury Lane, which was close to the rooms they rented in Vinegar Yard. Sarah's education had been gained from watching the actors during rehearsals, and she had learned to read by studying the programmes and billboards. The theatrical folk had taken her to their hearts, and by the time she was five years old she could recite whole passages from dramas by Boucicault without faltering. She had also been quite a favourite with the ballet dancers, especially when as a toddler she had climbed onto the stage during rehearsals and attempted to copy their graceful movements.

None of this helped her now as she stood for a painful hour, suffering muscle cramps and increasing exhaustion while the class was tested for spelling and times tables. Eventually the lesson came to an end and they were dismissed. Matron Trigg left the room, apparently having forgotten Sarah's existence, and she was left wondering what to do. Did she stand here all day and maybe all night, until someone discovered her? Or should she follow the rest of the girls?

Nettie was the last to file out of the classroom but she hesitated in the doorway and beckoned to Sarah. 'You'd best come with us. I think old bitch-face has forgotten you.'

Sarah would have giggled at this had she not been quite so scared. 'But – but she said I had to stay here.'

'You can if you like, but she'll have gone off to her office to drink tea and eat cake while we pick oakum in the yard.' Nettie held out her hand. 'Come on. I'll show you where to go and what to do.'

Sarah needed no second bidding. She ran to join Nettie and was about to rip the offending sign from her bodice when her new friend shook her head. 'I'd leave that on if I was you. She'll lock you in the cellar with the rats and spiders if you take it off. She might have forgot you now, but her memory ain't that bad, Sarah.'

Sarah smiled shyly. 'Ta, Nettie.'

'For what? I done nothing.'

'You called me by my proper name. I'm not Sal Scratch.'

Nettie grinned, revealing a missing eye tooth. 'Not to me, nipper, but if the old besom has anything to do with it you'll be Sal Scratch until you're old enough to be sold to the highest bidder.' She took Sarah by the hand and hurried down the dark corridor after the rest of the girls.

'Sold? They'll sell us?'

'They call us pauper apprentices, but it means the same. I've seen it happen often enough. You get these fat old mill owners who pay the workhouse master for boys and girls to work for them. I suppose it'll be my turn next.'

'No. You mustn't leave me,' Sarah cried, clutching her hand even tighter. 'What if Ma dies? I'll be all alone in the world.'

'Then you'll be the same as most of us in this place. Some of us, like me for instance, was dumped here as babies, and there ain't no escape unless we go to work at the mill or go into service. You just got to be brave, Sarah. Do what they tell you, but don't let them beat the spirit out of you.'

'You there. Nettie Bean.' A stentorian voice from the end of the passageway made them both jump. 'Stop talking and get to the women's yard now or you'll be on bread and water for the rest of the week.'

'That's Stoner,' Nettie whispered. 'He's the superintendent of outdoor labour. You don't want to fall foul of him. If you think that Matron Trigg is a dragon then he's a demon from hell.' She broke into a run, dragging Sarah behind her.

They arrived in the yard just in time to file in at the end of the line. The sight that met Sarah's eyes made her heart sink even further. Rows of women sat on wooden benches tugging at lengths of tarred rope with their bare fingers in order to extract the strands of hemp. The late autumn sun beat down on their heads and it was hot and airless in the enclosed area of the yard. Even from a distance Sarah could see that the women's fingers were raw and bleeding from picking at the salt-stiffened fibres.

'We do this until dinnertime,' Nettie whispered, seemingly regardless of the fact that the man Stoner was glaring at her beneath beetling black eyebrows. Sarah blinked, not daring to acknowledge this piece of information in case it brought his wrath down upon her head. She knew that she was an object of curiosity, if not pity, as she sported the damning sign. She had seen one of the women, who presumably could read, cross herself at the sight of the devil's child.

As she shuffled along behind Nettie towards the area set aside for the younger girls, Sarah glanced up at the building which towered five storeys above her. She had heard someone say that the lying-in ward was on the topmost floor beneath the roof. Ma was surely closer to heaven up there, but Sarah could only hope that she did not go there too soon.

'You there. Pay attention.' Stoner's loud bellow made her jump and she realised with a sinking heart that he was pointing at her. She huddled a little closer to Nettie but he reached out and grabbed her by the ear. 'So you're the devil's daughter, are you? Well, I'm Beelzebub hisself and if you don't behave yourself, little girl, I'll strike you dead on the spot.' He leaned over her and his breath stank of stale beer and tooth decay. 'D'you understand what I'm saying?'

'Y-yes, sir.' Sarah swallowed the bile that rose in her throat and threatened to make her vomit all over Stoner's dusty boots.

He gave her a shove that sent her sprawling on the bench beside Nettie. 'Show the brat what to do, Bean. I'll be round to check, so no slacking.' His cold grey stare encompassed the rest of the girls, who had already begun their onerous task. 'That goes for all of you.' With his hands clasped tightly behind his back he proceeded to walk slowly along the row and back again. Apparently satisfied with their prowess, he turned his attention to the older women.

Nettie waited until he was out of earshot before heaving a sigh of relief. 'He's a bastard, that one. We all hate him even worse than Trigg, and that's saying something.'

Sarah was doing her best to extract the fibres from the tarred rope, but her hands were small and her fingers were already beginning to hurt. 'Is it always like this?'

'No, love. Sometimes it's much worse.' Nettie bent her head over her work. 'You'll get used to it.'

By midday Sarah was exhausted and her fingers were a bleeding mass of broken blisters. She had been up before six o'clock that morning and had eaten nothing since a meagre breakfast of a slice of stale bread. After three hours in the schoolroom and two hours of picking oakum, she was barely able to stand when the dinner bell rang. Nettie helped her to her feet but Sarah had to walk to the refectory unaided, and she stumbled several times before she reached the large, echoing room filled with trestle tables and narrow forms. The meal of thin soup and a hunk of bread was barely edible but she was so hungry that by this time she did not care. There was silence except for the sound of the women and children slurping the tasteless broth and slapping their lips as though it were nectar from heaven.

Despite her physical discomfort, Sarah's only thoughts were for her mother. She was determined to get to the lying-in ward one way or another, but it proved almost impossible. Their every movement was watched by someone in authority, and after the tables were cleared and scrubbed until they were bleached bone-white, and the floors had been swept clean, it was time to return to work. The women went back to the yard to continue picking oakum, but the girls were divided up and some went to the sewing room and the others, including Nettie and Sarah, were given buckets and scrubbing brushes and strict instructions to clean the corridors and staircases until they were spotless.

This was something that Sarah had often done in the theatre when her mother was unwell or too far advanced in pregnancy. She filled her bucket and rolled up her sleeves. The cold water soothed her sore hands but the coarse lye soap stung when it touched the raw flesh. She did her best to ignore the pain as she made her way up five flights of stairs to the top floor. No one, it seemed, was eager to start at the top but it gave her the opportunity of sneaking into the female ward.

The heat beneath the rafters was suffocating, and the smell of blood almost knocked her sideways as she crept into the lying-in ward. The moans and screams of the women in labour filled her with horror, and she was tempted to turn and run, but somehow she forced herself to keep going. She tiptoed between the rows of iron beds, hardly daring to look at the tortured faces of the women as they struggled to give birth. The midwives were too busy to notice one small child in their midst, and Sarah was able to get to the far end of the room without being apprehended. She found her mother lying white-faced and still amongst blood-stained sheets. Her eyes were glazed and her lips moved silently as if in prayer.

Sarah went down on her knees at her mother's bedside, taking her hand and holding it to her cheek. 'Ma, speak to me.'

Ellen Scrase turned her head slowly, focusing her eyes on her daughter. 'My Sarah.'

11

'Ma, they wouldn't let me see you, but I came anyway.'

Ellen twisted her lips in a caricature of a smile. 'Don't cry, love. I can't bear to see you in tears.'

Sarah sniffed and wiped her eyes on the back of her hand. She glanced anxiously at her mother's flat belly, but there was no sign of the baby. 'Is it . . .'

'Gone to join his pa in heaven, darling. It wasn't meant to be, Sarah.'

'But you're all right, Ma. You'll be up and about soon.'

Ellen's eyelids fluttered and closed for a second but she opened them again. 'I think not, love.' Her voice was faint and her breathing laboured.

Fear greater than anything she had ever known created panic in Sarah's heart and she chafed her mother's cold hand. 'Don't die, Ma. You got to get well. You can't go to Pa and the boys and leave me in this dreadful place.'

'Come closer.'

Sarah leaned over and her tears mingled with her mother's. 'Please don't go. I love you, Ma.'

'I'm dying.'

'No, Ma. You're not.' Sarah clutched her mother's cold hand, holding it against her cheek. 'I won't let you die.'

'Come away from there.' A hand jerked Sarah to her feet. 'What are you doing up here, girl? Don't you know it's against the rules?'

Sarah kicked out but the nurse had her in an iron grip. 'Let me go. I won't leave Ma.'

The woman shook her like a terrier with a rat. 'She's

left you already by the look of her,' she said wearily. She picked Sarah up bodily and thrust her into the arms of one of her colleagues, who had rushed to her assistance. 'Take the kid away, Nurse Brown. I'll see to the dead woman.'

'No.' Sarah was carried, kicking and screaming, from the ward, and dumped unceremoniously outside the door.

'Get back to work,' Nurse Brown said, giving her a push towards the bucket and scrubbing brush which Sarah had left on the narrow landing. 'Take a tip from me and make yourself scarce. This ain't no place for a nipper of your age.' She closed the door, and the sound of the bolt being shot into place echoed in Sarah's ears. She sank down on her knees, bowing her head. She was alone in the world with no one to love and care for her. If only she could die too, and join her family in heaven.

The touch of a hand on her shoulder made Sarah jump. She raised her tear-stained face to see Nettie gazing anxiously down at her. 'I've been looking for you. What are you doing up here?'

'My ma's dead.'

'So is mine,' Nettie said in a matter-of-fact voice. 'You won't get no sympathy here, dearie. Don't let them see you cry or it'll make things worse.'

Sarah had to bite her bottom lip in order to stop it trembling. 'They can't get no worse.'

'I'll look after you.' Nettie helped her to her feet. 'Pick up your bucket and try to be brave. I know it's hard, but if they sees you got a weakness, the

13

stink-pots will make your life hell. Do as I do and keep your head down. You'll be all right.'

Sarah allowed herself to be led downstairs, moving like a sleepwalker, barely aware of her surroundings as the pain in her heart threatened to engulf her in a bottomless pit of misery. Nettie emptied her bucket in the back yard, tipping the contents onto the cobblestones. 'Go on, Sarah. Empty yours, there's a good girl. We ain't got all day.'

Sarah did as she was told, staring at the filthy water as it pooled at her feet. She had to combat the sudden urge to throw herself face down in the muddy morass so that she might drown, and join her family in that mystical place above the clouds. Above her the sun shone from an azure sky with tiny white clouds drifting across the celestial blue. She tried to imagine Ma reclining on one of them as she made her journey to heaven, but all she could see in her mind's eye was the waxen face of her dead mother, and she knew the image would remain with her for the rest of her life.

'Come on, Sarah,' Nettie said, prodding her gently in the ribs. 'We got work to do.' She led her unprotesting into the building where they deposited the empty buckets and collected dusters and polish. Blindly following Nettie's example, Sarah did her best but she was small for her age and undernourished. She was attempting to polish one of the benches in the refectory when the necessity to sleep was so overwhelming that she lay down on the floor and curled up in a ball. She was awakened by the strident tones of Matron Trigg. 'Nettie Bean. Come here, girl.'

'Yes, Matron.'

Sarah could hear the clatter of Nettie's shoes on the bare floorboards as she hurried from the far end of the room. She stretched cautiously, not wanting to draw attention to herself.

'Where is the new girl? Where's that wicked Sal Scratch? You were supposed to be keeping an eye on her.'

A screech of pain from Nettie brought Sarah to her senses and she sprang to her feet. 'Leave her alone. She ain't done nothing wrong, missis.'

Matron Trigg released Nettie's ear with a spiteful tweak and she advanced on Sarah, rolling up her sleeves. 'You were asleep, you lazy little brat. It'll be another taste of the Tickler for you.'

'No, please don't beat her again, Matron,' Nettie cried passionately. 'It were my fault. I'm the one what should be punished.'

'And you will be,' Matron Trigg said with a twist of her thin lips. 'There'll be no supper for either of you.'

'I don't care,' Sarah shouted, shaking her fist. 'My ma's dead. You can kill me too, if you want. I wish you would.'

'Wicked child.' Matron Trigg cast her eyes heavenward. 'You really are the devil's spawn, Sal Scratch. It's the coal cellar for you and Bean. After a night down there, you'll change your tune.'

Huddled against Nettie in the pitch darkness of the coal cellar, Sarah had no more tears to cry. Hunger and cold had numbed her small body, and she felt herself drifting in space like a dandelion clock. Nettie was shivering violently, but she wrapped her arms around Sarah and held her close. 'It's all right, dearie. There ain't nothing down here what can hurt more than old Tickler. Us can't see the spiders and the rats are too clever to come where there ain't no food.'

'I'm hungry,' Sarah whispered, 'and thirsty.'

'Me too, but we got to wait until bitch-face lets us out in the morning, so we'd best try to sleep.'

'I hate her and I hate this place.'

Nettie uttered a hollow laugh. 'You and me both, but one day I'll get out of here and I'll take you too.'

'Will you? Promise?'

'Cross me heart and hope to die.'

'Don't say that. It might come true.'

'Not me, Sarah. I'm going to live forever, and I'm going to see that bitch-face and her old man get what's coming to them. One day I'll be rich and famous, and I'll set all of them what lives here free. How about that?'

Sarah snuggled against Nettie's flat chest, resting her head against her shoulder. 'I believe you.'

'I'll marry a rich toff,' Nettie murmured, rubbing her cheek against Sarah's shorn head. 'You can come and live in me great big house, and have three square meals a day and all the chocolate you can eat.'

'Sing to me, Nettie. Ma used to sing me to sleep when I was little.'

'You ain't so big now, dearie.'

'Please sing a song. I'm scared of the dark.'

Nettie gave her a hug and began to croon a lullaby,

filling in gaps where she had forgotten the words by humming. Sarah tried to imagine that it was her mother's sweet voice singing her to sleep and eventually she drifted into a state of oblivion. But it was not to last. She was rudely awakened by the creaking of the hinges on the cellar door and the sound of heavy footsteps on the flagstone floor. Blinded by the light from a lantern held above their heads, Sarah and Nettie struggled to their feet.

'If you girls think last night was your punishment, you got another think coming.' Workhouse master Trigg raised his arm and the familiar sound of the Tickler swishing though the dank air made Sarah go weak at the knees.

Chapter Two

Matron Trigg hated her and did not bother to make a secret of it. Sarah suffered miserably at her hands, but there was nothing she could do to prevent the sadistic bullying that continued to make her life a living hell. She bore the name Sal Scratch with as much dignity as she could muster, but she often found herself wishing that she really was the devil's daughter. If that were the case she would invoke her satanic father and beg him to do his worst to Matron Trigg and the workhouse master. She would like to watch them suffer in purgatory together with Stoner and the midwife who would not allow her to say her last goodbye to her dead mother.

The only respite that Sarah could look forward to was the three hours she spent in class every morning except Sundays. Apart from Nettie, who was her only true friend, there was only one person in her small world who treated Sarah with any degree of humanity and kindness, and that was the schoolteacher, Miss Parfitt. The girls had nicknamed her Miss Perfect, and to Sarah she was the next best thing to a saint. With lustrous dark hair and smiling brown eyes, Pearl Parfitt was not only beautiful but she smelled of lavender and spoke in a soft melodious voice, quite unlike Matron Trigg's metallic tones.

It was rumoured that Miss Parfitt had been engaged to be married, but her fiancé had been killed in the Crimean War, and the gold-mounted mourning brooch which she wore at the neck of her starched white blouse contained a lock of her dead love's hair. Whether or not it was true, the notion of a broken-hearted young woman who had forsaken the world to devote her life to the poor and needy lent Miss Parfitt a romantic, almost mystical aura that was not lost on Sarah. She clung to every word her teacher uttered and did her utmost to earn her praise, working hard in every lesson and impressing Miss Parfitt with her ability to remember the passages from Shakespeare that she had learned parrot-fashion backstage at the Theatre Royal. If Miss Parfitt was curious about this fount of knowledge in one so young and underprivileged, she was too well trained to single Sarah out in a class of girls most of whom could barely write their own names. But as the months went by she gradually drew the information from Sarah and encouraged her to further her education.

After a year of enduring the torments of the workhouse Sarah had learned to live with the monotonous routine, the near starvation diet, the rigorous discipline and the punishments that were meted out with blatant disregard to fairness or clemency. There was one shining light in Sarah's blighted existence. She thought of her beloved Miss Parfitt as her guardian angel, although there was little that even an angel could do to protect her from continued persecution by Matron

Trigg, and there were the all too frequent beatings meted out by the Tickler. The cane had a mind and will of its own, according to the workhouse master, who simply provided the muscle.

Sarah survived with Nettie's help, but a few months before her tenth birthday she had to face a situation that threatened to destroy her fragile world. The older boys and girls were summoned to appear before the workhouse master, and Nettie was amongst them. Sarah clung to her hand, but a warning glare from Matron Trigg was enough to send Nettie on her way without a backwards glance. There was silence in the classroom until the door closed, leaving the younger children alone with Miss Parfitt.

'Please, miss,' Sarah said, putting up her hand. 'Where are they going?'

Miss Parfitt met her anxious gaze with an attempt at a smile. 'There are kind and generous mill owners and other men of business who take on pauper apprentices. Your friends are old enough to go out into the world and be trained to do useful work and earn their own living.'

'Nettie is only eleven, miss.'

'That's correct, Sarah. You will get your chance one day too. Now I must ask all of you to get on with your sums.'

'No.' Sarah leapt to her feet. 'I won't.' She ran to the door, wrenched it open and raced after the orderly procession of children as they marched towards the main hall. She caught up with Nettie, and despite Matron Trigg's efforts to prise them apart she clung to her friend, refusing to let go.

'What's going on there?' Trigg demanded from his lofty position on the dais which put him head and shoulders above the assembled businessmen, who were looking on in amazement. 'What's all that racket, Mrs Trigg?'

'Nothing that I can't handle, my dear,' Mrs Trigg said, tugging viciously at Sarah's hair, which had grown considerably in the past two years and had come loose when Matron slapped her round the head, knocking her cap to the ground.

'What sort of discipline do you call this, Trigg?' A rubicund gentleman with mutton-chop whiskers glared at Sarah, shaking his head. 'Appalling conduct.'

'Send the child back to the classroom, ma'am.' Trigg's fleshy features flushed crimson and his eyes bulged in their sockets. He ran his finger round the inside of his tight shirt collar. 'Get her out of here.'

Matron Trigg grabbed Sarah by the arm, tugging with all her considerable might but she only succeeded in pulling both girls off their feet and all three of them ended up in a heap on the floor. 'You'll pay for this, Sal Scratch,' she hissed.

Nettie scrambled to her feet and helped Sarah to stand. 'You got to let go, dearie,' she whispered. 'I can't take you with me. I dunno where I'll end up, and if you don't do as she says we'll both be sent to the cellar for a month on bread and water.'

'You'll be lucky if you're let out this side of Christmas,' Matron Trigg groaned as she floundered on the floor-boards in a tangle of hoops and red flannel petticoats. 'Help me up, someone. Don't gawp at me, you bloody fools.'

A dapper gentleman wearing a grey frock coat and top hat hurried to her assistance. With some difficulty he raised her to her feet. 'There you are, ma'am. No harm done, I think.'

'No harm?' Matron Trigg pushed him away. 'That daughter of Satan has been the cause of nothing but trouble since the day she came to this establishment.' She fanned herself vigorously with her hand. 'Mr Trigg, do something.'

'Stoner.' Trigg's voice echoed off the rafters. 'Stoner, get in here now and take that devil child away.'

'Just a moment, sir.' The gentleman who had come to Matron Trigg's assistance peered at Sarah. 'This person is very young and is in an obvious state of distress.' He leaned closer. 'Is this your sister, little girl?'

'No, sir. Nettie's me best friend. I ain't letting go of her. You can cut me arm off and I'll still cling on.'

'I am so sorry, Mr Arbuthnot.' Trigg stepped off the podium and hurried to his side, panting from the exertion. 'This has never happened before. We run the workhouse on very strict lines. Discipline is paramount when dealing with the scum from the gutters.'

'Harsh words indeed, Mr Trigg.' Mr Arbuthnot laid his hand on Sarah's shoulder. 'This child appears to be genuinely distressed.'

'She'll be punished severely, sir. Mark my words.' Matron Trigg moved to her husband's side. 'We won't tolerate such indiscipline.'

'That's not what I meant, ma'am.' Mr Arbuthnot turned to Nettie. 'How old are you, and what's your name, my girl?'

'Nettie Bean, sir. I'm eleven but I'll soon be twelve.'

He turned his attention to Sarah. 'And your name and age, my dear. Don't be afraid, I merely want to ascertain the facts.'

'Sarah Scrase, sir. I'm nine, but I'll soon be ten.'

Mr Arbuthnot's lips twitched but he maintained a straight face. He turned to the workhouse master. 'They're just children, Trigg. Is there no way these two girls could stay together?'

A murmur ran through the waiting gentlemen and one of them stepped forward. 'This is all very well, Arbuthnot, but we're here to do business. I want six strong lads for my manufactory at Wapping and I can't afford to waste time like this.'

'I'm sorry, Crawley, but this seems to me to be a matter of conscience.'

'We're all here to do our best for the poor unfortunates,' Matron Trigg said with an obsequious smile. 'Might we get on with the business in hand, sir?' She grabbed Sarah by the ear. 'Come with me, sweetheart. I'll take you back to the classroom where you were studying the bible.'

Taken by surprise and wincing as Matron Trigg pinched her earlobe, Sarah loosened her grip on Nettie's arm. 'No. Don't let her take me, sir.' She sent a pleading look at Arbuthnot. 'I can read and write, and I can recite Shakespeare. I work hard, sir.' She held out a calloused hand. 'I didn't get these from sitting on me backside all day, sir.'

A ripple of laughter ran around the room and some of the children sniggered. Trigg held up his hand. 'Silence. This is a serious matter.'

Arbuthnot took out a bulging wallet. 'Then to settle it, Mr Trigg, I'll give you ten pounds for Nettie Bean and five pounds for the younger girl.'

'She's too young, sir,' Matron Trigg said, tightening her grip on Sarah's ear. 'We can't allow a child of this age to leave us.'

Arbuthnot narrowed his eyes. 'Or is it that by keeping her in this sorry state for another year or two you'll get a higher price for her?'

'Slander, sir,' Trigg said, bristling. 'That is a slanderous remark.'

'Fifteen pounds.' Arbuthnot took the notes from his wallet. 'I'll have the indentures made out for the elder girl and the young one will be found suitable work in my house until she is old enough to join the other apprentices in the mill. Have you any further objections?'

'Get on with it, man.' One of the other gentlemen pushed to the front. 'Like Crawley I haven't got time for all this.'

Sarah could see that Mr Crawley was growing even more impatient, and the others were nodding in agreement. She held her breath, waiting for Mr Trigg's decision.

'Very well.' Reluctantly, Trigg shook Arbuthnot's hand. 'We're well rid of her. I just hope you don't live to regret your decision, sir.'

Mr Arbuthnot reached out to take Sarah's hand. 'You can release her now, Mrs Trigg. I'm relieving you of this young girl in the hope of giving her a better chance in life, and I'd prefer it if she came to us with both ears intact.'

Sarah and Nettie huddled together in the corner of Mr Arbuthnot's private carriage, clutching each other for comfort as the horses maintained a steady pace through the crowded streets. Mr Arbuthnot said very little during the journey and seemed to be more interested in the contents of *The Times* newspaper than he was in making conversation. Sarah stared out of the window and was finding it hard to take in the size and scale of the city. Until now her world had been centred on Covent Garden and St Giles, but she was beginning to realise that London was a much bigger place than she could ever have imagined. The roads narrowed as they approached the heart of the City and the buildings became even more impressive. Her eyes almost popped out of her head when they drove past a huge edifice that looked like a castle. 'What's that place, Nettie?'

'I dunno. Never seen nothing like it.'

Mr Arbuthnot looked over the top of his newspaper. 'It's the Tower of London. That's where wicked people were imprisoned and where traitors are sent to be executed on the block.'

Sarah had no idea what a traitor had done to receive such a terrible punishment, but she decided that she had better be good or she might end up in the Tower. She glanced at Nettie, who looked even paler than normal, and she squeezed her hand. 'Don't worry,' she whispered. 'It won't happen to us.'

'Not unless you do something really bad,' Mr Arbuthnot said with a wry smile. He folded his newspaper and laid it on the seat beside him. 'We're nearly there.'

'What will happen to us then?' Sarah had not meant to blurt out the question but she had been studying their mentor's face and had noted the crinkly lines at the corners of his eyes and mouth, which made him look as though he smiled rather a lot. He reminded her of Charlie Potts, who had played character roles in the theatre. Charlie had liked a drop or two of tiddley, but he was a good sort really, and he had a seemingly endless supply of sugared almonds in his dressing room. She licked her lips as she recalled the sweet crunch of the sugar shell and the delicious taste of the almond inside: Charlie could be very generous, especially when he had been taking a glass or two of gin to steady his nerves.

'I haven't quite decided yet,' Mr Arbuthnot said, eyeing her thoughtfully. 'You're very small for your age. We'll have to see, but I think my wife might have some ideas on the subject.' His gaze shifted to Nettie and he frowned. 'Perhaps I should have chosen a strong lad rather than a girl, but I'm sure we can find something for you to do in the sugar mill.'

'Sugar?' Nettie breathed. 'You make sugar, guvner? I love sugar.'

Sarah's mouth watered and she licked her lips, imagining endless supplies of sweetmeats. It sounded like heaven.

Mr Arbuthnot smiled benevolently. 'Perhaps you are

the right girl for me, young Nettie. I'm sure we'll find something to occupy you. However, the first thing on the agenda will be to find you girls something to wear other than that hideous uniform.'

Mrs Arbuthnot echoed these sentiments within moments of meeting them. Sarah had hung back, attempting to hide behind Nettie, but Mrs Arbuthnot's pleasant face was almost a mirror image of her husband's. Neither of them could be described as handsome, but kindness from an adult was something that Sarah had experienced very little during her time in the workhouse and she found herself melting beneath the nice lady's gentle smile. Mrs Arbuthnot turned to her husband with a determined nod of her head. 'You're quite right, James. These children must have new and more suitable clothes. I'll send Dorcas with a note to my dressmaker and she can come here and measure the girls for whatever they need.'

He leaned forward to kiss her on the cheek. 'I knew that you would want to help them, Sophia. I should have taken on a couple of boys, but when I saw these two poor little orphans clinging to each other as if they were drowning, I simply had to rescue them. I've a good mind to report Trigg and his abominable wife to the board of governors.'

'Quite right too,' Mrs Arbuthnot said firmly. 'You must do that as soon as possible, but what is more important now is to get the girls something to eat. I'm sure they must be hungry.'

'I daresay the food in that place leaves a lot to be

desired.' Mr Arbuthnot picked up his top hat and cane. 'I must get back to the mill, but I'll come home early and we can decide what's best for them then.'

'I think that's settled already, my love.'

'I had a feeling it might have been.' He left the room, closing the door behind him.

'If you please, missis,' Nettie said, bobbing a curtsey. 'What are we to do? We can scrub and clean and the like.'

'We'll talk about that later.' Mrs Arbuthnot tugged at an embroidered bell pull. 'In the meantime Dorcas will take you to the kitchen and Cook will look after you while I write a note to my dressmaker.'

Almost as if she had been summoned by the mere mention of her name, Dorcas entered the room. She bobbed a curtsey to her mistress. 'You rang, ma'am?'

Sarah shifted uncomfortably from one foot to the other beneath Dorcas's curious stare. She felt Nettie's fingers close around her hand and they moved closer together.

Mrs Arbuthnot gave them a reassuring smile. 'Dorcas will take you to the kitchen and Cook will give you something to eat.'

Sarah nodded mutely and Nettie squeezed her hand, grinning broadly.

'Tell Cook to make sure they are fed well,' Mrs Arbuthnot said firmly. 'Then I have an errand for you, Dorcas.'

'Yes'm. I'll be back directly.' Dorcas opened the door and beckoned. 'Come along then.'

'Thank you, Mrs Arbuthnot,' Sarah said, remembering

her manners. Ma had always been particular about how to behave and she did not want to let her down now.

'Yes'm, thank you,' Nettie murmured as she and Sarah followed Dorcas out of the room.

Once outside in the hallway, Dorcas stopped for a moment to look them up and down with a critical but not unfriendly expression. 'So where've you two come from then? Them duds look like workhouse clothes to me.'

'You're so sharp you must've spent the night in the knife box,' Nettie said, sticking out her chin as if spoiling for a fight.

Sarah tugged at her sleeve. 'She didn't mean nothing by it. Don't start a ruckus here.'

'Better watch your tongue, Ginger,' Dorcas said crossly. 'Take the little 'un's advice and mind your manners, especially in front of Cook. She'll take a ladle to your backside if you cheek her.'

Nettie tossed her head. 'I've had worse from the Tickler, and don't call me Ginger. Me name's Nettie Bean, and this here is Sarah Scrase.'

Dorcas sniffed and turned away.

'Please be nice,' Sarah whispered. 'Don't get us thrown out of this lovely house. I never seen anything like it afore.' She hurried after Dorcas, her small feet pitter-pattering on the polished oak floorboards. She wished that she could walk more slowly so that she could absorb every last detail of the richly patterned emerald-green wallpaper, the gilt-framed paintings of rather sombre pastoral scenes, and the brass candle sconces with expensive candles waiting to be lit at dusk. Mr Arbuthnot must be very rich to afford such a luxury, she thought, resisting the urge to run her finger down the velvet-smooth wax. At the workhouse they had used the much cheaper ones made from tallow, and when they lived in Vinegar Street Ma had soaked scraps of rag in tallow oil, which had given very little light and had filled their old lodgings with the smell of rancid mutton fat. 'This is a lovely house,' she whispered to Nettie. 'Mr Arbuthnot must be very wealthy.'

Dorcas glanced over her shoulder with a superior smile. 'The master's got the biggest and best sugar house in these parts. Come along, don't dawdle.' She led them down a narrow staircase to the basement kitchen.

The appetising aroma of roasting meat and fried onions made Sarah's stomach growl with hunger. She had eaten nothing but bread, gruel and thin vegetable soup for the past year and her diet in Vinegar Yard had been little better. Nettie licked her lips and sniffed the air like a ravenous hound.

'Well, now. What have we here?' A comely woman in her middle years stopped rolling out pastry to give them a steady look.

'These two are the master's latest charity cases, Mrs Burgess.' Dorcas propelled them forward with a gentle push. 'This one is Nettie Bean and the little 'un is Sarah something-or-other.'

'No,' Sarah said, alarmed at the prospect of being given yet another nickname. 'That's not me name, ma'am. I'm Sarah Scrase and I'm very hungry.'

'You may call me Cook,' Mrs Burgess said, beaming. 'I can see from your clothes that you've been rescued from one of those dreadful places, and you both look half-starved. Sit down and I'll find you something nice to eat.'

Sarah had to pinch herself to make certain she was not dreaming. She had almost forgotten that there were kind and generous people in the world other than her beloved Miss Parfitt. The only regret she had when leaving the workhouse was that she would never see her guardian angel again.

Nettie dug her in the ribs. 'Do as she says, or she'll think you're simple-minded or something.'

Dorcas snatched her bonnet and shawl from a wall peg. 'I've got to run an errand for the missis, Cook. I'll be as quick as I can.'

'All right, but don't stop to flirt with any of those big, good-looking German lads from the sugar house.'

Sarah glanced anxiously at Cook and was relieved to see her smiling, despite her stern warning, and Dorcas did not seem to be the least bit put out.

'I've got a gentleman friend, Cook, and well you know it. My Wally would take it very much amiss if I was to flirt with the sugar bakers, even if some of them are handsome, jolly fellows.' With a spirited toss of her head Dorcas pranced out of the room and her footsteps echoed on the wooden treads as she ascended the stairs.

Nettie and Sarah exchanged surprised looks, but Mrs Burgess merely laughed and moved to the range. Taking the lid off a large black saucepan she ladled soup into two bowls and placed them on the table. 'There you are, girlies. I'll cut you some bread and there's butter in the dish. Help yourselves.'

Sarah's heart sank when she realised they were to have soup, but one taste of the delicious broth filled with chunks of meat and vegetables was enough to dispel her fears. 'This is good,' she said, shovelling bread and butter into her mouth. She had learned to be quick in the workhouse or someone would snatch the food from beneath your nose.

Nettie was also gobbling her meal and had almost cleared her plate when Cook rapped on the tabletop with the ladle. 'I've seen better manners in a pigsty.' She pointed at them, frowning. 'Beware, for only fools in rags and beggars old in sin, mistake themselves for carpet bags and tumble vittles in.' Her sonorous tones echoed round the kitchen.

Sarah gulped and swallowed. 'Sorry, missis. But this is the first nice grub we've had for as long as I can remember.'

'Is there any more?' Nettie held up her empty plate.

Cook's stern expression melted into a sympathetic smile. 'Of course there is.' She lifted the pan to the table and refilled their bowls. 'The master never begrudges a penny spent on good nourishing food. Eat up, but don't make yourselves sick. There'll be more to come if you're going to stay here awhile, but that's up to sir and madam, not me.'

Sarah ate more slowly this time and was beginning to feel extremely full, but she managed to finish her meal. Nettie let out a loud belch and immediately apologised. 'Sorry, missis. It just came out.'

'I'll excuse you this time, young lady. But don't do it again. Bad manners don't get you anywhere in this world. You've got a lot to learn.'

'And I will,' Nettie said, sticking out her chin. 'One day I'm going to be a lady and wear silk gowns and travel in me own carriage.'

'You'll have to be very rich.' Sarah licked each of her fingers in turn and received a warning glance from Cook, who tossed a drying cloth at Nettie.

'That's as maybe, but in the meantime, miss, you can wash the dishes you've used and the little one can dry them and put them away. Everyone has to earn their keep and Betty, the scullery maid, has gone to the market to buy fresh vegetables, that's if the silly girl can remember what was on the list, for she cannot read or write.'

Nettie jumped to her feet and began piling up the dirty crockery. 'I'll do whatever you ask, missis. I'm not a shirker.'

'I can read and write,' Sarah said shyly. She did not want to boast but she felt that she must find some way to repay Cook's kindness. 'Perhaps I could go with Betty next time and tell her what you've written down.'

'At least they taught you something in the workhouse.' Cook picked up the rolling pin and sprinkled the pastry with a little flour. 'I've got work to do or Mr Arbuthnot won't get his favourite pie for dinner tonight, so you girls keep out of my way and then we'll all be happy.'

Nettie hurried through to the scullery carrying a pile of crockery. 'Come and help me, Sarah. Don't stand there doing nothing.'

'Coming.' Sarah rose from the table, but she did not follow immediately. She stood for a moment, twisting her apron into a knot as she plucked up the courage to continue the conversation. In the workhouse she would never have dared to speak unless spoken to by an adult. Such behaviour would have earned an instant reprimand from the Tickler. 'I never learned to read in the workhouse.' The words tumbled from her lips. 'I picked it up in the theatre where Ma worked.'

Cook looked up, her eyes widening and her mouth dropping open. 'What theatre was that?'

The sound of water gushing from the pump into the stone sink made Sarah jump. 'I'd best go and help Nettie.'

'Not till you tell me more. I go to Wilton's music hall on my nights off. It's just round the corner in Grace's Alley.'

Encouraged by Cook's sudden burst of enthusiasm, Sarah felt more at ease. 'We lived near the Theatre Royal in Drury Lane. That's where Ma worked, scrubbing floors.'

'Are you coming, Sarah?' Nettie shouted above the noise of the water swishing from the pump.

'She'll be with you in a moment.' Cook stared at Sarah as if she had said something incredibly interesting. 'You must tell me all about the goings on at the Theatre Royal. I saw Barney Williams in *Our Gal* and William Templeton as Robin Hood. It was magnificent and I was transported to another world. Oh, how I love the theatre.'

'I know Barney and Mr Templeton,' Sarah said, gulping back tears as the memories of happier times came flooding back. 'They was kind to me and let me watch them rehearsing while Ma scrubbed the floors.'

'And your ma is no longer with us?'

'She died in the workhouse, missis.' Sarah mopped her eyes on her apron.

'You poor little soul.' Cook's voice broke on a sob. 'Come here and let an old lady give you a cuddle.'

Enveloped in a large flour-covered bosom, Sarah could hardly breathe. She did not want to wriggle free and hurt Cook's feelings, but then Nettie burst into the room demanding to know why she was idling away her time when she should be wiping the dishes. Sarah broke away from Cook's warm embrace. 'I'd best help.'

'You do that, sweetheart,' Cook said, patting her on the head. 'You can tell me all about the theatrical folk after supper when the work is done. I like to sit by the fire and put me feet up for a bit before I go to my bed.'

'Yes. Thank you.' Sarah hurried off to appease Nettie.

They had just finished and were putting the plates away in the dresser when Dorcas came hurtling down the stairs. She came to a sudden stop, her bonnet awry and her shawl slipping to the ground. 'There's such a to-do upstairs,' she said breathlessly. 'I'm wondering whether I should run out and find a constable.'

'Why? What on earth has happened?' Cook hurried round the table to help Dorcas to a chair.

'Sit down and catch your breath, my girl. Tell me what's going on.'

'It's the master. I never seen him in a temper afore, but he's outside in the street having a set-to with a fat gent with a red face. I couldn't hear all what was said, but it were about them two.' She pointed to Sarah and Nettie.

'What did you hear?' Cook demanded. 'Pull yourself together, Dorcas.'

'The fat man was saying he'd been robbed. He said something about her being worth a tenner when she's a bit older or even more to the right buyer. I tell you, Cook, I couldn't hear most of it, but I thought the guvner was going to hit the other bloke.'

'Trigg,' Nettie whispered. 'It must be the workhouse master come to get you, Sarah.'

There was a moment of stunned silence and then Cook headed for the door that led into the area.

'Come on,' Nettie said, grabbing Sarah by the hand. 'We've got to see this. I'll put my money on Mr Arbuthnot.'

Chapter Three

'How dare you come here accusing me of foul play?' Standing in the street outside his house, Mr Arbuthnot faced up to a red-faced and furious Trigg.

Sarah clutched Nettie's hand even tighter. 'Don't let him take me.'

'Over my dead body,' Nettie said firmly.

Cook clutched at the area railings, fanning herself vigorously. 'Run and fetch a constable, Dorcas. The fellow should be taken to the watch house and locked up.'

Dorcas seemed frozen to the spot and despite a hearty shove from Cook she remained where she was, staring open-mouthed.

'You'll give the child back, sir,' Trigg shouted, fisting his hands. 'You've cheated me out of five pounds and I've got to answer to the governors for my actions.'

'You were quick enough to grab the money, workhouse master. We had an agreement and I'm holding you to it.' Mr Arbuthnot stood his ground. 'I'll be the one to report to the governors and it won't be favourable, I can tell you that.'

'I couldn't say anything in front of the other mill owners, but you took the child and it weren't legal.' Trigg took a step towards him. 'Give me the girl and we'll say no more about it.'

37

Sarah uttered a strangled cry and hid behind Nettie. 'I'm not going back to that place. I'd rather die.'

Mr Arbuthnot turned his head as if realising for the first time that he had an audience. 'Take the child indoors, Cook. She's going nowhere with this abominable bully.'

'Bully?' Trigg roared. 'I'll have you know I'm acting within my rights. That child is the property of the workhouse. It was an honest mistake when I allowed her to leave with you. It's kidnap, sir. Pure and simple.'

'Choose your words carefully, Trigg. I could have you for slander.'

Trigg made a strange gobbling sound deep in his throat. 'Hand her over, or pay me the five pounds as recompense for my loss.'

'That's blackmail.' Mr Arbuthnot turned to Dorcas. 'Fetch a constable. Run quickly.'

She danced up and down, wringing her hands. 'I dunno where to find one, sir. Me legs have turned to jelly.'

At that moment the front door of the house opened and Mrs Arbuthnot rushed out into the street. 'Don't touch my husband, you brute,' she cried, placing herself between them with her arms outstretched. 'You'll have to knock me down first.'

Mr Arbuthnot lifted her bodily and placed her behind him. 'Thank you, my dear, but I can handle this.'

Taking the opportunity provided by Mrs Arbuthnot's dramatic intervention, Trigg lunged at Nettie, pushing her aside and grabbing Sarah by the arm. 'You're coming with me.'

38

'I don't think so.' A huge fist landed on Trigg's jaw sending him spinning onto the cobblestones.

Dazed and terrified, Sarah gazed up at her saviour.

'You are safe, Liebchen.' A burly, fair-haired young man with startlingly blue eyes smiled at her and ruffled her hair.

'Franz.' Dorcas uttered his name with a sigh of relief. 'You was so brave.'

He smiled modestly. 'It was nothing. I cannot let the master down.' He stood over Trigg, folding his arms. 'You want to argue, mein Herr?'

Mr Arbuthnot slapped him on the shoulder. 'Thank you, Franz. That was good timing.'

'Yes, boss. I think you had trouble here. Shall I hit him again?'

'Take him away,' Mrs Arbuthnot cried, clutching her husband's arm. 'Take the fellow away before my husband does him some harm.'

Mr Arbuthnot patted her hand. 'I'm not a violent man, as you very well know, Sophia. I don't think we'll have any more trouble with the workhouse master, but he hasn't heard the last of this.'

Keeping a wary eye on Franz, Trigg scrambled to his feet. 'I'll sue you for assault, you Kraut bastard.'

Cook uttered a screech and hurried down the area steps. 'Bring the girls inside, Dorcas. Don't just stand there staring at the sugar baker.'

Dorcas sidled up to Franz, smiling. 'You was wonderful. I don't think my Wally could have done better.'

He nodded. 'Thank you, but it was nothing.'

39

'It was a timely intervention, Franz.' Mr Arbuthnot shook his hand. 'Is there a problem in the refinery, or were you just taking the air?'

'I was coming to find you, mein Herr. You are needed in the sugar house.'

'I'll be there as soon as this man goes on his way.' Mr Arbuthnot took a menacing step towards Trigg, who was dusting himself down.

'All right, I'm going, but you haven't heard the last of this.' With a malicious glance in Sarah's direction, Trigg lowered his voice. 'You'd better watch out. I'll have you, girl.'

Franz uttered a guttural growl and chased him down the street.

Nettie burst out laughing. 'That'll teach him.'

Mrs Arbuthnot kissed her husband on the cheek. 'You were so brave, James. I thought I was going to faint when I saw that brute attacking you, but you were magnificent.'

He puffed out his chest. 'Thank you, my dear, but it really was all in a day's work. I'm used to dealing with scoundrels like Trigg. However, I think we'd better be on our guard for the next week or so. I wouldn't put it past him to try to snatch the child.' His smile faded. 'Dorcas, I want you to keep an eye on both Sarah and Nettie. Don't let them go out alone.'

'No, sir.' Dorcas curtseyed. 'I'll take care of them.'

Mrs Arbuthnot held out her hands. 'Come indoors, girls. I've just seen Miss Gant, my dressmaker, coming down the road.' She ushered them into the house, hesitating on the step to give her husband a worried glance. 'You will be careful too, won't you, James? I don't trust that man. He might make trouble for you.'

His reply was lost on Sarah as she entered the hallway. She staggered and leaned against the wall as a feeling of faintness made the world spin dizzily around her.

'It's all right,' Nettie said, putting her arms around her and giving her a hug. 'I won't let the old bugger get you.'

'Ta, Nettie. I'm better now.'

'That's the ticket.' Nettie moved away to primp in one of the gilt-framed mirrors. 'I don't half fancy that big German bloke. I wouldn't mind working there if they're all like that.' She rolled her eyes and wiggled her hips.

'You're just saying that to make me laugh,' Sarah said, giggling.

'Well it worked, didn't it?' Nettie jumped to attention as Mrs Arbuthnot approached them, followed closely by Miss Gant.

'Go into the parlour, girls. Miss Gant will take your measurements and then Dorcas will show you where you are to sleep.'

The attic rooms were on the fourth floor at the very top of the house. Mrs Burgess occupied one of them, Dorcas another. A small space was used for storage, and the room allotted to Sarah and Nettie was at the back of the house overlooking a surprisingly large garden. Sarah went straight to the dormer window set beneath the eaves and peered out at what in her eyes appeared to be a small park. Despite the fact that it was late autumn, there were still a few sooty roses clinging to a pergola halfway down the garden, and a clump of bronze chrysanthemums created a pool of deep colour. The clouds had dispersed after a brief shower and the last rays of a pale golden sun played with the few remaining leaves on the trees, turning them into copper pennies dancing in the breeze. Having lived all of her life in the shadow of crowded tenements and dark alleyways where sunlight struggled to reach the pavements, Sarah could hardly believe her eyes as she gazed at the scene below. 'It's their garden,' she said breathlessly. 'I wonder if they'll let us go outside and play.'

'Stop gawping out of the window and feel the mattress on your bed,' Nettie said, flinging herself down on her iron bedstead with a chortle of delight. 'It's flock-filled unless I'm very much mistaken, and we got proper cotton sheets and pillowcases, and a coverlet. We'll sleep like princesses tonight.'

Reluctantly, Sarah left the view and went to sit on her bed. 'It's lovely up here,' she whispered. 'I used to sleep on the floor when I was with Ma in Vinegar Yard. She had the bed and the babies was put in a drawer while they was alive, and in little wooden boxes when they died.' She wiped her eyes on her sleeve. 'I can't believe they'll let us stay here, Nettie. It might be just for tonight and then we'll have to sleep on the bare tiles in the kitchen. That's what most servants do.'

Nettie lay on her back, staring at the sloping ceiling. 'You know a lot for a kid. I spent most of me life in the workhouse.'

'I don't really. It's just things I overheard in the theatre. They used to forget I was there.'

'Well, I don't care if this is just for tonight, and I don't mind if Miss Gant with the big sticking-out teeth makes me something even worse than this blooming uniform, I'm just going to enjoy each day of freedom as it comes and eat as much grub as I can get down me. If it all ends tomorrow, I'd still think it was worthwhile if only to have seen old Trigg lying in the horse shit and the rubbish in the gutter with his eyes rolling in fear of the sugar baker.'

Sarah was not so sure. She had a nasty feeling that Trigg would have his revenge. She had been in the workhouse long enough to learn that the master was the law as far as the inmates were concerned, and he was not used to having his authority questioned. She was also painfully aware that she had made an enemy of Mrs Trigg from the start, and that together the Triggs were a formidable foe. She did not think that either of them would give up easily once they had made their minds up about something. She wished she could be as confident as Nettie when it came to the future, but experience had taught her that she could take nothing for granted. Life had a way of playing nasty tricks on poor people, and no one was poorer than a pauper.

Next morning while it was still dark they were awakened by Dorcas, who burst into the room and shook them until they opened their eyes. 'Get dressed and come downstairs. I dunno what you're both supposed to be doing in the house but you can make yourselves useful.'

For a moment Sarah thought she was back in the workhouse and she fell out of bed, landing on the rag rug with a thud.

'Lord, you're eager,' Dorcas said, chuckling. 'I wish young Betty was as good at getting up as you are. I have to prod and poke that simpleton until she gets up from her bed by the hearth, and even then it's hard to tell if she's awake or not.'

Nettie stretched luxuriously and sat up. 'I never had a night's sleep like that in me whole life. I thought I was floating on a cloud, and I was snuggled up warm and comfy; it was lovely.'

'I'm glad, but don't run away with the idea that you're going to be spoilt rotten, because we work just as hard as any servants in the square. You'll be on your feet from before dawn until late at night if needs be, so you'd better start now. Nettie can fetch in the coal and you, Sarah, will help me clean out the grates and lay the fires.'

'Yes, Dorcas.' Sarah slipped her much-hated grogram dress over her head and put on her pinafore. 'I'm ready.'

Sarah was used to hard work, but she soon realised that Dorcas as the only housemaid in the establishment had duties that kept her fully occupied. There was the back-breaking task of carrying coal up several flights of stairs, not to mention the pitchers of hot water needed to fill the washbowl in the master bedroom. The chamber pots had to be emptied before the night soil collector called to take away the stinking human waste, and the potties had to be washed and dried before being replaced beneath the beds.

'We must feed you both up,' Cook said, filling Sarah's bowl with porridge when it was time to stop for breakfast. 'You and young Nettie are like a pair of skinned rabbits. You need more meat on your bones.'

It was hardly a flattering description, but Sarah took it meekly, although Nettie scowled as she spooned food into her mouth. 'I can work as hard as the rest of you,' she said sulkily. 'But I ain't going to be a housemaid all me life. I'll tell you that for nothing, missis.'

'You address me as Cook, or Mrs Burgess, and I don't want any of your lip, Nettie. It's up to the mistress if she chooses to employ you on a permanent basis, so if I was you I'd keep my mouth shut and only speak when spoken to. We're not interested in what you want or don't want. We all have work to do.'

Nettie subsided into silence and quickly mopped up a second bowl of porridge.

Dorcas came clattering down the stairs. 'The mistress wants to see you in the front parlour, Sarah.'

Sarah jumped to her feet and Nettie half rose but Dorcas shook her head. 'Not you, Nettie. Just the young 'un.'

'Have I done something wrong?' Sarah asked nervously. 'I done everything you told me to, Dorcas.'

'It's no use asking me. I don't know what she wants.' Dorcas took her seat at the table. 'My corns are killing me. It's these blooming boots; they're too small, but I can't afford a new pair until next quarter when I get paid.'

'I told you not to waste your money on that new bonnet, girl,' Cook said, slapping a plateful of porridge on the table in front of Dorcas. 'You only bought it to impress that young man of yours. You should have been more sensible.'

'Wally thought it was very pretty and he don't look at my feet.' Dorcas stared pointedly at Sarah. 'Why are you still here? The mistress is waiting for you.'

Sarah sent a mute plea for help to Nettie, but she shook her head. 'I can't hold your hand all the time, nipper. It seems you're the favourite round here and I'm just the skivvy.'

'That's enough of that talk,' Cook said severely. 'Perhaps you'd rather go back to the workhouse if you don't like it here? The master went there to get strong lads to help in the sugar house and all he brought back was two little girls, so watch your tongue, young lady.'

Nettie subsided into silence, her mouth pulled down at the corners and her jaw clenched. Sarah gave her a sympathetic pat on the shoulder before making her way to the parlour.

She hesitated outside the door, taking deep breaths as she plucked up the courage to knock. What would she do if Mr Arbuthnot had changed his mind and decided to give her back to Trigg and his wife? The mere thought of it made her feel faint with anxiety. She tapped gently on the oak door panel.

'Enter.' Mrs Arbuthnot's voice sounded friendly enough.

Sarah peeped into the room, half expecting to see the workhouse master, but to her intense relief Mrs

Arbuthnot was seated in a chair by the fire with an embroidery hoop clasped in one hand and a needle threaded with pink silk in the other. She was alone and she looked up, her face breaking into a smile. 'Come in, Sarah, and close the door.'

Sarah did as she was told but she hesitated, not knowing what to do next.

'Come over here and sit on the stool beside me. I want to talk to you.' She waited until Sarah was seated. 'Dorcas tells me that you've been helping her this morning.'

'Yes, ma'am.'

'I'm not sure that such heavy work is suitable for a girl of your age.'

'I'm nearly ten, ma'am. And I'm used to working hard.'

'Yes, I know, and it bothers me. I think a child of your age ought to be in school, even if you are a girl.'

'I can read and write, ma'am.'

'And my husband tells me that you can recite some Shakespeare.'

'Yes, ma'am.'

'Well, that is a talent in itself. You obviously have a retentive memory and I think you ought to have more schooling.'

'You're not going to send me away, are you?'

'No, Sarah. I intend to find a teacher who will give you at least two hours each morning, except Sundays, of course.'

'Miss Parfitt.'

'I beg your pardon?'

'I'm sorry, I didn't mean to interrupt, but she taught us at the workhouse. Miss Parfitt is lovely.'

'That's all very well, but it's unlikely that she'll be available. However, I'll see what I can do, and in the meantime you will continue to help Dorcas. I'll make certain that she gives you some of the lighter chores around the house.'

Realising that she had been dismissed, Sarah stood up but she did not leave the room immediately. She hesitated, twisting her hands together as she struggled to find the right words. Mrs Arbuthnot looked up from her sewing, her eyebrows raised. 'Have you got a question, Sarah?'

'Yes'm. What about Nettie? Will she have lessons too?'

Mrs Arbuthnot frowned. 'I think she's probably had all the education she will need in life, but you may send her to me. I'll have a word with Nettie.'

When Nettie returned to the kitchen she was looking distinctly downhearted. 'I've got to help Dorcas and do everything she says. I might as well be back in the blasted workhouse.'

'Language,' Cook said crossly. 'You should think yourself lucky to be here.'

'I suppose I am, but I don't want to be a servant all me life.'

'But it's lovely here,' Sarah protested. 'You know it is, Nettie. We got a comfy bed and three square meals a day.'

'It won't make me rich, though.' Nettie slumped

down at the table. 'No one got rich by cleaning privies and humping coal. Anyway, it's all right for you. You're going to have lessons and learn to be a young lady.'

Cook reached across the table and smacked Nettie's hand with a wooden spoon. 'That's for grumbling when you got no cause. I was going to take you and Sarah to Wilton's music hall on Saturday night as a special treat, but I've changed my mind now.'

Nettie leapt to her feet and rushed round the table to hug Cook. 'I didn't mean it. I was just being a grump. Please, please take us to the theatre, Cook. I never been to one in me life and I'm dying to see what it's like.'

'Oh, please,' Sarah whispered, clasping her hands together. 'Please forgive Nettie. She don't mean a word of it really. She's ever so grateful to the master and mistress and to you and Dorcas and even Betty.'

Betty popped her head out of the scullery. 'Who called me name?'

'No one,' Cook said hastily. 'Get back to your work, silly girl.' She waited until Betty was splashing about in the stone sink. 'She's not all there, poor little soul. We'll settle her down with a drop of Hollands when we go to the theatre. She'll sleep by the fire and Dorcas will keep an eye on her.'

Sarah and Nettie were both in a state of excitement as they made themselves ready to go to the theatre. Miss Gant had quickly run up two linsey-woolsey skirts for them to wear and Mrs Arbuthnot had sent Dorcas to a dollyshop in Well Street to purchase two white cambric blouses, which would have to do until their new clothes were ready. She had also given Dorcas enough money to buy two thick woollen shawls as the chill of autumn was making itself felt early that year.

Cook was in a good mood and she left Dorcas with a string of instructions for serving the evening meal above stairs. In the end Dorcas lost patience, which Sarah had observed was never her strongest point, and told Cook in no uncertain terms that she knew very well how to look after the master and mistress. She shooed them out of the door into the area. 'Go and enjoy yourselves. I'll look after young Betty.'

As Sarah left the warmth of the kitchen and followed Cook up the steep steps she could feel the cold and damp rising up from the ground. The air was thick with smoke-laden fog which made breathing difficult and filled her nostrils with an unpleasant acrid smell. She wrapped her shawl a little tighter around her shoulders and hurried after Cook and Nettie.

Wilton's music hall was situated in Grace's Alley, a narrow passageway which led from Wellclose Square to Well Street. The fog swirled about them and it was difficult to see anything more than a few feet away, but Cook marched ahead wielding her umbrella as if attempting to cut a path through the worsening pea-souper. If it had not been for the gas lights suspended over the doorway they might have walked past the theatre as it was rather oddly situated in the middle of a row of terraced houses. Figures emerged ghost-like from the murk as the audience began to arrive in twos and threes, but Cook pushed her way to the front, using her tightly furled umbrella to good effect. Sarah followed her into the foyer and was surprised at the smallness and simplicity of the area compared to the grand entrance of the Theatre Royal. Cook paid for their tickets and in her eagerness to secure a good seat she was up the stairs that led to the gallery with the agility of a mountain goat.

Nettie nudged Sarah. 'It looks like she's forgotten about her rheumatics.'

'Shh,' Sarah whispered, giggling. 'She might hear you, and it's very good of her to bring us here.'

Nettie took her by the hand. 'Come on, let's make a dash for it or we'll get killed in the crush.' She darted forward, dodging in between the crowds of people who apparently had the same idea as Cook. They made it to the gallery to find that Cook had already picked her vantage point and had settled herself on a wooden chair with her skirts spread out over the seats on either side of her. She beckoned furiously.

'Come and sit down or you'll lose your places.'

Sarah took her seat and leaned on the balustrade to watch the audience who were still arriving in the hall below. It was all so achingly familiar that it brought a lump to her throat. The theatre was neither as big as the one in Drury Lane nor was it as sumptuously decorated, but the sight and sounds of the small orchestra tuning up brought back memories of happier times. If she closed her eyes she could imagine that she was back in the Theatre Royal, waiting for Ma to finish her work and take her home to their humble lodgings in Vinegar Yard. It was no thanks to Pa, whose gambling had caused Ma such distress, but Sarah had seen how hard her mother had worked to keep food on the table and there had always been a fire to huddle round in winter. They had known hard times but Sarah had been happy.

She opened her eyes to concentrate on the scene below, forcing thoughts of her mother's sad end in the airless heat on the top floor of the workhouse to the back of her mind.

The orchestra struck a chord and then the master of ceremonies, wearing a rather shabby-looking tailcoat and over-tight breeches, introduced the first act.

Mrs Burgess craned her neck to get a better look as a rather large gentleman, also wearing evening dress that had seen better days, made his way onto the platform and took a bow. Sarah and Nettie exchanged grins as he fingered his cravat and glanced nervously at the orchestra, but the chatter in the theatre ceased when he started to sing 'The Girl I Left Behind Me' in a glorious baritone voice, and his performance was received with thunderous applause. He bowed several times and the next act was a pretty young woman wearing a white ball gown. Her dark hair was studded with white camellias and confined in a snood at the nape of her neck. She sang 'Flow Gently, Sweet Afton' in a pure soprano voice that throbbed with emotion. Sarah was enchanted by everything she saw and heard. The songs were new to her and refreshingly simple but touched her to the core. She could hardly believe it when the performers took their final bow to a standing ovation as the show ended.

Cook was sniffling into her hanky, apparently overcome by the emotion of the evening, and Nettie was unusually silent. She sat motionless with a rapt expression on her freckled face, and jumped when Cook tugged at her sleeve. 'I never saw nothing like it in me life,' she breathed. 'Did you see them gowns the women wore? They was so fine, and the way they sang. It made me go all funny inside.'

Cook tucked her hanky into her reticule. 'Yes, it was all wonderful, but we'd best get home. It's late and you never know who's lurking around in the dark. It's lucky we haven't far to go. Get up, girl. Everyone's leaving and we don't want to spend the night locked in an empty theatre.'

Nettie stood up and stretched. 'I could live me whole life in here, smelling the perfume and the cigar smoke. I like watching the rich people in their fine clothes. I want to be one of them and wear fine gowns and ride in a private carriage.'

'Get on with you.' Cook gave her a gentle shove. 'There's only one way a girl from the workhouse could earn enough money to look like that and it's not for you, young Nettie. You're going to grow up to be respectable or my name ain't Hepzibah Burgess.'

Sarah stifled a giggle and dared not look at Nettie in case she burst out laughing and offended Cook, who had been kind to them.

'Yes, Cook,' Nettie said, winking at Sarah. 'If you say so.'

'I do indeed.' Cook plucked her shawl from the back of her chair and slipped it around her shoulders. 'Let's go home. I'm looking forward to a cup of cocoa and my nice warm bed.'

They joined the queue for the stairs and were almost the last to leave the theatre. The darkness outside had swallowed up the stragglers and it was eerily silent. The fog was even thicker now and suffocating in its greenish yellow density. Sarah put her hands out in front of her, feeling her way along the walls of the terrace. Nettie and Cook were a little way behind her but she could barely hear their muffled footsteps and she was suddenly scared. The pleasant evening had taken on a sinister note and it could not just have been the pea-souper that had blanketed the city which made her feel nervous and ill at ease.

She stumbled over a doorstep but managed to save herself from falling by clutching at a protruding windowsill. Then through the murk she could just make out the faint greenish shimmer of the gas lamp at the corner of Grace's Alley, and she started to run. Although there was no obvious reason for her panic, she raced over the cobblestones, slipping and sliding in her desperate attempt to get out into the square and the safe haven of her new home. She saw a shadow in the hazy pool of light but it was not until it moved that she realised it was the burly figure of a man wearing a caped greatcoat. She came to a sudden halt, turning her head in the hope of seeing Cook and Nettie, but the wall of fog and darkness obliterated everything. Before she realised what was happening a large hand clamped over her mouth and she was lifted bodily off her feet.

Chapter Four

Sarah kicked and struggled, but with the hand covering the lower half of her face it was almost impossible to breathe. The sulphurous smell of the fog only added to her distress and she was beginning to feel faint when without warning her captor uttered a grunt and she fell to the ground. She landed with a thud that momentarily knocked the wind from her lungs. Gasping for air she raised herself on her elbow and saw Cook attacking the man with her umbrella. He was about to snatch it from her but Nettie put her head down and butted him in the stomach. He doubled over, clutching his belly.

'Come on, Sarah,' Nettie cried, dragging her to her feet. 'Run.'

Sarah yelped with pain as she put her right foot to the ground. 'I twisted me ankle.'

Wielding her umbrella, Cook clouted the man round the head, sending his hat flying to the ground. 'I dunno who you are, mister, but you got no right to attack little girls and defenceless old women.' She took another swipe at him. 'And that's for using bad language in front of ladies.'

He scrabbled around trying to find his battered hat, which had rolled into the gutter. 'Defenceless,' he gasped. 'You're a vicious old cow, but I got her mark and I'll get her sooner or later. No one gets the better of me, let alone a nipper.' He struggled to his feet but Nettie pushed Cook out of the way and kicked him on the shin.

'You just try it, mister. I grew up in the workhouse. I learned to take care of meself and I ain't afraid of you.'

'Come on, girls,' Cook said firmly. 'We're going home and if he tries to follow us I'll set the German sugar bakers on him.'

Taking advantage of the fact that their attacker was hopping up and down in pain, Nettie grabbed Cook's umbrella. 'Follow me.' She ran on ahead, trailing the ferule along the railings so that even as she disappeared into the wall of fog the metallic sound rang out like a peal of bells, leading them home.

When they were safely indoors with the door bolted, Sarah sank down on the nearest chair and Cook stepped over the sleeping Betty to take the simmering kettle off the hob. 'We'll have a nice hot cup of cocoa, and you can tell me why that ruffian wanted to take you from us, young Sarah.' She reached up, taking the cocoa tin from the mantelshelf. 'Pass me some cups from the dresser, Nettie.' She frowned, turning her gaze on Sarah who was shivering even though the kitchen was warm. 'Had you ever seen that man before?'

'N-never.' Sarah wrapped her arms around her body in an attempt to control her shaking limbs. 'I dunno why he wanted me.'

Nettie placed the cups on the table. 'It don't take a clever person to work that out, duck. Who was here just a few days ago, making a fuss and demanding his rights?'

'Mr Trigg, but that wasn't him.'

'No, silly, but I'll bet it was the workhouse master what sent him to get you. Trigg ain't the sort to give up easily, and he's greedy. He'll be in trouble if the governors find out about his crooked business dealings, and I'll warrant it don't stop at selling the odd kid into slavery.'

Cook stopped what she was doing and her eyes narrowed. 'The master should be told about this.' She pushed the kettle towards Nettie. 'Finish making the cocoa. I'm going to see if Mr Arbuthnot is still up. He should be told.'

'He might send me away,' Sarah whispered, her bottom lip trembling. 'He might even send me back to the workhouse.'

Cook stepped over Betty, who had not stirred from her straw-filled palliasse by the range and was snoring loudly. 'He won't do that, but he might well report the matter to the governors.' She left them staring helplessly at each other as she went upstairs.

'I hope he's gone to bed,' Sarah said, biting her lip. 'I don't want any trouble.'

Nettie finished making the cocoa and passed a cup to her. 'Looks like you got it, whether you wants it or not, love.'

Cook returned just as they finished their warming drinks. She was flushed with triumph and slightly out of breath. 'The master was in his study and he was horrified and then furious. He said he's already told the board of governors about Trigg but he'll let them know about the attempted kidnap. It might not be anything to do with the workhouse master, but he's going to report the matter to the police in case the man is known to them. I can certainly give a description of him, and you two might be asked to put your twopenn'orth in as well. Anyway, off to bed with you.'

The constable noted down everything that Sarah said. Mr Arbuthnot sat behind his desk, making encouraging noises when she was at a loss for words, and Mrs Arbuthnot sat beside her, holding her hand.

'That will be all for now, sir.' The constable closed his notebook. 'I've taken a description from Mrs Burgess and the other young girl and it will be circulated, although I have to say it could fit any number of the criminals known to us.'

Mr Arbuthnot rose from his seat. 'I understand, constable. Anyway, thank you for attending so promptly.'

'The officer on the beat will keep an eye on the house, sir.'

Mrs Arbuthnot squeezed Sarah's fingers. 'That makes me feel much better. At least we'll be safe in our beds at night.'

'Yes, ma'am.'

Mr Arbuthnot moved to the door and opened it. 'I'll see you out, constable.'

Sarah gazed anxiously at Mrs Arbuthnot. 'I'm sorry to have brought trouble to your door, ma'am.'

'Nonsense, my dear. None of this is your fault, and you mustn't be afraid. We will see that no harm comes to you.' She released Sarah's hand with an encouraging smile. 'You may go about your duties as usual, but you must on no account go out alone. I don't know why the workhouse master is causing us so much trouble, but I promise that we won't ever send you back to that dreadful place.'

Sarah bobbed a curtsey. 'Thank you, ma'am.' She left the room and went to find Dorcas, who was dusting the drawing room on the first floor.

'I seem to have missed all the excitement,' Dorcas said, tossing a duster to her. 'Be careful with Mrs Arbuthnot's Dresden figurines. She'll be very upset if they get damaged.'

'Yes, Dorcas.' Sarah picked one off the side table, hardly daring to breathe as she dusted the soot from the fragile piece.

'So what did the peeler say? Did he know who it was who leapt out at you?'

'I don't think so. He said it could be any one of the villains known to the police.'

'But the master thinks it has to do with that horrible man Trigg.'

'I think so, but I can't understand why he would want me back. Mrs Trigg used to call me Sal Scratch and made me wear a placard with my name written on it for everyone to see. She said I was the devil's daughter.'

Dorcas uttered a hollow laugh. 'Did she now? Maybe she's the one related to Old Nick; it certainly sounds that way.' She gave a start as Sarah picked up a dainty porcelain shepherdess. 'Oh, do be careful of that one, that's her favourite of all.'

Sarah put the ornament back on the table and when Dorcas was not looking she blew the dust off the delicate face and fingers. Before she came to Wellclose Square she would never have considered that keeping house was such a nerve-racking task, but she was rapidly learning its dangers and pitfalls, although so far she had not broken anything.

Dorcas lifted the sash and shook her duster out of the window. 'At least the fog has cleared. It's my afternoon off and I'm stepping out with my gentleman friend.' She leaned out further. 'There's a lady knocking on the front door.' She withdrew her head, turning to Sarah with a pleading look. 'Run down and answer it, there's a good girl. She looks like one of them church-going ladies who raise money for orphans and foundlings. The master always gives something; that's why they make a beeline for this house.'

'Perhaps you ought to go,' Sarah said nervously. 'I wouldn't know what to say.'

'I've got to get done or I'll be late meeting Wally, and he's a stickler for time. Just be polite and let her do the talking.'

Sarah was glad to be relieved of the onerous task of dusting precious things, and she raced downstairs hoping that she could remember everything that Dorcas had taught her. She stopped to check her appearance in the wall mirror by the hallstand before opening the front door. A housemaid had to appear clean and tidy at all times; that was what Dorcas always said. She opened the door and her breath hitched in her throat when she saw who was standing on the pavement outside. Forgetting everything that Dorcas had taught her about how to behave in public she threw her arms around the startled visitor, almost knocking her over. 'Miss Parfitt. You came to see me.'

Disengaging herself from Sarah's frantic grasp, Miss Parfitt straightened her bonnet, which had almost been knocked off in the embrace. 'I had to come, Sarah, but my business is with Mrs Arbuthnot.'

Sarah stared at her in amazement. 'You know the mistress?'

'Not exactly, but she sent a message to the workhouse asking me to come here today, although she didn't say why exactly.' Miss Parfitt glanced over Sarah's shoulder. 'I think you'd better let me in, dear.'

'Oh, yes. I'm sorry. I'm not used to doing this. It's Dorcas's job really but she's getting ready to go out and meet Wally, her gentleman friend.' Sarah stepped aside. 'I've forgotten what I'm supposed to do next. I'm so pleased to see you, miss.'

'And I you, Sarah. I think you ought to find Mrs Arbuthnot and tell her that I'm here.'

'I expect she's in her parlour. That's where she spends most of the time on Sundays after dinner. We all went to church this morning. Nettie and me went with Cook and Dorcas, and Mr and Mrs Arbuthnot went on ahead. They sat in the front pew and we was at the back of the church, but the singing wasn't nearly as good as it was in the theatre last night.'

Miss Parfitt smiled and her pansy-brown eyes danced with amusement. 'I'd love to hear about it, dear. But I think you should knock on the parlour door and announce me. Then if Mrs Arbuthnot says so, you come and tell me she'll see me, and show me into the room. Can you remember all that?'

'Of course I can.' Controlling the urge to run, Sarah crossed the hall and knocked on the parlour door.

'Come in.'

Sarah opened the door and went inside. 'Miss Parfitt is here to see you, ma'am,' she said, bobbing a curtsey.

'I was expecting her and I'm glad to see that she is on time. I hate unpunctuality. Show her in, please.'

Sarah ushered Miss Parfitt into the parlour and closed the door on them. She had to resist the temptation to listen at the keyhole, but she had no intention of going below stairs until she had found out if her suspicions were correct. She crossed her fingers, hoping that Miss Parfitt would agree to be her tutor, and then one day, if she worked really hard, maybe she might be able to find work as a teacher or even a governess. Of one thing Sarah was certain: she would do something that would make her mother proud of her, and if they met in heaven Ma would say, 'Well done, love. I always knew you'd amount to something.' She paced the floor, waiting for what seemed like hours until the parlour door opened and Miss Parfitt emerged, followed by a smiling Mrs Arbuthnot.

'Sarah, I have good news for you. Miss Parfitt has agreed to come here once a week, on her afternoon off, to continue your lessons.'

Miss Parfitt nodded. 'I'd happily spend more time with you, Sarah, but my duties at the workhouse have to come first. However, you're a bright child and I'll set work for you to do on your own. Mrs Arbuthnot has offered to provide everything you'll need to further your education. You are a very lucky girl.'

'I know that, miss. When do we start?'

Miss Parfitt came once a week as promised and Mrs Arbuthnot purchased the necessary books, a slate and slate pencils and even some expensive paper so that Sarah could learn to draw. Nettie was envious at first, but she changed her mind when she saw the amount of time that Sarah spent reading and doing sums.

On the Sunday before Christmas, Miss Parfitt arrived earlier than usual. Her cheeks were flushed and her eyes bright with excitement as she took off her bonnet and cape. 'Such news,' she said, peeling off her gloves and handing them to Sarah. 'You'll never guess what's happened at the workhouse.'

'Are you all right, miss? You're not sick, are you?'

Miss Parfitt threw up her hands and laughed. 'I'm absolutely fine, my dear. It's the Triggs. They've been sent packing. They're leaving the workhouse in disgrace. Can you imagine that?'

Sarah could, quite easily. She had been forbidden to venture out alone since the failed kidnap attempt, and she was certain that the man had been sent by Mr Trigg. 'I'm glad, miss. They were bad people.'

'I think everyone at the workhouse would agree with you there, Sarah. No one knows quite how it happened, but the board of governors called a special meeting and they sent for both Mr and Mrs Trigg. That was yesterday, and they've been given until tomorrow to pack their bags and leave.'

'But that's Christmas Eve.'

'I know. It does seem a little hard, but I can't find it in my heart to pity them. I myself have been thinking of leaving because I couldn't stand watching the poor children suffering. The only reason I stayed on was to try to make things better for them, but we must hope that the next workhouse master is a better person.'

Sarah's hands trembled as she hung Miss Parfitt's outer garments on the hallstand, but it was relief that made her shake from head to foot. The Triggs would have nothing to gain by abducting her now. She was free from them forever and she wanted to sing and dance, but her time in the workhouse had taught her how to control her emotions and she resisted the temptation. 'Do you know where the Triggs are going, miss?'

'No, but I hope it's somewhere far away from here. I never want to see them again.' Miss Parfitt opened the parlour door. 'Let's start our lesson. It will be the last one before Christmas and I must say you're doing very well.' She opened the cupboard where the books were put away in between sessions and selected one. She spun round to face Sarah, her dark eyes lustrous with excitement. 'Actually I have a surprise for you and Nettie. I was going to wait until we had finished, but I can't keep it to myself any longer.'

'What is it, miss?'

'Mrs Burgess told me how much you enjoyed your visit to the theatre, even though it very nearly turned into a disaster, but we won't speak of that.'

'I'm safe now that the Triggs have gone. They won't want me any more.'

'We must hope not, but that's not what I intended to say.' Miss Parfitt clasped her hands together and took a deep breath. 'I'm putting this very badly and it's so simple. Your very kind employer has bought tickets for the show tomorrow evening at Wilton's music hall. He's treating you and Nettie, Mrs Burgess, Dorcas and myself, and just in case that evil man is lurking in the shadows, Mr Arbuthnot has arranged for one of the sugar bakers to escort us.'

Forgetting that she was supposed to behave with decorum during classes, Sarah danced up and down clapping her hands. 'May I be excused so that I can tell Nettie?'

Miss Parfitt put the book down. 'Of course you may, and when you return we'll read another chapter of *The Old Curiosity Shop* by Mr Dickens.'

'I can't wait to find out what happens to Little Nell,' Sarah said, hesitating. 'But I must tell Nettie about our Christmas treat. I never had one before and I don't suppose she has either.'

'I understand. Hurry along, and perhaps Cook would be kind enough to let us have a cup of tea and some of her delicious gingerbread. It's nearly Christmas.'

The next evening Sarah and Nettie put on the dresses that Miss Gant had made for them to wear on Sundays and special occasions. Nettie's gown in blue and crimson tartan was worn over a small crinoline and just skimmed the tops of her high buttoned boots. Sarah's was identical, but shorter.

'I never had anything so grand,' Nettie said, executing a twirl and almost knocking the milk jug off the kitchen table.

'You're supposed to be a young lady,' Cook said severely. 'If you don't act like one I'll ask Miss Gant to make your skirt shorter, like Sarah's.'

Sarah glanced down at her beautiful dress and frowned. 'Why do I have to wear short skirts like a little nipper?'

'Because you are just a nipper.' Dorcas tweaked the bow on Sarah's bonnet. 'You're not ten yet and Nettie's had her twelfth birthday, although she acts like a six-year-old at times.'

Nettie opened her mouth as if to argue but Cook held up her hand. 'That was the doorbell. Run up and answer it, Nettie. It'll be Miss Parfitt, I expect.'

Nettie flew up the stairs, taking two at a time and almost tripping over her skirts as she ran. Moments later she reappeared, her face shining with excitement. 'Miss Parfitt's here and Franz, the head sugar baker.'

'Mr Beckman to you, miss,' Dorcas said, pursing her lips.

Nettie shrugged her thin shoulders. 'Anyway, the mistress says come upstairs, all of you, including Betty.'

'Are you sure that's what she said?' Cook turned to glare at Betty who had covered her face with her apron and was uttering a sound like a braying jackass. 'I'm sure she doesn't mean you, you stupid girl.'

'Madam said everyone; even her.' Nettie shot a disdainful look at Betty. 'Madam said we should all partake of a little Christmas cheer before going out into the cold night.'

'Oh lawks!' Betty screeched through the folds of material. 'I never had no Christmas cheer.'

Cook seized her trusty umbrella and hooked the apron from Betty's grasp. 'You may come upstairs, but only if you promise not to say a word.'

Betty's eyes widened until they seemed in danger of popping out of her head. Sarah could see that she was frightened and she held out her hand. 'Come with me. I'll take you upstairs.'

Dorcas pushed past her, tut-tutting. 'Leave the silly thing down here where she's content to stay by the fire. I'm not going to miss my night out for anyone.' She marched up the stairs with Nettie racing after her and Cook following at a slower pace.

Sarah took Betty by the hand. 'There's nothing to be scared of. If I can do it so can you. There's nothing to worry about.'

'I won't say nothing.' Betty plugged her thumb in her mouth.

'Good girl.' Sarah led the way and they found everyone assembled in the front parlour. The aroma of hot spiced wine wafted through the open door and Sarah gave Betty a gentle push over the threshold.

Mrs Arbuthnot smiled benevolently. 'Merry Christmas, girls.'

Sarah was about to return the compliments of the season but she stopped short, gazing at Miss Parfitt in admiration. Her teacher had abandoned the severe grey poplin dress and cape she wore on schooldays for a gown of magenta cotton sateen with a matching velvet cape and a bonnet trimmed with cream rosebuds. 'Oh, Miss Parfitt, you look so fine,' she breathed.

Miss Parfitt blushed prettily. 'Thank you, Sarah.'

'You are beautiful. Like an angel.'

'That's not true, dear, but it's kind of you to say so.'

'The little girl is right.'

Everyone turned to stare at Franz Beckman who until that moment had been standing quietly by the fireplace with an empty glass clutched in his hand.

'Well now,' Mrs Arbuthnot said hastily. 'This is all very pleasant and I hope everyone has a truly wonderful evening. It is Christmas, after all.'

Cook raised her glass. 'Merry Christmas, ma'am. And thank you for giving us such a wonderful treat. I'm sure we are all very grateful.'

Mr Arbuthnot acknowledged the toast, smiling broadly. 'It's a pleasure to reward our loyal servants for all their hard work during the year, Mrs Burgess.'

'Perhaps we had better leave, sir,' Franz said, placing his glass on the table. 'We don't want to be late for the show.'

'No indeed.' Dorcas directed a pert smile in his direction. 'How right you are, Franz, and we all feel much safer knowing that you are accompanying us.'

He inclined his head. 'Thank you, Miss Dorcas.'

'Then off we go,' Cook said, tucking her umbrella under her arm. 'Go back to the kitchen, Betty.'

'Not fair,' Betty wailed. 'Want to go. Always left behind.' She began to sob loudly.

'Now, now, dear, there's no need to get yourself in a state.' Mrs Arbuthnot laid her hand on Betty's shoulder. 'You may have an orange and some walnuts if you do as Cook says.'

'Perhaps we ought to leave quickly,' Miss Parfitt said, gently. 'It won't be so upsetting for her once we are gone.'

Franz moved swiftly to her side, proffering his arm. 'May I?'

With a sidelong glance at Miss Parfitt that spoke volumes, Dorcas marched out of the room. 'Some people have all the luck,' she muttered, tossing her head.

'Behave yourself, Dorcas.' Cook hurried after her. 'Come along, girls.'

Sarah put her arm around Betty's heaving shoulders. 'Do you want me to take you back to the kitchen?'

'Want to go too,' Betty said, hiccuping. 'Want to see the show.'

'For heaven's sake come on.' Nettie caught Sarah by the edge of her cape. 'She'll forget what she was making a fuss about afore we've got halfway down the street.'

Mr Arbuthnot stepped forward to pat Betty on the head. 'There, there, girl. You heard what the mistress said. Go downstairs and you will have a treat.'

Mrs Arbuthnot snatched an orange, some nuts and an apple from the fruit bowl. She offered them to Betty. 'Here you are, child. Let Sarah go and you shall have all these nice things to eat.'

Betty howled even louder and Sarah was close to tears herself. She disengaged her hand from Betty's clutch and took off her new cape. She wrapped it around Betty's shoulders. 'It ain't fair that I get all the good times and you get none. You go with them and enjoy yourself.'

'Really, my dear, that's not necessary,' Mrs Arbuthnot

said hastily. 'I'm sure you've been looking forward to the outing just as much as anyone, if not more.'

Taking off her bonnet, Sarah placed it on Betty's head and tied the ribbons beneath her chin. 'I was very nearly born in the theatre, ma'am. I seen more actors, dancers and singers than I've had hot dinners, so it don't seem right that I should go and poor Betty should not.'

Mrs Arbuthnot opened her mouth to speak but her husband held a finger to his lips. 'Sarah has a point, my love. It's a noble gesture and I applaud the generosity of spirit shown by such a young child.'

Nettie put her head round the door. 'Come on, Sarah. The others have left and we need to run to catch them up.'

'I'm staying here, Nettie. You take Betty with you. She's never seen a show and it is Christmas.'

'What? Me take the simpleton?'

Mr Arbuthnot's brows drew together in a frown. 'Sarah has made a kind gesture, Nettie. I'm sure you would not want to upset the mistress and me.'

'I don't mind staying behind,' Sarah said earnestly. 'You can tell me all about it when you come home. I'd like that.'

'All right, but I think you're nuts. C'mon then, stupid.' Nettie stomped out of the room, dragging Betty by the hand.

Mrs Arbuthnot gave Sarah a hug. 'You are a dear, sweet child. That was a very nice thing to do.'

Sarah heard the front door close and was already regretting her decision. She had to bite back tears as she waited for Mrs Arbuthnot to wrap the fruit and nuts intended for Betty in a table napkin.

'There you are, my dear.' Mrs Arbuthnot pressed the bundle into her hands. 'You may take this down to the kitchen and make yourself a cup of hot chocolate as a special treat.'

Sarah bobbed a curtsey. 'Thank you, ma'am.' She retreated below stairs and settled herself in Cook's rocking chair by the range. Sending Betty in her place had been the right thing to do, but she could not help wishing that she was seated in the gallery, watching the show and clapping madly at the end of each act. She wiped her eyes and took a bite from the apple, which was sweet and delicious. She ate it down to the core and tossed what remained into the fire. She was just deciding whether to peel the orange or save it for later and share it with Nettie when the sound of a bell jangling made her jump. She looked up and saw that it was the front door. Perhaps it was carol singers, she thought with a frisson of excitement. They would certainly liven up a dull evening. She leapt off the chair, placed the napkin and its contents on the table and ran upstairs, but as she stopped to check her appearance in the hall mirror she realised that she was still wearing her best frock. She hesitated, but the caller was obviously growing impatient as they hammered on the knocker.

Composing herself, Sarah went to open the door, but it was not carol singers who were standing on the steps. The mere sight of workhouse master Trigg was enough to make Sarah open her mouth to scream, but he clamped his hand over her face and lifted her off her feet before she could make a sound. She felt herself spiralling helplessly into a black pit of oblivion.

Chapter Five

Sarah opened her eyes to almost total darkness. One moment she had been safe at home and now she was in a conveyance of some kind, hurtling through the city streets at an alarming speed. Then, in a terrifying flash, she remembered everything. Workhouse master Trigg had kidnapped her. She could feel his evil presence even if she could not make out the features of the man slumped in the seat opposite her. The smell of unwashed bodies and stale tobacco lingered in the confines of the hackney carriage, and she wrinkled her nose in distaste.

'Don't move a muscle.'

She recognised that voice and was stricken with fear. 'Where are you taking me?'

Trigg leaned towards her and she was sickened by the stench of his foul breath. He clamped his hand on her knee. 'That would be telling.'

She shrank even further into the leather squabs. 'Mr Arbuthnot will be cross.'

Trigg released her with a coarse laugh. 'He'll be cross? He's the one who ruined me and the missis. It was his lies to the workhouse governors that got us dismissed without a character between us. I want Mr Arbuthnot to suffer and I've only just begun.'

'It's not my fault,' Sarah whispered. 'It's got nothing to do with me. Please let me go home, sir.'

'I should have got ten pounds for you. Arbuthnot owes me a fiver and if I can't get if off him then I'll have to look elsewhere. Now shut up or you'll feel the back of my hand.'

Sarah cowered away from him, curling up in an attempt to keep warm. Her teeth were chattering, and the fine woollen dress so carefully made by Miss Gant was no protection against the bitter cold. She wished that she had not given her cape to Betty, and if only she had gone to the theatre as planned she would have been safe now. Her good deed had gone horribly wrong. She covered her face with her hands and stifled a sob.

The rumbling of the carriage wheels and the clatter of the horse's hooves on the frosty cobblestones seemed to go on forever, but then suddenly the rhythm changed and the carriage slowed down and came to a halt. Trigg thrust the door open and scooped her up with one arm as if she weighed less than a feather. He clambered to the pavement. 'Say one word and I'll snap your neck,' he growled as he hitched her over his shoulder. 'How much, cabby?'

Upside down and fearing for her life, Sarah did not hear the response, but she felt Trigg reach into his pocket and hand the money to the cabby, who drove off without a word. She was tempted to put up a fight or scream for help, but there did not seem to be anyone about. Trigg began to stride along and she was left hanging over his shoulder like a sack of coal. Each jolt made it even harder to catch her breath, and by the time he set her on her feet she was feeling sick and dizzy. He unlocked a door and thrust her into a dark passageway. 'Move along there or I'll help you with the toe of me boot.'

As she felt her way along the damp wall her feet crunched on the carapaces of a seething mass of what could only be cockroaches: no other insect was as large or smelled as bad. The floor seemed to be alive with them and she had to stifle a cry of horror as something large and furry ran across her feet. The alarming thought crossed her mind that they must be breeding rats the size of feral cats in this dreadful place. The sounds of raised male voices and women's screams filled her ears, and somewhere in the building a baby was crying.

'Stop there.' Trigg leaned across her to thrust a door open, and he gave her a shove that sent her sprawling onto the flagstone floor.

'So you got her then?' Mrs Trigg rose from a stool by a desultory fire.

'Yes, my love. Trigg always does what he promises.'

She crossed the room to drag Sarah to her feet. 'That dress will fetch a bob or two. Take it off, girl.'

Sarah stared at her in horror. 'What?'

'You heard me.' Mrs Trigg stood arms akimbo. 'D'you want to feel the Tickler's anger?'

'N-no, ma'am.' Sarah's hands were trembling violently as she attempted to undo the tiny pearl buttons at the back of her bodice.

Losing patience, Mrs Trigg whipped her round and finished the task. 'Now take it off.'

Too frightened to offer any resistance Sarah stepped out of the gown and wrapped her arms around her thin body. The cold air seemed to bite into her flesh as if an unseen entity was trying to eat her. She glanced anxiously at Mrs Trigg, who was staring greedily at her underwear. 'I'm freezing cold, ma'am.'

'Why would I care?' Mrs Trigg bent over to pick up the dress. 'Take them petticoats off too.' She draped the frock over her arm. 'This lot will keep us in gin for a week, Trigg.'

He was about to light his clay pipe with a spill from the fire but he paused, frowning. 'We don't want the brat to die of pneumonia. She's worth more alive than she is dead.'

Mrs Trigg uttered a humourless cackle of laughter. 'I thought of that, Mr Trigg.' She snatched the red flannel from the floor as Sarah took off her petticoat. 'I went to the dollyshop on the corner earlier. I didn't think she'd turn up wearing the workhouse duds.' She waddled over to a chest of drawers on the far side of the room and took out a couple of garments, tossing them to Sarah. 'Think yourself lucky to have any rag on your back, and stop complaining.'

Sarah was too cold and scared to argue and she dressed hurriedly. The skirt was made from shoddy and smelled like the coat of a wet dog. The coarse material scratched her bare legs but at least it gave some protection from the cold rising from the stone floor. The calico blouse was soiled and patched with

75

oddments of material, but it was infinitely better than nothing. Mrs Trigg eyed the result with pursed lips. 'You look like a ragbag, Sal Scratch. But it's only what you deserve. If we wasn't God-fearing people you'd have ended up in the river with a lead weight tied to your ankles.'

'But I never did you any harm.'

'We lost everything because of you.' Mrs Trigg's eyes narrowed to dark slits in her pudgy face. 'We had a good living at the workhouse, but the mill owner's words carried more weight than ours. We was sent packing just afore Christmas and we ended up here in this disgusting hovel. You're going to pay for that for the rest of your life, devil's daughter.'

'What are you going to do to me?' Sarah's lips were dry and her heart was beating so fast she thought that her captors must be able to hear it thudding against her ribs.

Trigg puffed smoke at the soot-blackened ceiling. 'You'll find out soon enough.'

'You've got too much to say for yourself,' Mrs Trigg added, giving Sarah a push that sent her staggering against the wall. 'Sit down and keep quiet or the Tickler will have his revenge, and you know what the Tickler can do to unruly children.'

Sarah slid to the ground, huddling up in an attempt to keep warm. She glanced round the room, looking for a way of escape, but the windows were shuttered on the outside, and Trigg had locked the door when they came in. The dank room was filled with moving shadows created by the guttering of a single candle, which was the only illumination other than the feeble flames from the coal fire. Three ill-assorted wooden chairs were set around a deal table in the centre of the room, and there was an iron bedstead in the far corner. A crust of bread and a heel of cheese were the only evidence of food, but Trigg had taken a bottle from the mantelshelf and was taking swigs from it in between puffs on his pipe.

'Save some for me,' Mrs Trigg said, tossing a shoe at her husband. 'And it's time we had supper. You'll have to go to the pie shop afore it closes.'

Trigg rose somewhat unsteadily to his feet. 'I'm going to the pub to meet Grey. We got some haggling to do.'

'Then I'm coming with you.'

'What about her?' Trigg pointed the stem of his pipe at Sarah. 'We can't leave her on her own.'

Mrs Trigg bared her teeth in a semblance of a grin. 'What's she going to get up to here? We'll lock her in.'

'Supposing she makes a noise and shouts for help?'

'Who is there to hear her? Those that are in their rooms will be too drunk to care, or too befuddled with opium to notice, and even if they did they wouldn't interfere.' Mrs Trigg turned to Sarah, scowling ominously. 'Try anything and it'll be the worse for you.' She snatched her cloak from the back of a chair. 'There's bread and cheese on the table and if he's left any there's some gin in the bottle. Drink that and it'll shut you up for the night.' She made for the door, pausing with her hand on the key. 'You'll sleep on the floor. If I find you in my bed I'll throttle you with me bare hands and enjoy doing it.' She unlocked the door and stepped outside, followed by Trigg.

The door closed on them and Sarah heard the key scrape in the lock. She rose stiffly to her feet and went to warm herself by the fire.

She sat on the hearth and buried her face in her hands, giving way to the tears that she had so far held back. She cried for her mother and father and the little siblings who were laid to rest in a pauper's grave. She cried for Nettie and Miss Parfitt, whom she loved, and for Dorcas and Cook who had been kind to her. She cried for her kind employers who had taken her in and had treated her more like a daughter than a servant. They would all be wondering where she was and why she had left the house without a word. Perhaps they would think that she had run away. One thing was certain: no one would know where to look for her. And it was Christmas Eve. There were presents under the tree in Mrs Arbuthnot's parlour and she was certain that one of them was for her. Who would have it now? Fresh tears spurted from her eyes and she curled up on the floor, her small body racked with sobs.

She was awakened by a sudden burst of sound as the door opened and Mrs Trigg staggered into the room with Trigg and another man close on her heels. The candle had gone out but there was enough light from the dying embers of the fire to see that the third party was no stranger. It was the man who had attempted to snatch her on the night of the pea-souper, and Sarah stuffed her hand into her mouth to stifle a scream. She lay very still, closing her eyes again and feigning sleep, but a sharp kick in the ribs from Mrs Trigg made her yelp with pain and she sat up.

'Light the candle, Trigg. We'll have another drink with our good friend afore he sets off.' Mrs Trigg bent over to grab Sarah by the ear and yank her to her feet. 'See here, Grey. This is the nipper you were supposed to bring to us.'

'Never mind that now,' Trigg said, pulling the stopper from a bottle with his teeth. 'Let's have something to keep out the cold.'

Grey pulled up a chair and sat down. He put his battered top hat on the table and unwound his muffler. 'It'll be a long night. I need something to keep me going. Are you sure it won't wait until daybreak, Trigg?'

'Very sure. Old Arbuthnot will have the peelers out looking for the kid the moment they realise she's missing.' Trigg handed the bottle to him. 'Help yourself but don't get so swipey that you lose your way, cully.'

Mrs Trigg abandoned Sarah and went to the table, snatching the stone bottle from Grey before he had taken more than a sip. 'That's enough of that. You'd best hand over the money and be off.'

'All right, Mrs T. I don't want to hang around here anyway. I need to get away from town for me health, if you know what I mean.' Grey thrust his hand into his pocket and took out a leather pouch.

Sarah watched helplessly as he opened it and counted out the coins, laying them in a line on the table. 'There you are. There's your blood money.'

Mrs Trigg clipped him round the ear. 'Less of your cheek. And there's only five sovs there. Where's the rest?'

He grinned. 'Expenses, Mrs T. A chap's got to live.'

'You was supposed to get ten quid off the person in question.'

'She's no fool,' Grey said, shaking his head. 'She knows the score and she wouldn't cough up any more. Seven sovs was her final offer.' He rose to his feet, turning his gaze on Sarah. 'We'll have to gag the kid and tie her up. I got enough to do driving all the way to the Essex coast without having to act as nursemaid.'

Mrs Trigg reached out and grabbed Sarah by the hair. 'Fetch some rope, Trigg.'

He raised himself from his seat. 'Where am I going to find rope at this time of night, my love?'

She curled her lip. 'Tear up a sheet then, Mr Trigg. Do I have to think of everything?'

Sarah tried to resist but it was useless and she was gagged and trussed up like poultry ready for the roast. Grey wrapped her in his caped greatcoat and once again she found herself tossed over a man's shoulder, where she hung helplessly until he threw her into the back of a cart. She landed with a thud on bare boards which temporarily winded her. She struggled to free herself and after several minutes of wriggling about she managed to stick her head out of the smelly material and inhale the cold night air. Exhausted, cramped and sore, she could do nothing other than lie still, staring up at the stars as the cart rattled and bumped over the cobblestones. She was uncomfortable but at least she was reasonably warm and eventually she fell asleep.

She was awakened by birdsong and opened her eyes to a cold, white morning. Above her head she could see the bare branches of a tree with a robin perched on one singing his head off. Frost decorated the leafless twigs in the hedgerows and dusted bunches of scarlet berries with glittering diamonds. The air was fresh and clean with a hint of fragrant woodsmoke, and that alone was enough to convince her that they were far away from the putrid stench of the city. She tried to move, but her limbs were stiff and she could not feel her feet at all.

Grey loomed above her and she saw a knife clasped in his hand. She thought he was going to kill her, but the gag prevented her from uttering a sound. He leaned over the side of the cart and with a swift movement slit the cotton sheeting tied over her mouth. He reached in and pulled her to a sitting position. 'I ain't going to hurt you, kid,' he said gruffly. 'You've been a good girl, so I'm going to trust you not to try to run away.' He cut her bonds and sheathed the knife before lifting her out of the cart, setting her on her feet. She would have fallen but he steadied her and helped her to the hollow beneath the tree. He took a pile of sacks from the cart and spread them on the ground. 'Sit there and I'll give you something hot to drink.'

She had no choice other than to obey him and she sat down, chafing her legs in an attempt to get the blood circulating. She watched him as he made a fire and hung a tin can from a metal hook over the flames. Within minutes its contents were bubbling and sending clouds of aromatic steam into the frosty air. He poured the brew into two tin mugs. 'Got no milk or sugar,' he said, handing one to Sarah. 'Be very careful, it's hot.'

She took it gratefully, blowing on the tea until it was cool enough to sip. She kept a wary eye on Grey, but he seemed a different man now that he was away from the evil influence of the Triggs. He busied himself hacking slices of bread from a loaf and he passed one to her with a slice of cheese. 'Eat up. We've got a long way to go yet.'

She would have liked to refuse, but she was hungry and she took a bite. The bread was a bit stale but the cheese was tasty and she savoured each mouthful, washing it down with tea. 'Where are you taking me?' she said at last. The food and drink had given her courage, and it was hard to be scared of a man who had given up his overcoat for her benefit and was munching bread and cheese with evident enjoyment.

His stern expression was tempered with a hint of a grin. 'Don't bother your head with details, kid. You'll find out soon enough, and no one's going to harm you.'

'Well, where are we now?'

'Questions all the time; don't you never shut up?'

'We're not in London. I know that.'

'Sharp little thing, ain't you?' He gulped down the last mouthful of tea and shook the dregs from the mug. 'We've wasted enough time. Get in the cart and we'll be on our way.'

Sarah scrambled to her feet, but she was reluctant to leave the warmth of the fire. She remained motionless, shivering despite the thickness of his greatcoat, which hung about her like a tent. He doused the flames and was busy stamping on the embers when he looked up and saw her staring at him. 'You look perished. The old bitch should've given you something warm to wear.' He picked her up and lifted her onto the driver's seat, wrapping the sacks around her legs for added warmth. 'That'll have to do.' He stowed his belongings in the back of the cart and climbed up beside her. 'Sit tight and keep quiet or I'll have to tie you up again. I can't afford to lose you, Sal Scratch. You're worth two quid to me.'

'My name is Sarah Scrase, not Sal Scratch.'

His hazel eyes twinkled but he kept a straight face. 'It's all the same to me, kid. You're just market goods to my way of thinking. You're a barrel of molasses or a tub of lard – I'm just the delivery man.'

'If that's the case then why did you give me food and drink?' Sarah said, eyeing him curiously. 'You didn't have to wrap me in your coat. You've only got your jacket and you must be cold.'

'I'm tough and you're just a little girl.' He flicked the reins. 'Walk on, Boxer.'

'You must have been chilly, but you let me sleep. You wouldn't have done that if you were really a bad man.'

He shot her a sideways glance. 'I am a bad man. Don't ever doubt it, Sarah Scrase.'

She was warm beneath his coat and the sacking and

she had seen enough of life to know the difference between someone who was inherently bad and a person who could on occasions show kindness and understanding. 'I know what I know,' she said, nodding her head. 'And if you take me home to Wellclose Square, Mr Arbuthnot will reward you. He's got a big sugar mill and lots of money.'

'And I'll end up dancing a Newgate hornpipe.'

'I don't know what that is.'

'Keep it that way.' He reached into his pocket, took out a clay pipe. 'Now shut up. I can't be doing with all this talk.' He stuck the pipe in his mouth and stared at the road ahead.

Sarah lapsed into silence, but her mind was busy planning ways of escape. She had no idea where they were or how far they had come from London. They seemed to be travelling along country lanes miles from anywhere, but when they came to a town or a village she would take the first opportunity to leap off and ask for help. There must be kindly citizens who would take pity on a girl, especially on Christmas Day. She bit her lip as she thought of the house in Wellclose Square, and the large goose that Mrs Burgess would have put in the oven to roast. She had helped to make the plum pudding and it would be simmering in the washhouse copper. Her present would still be under the tree and she wondered what it could be. Perhaps it was something to wear? It might be a muffler and a pair of woollen gloves: she could really do with them now. Or perhaps it was a storybook. That would be lovely, especially if it had pictures in it. She wrapped

84

the sack closer round her knees as a cold east wind whipped her hair around her face and slapped her cheeks with spikes of sleet.

Grey unwound his muffler and thrust it into her hands. 'Put it on or you'll freeze.'

She wrapped it around her head and neck. It smelled of the stables and pipe tobacco but it was warm and she managed a smile. 'Ta, mister. You're a toff.'

He grunted something unintelligible and put his arm around her, pulling her close to his side so that she was sheltered from the worst of the weather. She was tempted to resist, but it was cold and getting colder. She leaned against him, working out her plan of action, but when they did pass through habitation there was no one about. It seemed that they were the only travellers on the road, and that everyone was indoors taking advantage of the holiday to sit round the fire in festive mood. She spotted the occasional farm worker in the fields tending to the livestock, but they were always too far away to be of any help.

Grey stopped several times to allow the horse to drink from a stream or a river, and to make a fresh brew of tea. He produced a cold pie from the back of the cart which they ate at midday, and he gave Sarah an apple. 'Merry Christmas. I ain't forgotten the day, but there's not much to celebrate. It's all a sham if you ask me.'

Sarah took the piece of fruit. 'Why is it a sham?'

'Because it's supposed to be a time for the family.'

She digested this in silence for a moment, but it did not seem to make sense. 'I don't know what you mean, Grey. I lost my family and that makes me very sad.'

'Think yourself lucky, kid. Families fall out with each other. They might make a show of everything being all right just for a day, and then it's all over again. Christmas is a nonsense, if you ask me.'

'Did you fall out with your family? That would be sad too.'

'I've told you not to ask so many questions. Eat your apple.'

She bit into the firm flesh, chewing thoughtfully. 'Is that why you haven't got anywhere to go on Christmas Day? Don't you have a home to go to?'

He shot her an exasperated glance. 'It's none of your business.'

'I don't think you're as bad as you make out. You've been good to me in your way, and it's not too late for you to take me back to Wellclose Square. You could leave me outside and drive off.'

'And your master would have the coppers on me before you could blink.'

'I wouldn't peach on you, Grey. I wouldn't want you to go to prison.'

'You're goods to be transported, nipper. That's what you are to me; nothing else.' He stared at her for a moment and then turned away. 'We've got a few more miles to go and it gets dark early this time of year. Get back on the cart.'

They travelled on again, and Sarah lapsed into silence. She knew that it was useless to appeal to his better nature, but she continued to hope that something might happen to make him change his mind. Perhaps Mr Arbuthnot would offer a reward for her return. She would put this to Grey at the first opportunity, but he was deliberately ignoring her and she decided to wait until he was more amenable.

She closed her eyes, and although she was conscious of every rut in the road she must have dozed off, as when she opened them again she noticed a change in the landscape. The flat, wooded countryside had opened out into marshland with a salty tang in the air. Tussocks of reed and grass created small islands surrounded by turgid water, and the mournful cries of seabirds soaring above their heads sent shivers down her spine that had nothing to do with the ice-cold air.

'We're almost there,' Grey said, pointing to what looked like the ruins of a cottage in the half-light.

'This is where you're taking me?' Sarah stared at it in dismay. They seemed to be in a wet wilderness miles away from anywhere, and the building appeared to be in a tumbledown state close to dereliction. 'Take me home, please,' she cried, clutching his arm. 'Don't leave me in this terrible place.'

He pushed her away. 'Shut up.' He flicked the whip above the horse's ear and it plodded wearily on along a narrow track until it came to a halt in front of the building. 'This is it,' he said tersely. 'Get down.'

She shook her head and clung to the seat. 'No. I won't. You can't make me.'

He leapt from the cart. 'There's nowhere to run to, kid. These salt marshes are deadly if you don't know where to put your feet. One false step and you'll be sucked down into the mud and never seen again.' He held out his arms. 'Don't make me drag you off that seat.'

She realised that it was useless to argue and she allowed him to lift her to the ground. 'But where is this place? What am I doing here?'

'It's not for me to say.' He stared at her for a long moment. 'What a sight you look, kid. Maybe she'll demand her money back.'

'And you'll take me home?'

'Maybe, or perhaps I'll sell you in the market. You can't trust me. I'm no good and never will be.' He seized her by the hand and dragged her up the steps onto the wooden platform that ran the width of the building. A thatched lean-to had been added in an attempt to shield the front of the building from the worst of the weather, but it had begun to rain and water dripped through huge gaps where the straw had rotted away. Grey hammered on the door. 'Ho there, Elsie. Anyone at home?'

Sarah's stomach churned and she felt sick with apprehension. She wanted to run away but Grey's timely warning about the marshland had terrified her, and she slipped her small hand into his. She hoped that no one would come and then he would have to take her away from this dreadful place. She waited, hardly daring to breathe, but just as she thought that her prayers had been answered she heard footsteps and the door opened slowly, grinding on rusty hinges.

'Who's there?'

'It's me, Grey. I've brought the goods you ordered.'

A slatternly woman of indeterminable age held up

an oil lamp, peering at them through strands of lank auburn hair. 'Come inside.'

Grey gave Sarah a gentle push and as she stepped over the threshold a dreadful stench caught her at the back of her throat, causing her to retch. He followed her into the dark, evil-smelling interior. 'Good God, woman. What in the devil's name have you been cooking?'

'Close the door. You're causing a draught.' She backed towards the rusty range where a cauldron hung above the open fire.

Sarah covered her mouth and nose with her hand. The lines from Shakespeare's *Macbeth* came forcibly to mind. She had seen it being rehearsed by Charles and Ellen Kean, and it had given her nightmares for weeks afterwards. 'Bubble, bubble, toil and trouble'; never had a quotation seemed more appropriate. The old woman was undoubtedly a witch – there was no other explanation. She huddled closer to Grey. 'Please take me with you,' she whispered. 'Don't leave me here.'

'Not now, nipper. This is Miss Fitch and you're going to be her apprentice.' He moved closer to the woman, who had set the lamp on the table and was attempting to take the cauldron off the heat. 'That don't smell too good, Elsie.'

She brushed her hair back from her face. 'Give us a hand, you great lump. It's about to boil over.'

He lifted the pot off the flames. 'Looks like whatever you're cooking is trying to escape. I hope that's not your supper.'

'Don't be so cheeky. This is a tried and tested remedy for foot rot.'

'My feet are fine, I'm glad to say.'

Miss Fitch glared at him, her thin features contorted so that her eyes, nose and lips seemed to form a single feature. 'It's for sheep, you fool.' She pushed past him and picked up the oil lamp, holding it so that she could examine Sarah from head to toe. 'So this is my new pupil. She won't do. Take her back – she's too young.'

'That's your problem, not mine,' Grey said, ramming his hat back on his head. 'I've done my bit by delivering her, and that'll be ten sovs, as agreed.'

She poked a finger into Sarah's ribs. 'This girl can't be more than nine or ten years old. I asked for someone older and bigger. She'll not last the winter here.'

'I'll be ten January.' Sarah gulped and swallowed. 'But I shouldn't be here, miss. I was taken by force and I want to go home.'

Miss Fitch turned to Grey. 'So that's it. The child was abducted.'

'Take it up with Trigg,' he said, shrugging. 'I paid him and now you pay me. That was the agreement.'

'I wanted a worker, and you've brought me a child.'

Grey flexed his fingers and was glaring at Miss Fitch, Sarah observed nervously, as though he would like to wring her skinny neck. 'I've had a long drive and I need to get off these bloody marshes before dark. Now pay up and let me be on my way.'

'I was wrong to put my trust in that blackguard Trigg.' Miss Fitch squared up to him, seemingly unafraid. 'Five sovs and we're done.'

'Seven,' Grey said, holding out his hand.

'You don't get a penny until you've delivered my stuff.'

Grey raised an eyebrow. 'And what would that be, Elsie?'

'Don't play games with me, you reprobate. Hand it over.' She snatched a knife from the table and held it to his throat. 'If you're trying to extort money from me, Tobias, I swear I'll use this to good effect.'

He produced a small paper package, holding it above her head as she tried to snatch it from him. 'Let's see the colour of your money first.'

She fished in her pocket and drew out a handful of coins. 'Seven it is then, you dreadful fellow. Now give it to me.' He passed it to her with a wry quirk to his lips and she dropped the money into his hand. 'Take it and be off.'

'No,' Sarah cried, throwing herself at Grey and clinging on for dear life. 'Don't leave me. I'll die if you leave me here. You heard what the old witch said.'

Miss Fitch let out a shriek of laughter. 'Witch. Yes, I've been called that and worse, but you've nothing to fear from me, girl. Unless of course you don't do as you're told and then I might well turn you into a toad.'

'No,' Sarah wailed. 'Take me with you, Grey.'

He extricated himself from her desperate grasp, taking her by the shoulders and giving her a shake. 'I can't do anything about it, kid. She might look like a witch but she's a healer. She makes medicines for people and animals. You'll work for her and learn.' He headed for the door but Sarah ran after him, catching him by the coat tails.

'Take me and sell me in the marketplace if you like. I don't want to be turned into a toad.'

He hesitated, staring down at her, and for a moment she thought that he was weakening, but he shook her off. 'Think yourself lucky that I didn't do as the Triggs asked and sell you to a whorehouse.'

He wrenched the door open and a gust of cold air almost knocked Sarah off her feet. Seized by panic she tried to run after him but a bony hand grabbed her by the muffler that Grey had wrapped around her neck, and she was jerked backwards with such force that she fell to the floor. 'Don't leave me,' she gasped. 'Grey. Come back.'

Chapter Six

'Be quiet.' Miss Fitch prodded Sarah with the toe of her boot. 'I can't stand the sound of caterwauling, which is why I wanted someone older with a bit of sense.'

Sarah loosened the muffler so that she could breathe more easily. 'You can't keep me locked up, miss. I was taken from my rightful master, Mr Arbuthnot of Wellclose Square.'

'That's got nothing to do with me. You're here now, bought and paid for, so you'll do as you're told. Get up.'

'It was the workhouse master who ordered it,' Sarah said, getting slowly to her feet. 'He's a bad man, miss.'

'All men are bad, if you ask me.' Miss Fitch folded her arms across her flat chest, giving Sarah a calculating look. 'Can you read and write?'

'Yes, miss.'

'That's something. Have you got a neat hand?'

'Miss Parfitt seemed to think so.' Sarah's eyes filled with tears at the mention of her idol's name. She would never see her again and Miss Parfitt would forget all about her.

'Why are you crying? I can't stand babies.'

'It's Christmas Day and I don't know why I'm here.'

Miss Fitch raised her thin eyebrows. 'Is it really? I had no idea, but then time matters little out here on the marsh.'

'I want to go home, miss.'

'This is your home now, silly child. You will live with me and learn to be an apothecary. If you are quick and bright I can teach you how to heal the sick. Doesn't that appeal to you?'

Sarah shook her head. 'I want Nettie and Cook and Dorcas.'

'Stop that now. I won't listen to you drivelling on about what is past and gone. You are here and here you will stay. Tomorrow we will start work, but I can see that you're tired and probably hungry too.' Miss Fitch gazed around the untidy room with a perplexed frown. 'I can't recall where I put the china bowls.'

Sarah was about to suggest the dresser might be a good place to start, but Miss Fitch had obviously had the same thought. She began to rummage amongst the jumble of items piled one upon the other, tossing notebooks, scraps of paper, quill pens and bunches of dried herbs onto the table until she found two cracked and chipped basins. She filled them from a saucepan that had been simmering on the hob and placed them on the table, pushing one towards Sarah. 'Sit down and eat.'

'It's not for foot rot, is it, miss?' Sarah asked nervously, staring at the swirling contents of the bowl. She sniffed, but the smell of the cauldron still lingered in her nostrils and the soup, if that was what it was, did not look much different.

'It's my own recipe,' Miss Fitch said, hacking a slice from a loaf that she produced from an earthenware crock. 'It's vegetable broth and it will do you good.' She speared a piece of bread with her knife and flicked it onto the tabletop beside Sarah's plate. 'You'll feel better with food in your belly.' She took a seat and began to spoon the soup into her mouth. 'Go on, it won't poison you.'

Sarah screwed up her face and sipped the hot broth. It was surprisingly tasty and she smothered a sigh of relief. 'It was the smell of the medicine, miss,' she said apologetically. 'It turned my stomach.'

'You'll get used to it. I make all my own remedies from herbs that I gather during my excursions into the countryside. I'll take you with me when the weather permits.' Miss Fitch laid her spoon down, staring hard at Sarah. 'But if you prove to be lazy I will be very strict and punish you, and if you are stupid I will sell you to the raddle man. You know what he is, don't you?'

Trembling, Sarah pushed her plate away. 'No, miss.'

'He is red all over and folks say that he is the devil incarnate. If you are bad he will come and get you. Do you understand?'

'Y-yes, miss.'

'Good.' Miss Fitch stared at Sarah, chewing the tip of her finger with a thoughtful expression. 'I think I might grow to like you, given time.'

Sarah decided that the safest option was to agree to everything this strange person said, and she nodded. 'Yes, miss.'

95

Miss Fitch rose to her feet. 'My name is Elsie Fortunata Fitch,' she proclaimed, flinging both arms open in a dramatic gesture. 'But as I hate standing on ceremony you may call me Elsie. What is your name, girl?'

'At the workhouse they called me Sal Scratch, but my name is Sarah Scrase and I'm not afraid of the raddle man.'

Elsie threw back her head and roared with laughter. 'You may be just a child, Sarah Scrase, but you've got spirit. Finish your meal and then you can start helping me by clearing up some of this mess.' She jerked her head in the direction of the overloaded dresser and her bed in the corner, which was piled high with what looked to Sarah like rubbish. 'There's no need to pull a face,' Elsie said sternly. 'I may not be the tidiest person in the world, but I am a woman of science. I answered my calling when I was a girl and I have never regretted my decision to devote my life to healing the sick, whether they be human or animal.'

Sarah finished off her soup and wiped the bowl with the last of her bread. She stood up. 'I'm ready, miss – I mean, Elsie.' She frowned. 'Are you sure you want me to call you by your Christian name, miss?'

Elsie had moved to the range and was stirring yet another pan which was bubbling away on the hob. 'Ah, but I'm not a Christian, Sarah. I am a child of the forest, a pagan princess. Herne the Hunter and the Greek god Pan are amongst those whom I worship.' She paused, waving the spoon in the air so that droplets of something brown and sticky fell onto the flames and ignited with a fizz and a pop. 'I am kin to the green man and he shares his bounty with me.' She took the pan off the hob and made a dash for the table, setting it down on a charred wooden board. 'Now find me some bottles, Sarah. There should be some on the dresser, or maybe I put them under my bed. On the other hand they might be outside on the deck.' She chuckled. 'I call it the deck because my home is like a small boat, floating on the marsh.'

Sarah scuttled about, searching everywhere for the bottles and discovering them one by one in the most unexpected places. She set them in a neat row on the table and watched Elsie fill them from the saucepan, spilling more of the liquid than she was actually getting in the bottles. 'What is that stuff, Miss Elsie?'

'Miss Elsie! I rather like that title. It has a certain ring to it. You may call me that, Sarah, if it suits you better.'

'Thank you, Miss Elsie.'

'I do rather sound like a stage actress of some repute.' Elsie brushed her curtain of hair back from her forehead. 'I was not always a recluse. I had a different life once upon a time, but that was many years ago before I turned my back on society, and men in particular.' She leaned towards Sarah, breathing heavily. 'They're all rotten to the core, Sarah Scrase. They'll break your heart if you let them.'

Sarah decided that it would be wiser not to argue and she perched on the edge of a chair, leaning her elbows on the table and watching Elsie bottle the noxious-smelling brew. She still did not know what the mysterious elixir was, or what it was for, but her eyelids were growing heavy and her limbs felt leaden.

Elsie put the cork in the last bottle with a satisfied sigh. 'There. This is my remedy for coughs and colds. It will soothe a sore throat and lull the sufferer into the arms of Morpheus.' She looked up, frowning. 'You're half asleep already, child.'

'We were travelling all night and it was cold. I wish Grey would come back.'

'I've just told you that men are dangerous,' Elsie said sternly. 'Keep away from the male of the species. They'll be nice to you until they get what they want and then they'll abandon you. Tobias won't be coming back until the spring when he brings me a fresh supply of things that can only be purchased in London. He has his uses, but like all of his gender, he is not to be trusted.'

Sarah nodded. 'Yes. I mean, no.'

Elsie moved to Sarah's side just as she was about to slide off the seat. She lifted her in her arms and carried her to the bed where she dumped her unceremoniously on a pile of old clothes. 'You can lie there for now,' she said, covering her with a greatcoat that smelled of rotten fish. 'Tomorrow we'll arrange things differently, but I have work to do before I can rest.' She moved away and Sarah closed her eyes, sinking immediately into a deep and dreamless sleep.

In the weeks that followed Sarah realised that there was little or no chance of escaping from her present situation and returning to London. The vast expanse of saltings was covered twice daily by the incoming tide, and the marsh interlaced with channels of brackish water created an effective prison. The cart track was the only route to freedom, but as far as she could remember it was several miles to the nearest village.

She had to come to terms with the fact that she was ill-equipped to undertake the long journey back to London as she had neither money nor warm clothing, and the worst of the winter weather was yet to come. The garments that Mrs Trigg had forced upon her were no protection against the cold, and she dressed herself in oddments taken from the pile of clothing that Elsie used as bedding. These were moth-eaten and in desperate need of a wash, but that presented yet another problem. Water had to be fetched from a stream more than a mile away and it was too precious a commodity to waste in the washtub, which was used for anything other than the purpose for which it was originally intended. Elsie's personal hygiene was questionable, but Sarah had been brought up to value cleanliness. 'We might be poor,' her mother had often said, 'but it costs us nothing to keep clean.' This, Sarah thought now, might have been a slight exaggeration, but she could recall her mother's work-worn hands, chapped and sore from constant washing and scrubbing floors, and she vowed that she would never let Ma down. All she had now of her early years were memories of days before they were forced into the workhouse, and she clung to them steadfastly.

Every morning as she trudged across the marsh to fetch fresh water she hoped that Ma was looking down at her from heaven with a smile of approval. Even in the worst weather she washed her hands and face in the cool spring water before filling two wooden buckets and hefting them back to the place she now called home. Her next duty was to follow the track to the edge of the marsh where stunted trees and bushes grew in abundance. She collected wood for the fire and stacked it on a pallet, securing it with a length of rope which she then tied around her waist, dragging her load homewards like a beast of burden.

It was only at night, when she lay on a straw-filled palliasse by the range and settled down to sleep, that she allowed herself to think of Nettie and everyone in the Arbuthnots' house in Wellclose Square. She struggled with the agonising pangs of homesickness and tried hard not to give way to tears. She wondered if they missed her, or if they had given her up for lost. In the beginning she had looked out across the marshes, hoping to see a search party scouring the countryside in their efforts to find her, but no one came. There was only Miss Elsie, who with her labours for the day ended would sit in the rickety rocking chair by the range, smoking a strange-looking pipe, the detachable bowl of which she heated over a small lamp before putting it back on a bamboo stem and inhaling the vapour. It was not long before she sank into a state of oblivion and Sarah would eventually fall asleep.

One cold winter's morning when she had nothing better to occupy her time, Sarah was tidying the dresser when she discovered some writing paper in one of the drawers and a bottle of ink. She waited until Elsie had left the cottage to go outside and commune with nature, which she did regardless of the weather, and, safe in the knowledge that she would be undisturbed, she wrote to Mr Arbuthnot, begging him to come and take her home. The only problem was that she had no way of getting the letter to him. She shed a few tears and folded the note carefully before hiding it in her palliasse, although she feared that it would remain there for some time. Elsie had promised to take her to market when she made her next trip to the nearest town, but it had snowed heavily and now they would have to wait until the roads were passable.

By the end of February they were running out of rations and survived mainly on bread and vegetable soup. Elsie had a sack of flour stowed away in a cupboard and another filled with carrots, turnips and potatoes, but supplies were dwindling away. There were a few strings of onions still hanging from the beamed ceiling together with bunches of dried herbs, and the remains of a flitch of bacon smoked gently in the chimney breast. They would not starve, but their diet was frugal and monotonous. Occasionally Elsie braved the elements and made forays across the marshes to the estuary, where she bartered her potions for fresh fish. At first she went alone, but in March when the worst of the winter weather appeared to be over, she offered to take Sarah with her.

It was cold inside the cottage that morning, even though Sarah had lit the fire earlier than usual. The bitter east wind soughed through gaps in the weatherboard and a chill rose up from the floor. Her teeth were chattering as she made herself ready to go out, but she had to stifle a giggle at the sight of Miss Elsie dressed for the occasion in men's breeches and a leather jerkin with three multi-coloured woollen mufflers wound around her neck. This was comical enough, but her hair seemed to have a life of its own, and even with a man's felt hat pulled down over her ears Elsie's fiery locks managed to escape and twined snake-like around her weathered features.

Sarah knew that she had managed little better, and she was glad that there were no mirrors on the walls to confirm her suspicion that she looked just as odd as her mistress. She had searched the tangled mass of garments on Elsie's bed and discovered a red velvet gown, which must once have been someone's Sunday best but was now patched and threadbare. There was a hooded fur cape that had also seen better days and now resembled the pelt of a mangy fox, but it was warm and would protect her from the biting east wind.

As they set off in the pearl-grey light of dawn she could not help thinking that they must present a very odd sight as they trudged across the boggy terrain. It was hard going and her legs ached as she tried to keep up with Miss Elsie's mannish strides, but she knew better than to complain. They arrived at the muddy foreshore as the boats were being dragged onto the beach and unloaded. Seagulls hovered overhead in great white clouds of flapping wings, and their mournful cries filled the air as they waited for their chance to seize the odd fish. Elsie strode amongst the fishermen with her basket of medicines and to Sarah's astonishment they greeted her like an old and valued friend. They seemed eager to take her patent remedies for everything from warts to inflammation of the lungs and paid her with fish and a large crab, which she passed to Sarah. She took it gingerly but when the creature snapped its huge claws she dropped it onto the mud with a cry of fright. This caused the fishermen to guffaw with laughter and demand to know where the funny little maid had been living all her life.

'Don't be a baby, Sarah,' Elsie said with an amused smile. 'Pick it up. That's our supper tonight.'

Sarah bent down to retrieve it but the crab scuttled towards the water and as she attempted to chase it her boots became stuck in the mud. 'Help,' she cried. 'I'm sinking.'

Elsie merely laughed and turned back to haggle with a fisherman over the price of one of her nostrums. By this time the crab had reached the water and was swimming for its life, but the more Sarah struggled, the deeper she sank. She uttered a shriek of despair, thinking that she would be sucked into the morass, but suddenly a pair of arms seized her round the waist and she was dragged free and deposited on firm ground. She spun round to thank her rescuer only to discover that it was a boy of perhaps thirteen or fourteen and he was doubled up with laughter. 'I'm glad you think it's funny,' she said crossly. 'I could have drowned.'

He shook his head. 'I never seen anything the likes of you before. I thought you was a funny little dwarf or something.'

'I'm a girl. My name is Sarah Scrase and you are very rude.'

'Well, young Sarah, you got to admit you look a bit comical in that garb.' He held out his hand. 'Davey Hawkes.'

His smile was infectious and she shook his hand. 'Thank you for saving me.'

'It was nothing, but I'm afraid you lost your supper. Looks like the crab got away, but I daresay I could find you another one.'

Sarah recoiled at the thought. 'Maybe not.'

'I'll tie its pincers up and then it won't snap at you.' He went over to one of the boats and leaned in to pick up an even larger crab. 'This one will be tasty.' He proceeded to tie the claws with lengths of twine. 'Here, you can take it now.'

She did not want him to think she was a coward, but she did not like the way the animal was waving its legs and swivelling its eyes in obvious distress. She felt sorry for the poor creature and would have liked to return it to the water so that it could swim free again. She could sympathise with its plight, which was similar to her own. She was just like that crab when it was out of its element. She too was in a strange place and did not fit in. She found herself longing for the cobbled, gaslit city streets, and the smell of hot molasses that wafted from the sugar mills in Wellclose Square. At this moment she would have swapped the sharp, briny air for a pea-souper, and a crippling wave of homesickness washed over her. She bit the inside of her lip so that she would not let herself down by crying in front of the grinning boy, and she held out her hand. 'All right. Give it to me then. I'm not afraid.'

He stared into her face, his smile fading. 'Tell you what, young 'un, I'll put it in the old woman's basket. It'll rest easier there.' He strode off to deposit the crab out of sight amongst the remaining bottles and paper pokes.

Overwhelmed by such a simple act of kindness, Sarah turned away to wipe her streaming eyes on her sleeve.

'What's up now?' Davey said, patting her on the shoulder. 'Are you poorly?'

She shook her head. 'It's the wind. It makes my eyes sore.'

'You don't come from round here, do you?'

'How did you know?'

'You talk funny.'

'I used to live in London.'

'Ah,' he said wisely. 'That would account for it then. How come you're here?'

She could see Miss Elsie beckoning to her. 'I have to go now, Davey. Thank you for helping me.'

He shrugged his shoulders. 'Weren't nothing, Sarah. I'd have done the same for anyone who was scared.'

'I wasn't scared.'

'Of course you weren't.' He patted her on the head. 'I meant anyone who didn't know how to handle a live thing fresh from the sea.'

'Come along, Sarah. It's time we were on our way.' Elsie's voice was tinged with impatience.

'I'm coming.' Sarah made a move to leave but Davey caught her by the hand.

'You still haven't told me how you got to live with Miss Witch.'

'Miss Fitch,' Sarah said, trying not to laugh. 'She's really quite nice, even if she is a bit strange.'

'Everyone calls her that,' Davey said, chuckling. 'It fits, don't it?'

'Sarah, I'm not waiting a moment longer.'

Elsie sounded angry now and Sarah dared not disobey. 'Got to go.' She bundled her long skirts up in her arms and ran after her. 'Coming, Miss Elsie. Wait for me.'

'You don't want to get too friendly with the locals,' Elsie said sternly when Sarah caught up with her. 'They're good fellows in their way, but they're simple folk and have a limited understanding of the way others live.'

'I was just talking to the boy.'

'Be polite at all times. Good manners are very important, but remember that you are not one of them and never will be. I am bringing you up to be a woman of science, like myself. I know that you have intelligence, Sarah, and I am determined that it will not be wasted. Women of my class are brought up to be little more than slaves to their husbands' whims and wishes. Many a clever female has had to deny her own abilities in order to flatter and placate a dominant male. That wouldn't do for me and I'll make certain it does not happen to you.' Elsie lengthened her stride as she made her way across the tufts of cord grass and glasswort.

Sarah had to quicken her pace in order to keep up with her. She had only partly grasped the meaning of Miss Elsie's angry tirade, but she was growing tired and her legs were aching. She was cold and hungry, but despite everything she had a warm feeling inside.

They settled back into their daily routine but Sarah had not forgotten Davey Hawkes. He had shown her kindness and she felt that she had found a friend. Maybe one day she would have the opportunity to tell him her story and he might help her to get the letter to Mr Arbuthnot. The thought cheered her through the long days that followed, and the even longer nights when she awakened thinking she was in her comfortable bed in Wellclose Square. It was always something of a shock to realise that she was curled up on a lumpy palliasse in front of the range, with draughts whistling around her ears and the smell of Miss Elsie's latest noxious brew filling her nostrils.

As the weeks went by it seemed to Sarah that whenever she had a chance to be happy, as she had been in the days when her mother was still alive and in the brief months she had spent in Wellclose Square, it was snatched from her. She missed her lessons with Miss Parfitt and the motherly ministrations of Cook, but being separated from Nettie was the worst thing of all. Nettie had been her saviour during their time together in the workhouse, and parting from her had left a pain in her heart that would not go away. She was not exactly unhappy with her eccentric new mistress but she desperately wanted to go home.

One dismal afternoon, when a sudden rainstorm pelted the window like naughty children throwing handfuls of gravel at the glass, Sarah tried to tell Miss Elsie how she felt. 'Can I at least let the Arbuthnots know that I am safe and well? I need not tell them where I am, but it would set their minds at rest.'

Miss Elsie smiled vaguely and fluttered her expressive hands but she did not look up from the dog-eared notebook that she was studying. 'We will talk about it later,' she murmured. 'Fetch me a bunch of hyssop and liquorice root.' She paused, running her fingers through her matted hair. 'My nerves are on edge. I need more opium. That wretched fellow should be here soon with a fresh supply.'

Sarah had climbed onto a chair and was unhooking a bunch of the dried herbs but she hesitated, teetering dangerously above the tabletop. 'Do you mean Grey?'

'Who else? Hurry up, child. Don't gawp at me like an idiot. I need to make this batch of medicine. If I have nothing to sell, we'll starve. It's as simple as that.'

Sarah leapt to the ground and laid the hyssop on the table. 'We could make another trip to the shore and get some fish.'

'We could but, as I've just said, only if I have something to barter with. No one gives you anything for nothing in this life. Remember that as one of your lessons.'

'Yes, Miss Elsie.'

'I need liquorice root now. You'll find some in the cupboard, and while you're there see if there's anything left in the brown paper packet that Tobias gave me.'

Sarah found the withered root of liquorice but the package was empty. Miss Elsie swore volubly as she worked, and Sarah knew better than to disturb her again. She finished tidying up, but the rain had ceased and shafts of sunlight were forcing their way through the salt-encrusted windowpanes and she felt restless. There had been a hint of spring in the air that morning when she went to collect water from the stream. She had noticed tightly furled buds on the bushes and trees in the copse where she collected the wood, and there had been rustling in the undergrowth as if the animal world was just waking up from a long winter's sleep. The birds had been carolling from the branches and she had found clumps of primroses bursting into bloom. She had barely noticed the changing of the seasons in London, and she had never seen flowers growing wild or green shoots pushing their way through the cold dark soil. It was new and exciting and now she longed to feel the sun on her face.

She shot a wary glance at Miss Elsie but she was absorbed in her task, frowning as she concentrated on the preparation of her patent remedy and oblivious to her surroundings. Sarah seized the opportunity to go outside and stand on the deck, taking great gulps of the bracing air. She gazed at the wide expanse of flat-land, seeing it with new eyes. Rain-washed and spark-ling, the saltings possessed a beauty of their own, far different from the bleak picture they presented mid-winter. The sunlight played on the pools of brackish water, and wading birds strutted about in their constant search for food, bending their long necks and making sudden stabbing movements in order to catch a tasty morsel. She closed her eyes, raising her face to the sun and wishing that she could fly like one of the gulls that circled overhead. She opened her arms wide, standing on tiptoe as if poised for flight.

'You'll need wings if you're going to take off, kid.'

She recognised his voice instantly and she opened her eyes, shading them against the glare. 'Grey, is that you?'

He came round the side of the cottage and took the steps two at a time. 'It's me, nipper. I've come to see the old witch. Is she in or is she flying around on her broomstick?'

A gurgle of laughter escaped from Sarah's lips. 'Hush, she's inside. She'll hear you.'

'It smells like she's making one of her brews,' he said, sniffing the air. 'How are you getting on with the old crone?'

'What do you care? You left me.'

He ruffled her hair. 'Come on now, kid. I was just doing what I was paid for, but I knew she wouldn't hurt you. She's quite mad but she's harmless, and I thought you'd be safe from the Triggs out here.'

'Take me home, Grey. Please take me back to Wellclose Square. I'm sure you'll be rewarded for your trouble. Mr Arbuthnot's a generous man.' She hesitated, staring up at him as his smile faded and a troubled look crossed his rugged features. 'What's the matter?'

He took both her hands in his. 'I couldn't forget you, little 'un. After I left you on Christmas Day I kept seeing your face, and I felt bad about leaving you all alone with a crazy woman. I tried to put you out of my mind but I couldn't, so a couple of days ago I went to the sugar mill. I was going to see the boss and tell him where you were.' He hesitated. 'I don't know how to tell you this.'

'You're scaring me. What's wrong?'

His hazel eyes darkened to the colour of rain-washed slate. 'I'm afraid it's bad news, kid.'

Chapter Seven

'What is it, Grey? What's wrong?'

'There was a fire in the mill shortly after Christmas. It was burned to the ground.'

Sarah stared at him in horror. 'Was anyone hurt?'

'It happened at night. The watchman got out unharmed but the building was gutted.'

'But Mr Arbuthnot is all right, isn't he?'

'Tobias. Is that you?' Elsie opened the door, squinting into the sunlight. 'About time, you wretched fellow.'

'That's a nice way to greet your sister's only son.'

Sarah looked from one to the other, hardly able to believe her ears. 'You never said he was your nephew, Miss Elsie.'

'I wasn't in the best of moods when Tobias brought you here. Besides which, he's a disgrace to the family name. Sometimes I choose to forget that we're related.'

Sarah turned to Grey. 'You really are her nephew?'

He grinned. 'Why d'you think I bother driving all the way here from London? It's not because Miss Elsie Fortunata Fitch is such charming company. If it weren't for my sweet mother who died when I was just a child, I'd leave Aunt Elsie to her own devices.'

'Never mind that, Tobias,' Elsie said impatiently. 'Have you brought what I asked for?'

'It's in the cart, which I left on the edge of the marsh in case you'd gone off on one of your jaunts. Anyway, I see that you're here so is it too much to ask for some refreshment after my long journey?'

'There's soup in the pot and I'll make some herbal tea, but only after I've checked to make sure that you've completed your part of the bargain.'

'You're a hard woman, Elsie,' Grey said, tipping his hat. 'I'll fetch it now.'

Sarah followed him down the steps. 'I'm coming with you. I want to know what happened in London. Did you speak to Mr Arbuthnot? Did you tell him what happened to me?' She quickened her pace in an attempt to keep up with his long strides. 'Please tell me. I must know.'

'When I saw what the fire had done I went looking for the owner.' He slowed his pace, matching it to her smaller steps. 'I found the house easily enough and I spoke to one of the servants.'

'Really? Who was it? What did she look like? It might have been Dorcas, or even Nettie.'

'It was a young woman with dark hair and a pretty little tip-tilted nose.'

'Dorcas,' Sarah said, smiling. 'That would be her. She's very pretty and she's got a gentleman friend called Wally, although she has a soft spot for Franz Beckman, the master sugar baker.'

'Then it was Dorcas who answered the door. I asked to see the master, but she burst into tears.' He held up his hand as Sarah uttered a cry of alarm. 'Don't upset yourself, Sarah. He's alive, so I was told, but he had some kind of seizure after the fire and has taken to his bed.'

'That's awful.' Her bottom lip quivered but she was determined not to cry. 'Poor Mr Arbuthnot; he's such a nice gentleman.'

'It could have been worse, kid. At least he wasn't in the building when the fire broke out.'

'I suppose so,' she said doubtfully. 'Did you tell Dorcas where you'd taken me?'

He shook his head. 'No. I wanted to speak to the mistress and explain my part in the business. I'm not proud of what I did, but I can't undo what's already been done.'

'So did you see Mrs Arbuthnot? Does she want me to go home?'

'I was shown into the parlour, where I waited for a good ten minutes before the good lady put in an appearance.'

'And then you told her about me?'

'Of course I did.'

Sarah grasped him by the hand. 'So what did she say? Don't keep me in suspense, Grey.'

'She was shocked but not surprised to learn that the Triggs were to blame. She told me that the police suspected Trigg had set fire to the sugar mill, but they had no evidence that would stand up in court.'

'The Triggs are wicked people. How could they do such a thing to a wonderful person like Mr Arbuthnot?'

'I can't answer that, young 'un. Anyway, there's Boxer over yonder, nibbling the grass, which is something he doesn't get in London.'

'You still haven't answered my question, Grey. Am I to go home now?'

He squeezed her fingers. 'Not yet, kid. I told Mrs Arbuthnot that you were living with my aunt, who might be a bit eccentric, but she would take care of you.'

Sarah's hopes were fading fast. 'What did she say then?'

'She said she was glad you were safe and well, but it wasn't a good time for you to return to Wellclose Square. With the sugar mill gone and her husband not quite himself, she said that it would be best if you stayed with Elsie for the time being.'

Sarah digested this in silence. Suddenly the bright day seemed like a mockery. It should have been overcast, with the clouds spilling rain like tears upon her upturned face. Grey shot her a worried glance. 'Are you all right, nipper?'

She nodded, although it was untrue; she could not have felt worse. All her hopes of returning home had been cruelly dashed and, yet again, the workhouse master's evil influence had blighted her life. She took a deep breath. 'Did she mention Nettie?'

'Not in so many words, but she did say that they all missed you, and would rest easier now they knew you were all right.'

'But I'd rather go home, Grey. I like Miss Elsie well enough but it's lonely out here on the marshes and she acts oddly after she's smoked that funny pipe of hers and she goes out at night, dancing about in the moonlight. I've seen her.' Sarah lowered her voice. 'And sometimes she forgets to put any clothes on.'

He threw back his head and laughed. 'That sounds like the sort of thing the mad woman would do.'

'It's not funny,' Sarah said angrily. 'I don't belong here, Grey. If I went back to Wellclose Square I wouldn't need to have lessons from Miss Parfitt. I could go out cleaning like my mother used to do, and I'd give my wages to Mrs Arbuthnot to pay for my keep.'

'We'll have to wait and see how it goes, nipper.' He linked her hand through the crook of his arm. 'I'll keep an eye on you from now on. I'll leave it awhile, but give it a couple of months and I'll pay another visit to Mrs Arbuthnot and see how matters have progressed. Maybe I can do something to help them.'

'You'd do that for me?'

'As I said before, I've felt guilty for my part in the Triggs' schemes and I want to make amends. I can't promise anything, but I won't abandon you here on the marsh with my mad aunt. On the other hand, she's not a bad old stick, and you could do worse than stay here for a while, especially while the Triggs are at large. I'll do everything I can to see them put away for a very long time.'

'You told me that you were a bad man, but you were wrong, Grey. I think you're a good man pretending to be bad.'

He threw back his head and laughed. 'That's the first time anyone's said that about me, kid. I don't think Elsie would agree with you.'

'She calls you Tobias. Is that your real name?'

'That's what I was christened, twenty-three years ago.' He came to a halt at the edge of the copse where

Boxer had been waiting patiently. 'Climb up on the cart and I'll show you how to handle the reins. We'll make a country woman out of you yet.'

'Are you a country man, Grey?'

He picked her up and tossed her onto the seat, climbing up to sit beside her. 'I was once, but now I'm a man from nowhere in particular.'

'That sounds very lonely.'

He thrust the reins into her hands. 'Tell Boxer to walk on. I'm hungry and Elsie makes good soup.'

Sarah flicked the reins. 'Walk on, Boxer.' She uttered a cry of delight as the animal obeyed her command.

'Give him his head,' Grey said, leaning back in the seat. 'He knows the way.'

Grey left soon after he had finished his meal, promising to return soon. Sarah wished that he would stay longer, but there was barely room for her and Miss Elsie in the cottage and Grey's presence seemed to make everything seem smaller than usual and more crowded. It was not until the cart disappeared into the evening mist that the full impact of the disaster that had befallen the Arbuthnots began to dawn upon her. With the factory razed to the ground they would have lost their livelihood. They might even lose their home and what would happen to Nettie and the others then? If only she were older she might be able to help them, but if she tried to return home now she would only add to their burden. She leaned on the railing watching the fingers of fog curling around the reed beds and swallowing up the tufts of sedge. She shivered as the sea fret chilled her bones and she was about to go indoors when a shout from the marsh made her turn her head, and she saw Davey Hawkes leaping from tussock to tussock as he crossed the boggy ground. 'Ho there, Sarah. It's me, Davey.'

She waved and waited eagerly for him to join her on the deck. He dumped a creel at her feet. 'Herring,' he said breathlessly. 'Is the old lady in? My dad needs some of her linctus for his cough. He was took bad again last night.'

'Come inside.' Sarah glanced at the wicker basket. 'We'll leave it out here where it's cooler.'

'There's a dozen or more fish. The ones you don't eat can be salted or pickled, if you know how.'

'I don't, but I'm sure Miss Elsie does.' Sarah opened the door. 'Miss Elsie, there's someone to see you.'

'What do you want, boy?' Elsie peered at him. 'It's Davey Hawkes, isn't it?'

'Yes, miss.'

'Your father's poorly again?'

'It's his chest, miss. He can't sleep for coughing.'

She frowned. 'Has he seen the doctor?'

'Can't afford it, miss.'

She rose from her chair and selected a bottle from the shelf above the mantelpiece. She thrust it into his hand. 'This will help.'

'Thank you, miss.' He clutched the medicine in his hand, shifting from foot to foot.

'Was there something else, boy?'

'I'm worried he might have the same disease that took Ma and me brothers.'

'I'm not a physician, but I've seen many cases of consumption, Davey.' Elsie moderated her tone. 'I think that your father is suffering from bronchitis or bronchial catarrh, which is debilitating but not fatal.'

Davey's grin almost split his face in two. 'Thank you, miss. It's been difficult at home since Ma was took.'

'That's very sad,' Sarah murmured, knowing only too well the suffering caused by the loss of a beloved parent. She wanted to give him a hug, but decided against it as Davey was a big boy and might not appreciate the gesture.

'You are the eldest child, are you not?' Elsie said thoughtfully.

'I am, miss.'

She took another bottle from the shelf. 'Laudanum, Davey. Your father will know how much to take.'

'Does that cost more than a dozen herring, miss?'

'There's no need to worry about that, but you could do something for me in return.'

'What's that, miss?'

'I believe your father has use of a vehicle when he takes the catch to market.'

'The fishermen have an arrangement with the butcher. He lets them borrow his horse and cart on market days in return for part of the catch.'

'Do you think you could drive me there next week? If I can sell my stock of medicines I'll be able to buy some much needed supplies. Would that be possible?'

'It would, miss. Can Sarah come too?'

Sarah clapped her hands. 'Oh, please say yes.'

A rare smile creased Elsie's features. 'I suppose so.'

As he had promised, Davey arrived on market day to drive Sarah and Elsie to Maldon. The butcher's cart was stacked with wicker baskets filled with glassy-eyed fish which smelled of the sea, but a lingering odour of animal fat and dried blood emanated from the scrubbed boards. Wedged between Davey and Miss Elsie on the driver's seat, Sarah was too excited to care about minor discomforts and she was filled with the simple joy of being out and about on a beautiful day. The narrow lanes had been touched by the magic of springtime, and the whole world seemed to be coming alive again. The stark black branches of the blackthorn were disappearing beneath a creamy-white burst of blossom, and hazel catkins danced in the breeze. In the fields ploughed furrows were misted with green shoots and the sun shone from a cloudless sky.

For the first time since she had been snatched from her home in Wellclose Square, Sarah felt a surge of optimism well up inside her, and she wanted to sing like the skylark hovering overhead. When they arrived in town it was a relief to climb down from the cart and stretch her legs. The market was already in full swing and Davey had barely finished unloading the fish before they were surrounded by eager customers. Many of them had come to see Elsie and she was soon lost in a press of people who wanted her attention and advice. She listened patiently as each one described their symptoms and revealed a variety of rashes, septic cuts and swollen limbs. She prescribed the appropriate medication and some paid with cash while others struck a bargain with goods. This, Sarah discovered, was how Miss Elsie came to have such a wide selection of second-hand clothes. The baker's wife complained of crippling headaches and insomnia and was willing to exchange a bundle of her daughter's outgrown clothing in return for a bottle of medicine made from meadowsweet, and another containing a tincture of valerian.

Sarah could not wait to examine the clothes and to her delight she found herself the proud possessor of an almost new cotton print gown, a red flannel petticoat similar to the one that Mrs Trigg had taken from her and a crocheted shawl that was very nearly perfect, apart from a few moth holes.

By midday Elsie had either sold or bartered her entire stock and she treated them to hot pies from the bakery. She had even been moved to give Sarah a halfpenny to spend on sweets, and after much indecision Sarah purchased a poke of barley sugar and some peppermint creams.

Davey had sold all the fish, although most of the money would go to the other fishermen. He offered to pay for his food but Elsie waved the coins aside, telling him that it was in payment for transport to and from the market. 'We will eat like kings when we get home,' she said, heaving a sack of potatoes into the trap. 'And tomorrow, Sarah, I'm going to take you for a long walk and we'll collect the plants I need for my medicines. You may come too, young Davey, if you are not going out in your father's boat.'

'Thank you, Miss Elsie,' he said with an apologetic smile. 'But I'm to crew for Saul Samson until my dad's well enough to go to sea again.'

Sarah was quick to hear the note of despair in his voice and she patted him on the shoulder. 'You will come and see us again, won't you?'

'I'll need medicine for Dad, so I expect you'll be seeing a lot of me from now on.'

Elsie hitched up her skirts and climbed into the trap. 'Your father is a good man, Davey. If you need more medicine for him you only have to ask.'

'My dad's a proud man. He won't take what he can't pay for.'

'Then I will visit him at home and give him a talking-to. In fact, I'll call in first thing tomorrow morning and Sarah will accompany me. It's time she met the locals.'

The Hawkes family lived in one of the terraced weather-board cottages that overlooked the creek and the wooden landing stage where the larger boats and barges unloaded their cargoes. Elsie walked purpose-fully down the main street of Blackwood village, acknowledging a group of women who were chatting while they waited to take their turn at the village pump. Sarah followed more slowly, taking in the scene, which was new and strange to her. Used as she had been to the noise and stench of the crowded city streets, this quiet backwater came as something of a surprise. Life seemed to move at a much slower pace in the country, but there was poverty here too albeit in pleasanter surroundings.

Cats basked lazily in the sunshine as if sleeping off the night's excesses of hunting and gorging on small rodents, largely ignoring the group of small children who were playing a game of tag. They were grubby and their clothes were patched and shabby, but they did not have the hungry feral look of the ragged urchins that Sarah had seen in London. She smiled at a tousle-haired child in petticoats who could have been a girl or a boy, and received a blank look in return. The others stopped in the middle of their game to gaze curiously at Elsie, who was wearing boots and breeches. She strode along like a man, but her flame-coloured hair hung loose around her shoulders in a riot of tangled curls. Her androgynous appearance was confusing to say the least and Sarah could hardly blame them for staring.

Oblivious to anything other than her own purpose, Elsie marched up to the cottage and knocked on the door. When no one answered she lifted the latch and went inside. Sarah made to follow her but she hesitated on the threshold, blinking as her eyes grew accustomed to the dim light. The room was simply furnished with a table, two chairs and several three-legged stools. In the far corner she could just make out the figure of a man lying on a bed covered with a tattered patchwork quilt. The air was thick with dust and the smell of unwashed bodies, stale food and sour milk.

A girl of about five or six was sitting on the packed earth floor playing with a wooden doll that had lost one arm. She jumped up and ran to the bed. 'Dada, there's someone here.'

He raised himself on his elbows, peering into the shaft of light from the open door. 'Is that you, Elsie Fitch?'

'Yes, Alfred.'

'I don't owe you any money, do I?'

'Certainly not. Your son paid me in kind for the medicines. I've come to see if there's anything I can do for you or your children while you're unwell.'

A bout of coughing prevented him from answering immediately and the little girl snatched a tin mug from the table and held it to his lips. 'Have a sip, Dada.'

He drank thirstily. 'Thank you, Mary, love. You're a good girl.'

She puffed out her chest. 'I'll look after you, Dada.'

Elsie beckoned to Sarah. 'Would you take Mary outside for a moment, please? I need to speak to her father in private.'

Mary backed away. 'I don't want to.'

'But I've got some barley sugar in my pocket,' Sarah said, holding out her hand. 'We could share it with your brothers, but I don't know their names. We don't want to give it just to anyone, do we?'

Mary shook her head.

'I'll come out when I'm done,' Elsie said, shooing them out of the door. 'Keep them occupied for a while.'

It was no hardship to escape from the confines of the stuffy room into the sunlit street and Sarah waited outside the cottage while Mary ran off to fetch her two younger brothers. A sudden feeling of sadness threatened to engulf her when she saw Mary pick up the smaller of the twins who had fallen over, comforting him with a hug and a kiss.

She would have been the big sister like Mary had her infant siblings survived, and seeing them together made the loss of her family seem even more poignant. She could only hope that their father would regain his health and keep the family together, but having grown up in the slums Sarah was only too familiar with death and disease. She had seen first hand the debilitating illness that affected the lungs and killed indiscriminately, but she knew that Miss Elsie was doing her best for Mr Hawkes.

In an odd sort of way Sarah thought her mother would have approved of Miss Elsie and her valiant attempts to heal the sick. Perhaps Ma and Miss Elsie were alike in their courage and single-mindedness. The comparison had not occurred to her before, but there was comfort in the idea and it made Ma seem a little bit closer.

Holding her younger brothers by the hand, Mary crossed the street. 'Here they are,' she said, smiling proudly. 'Jonah and Lemuel, I want you to meet this nice lady. Her name's Sarah and she's brought you some barley sugar.'

Sarah put her hand in her pocket and took out the poke. She had intended to eat the sweets herself but the sight of the motherless children, younger even than herself, filled her with pity. She gave the boys one each and they stuffed the sweets into their mouths like young animals gobbling a titbit before it could be taken from them. Sarah was suddenly aware that the other children had stopped their game of tag and were advancing upon her with eager looks on their faces. She had not nearly enough treats to go round and she was outnumbered.

'Give us some.' One of the bigger boys rushed at her but a shout from Miss Elsie sent him scurrying away. She strode out of the cottage gesticulating wildly.

'Go away, you young rapscallions.'

They fled.

'She's a witch,' Mary whispered through a mouthful of barley sugar. 'Everyone says so.'

'That's nonsense,' Sarah said sharply. 'Miss Elsie is an apothecary.'

'Is that like a witch?' Mary stared nervously at Elsie, who had moved away to speak to an elderly woman.

Sarah lowered her voice. 'Of course not, silly. She makes medicine to cure sick people like your dad.'

'He's going to go to heaven to join Ma.'

Jonah and Lemuel began to snivel in unison, wiping their runny noses on their sleeves.

Sarah was moved by pity for the motherless children and she shook her head. 'Your dad is not going to die,' she said firmly. 'Miss Elsie will make him better. Now stop crying and let me take you to the pump and wash your faces.'

'No.' This time all three of them spoke as one.

Sarah grabbed the boys by their shirt collars and led them to the communal pump. 'Come along, Mary. You can work the handle while I wash your brothers. Then it's your turn.'

Reluctantly, Mary heaved on the wooden handle

until water spilled into the stone trough. Sarah thrust Lemuel's head beneath the water spout, ignoring his cries for mercy, and leaving him to shake himself like a wet dog she turned her attention to Jonah. She released him and he wiped his face and hands on Lemuel's shirt tails before scurrying out of reach. She took the pump handle from Mary. 'You're next. Show them that girls are braver than boys.'

Mary did not look too certain but she allowed Sarah to sluice her with water. 'I didn't make a fuss,' she said, wiping her face on her grubby pinafore.

Sarah took the poke from her pocket and gave it to Mary. 'That's for being good. Next time I come here I'll expect to see clean faces and hands.'

'Will you bring more sweets?' Mary asked eagerly. 'I'll make 'em wash.'

'I'll see what I can do.' Sarah bent down and kissed Mary's cool cheek. 'You're a good girl. I'll come again, I promise.'

Elsie raised no objections and Sarah visited the Hawkes family at least twice a week until Mr Hawkes had recovered his health and was able to return to sea. She tried to remember everything that Dorcas had told her about dusting and sweeping, although luckily there were no precious porcelain ornaments to worry about now. On washdays Sarah carried the family's soiled clothing to a nearby stream where the village women did their washing, and under their instruction she and Mary learned how to beat the garments on stones and rinse them in the fast-flowing water. It was laborious work for small hands but they managed it between them.

Sarah had become firm friends with Davey but she was shocked to discover that he could neither read nor write. His mother had tried to teach him but her health had always been fragile and he had never had the opportunity to attend school. He was eager to better himself by learning to read and wanted more from life than hauling nets of fish from the sea. Sarah was only too happy to help and she spent many warm summer evenings with the family teaching them their letters. She put into practice everything that Miss Parfitt had taught her and soon Davey was able to read the primer that he had bought from a stall in the market.

On an afternoon in early September Sarah and Davey arrived back at the cottage having spent the morning on the mudflats picking cockles. Sarah had abandoned her cotton sunbonnet and strands of hair bleached to the colour of tow curled around her tanned face and neck. She had looped her skirts up to prevent them from trailing in the mud and was barefoot, as was Davey, who had rolled his breeches up above his knees. They were laughing at something he had said as they hefted their catch onto the deck but Sarah paused, holding her finger to her lips. 'I can hear voices.' She cocked her head on one side. 'It sounds like a man. It might be Grey – he promised he'd come to see me.' She pushed past Davey to fling the door open. 'Oh!' She could not hide her disappointment as she saw that it was the schoolmaster, Mr Wills. 'I'm sorry. I thought it was Grey.' She was about to retreat when Elsie called her back.

'Don't go, child. Mr Wills has something he would like to say to you.'

'Yes, sir?' Sarah paused on the threshold, staring at the young man who had only recently come to the village.

His frock coat seemed to have been made for a smaller man, exposing frayed shirt cuffs, and his ink-stained fingers were clamped around the brim of his top hat as if he were afraid to put it down amongst the clutter on Elsie's table. He peered at her over the top of his steel-rimmed spectacles, but there was a hint of a smile in his myopic blue eyes. 'I've heard that you've been teaching the Hawkes children to read, Sarah.'

'I have, sir.'

'How old are you, Sarah?'

She shot a wary glance in Elsie's direction and received a nod of approval. 'I'll be eleven next birthday, sir.'

'You appear to have received a good education, and Mary has done well under your tutelage as have her brothers who are now old enough to attend school.'

'I'm sorry, sir. I don't understand what you're saying.'

'You may know that the Church of England has seen fit to appoint me as schoolmaster in charge of the new village school. The local children will receive a free education at last.'

'I've seen the new buildings, sir.'

'Well, to put it simply, I cannot afford to employ another qualified teacher but I'm prepared to take you on to help me with the younger children. You may be little more than a child yourself and a female, but I think you might prove very useful.'

Elsie bridled, clearing her throat noisily. 'Just because Sarah is a girl does not mean that she is brainless, Mr Wills. There will come a time when all female children will receive the same advantages as those given to their male siblings.'

'Yes, no doubt,' he said, coughing nervously. 'But I can assure you that is not the case now. In the normal course of things Sarah would be working in a manu-factory or in service, and I think she is very fortunate to have been taken on as an apprentice by someone with your background, Miss Fitch.'

'She is indeed.' Elsie nodded vehemently. 'But nothing is for nothing, Mr Wills.'

Davey stuck his head round the door. 'What's going on?' He spotted the schoolmaster and frowned. 'What's old inky doing here?'

'Less of your cheek, young Hawkes.' Mr Wills flushed to the roots of his light brown hair, which was already receding at the temples, giving him the appear-ance of a much older man. 'This has nothing to do with you, my boy.'

Davey moved swiftly to Sarah's side. 'She's my friend and she needs a man to stick up for her.'

Mr Wills raised a sandy eyebrow. 'You're nothing but a callow youth, Hawkes. I'm offering Sarah a chance to better herself and to further her education.'

'Go on, schoolmaster,' Davey said, slipping his arm around Sarah's shoulders.

'I'm speaking to Sarah, not you.' Mr Wills leaned towards her. 'You will spend two hours a morning at the school helping the younger children with their lessons, and I will see to it that you have all the reading matter and extra tuition that you require to help you in your studies. Miss Fitch tells me that you would make an excellent apothecary and one day you might want to set up your own pharmacy.'

Sarah stared at him in surprise. 'I've never given it a thought, sir.'

'I may not always be here,' Miss Fitch said wearily. 'I might fly away like a migrating swallow, never to return. You won't be with me forever, Sarah.'

Mr Wills shot a warning glace at Davey. 'Let the girl speak for herself, Hawkes.' He turned his attention to Sarah, curving his thin lips into a smile which was not mirrored in his eyes. 'May I have your answer? I need to know now, or I will have to look elsewhere for an assistant.'

Chapter Eight

Sarah went round the schoolroom collecting up the slates and slate pencils. The children had gone and the room seemed empty without their bright faces and incessant chatter. It was five years since Mr Wills had asked her to spend a couple of hours a day helping the younger children with their letters and numbers, and she had loved every minute of it. In the beginning Elsie had been reluctant to allow her to devote time to the school, but earlier that summer, when Mr Wills was thrown from his horse and suffered a broken arm and leg, she had grudgingly given her permission for Sarah to take all his classes, and Sarah had been only too happy to oblige. She could still recall Pearl Parfitt's lessons and if there was one person in the world whom she would like to emulate, it was her beautiful Miss Perfect. Memories of the good times in the Arbuthnots' household had gradually faded into a pleasant dream, but Sarah still missed Nettie. Just thinking about her old friend made her smile as she stacked the slates in the book cupboard.

She took a last look round the room to make certain that nothing was left out of place. It would never do if Mr Wills came in on Monday morning and found disorder in his beloved school. Satisfied that everything was in order she took her bonnet from its peg and put it on, tying the blue satin ribbons into a bow beneath her chin. She did not need to check her appearance in the mirror to know that it was becoming; Davey had told her so on numerous occasions, making her blush but pleasing her all the same. She picked up her reticule and stepped outside, locking the door behind her. Taking deep breaths of the autumnal air filled with the fruity richness of damp earth and a hint of bonfire smoke, she started out across the school yard. The leaves on an ancient oak tree at the edge of the main street were beginning to change colour, and silhouetted against the blue sky a skein of wild geese flew in perfect formation, heading towards their winter breeding grounds. Although the sun was warm on her face she knew that winter would soon be upon them, and there was little time left to gather herbs for Elsie's potions before the frosts came.

Sarah was careful to divide her time so that she could continue to help Elsie, but since a tragic accident at sea that took the life of their father there was also Davey's family to consider. Alfred Hawkes had been lost overboard during one of the vicious winter storms two years previously. Davey had been on the boat at the time but there had been nothing he could do to save his father's life. Sarah had helped him through the bitter grieving process, and even though she was only a few years their senior she had become a surrogate mother to the younger children. She had seen Davey grow to manhood almost overnight, and they had become even closer as a result of the tragedy. She knew only too well what it was like to lose both parents at a young age, and she was always ready to listen to his problems, which were many as he was now the father figure in his small family and the main provider. Times were often hard for the east coast fishermen, and despite his impressive physical stature and strength Sarah knew that Davey at nineteen was still a boy at heart. Just thinking about him brought a smile to her face, but there was nothing romantic in their relationship even though the village gossips seemed to think they were sweethearts.

She set off for the cottage to check on the Hawkes children as she wanted to be certain that Mary had given the twins their midday meal of bread and cheese, and that they could manage on their own until Davey returned from his fishing trip later that day. She walked along the main street, acknowledging the friendly greetings of the women who were chatting in their doorways or waiting at the pump to draw water. It gave her a warm feeling to know that she was now accepted as one of them. It was strange to think that a few short years ago she had been a frightened child, longing to return to the life she knew in London, and now this was her home.

Although they had never talked about the future it seemed like a foregone conclusion that one day she and Davey would marry and raise their family in the tiny cottage overlooking the creek. There were other young men in the village who had shown her marked attention, asking her to dance at the church social or offering to take her to the fair when it came to the nearby town, and on these occasions Davey had stepped in and her would-be suitors had melted away. But the attitude of one person in particular was causing her concern. She had noticed that before his accident had kept him housebound Mr Wills had been very keen to ask her opinion on a number of different topics, and had made excuses to detain her after school, although on each occasion he had behaved like a perfect gentleman. He had given her a leather-bound prayer book for her last birthday, about which Davey had teased her mercilessly, saying that Wills was old enough to be her father and did she really want to be an old man's darling? She had tossed her head and turned away to hide her blushes, but she had seen her employer in a new light and had not felt entirely comfortable in his presence since that day. His absence due to the accident had given her some respite and she tried to convince herself that it was all her imagination, but now his return approached she was not so sure.

Putting such thoughts out of her mind, she entered the cottage to find the children seated on their stools munching their food with evident relish. 'Good,' she said, smiling. 'You're looking after the boys like a little mother, Mary.'

'She's bossy,' Lemuel said with his mouth full.

'She won't let us have cake,' Jonah added, frowning.

Mary pulled a face. 'The baker's wife gave us some fruit cake in exchange for a dozen herring, but it's for tea tonight when Davey comes home.'

'That's right,' Sarah said, trying not to laugh at the

expression on the twins' faces. 'You must be firm with these two, Mary. But I can see that you're managing very well without me.'

Mary leapt up from her seat. 'Won't you stay for a while, please, Sarah?'

'I can't, love. I wish I could but I promised Miss Elsie that I'd help her this afternoon. Maybe I'll come back this evening when I've done all my chores at home. How about that?'

'You can have some cake if you do,' Jonah said, winking.

She ruffled his short hair. 'You're a cheeky boy, Jonah Hawkes.'

'I'll save you a slice.' Mary rushed over to her and gave her a hug. 'Please come. Davey's always in a better mood when you're here.'

'Is he now? Well, I'll have to tell him off if he's grumpy with you when you all work so hard.' Sarah retreated to the doorway, blowing them a kiss. 'Boys, you can practise your alphabet and show Mr Wills how clever you are when he returns on Monday.' She paused as she was about to step outside. 'And do what your sister says. It won't only be Davey who gets cross with you if I hear bad things when I return.' She left with the sound of their promises ringing in her ears, although she doubted very much whether they would remember her words once she was out of sight. The boys were a handful and Mary had only just celebrated her tenth birthday, but at least the woman who lived next door was always ready to step in when needed. Mother Johnson had raised eleven children of her own and was a kindly soul who would have done more for the orphans had it not been for her rheumatics.

Sarah made her way towards the saltings with a spring in her step. It was still a lovely day and tonight she would see Davey. They would eat cake and drink tea together as they sat by the fire discussing the day's events, and when the young ones were safely tucked up in their beds Davey would walk her home across the marsh. She felt like singing as she took the shortcut through the woods, and when she came across Grey's cart with Boxer placidly nibbling at the grass she was doubly happy. She had not seen him since Easter and she always looked forward to his visits. She stopped to make a fuss of the old horse but then she smelled something that made the hairs on the back of her neck prickle with fear. She turned and saw smoke rising in the air above the trees. The acrid odour of burning wood and pitch could only mean one thing. Fire!

She raced across the clearing and emerged from the trees at the edge of the track. A cry of horror was wrenched from her lips. The cottage was ablaze sending pillars of black smoke billowing into the azure sky. For a moment she was frozen to the spot but then she saw Grey stagger out of the building carrying Elsie in his arms. Sarah broke into a run. 'Is she all right?'

He shook his head. 'She's badly burned.'

'Let me help you.'

'Go and lay some sacks on the floor of the cart. We've got to get her to a physician as quickly as possible.'

Sarah did as he asked although her hands were trembling violently and she had difficulty in completing the simple task. As Grey laid Elsie's unconscious form on the crude bed Sarah noticed that his own hands were blackened and blistered. Elsie was almost unrecognisable beneath a layer of soot and she was barely breathing. Sarah struggled against a bubble of hysteria that threatened to overcome her. 'You both need to see a doctor and there isn't one in the village. We'll have to go to Maldon.'

'No, we won't.' Grey heaved himself onto the driver's seat. 'We're going to London where they have hospitals and specialists. You only have to look at her to see that she's close to death.'

'You can't drive that far with those injuries.'

He gave her a pitying glance. 'Of course not. You'll have to take the reins.'

'But I can't go to London. I've a job to do, and who will look after the children if I'm not there?'

'So you'll let Elsie die, will you?'

'No, of course not,' she said angrily. 'But I can't leave without telling anyone.'

'You bloody well can, and you will. Now stop arguing and get up beside me. You owe Elsie that, at least.'

'I must let Davey know where I'm going.'

Grey closed his eyes and his skin paled beneath his tan. 'You can send a message later. For God's sake stop arguing.'

With the greatest reluctance she climbed up beside him. 'All right. Give me the reins, but we're going to get help before I even think about driving all the way to London.' She glanced over her shoulder as the sound of roof timbers collapsing echoed across the saltings and flames consumed the last of her home and her belongings.

'Must have been all that rubbish she kept in the place,' Grey said grimly. 'There's nothing left here for either of you.'

'Walk on,' Sarah said, flicking the reins. Grey was right: everything had gone and her few worldly possessions would soon be nothing but ashes. Once again she had lost her home and was on the road with him, but this time she was returning to London.

Grey was silent for a while, grimacing with pain. 'Elsie doesn't stand a chance unless she sees one of the best physicians,' he said hoarsely. 'Anyway, I've got to get back by nightfall. I'll be a dead man if I don't pay a certain somebody what I owe him, and that's no exaggeration.'

Sarah allowed Boxer to have his head as he followed the narrow track through the woods. 'Who are you talking about?'

'You know Trigg – he's evil to his rotten core.' Grey stared down at his injured hands. 'This is nothing compared to what his men will do to me if I don't pay up.'

She shot him a curious glance. 'What has Trigg got to do with you?'

'When he couldn't get another job after being sacked from the workhouse he found another way to keep him and his hag of a wife in comfort. He lends money to desperate people and then charges them high interest. If they don't pay up on time he sends his thugs round.'

'And you owe him money?'

Grey shrugged his shoulders. 'Business was slack. I owed money and my creditors were growing impatient. I thought I was on to a sure thing but the wretched fellow went down in the fifth round and so did my hopes of paying Trigg.'

'I thought you were cleverer than that,' Sarah said angrily. 'How could you be so stupid? I thought you were trying to earn an honest living, but I can see I was wrong.'

A bitter smile twisted his lips. 'You sound like Elsie.'

'Maybe I do, but it looks as though you've proved her right.'

'That's what she said when I asked her for a loan.'

'Is that why you came to see her today?'

'I knew she had cash stowed away. Poor old Elsie has always been a miser and this is what it's done to her.'

'I don't understand.'

'I told her why I'd come to see her, and I didn't mince my words.'

'You didn't steal her money, did you?'

'I may be a bad 'un but I wouldn't do that, even though most of my relations are skinflints.'

'So how did the fire start?'

'I asked her for a loan and at first she seemed willing to help. She pulled up a floorboard and took out a leather pouch. Did you know it was there?'

Sarah shook her head. 'What was in it?'

'Elsie tipped the contents on the table. It would have paid off Trigg and bought me a stake in the future.'

'And she gave it to you?'

'Not Elsie. She scooped the coins into the bag and put it back in its hiding place. She'd been smoking that filthy stuff she loves so much and she was laughing and waving her arms about like a madwoman. She fell against the range and one of her sleeves caught light. I tried to get to her but she panicked and knocked a bottle of spirits into the fire where it exploded and sent live coals flying into the air like rockets.' He paused, shuddering at the memory. 'I threw her on the floor and beat out the flames, but by this time the fire had taken hold. I managed to get her outside, and the rest you know.'

'She would wear those strange flowing garments,' Sarah said sadly. 'I've warned her about them often enough but she would never listen, and she falls into a stupor at night after she's been smoking that filthy opium.' She cracked the whip to encourage Boxer into a trot. 'I still think we ought to get help more quickly. She might die if we leave her like this.'

'It's London or nothing. I've got a room in Wych Street. D'you know how to get there?'

'Yes, as it happens I do. It's not far from Drury Lane, but why go there when you haven't got Trigg's money?'

Wincing, he put his hand into his pocket and pulled out a leather pouch. 'I grabbed it as I was leaving. This will buy my freedom and it might save her life. It means I can pay for the best treatment and . . .' He slumped forward and was silent.

'Well, we're going to find a doctor and the sooner the better.' She glanced at his inert form. 'It was a brave thing you did, Grey, and I'm not going to let either of you suffer unnecessarily.' She looked over her shoulder to check on Elsie, and was relieved to see that she was still breathing even though she had not yet regained consciousness. 'Giddy-up, Boxer. We're going to Maldon. There must be a doctor there, and I can send a message to Davey.'

The aged doctor shook his head when he saw the extent of Elsie's injuries, but he did what he could and dosed her with laudanum. He attended to Grey's injured hands, and said that nature must be allowed to take its course. Sarah paid him for his services, and ignoring Grey's protests that they should be on their way immediately, she set off in search of a second-hand shop. She returned ten minutes later laden with coarse woollen blankets and a couple of pillows. 'I've one more thing to do before we leave,' she said, adjusting the bedding around Elsie so that it formed a warm cocoon.

'Where are you going now?' Grey demanded as she was about to hurry off.

'The doctor gave me paper and ink and I wrote a note to Davey while I was waiting for you. I must find a messenger who will deliver it.'

Grey raised his eyes to heaven. 'For God's sake, girl. Haven't we wasted enough time already? It'll be after midnight before we reach London.'

'I don't care. This is important, and we need food and drink too. I don't suppose you've got a well-stocked larder in your lodgings.'

'Women!' He frowned, staring at her as if seeing her for the first time. 'You were just a child when I last saw you, and now you're telling me what to do.'

'I've grown up.'

He gazed sorrowfully at his bandaged hands. 'I'm bloody useless like this.'

'You saved Elsie's life.'

'But it was my fault it happened in the first place. I'm a worthless piece of work and maybe I ought to let Trigg finish me off.'

Sarah took him by the shoulders and shook him hard. 'Stop it. That sort of talk won't get us anywhere and we're wasting time.'

'You're right.' He held his hand out. 'Give me the note and I'll find someone to take it to your friend. You get the food, and hurry.'

Sarah's first impression as they arrived in Wych Street was one of noise, filth and the long-forgotten noxious city odours. The narrow cobbled road was lined with timber-framed four-storey Elizabethan buildings which must once have been town houses for prosperous merchants, but now provided cheap lodgings above shops and rowdy public houses.

Grey nudged her with his elbow. 'Stop here. This is where I live.' He indicated a tall narrow building with an apothecary's shop situated on the ground floor.

'Why here?'

'It's cheap,' he said brusquely.

She drew the sturdy carriage horse to a halt. Boxer had been exchanged for a faster steed at a coaching inn, although Grey had been reluctant to leave him and had paid the ostler good money to take care of the animal until he was able to return. He climbed stiffly to the pavement. 'I'll take Elsie inside. You stay here and keep an eye out for thieves. Use the whip if you have to. They'll steal the clothes off your back given half a chance.' He went round to the back of the cart and lifted Elsie gently in his arms. She uttered a faint moan, but she was heavily sedated and she did not protest as he carried her into the building.

Sarah sat hunched up on the driver's seat with the horse whip clutched in her hand. The clock on the tower of St Clement Danes church had just struck midnight, but this part of London was still very much awake. Drunks stumbled out of the Angel Inn and the Rising Sun, laughing and singing, swearing and brawling. Prostitutes lingered in doorways offering their services to anyone with the money to pay for them. Feral cats and dogs scavenged for scraps of offal or anything that was remotely edible in the ankle-deep detritus in the gutters, and a couple of ragged street arabs skulked in the shadows dipping the pockets of unwary passers-by who were too inebriated to notice.

Sarah waited anxiously for Grey to return and breathed a sigh of relief when the door of the apothecary shop opened and he reappeared.

'Get down,' he said, holding up his arms. 'I'll take the horse to the stables. It's not far and I can manage to drive a short distance.'

Her limbs ached and her hands were blistered. She allowed him to help her to the ground. 'Where is Elsie?'

'She's safe in bed. Go down the passage and my room is at the back of the building, the last door on your right. I've left it open so you can't miss it. Put the bolt across and don't open it until I get back.' He reached for the basket containing their provisions and handed it to her.

She hesitated. 'What about Trigg? You said you had to see him tonight.'

'He'll be in the Rising Sun. I won't let on that you're here, so don't worry.'

Sarah nodded vaguely. 'Good luck.'

'Don't fret. I can repay my debt and that'll be the end of it.'

Sarah was too tired to worry about Trigg, who would almost certainly have forgotten about her after all this time. He had had his revenge on poor Mr Arbuthnot and she was a person of very little importance. She realised that Grey was waiting to see her safely into the building, and the reason for his concern was obvious when she saw a group of drunken men staggering towards her. She hurried inside and closed the door, hoping that they had not seen her. She breathed a sigh of relief when the sound of their boots thudding on the paving stones faded into the distance.

It was extremely dark and the floorboards were uneven, creaking noisily each time she took a step. She had to feel along the walls, dislodging flakes of plaster and stifling cries of disgust as her fingers came in contact with damp patches and the odd snail or two. After what felt like an eternity, she came to the end of the long passageway. True to his word, Grey had left the door open and she stepped inside, shutting the door and bolting it as he had instructed. As her eyes become accustomed to the darkness she could just make out the square panes of a window on the far wall. A glimmer of light from the street lamp outside revealed a single wooden chair close to an empty grate and a narrow bed in the corner of the room. A table was pushed up against the wall and amidst the clutter of plates, mugs and empty bottles she found a candle and a box of vestas.

She discovered that candlelight did nothing to improve Grey's lodging place. Cobwebs festooned the ceiling and veiled the window. Ashes spilled from the grate onto the tiled fire surround and the air was stale. Cockroaches scattered in all directions as she crossed the floor to take a closer look at Elsie, who was stirring and groaning. Sarah stuck the candle in an empty beer bottle and set it on the windowsill, leaving her hands free to tend Elsie, but there was little she could do other than give her a few drops of laudanum diluted in water.

'We'll get you to hospital first thing in the morning,' she said, hoping that Elsie might be able to hear her and understand that she was doing everything in her power to make her well again. 'You'll be better soon, and we'll go home. We'll find somewhere else to live and I'll take care of you. Grey will help us. He owes you that, Elsie.' She pulled up the coverlet, wrinkling her nose. The lack of female touches and the disorder in the room spoke volumes about Grey's bachelor existence. She began by tidying up the mess on the table, filling an old sack that she found stuffed in a broken windowpane with rubbish and cinders from the grate.

It was cold in the room and she could feel dampness rising through gaps in the floorboards. There were a few lumps of coal in the scuttle and a bundle of kindling stacked on the mantelshelf. She was in the process of lighting the fire when she heard someone tapping on the door.

Forgetting Grey's warning she rose to her feet and ran to open it. 'Thank goodness. I thought you were never coming back.' Her hand flew to her mouth as the man barged past her and strode over to the bed. He wrenched back the covers and uttered an oath.

'Who are you?' Sarah demanded nervously. 'What are you doing here? This isn't your room.'

He had his back to her but he snatched the candle from the table and turned slowly to face her. His face was in shadow but she knew him instantly. Her heart was pounding and her legs threatened to give way beneath her. 'What do you want?' she whispered. 'Go away.'

Chapter Nine

Trigg held the lighted candle close to her face. 'I know that voice. It's bloody Sal Scratch.' He threw back his head and laughed. 'So he couldn't keep his filthy hands off you. I always knew that Grey was a man after me own heart.'

She felt sick. The bitter taste of bile filled her mouth but she held her head high. 'I'm Sarah Scrase and you couldn't be more wrong. Grey is my friend. He's looked out for me all these years since you stole me from my home.'

Trigg glanced over his shoulder. 'Who's that in the bed? I know it ain't your ma because we buried her in a pauper's grave together with her bastard child.'

'Don't you dare speak ill of Ma. She was a good woman.'

'She was a whore and it looks like you're going down the same path.'

'That's a wicked lie. You don't know anything about me.'

'Well, if you ain't Grey's doxy, what are you doing here?'

'You're a bad man to even think such dreadful things,' Sarah cried angrily. 'I owe my life to him. I don't know how he came to be mixed up with a brute like you, but Tobias Grey is a good man and you are evil.'

He guffawed with laughter and his hand shook, spilling candle wax onto the floor. He put it down and his face was left in shadow, but the menace in his expression was imprinted in her mind and she was nine years old again and terrified. He took a step towards her. 'You've grown into a cheeky little madam, Sal. A good slapping would knock that out of you.'

She was not going to give him the satisfaction of seeing that she was afraid and she forced herself to remain calm. 'What do you want? Grey isn't here.'

'I can see that, sweetheart. But I'll bet a golden guinea that he won't be far away from his lady love. The bastard owes me money and I ain't going nowhere until I get what's due to me.'

A footstep in the doorway made them both turn to see Grey, half hidden beneath the pile of bedding he had brought from the cart. Sarah raised her hand in warning. 'Don't come in.'

He dropped his burden and kicked it out of the way. 'Keep out of this, Sarah. It's between him and me.'

'Yes, it is.' Trigg made a move towards him, fisting his hands. 'I want what I'm owed.'

Grey stood his ground. 'And you shall have it, but we'll go to the pub as arranged and leave the ladies in peace.'

'Ladies!' Trigg spat on the floor. 'I don't know about the old 'un. But it seems to me you've taken full advantage of young Sal.'

Grey would have lunged at Trigg but Sarah threw

herself between them. 'Don't play his game. That's exactly what he wants.'

'She's a bright girl. I'm sorry I got rid of her, but it's not too late. If you can't pay up, I'll take her instead.'

'I can settle the debt, but I'm warning you, Trigg. Lay a hand on Sarah and you'll have me to answer to.' Grey moved swiftly to the door, holding it open. 'Let's go.'

'You would do better with me, darling.' Trigg looked her up and down with a lascivious grin. 'The missis is past her best and I could do with some young blood.'

'You'll taste your own if you carry on like that.' Grey's voice was controlled but his eyes glittered angrily.

Trigg raised his hand to touch Sarah's cheek as he walked past her. 'You'll keep, little girl.' He lowered his voice. 'But don't think you've seen the last of me.'

'Come along, man,' Grey said impatiently. 'The pub will be closed if we don't hurry.'

'The landlord will stay open if I tells him to.' Trigg stared pointedly at Grey's bandaged hands. 'You're not in any condition to stand up for yourself. I could take her and your money right now, if I felt so inclined.'

'Just try it.'

Sarah watched helplessly as they squared up to each other. She could tell by the pallor of his skin, and the white lines etched from the corners of his mouth to his chin, that Grey's hands must be causing him a great deal of pain. It would only take one punch from Trigg's huge fist to knock him senseless.

'But I give my word,' Trigg said, chuckling. 'Honour

amongst thieves and all that, Tobias my boy. I'll settle for the money and a glass of brandy, this time.' He pushed Grey into the passage and they both disappeared into the darkness.

Sarah ran to the door and closed it but the smell of Trigg lingered in the room, tainting the atmosphere as if part of him remained there to haunt her. She paced the floor, too agitated to even think about sleep. She had never thought to meet Trigg again but he was even worse than she remembered. Her childish fear of the workhouse master was even greater now that she was a young woman. His whole attitude to her had changed and was even more terrifying than before. The look in his eyes had sickened her and his assumption that Grey had taken advantage of her youth and innocence was revolting.

She came to a halt by the bed, gazing down at Elsie's inert form with tears in her eyes. She was an unlikely surrogate mother, but despite her odd ways they had dealt well together through the years. Sarah drew the covers up to Elsie's chin. Now it was her turn to look after the woman who had taken her in and had taught her all she knew. As soon as morning came they would take her to hospital and pray for a miracle. The doctor in Maldon had not held out much hope, but Elsie was a strong woman and a determined one. She, the healer, needed a power greater than her own to save her now. Sarah knelt by her bedside, murmuring the prayers that her mother had taught her when she was a small child. Elsie might worship the pagan gods but Sarah did not think that would be held against her in heaven.

She rose to her feet and put one of the pillows under Elsie's head. She laid the remainder of the bedding on the floor, one blanket for herself and one for Grey, spacing them as far apart as was possible in a small room. It was difficult to forget Trigg's vile accusations but she did her best to put them out of her mind. She stoked the fire with the remainder of the coal and sat down to await Grey's return. After a while she was beginning to feel sleepy, but the sound of approaching footsteps made her suddenly alert. The door opened and she leapt to her feet. 'Grey?'

'Yes, it's me.' He closed the door and bolted it. 'You should be asleep, kid. It's almost two in the morning.'

'I had to be certain that you were all right.'

He took off his hat and jacket and hung them on a nail high up on the wall, out of reach of nibbling rodents and the armies of ants and cockroaches that skittered across the floor. 'I've paid him, that's all that matters. He won't bother me again unless there's a job he wants me to do, but I've had enough of Trigg. I'll not be working with him again.'

'He's a brute.'

'He's a villain and you do right to be scared of him. I'll get you away from here as soon as possible, Sarah. This isn't the place for you.'

'But we must get Elsie to hospital.'

'As soon as it's light I'll bring the cart round and we'll take her to the Charing Cross hospital. That's the nearest.'

'I want to stay with her. I don't want her to wake up in a strange place. She'll be alone and frightened.'

'I don't think Elsie has ever been scared of anything, kid.' He sat down suddenly. 'As soon as Elsie's taken care of I'll go and get Boxer. The ostler only promised to keep him overnight and I wouldn't want him to fall into the hands of strangers who might ill-treat the poor brute.'

She was too tired to argue or to challenge his decision. 'All right. We'll sort everything out in the morning.'

'Good girl. Now make yourself comfortable. I'm afraid it'll have to be the floor, but you take the bedding. I'll sleep in the chair.' He smiled. 'It won't be the first time. Now get some sleep.'

Elsie was admitted to hospital next morning and Sarah waited outside the cubicle while the doctor examined her. She wished that Grey had been able to stay and give her moral support, but he had left for Essex promising to return as soon as possible. She kept glancing at the clock on the wall but the hands seemed to be stuck in one position. Time was leaden and the heaviness of it pressed in upon her. She tried to keep calm but she was becoming increasingly agitated. Surely they would know something after all this time. She glanced at the clock yet again and was about to get up to make enquiries when the door opened and the doctor stepped out into the corridor. The shred of hope she had been harbouring faded when she saw his grave expression. 'How is she, doctor? Will she be all right?'

'In cases like these the patient often succumbs to shock,' he said, shaking his head. 'Or else infection sets in and there is very little we can do other than keep them sedated and apply dressings soaked in turpentine.'

'Can I stay with her, doctor?'

'I'm sorry, miss. It's against the rules, but you may visit your mother this afternoon between four o'clock and five o'clock.'

She did not bother to explain her relationship to Elsie; it hardly seemed to matter whether or not they were blood relations. She left the hospital in a daze. Having put so much faith in the miracles of modern medicine it was almost impossible to believe that the doctors could fail now. She was beginning to wish she had used the tried and tested salve made from lard, mutton tallow, beeswax and carbolic acid which Elsie had used to treat burns. The mere thought of bandages soaked in turpentine made Sarah wince.

She set off along the Strand, heading in the direction of Wych Street. Grey had given her strict instructions to return to his lodgings and not to open the door to anyone but himself. She intended to do as he asked, but he had given her some money and she wanted to purchase a nightgown for Elsie and a shawl for herself. If she could find a second-hand shop she might be able to afford a change of clothes as well, but it had begun to spit with rain and her straw bonnet would be ruined if she did not take shelter.

She took a short cut through Drury Court, although she knew it to be a dangerous area, the haunt of criminals and families living with crippling poverty in filthy, rat-infested tenements. Men were huddled round a brazier, and women with babies in their arms and toddlers clinging to their skirts stared at her with hostile expressions on their hollow-cheeked faces. Some of them jeered at her, but a few of them held out their hands, begging for money. It was hard to ignore their pleas, which were genuine enough, but if the pickpockets thought she had anything of value about her person she would soon be relieved of her purse, and they might not stop at that. Unwary trespassers in the rookeries could find themselves stripped of their clothing and left to wander the alleyways barefoot and shivering.

The drizzle had turned into a downpour, but at least it saved her from being set upon. The women and children took shelter in the dilapidated buildings and the men gathered in a tighter knot around the fire. Sarah raced across the slippery cobblestones, avoiding the worst piles of filth and excrement that littered the street. She could see the spire of St Mary le Strand, but as she turned the corner into the comparative safety of Wych Street she cannoned into someone coming from the opposite direction and they both tumbled to the ground.

'Look where you're damn well going.' The young woman's crinoline cage hampered her attempts to rise and she lay on her back, flailing her legs like an upturned beetle.

Sarah scrambled to her feet and proffered her hand. 'Catch hold.'

'Ho. There's a pretty sight.'

Sarah looked up and frowned at a group of men standing nearby who were openly laughing at their plight. 'If you were gents you'd help a lady in distress.'

'If we was gents we wouldn't be enjoying the sight of a young lady's drawers.' The younger of the men tipped his cap. 'And as fine a pair of props as I ever saw.'

The girl grabbed Sarah's hand and struggled to her feet, adjusting her skirts. 'Shut up you idiot,' she cried, shaking her fist. 'These are my best duds and they're ruined.'

The young man grinned. 'A bit of mud won't hurt you, love.'

'Good for the complexion,' his mate added, chuckling. 'You'll have a lovely arse when it's washed clean. I'll volunteer for that job, miss.'

'Oh, will you now.' She bent down and scooped up a handful of mud mixed with straw and rotten vegetables and threw it in his face. 'How d'you like it, cully?'

Coughing and spluttering he made as if to strike her but his friend caught him by the arm. 'You asked for that, chum. C'mon, let's get you cleaned up or we'll be late back at work and we'll be for it.' His companion allowed himself to be dragged away, still uttering dire threats.

Sarah stared at the girl, who was tut-tutting and twisting round in an attempt to see the damage to her green satin gown. Her hat had come off and her copper curls cascaded around her shoulders. Sarah could hardly believe her eyes and her breath caught in her throat. 'Nettie? Is it really you?'

'Who's asking?' Nettie turned her head and her eyes widened. 'Little Sal Scratch? Is it you, all grown up and covered with mud?'

They fell into each other's arms, laughing and crying. 'I can't believe it,' Sarah gasped. 'I never thought I'd see you again.'

'And you almost killed me,' Nettie said, wiping tears from her cheeks and leaving smudges of dirt in their place. 'What was you running from? It couldn't have been Trigg this time.'

'Oh, Nettie. I've got such a lot to tell you and I'm getting soaked to the skin.'

'So am I, but who cares? I've found me little sister and she's even prettier than she was all those years ago. I'd be jealous if I wasn't such a beauty meself.' She slipped her arm round Sarah's waist. 'Come with me. We'll get you cleaned up and we'll have a nice hot cup of tea with a slug of gin in it, and you can tell me how you come to be in London. I thought you was living the life of a country lady, but you look a bit of a mess if I'm to be honest.'

'We could go to Grey's lodgings,' Sarah said shyly. 'It's not very grand but at least it'll be out of the rain.'

'You're not . . .' Nettie stared at her, eyebrows raised.

'Oh, no. Nothing like that.'

'We'll go to my dressing room and you can tell me everything.' Nettie pointed to the impressive façade of the Olympic Theatre. 'I'm an actress now, Sarah. I told you I would be famous one day, and I'm well on me way. Come inside and we'll get you out of those terrible duds and into something that don't look as though it came from a dollyshop.'

She led Sarah through the stage door, past a grumpy-looking doorkeeper who glared at them and told them to be quiet, which made them giggle even louder. They were helpless with laughter by the time they reached the stuffy dressing room shared by the younger and least important members of the cast. The stale air was filled with the smell of greasepaint, cheap perfume and the rancid odour of tallow candles, but Nettie seemed not to notice. She dragged Sarah in and closed the door. 'This is where we get made up to go on stage,' she said with an expansive gesture. 'We have all sorts of lovely costumes and satin shoes dyed to match. That's when we're doing musical burlesques. Sometimes we do serious plays and I've only had small parts so far, but I'm going to be a star like Nellie Farren or die in the attempt.'

Sarah was left breathless by Nettie's enthusiasm as much as the suffocating atmosphere in the windowless room. She gazed round at the racks of brightly coloured costumes and shelves piled high with hats, shoes and plumes made of ostrich feathers. 'Well, I never.'

Nettle chortled with delight. 'I can tell that you're impressed, nipper.' She gave Sarah an affectionate hug. 'Not so much a kid now though, are you? But if you don't mind me saying so, you look a fright, although I daresay you'd clean up nicely.'

'This is all I've got,' Sarah said, taking off her soggy straw bonnet. 'There was a fire and we lost everything. I was looking for a dollyshop when it started to rain.'

'That dress is awful anyway.' Nettie turned her back to Sarah. 'Undo me buttons, there's a love. I'll have to bribe the wardrobe mistress with some bonbons so that she'll wash my gown for me. She's a miserable old cow, but she's got a sweet tooth.' She pulled a face. 'Actually she's got hardly any teeth at all but she can suck a piece of barley sugar and smack her gums together on a slice of cake, but no one dares laugh at her because she's got a temper and she's not above taking the scissors to a costume if someone gets on the wrong side of her.'

Sarah frowned as she concentrated on undoing the row of tiny satin-covered buttons. 'She sounds terrifying.'

'Hurry up, do. I'm shivering and it doesn't do my voice any good.' Nettie cleared her throat. 'Do re mi fa so la te do,' she sang as if to prove a point. 'See what I mean?'

'I'm doing my best, and you've got a lovely voice so I wouldn't worry if I were you.' Sarah did not add that she was also soaked to the skin and equally cold, but then Nettie always had to be the best. She did not mind. It was wonderful to see her again and she could still hardly believe the piece of good fortune that had caused their paths to cross.

Nettie turned her head to stare at her. 'Who taught you to talk like a toff?'

'I didn't know that I did.'

'Well, you do and it sounds funny. I'm trying to lose me cockney accent so I can act proper but it ain't easy.'

'How long have you been an actress? Do you still live in Wellclose Square?'

Nettie tossed her head. 'I should think not. I share digs with Nellie and three of the other girls.' She glanced at Sarah's reflection in the dressing table mirror

159

and smiled. 'But I do visit them on my days off. It was Cook who introduced me to the manager of this theatre and he gave me an audition. I'm understudy to Nellie in *Faust* and *Marguerite* this coming week.'

'That's wonderful,' Sarah said enthusiastically. 'Cook must be so proud of you.'

'She is, and I have to tell her everything that goes on in the theatre. If it weren't for her taking us to Wilton's music hall I'd probably still be a housemaid.'

'So Mrs Burgess is still working for the Arbuthnots?'

'Yes, and Dorcas too.' Nettie twisted round in an attempt to see what Sarah was doing. 'Aren't you finished yet?'

'Nearly.' Sarah's cold fingers fumbled with the buttons but she managed to undo the last one. 'There you are.'

Nettie shrugged the gown off her shoulders and allowed it to slide to the floor. She plucked a cotton wrap from one of the rails and slipped it on. 'Now you, Sarah. Your teeth are chattering and you're turning blue. Get that awful print frock off and I'll find you something else to wear.'

Minutes later Sarah was dressed in a pale blue cambric gown with a lace collar and cuffs. Nettie looked her up and down with a satisfied smile. 'There, you look half decent and it suits you better than it did me.'

'It's your dress?'

'Miss Gant made it for me and I always felt like a Sunday school teacher in it, so now it's yours.'

'Thank you, but are you sure?'

'Stop fussing and take a seat while I sort out your hair. Gawd knows what you do in the country but it looks like a bird's nest.'

Sarah stared into the mirror, watching in amazement as Nettie brushed her fair hair until it shone like silk and wound it into a coil at the nape of her neck. She put the last pin in place with a cry of triumph. 'There! That's a miracle in itself. Just look at yourself, Sarah Scrase. What d'you think?'

'It's amazing,' Sarah said, turning her head from side to side to get the full effect. 'You're so clever, Nettie.'

'I know I am. I've many talents, duck. If I don't succeed in the theatre I could always get a job as a lady's maid. But I'll make it, I know I will. My name will be top of the bill one day.'

'I'm sure you're right.' Sarah stood up, marvelling at her altered appearance. 'I've only ever seen bits of me in a looking glass,' she confessed shyly. 'Miss Elsie's house was very small and we were quite poor.'

Nettie pulled up a chair. 'Tell me everything that's happened to you since you was taken from us. Mrs Arbuthnot told Cook that you was safe in Essex and that it was best that you stayed there until such time as the sugar mill was rebuilt.'

'That's what Grey told me.'

'We all suspected Trigg, but no one could prove the bastard did it.'

'He blamed me for everything. I think he would have killed me if he thought he could get away with it, but he left it to Grey to get rid of me.'

161

'You was lucky; that's all I can say. But we didn't know what had happened to you for ages. The master had the police looking for you and the mistress cried for days. We was all upset, even Betty, although the poor soul didn't really understand what was going on.'

'It was bad enough for me and I was scared stiff, but Grey was kind in his own way. I'll never forget that he gave me an apple as a Christmas present because that was all he had to give, but then he left me with Miss Elsie in a tumbledown cottage in the middle of the marshes. I was really scared in the beginning but he came back every now and again and I got used to Miss Elsie and her strange ways. Now I'm really fond of her and I can't bear to think of her suffering.'

Nettie cocked her head on one side, looking thoughtful. 'Sounds to me like you've got a soft spot for Grey as well as the old lady.'

'No, of course I haven't,' Sarah said hastily. 'And he only came back because he was doing business for Miss Elsie. I found out later that they were related, although you wouldn't think so if you saw them together.'

'It all sounds like a rum do to me, but here you are now and seemingly none the worse for it.'

'That's enough about me, Nettie. Tell me more about Wellclose Square. Did the master rebuild the sugar mill?'

'He's never recovered completely from the seizure he suffered after the fire. There was no money coming in, so the mistress was forced to take in gentlemen lodgers. She and the master have use of the front parlour, but all the best rooms are given over to commercial travellers and suchlike. She kept Cook, Dorcas and Betty on, although they don't always get their wages.'

'I thought Dorcas would have married her young man by now.'

'She keeps poor Wally dangling, although between you and me I think she's always had a soft spot for Franz Beckman, but he has a fancy for Miss Parfitt.'

'And does Miss Parfitt like Franz?'

'Who's to say? She's always so sweet and calm. I can't imagine her being passionate about anything or anyone. She teaches at a school in Princes Street, near London Docks, but she comes to tea with Mrs Burgess and Dorcas once a week.'

'I'd like to see them all again, Nettie. D'you think it would be all right if I went to call on Mrs Arbuthnot?'

'More than all right, nipper. I'm sure she'd be happy to see you again, and so would the others.' Nettie looked round as the door opened and three girls rushed in, chattering and laughing like a horde of brightly coloured parakeets. Nettie rose to her feet and took off her wrap. 'You'll have to go, Sarah. It's rehearsal time.' She reached out her hand and snatched a costume from the rack.

'Who is this?' One of the girls stared curiously at Sarah. 'Are you a performer, love? What's your speciality? The cancan? They do it in Paris with bare bums, or so I've been told.'

Nettie scowled at her. 'Leave her alone, Mabel. She's my friend.'

'Sorry, I'm sure,' Mabel said, shrugging. 'I only asked.'

'I'd best go.' Sarah backed towards the doorway. 'Maybe I'll see you later.'

'They're a nosey lot,' Nettie said loudly. 'Tell me where you're lodging and I'll come to call for you tomorrow morning. There's no rehearsal so I won't be needed until the evening performance. We'll get the omnibus to Wellclose Square and give them all a lovely surprise. How about that?'

'Best get your costume on, Beanie,' Mabel said, nudging Nettie in the ribs. 'You know how cross Mr Wigan gets if we're late on stage.'

'All right, don't keep on so.' Nettie put her arms around Sarah, giving her a hearty hug. 'What number Wych Street?'

'I'm not sure, but it's at the back of an apothecary's shop, the last door on the right.' Sarah picked up her gown and ruined bonnet.

Mabel looked her up and down. 'Ain't that one of Beanie's old gowns?'

'Mind your own business, Mabel Smith.' Nettie gave Sarah a gentle shove towards the door. 'Off you go then. I'll see you tomorrow morning.'

'It's raining cats and dogs out there.' Mabel snatched a coarse grogram cape from the clothes rack and tossed it to Sarah. 'Here, young 'un, put this on with my compliments. I've always hated the bloody thing anyway.'

'Thank you.' Sarah slipped it around her shoulders. 'I'm most grateful, but may I pay you for it?'

164

Mabel threw up her hands in mock surprise. 'Lawks, we got a lady in our midst, girls.' She patted Sarah on the shoulder. 'It's seen better days, like most of us here, but you're welcome to it. We can't have a delicate little thing like you falling sick with lung fever.'

'I don't know what to say.' Sarah glanced anxiously at the other girls, who were grinning with approval. 'You're all very kind.'

Nettie opened the door. 'Time you wasn't here, girl.'

Sarah found herself alone in the dark corridor but she had a warm feeling inside and now she had a hooded cape to keep off the rain. She made her way out of the theatre, scurrying past the stage doorkeeper with her head down.

She found a second-hand clothes shop in Houghton Street where she bought a cambric nightgown for Elsie and a woollen shawl for herself. She was about to leave when she saw a pink silk bonnet trimmed with satin ribbons, and although it seemed like sheer extravagance she simply had to have it. Tucking it under the cape to protect it from the rain, she hurried back to Grey's lodgings.

The elegant bonnet might have had at least one previous owner, but it was new to Sarah and the first really pretty thing that she had owned. She was wearing it when she left for the hospital that afternoon and she held her head high. She was no longer the girl from the workhouse who lived with the crazy woman on the marsh. She was back home in her native London, and she had as fine a bonnet as any lady from one of the mansions up West. Despite the seemingly ever-present threat posed by Trigg and her concern over the injuries that Elsie had received during the fire, Sarah felt a surge of optimism as she walked briskly along the Strand.

She arrived at the hospital on the stroke of four and was shown into a ward with six beds, the occupants of which lay tucked up beneath white coverlets. Pale faces were turned hopefully towards her as she tiptoed across the scrubbed floorboards but none of them was Elsie. The last bed was hidden behind closed curtains and Sarah was about to draw them back when a nurse appeared at her side. 'Have you come to see Miss Fitch?' she asked in a low voice. 'Would you accompany me to the office, please, miss?'

Chapter Ten

Sarah could barely take it in. Elsie, the rebel who had worshipped pagan deities and had spent her life making medicines to cure the sick, had succumbed to her injuries. She would not have believed it had she not seen her lying in the mortuary, stiff and cold. In death Elsie had the appearance of a wax effigy, but Sarah was certain that the untamed spirit who had danced naked in the moonlight and shunned polite society had gone to another place. Perhaps Elsie had joined the green man and Herne the Hunter in the greenwood. Sarah hoped so, although it was little comfort to her.

'Will it be a pauper's burial, miss?'

Sarah came back to reality with a start. She stared at the mortuary attendant, momentarily at a loss, but the thought of Elsie's fragile body buried in a common grave was too appalling to contemplate. 'No, certainly not. I'll make the necessary arrangements.'

She returned to Wych Street in a state of shock. Despite her confident assertion that Elsie would receive a proper send-off, she had no idea how they would find the money to pay for a decent burial, let alone a headstone.

Grey returned that evening and his smile faded as

he walked into the cold room where only a single candle relieved the darkness. 'It's not good news, then?'

Sarah shook her head. She could not speak. If she opened her mouth it would all flood out, the bitter resentment that she felt at the unfairness of Elsie's untimely death, the sorrow she felt for a lost friend and mentor and her fear of being alone and abandoned for a second time.

'Have you eaten today, Sarah?'

'I can't remember.'

'It's freezing in here,' he said, taking in the empty grate and frowning.

'There's no coal,' she said dully.

'Get up.' He held out his hand.

'What?'

'I'm truly sorry that Elsie's gone, and I'll miss the old girl, but I know one thing for certain.'

'What's that?'

'She would want me to take care of you. She might not have shown it, but Elsie thought the world of you, Sarah.'

'Don't,' Sarah said with a muffled sob. 'You're making me feel even worse.'

'That's because you're tired and hungry. I'm taking you to the Albion supper house in Russell Street. You've got to eat or you'll be joining Elsie in heaven or wherever the old girl's ended up.' He lifted her to her feet. 'She wouldn't want you to waste away.' He held her at arm's length. 'You look different, kid. I see you bought yourself a new gown. That's good.' He spotted the cape draped over the back of the chair and he picked it up. 'But you could have found something a bit less like an old horse blanket. I'll have to take you shopping next time.'

Sarah allowed him to drape it around her shoulders. She realised that his unusually conversational mood was for her benefit and she managed a wobbly smile. 'It was a gift. The dress was too.'

His fingers tightened momentarily on her shoulders. 'You don't know anyone in this part of London.'

'Yes, I do. I met an old friend today. Nettie and me were in the workhouse together and Mr Arbuthnot took both of us to Wellclose Square. We met by accident outside the Olympic Theatre where she's performing in a play.'

'Well it's a pity you won't be here long enough to see it. Put on your bonnet and let's go. I'm starving.'

'I did buy the bonnet,' she said guiltily. 'It was expensive, and I bought Elsie a nearly new nightgown . . .' She broke off, choking back a sob. 'I can't believe she's gone.'

'Don't cry. I can't bear to see a woman crying.' He patted her clumsily on the shoulder. 'You'll feel better when you've got some food in your belly.'

Sniffing and wiping her eyes on her sleeve she put her bonnet on, but she lacked the will to tie the ribbons and would have followed him outside with them dangling had he not stopped, shaking his head. 'You can't go out to supper looking like something the cat dragged in, girl.' He tied the satin ribbons into a bow. 'That's better. Now you look presentable and your expensive hat won't blow off in the first gust of wind.'

Surprised and diverted, she stared at him. 'I never knew you were so particular.'

'I wasn't raised on the streets.' He held the door open. 'But I was the black sheep of the family and still am, so don't get any false ideas about me, kid. If I could choose your friends for you I certainly wouldn't pick a man like me. Now come on. We need to hurry or they'll stop serving and I fancy a large steak and a glass or two of claret. There's nothing we can do for Elsie now, but we'll raise a toast to her.' He closed the door and locked it.

'That's part of the trouble, Grey,' Sarah said nervously. 'I told them at the hospital that we'd be making the funeral arrangements. Is there any money left?'

He shook his head. 'Not enough for that, but we'll see her right, kid. You mustn't worry.'

'You won't borrow from Trigg, will you?'

'No, I won't make that mistake again. I suppose I'll have to go cap in hand to the family.' He led the way along the dark corridor and when they reached the street he tucked her hand in the crook of his arm. 'Hold on to me, kid. You can't be too careful round here, especially at night.'

'What did you mean about Elsie's family? I thought there was only you.'

He uttered a sharp bark of mirthless laughter. 'If only that were true. The Fitches and the Greys populated half of Essex and moved on to London. Elsie's nearest would be her brother, my uncle George, who lives in Spital Square. We don't get on.'

'But you will go and see him?'

'It's unavoidable.' He pulled her out of the path of a drunken man who was thrown bodily from a pub door and landed in the gutter, swearing and shaking his fist at the men who had perpetrated the assault.

'There's the theatre,' Sarah said, pointing across the street. 'I promised to go to Wellclose Square with Nettie tomorrow, but that was before I knew about poor Elsie.'

'She wouldn't want you to do anything different, and that doesn't change because she's gone to meet her maker. I'll go to the hospital in the morning and make the necessary arrangements and worry about the funds later.'

'Don't you want me to go with you?'

'No. I'll manage, but you can come to Spital Square later in the day. There's your future to think about as well as doing the decent thing by Elsie.'

'What are you saying?'

'We'll discuss this over supper. I'm not going to abandon you, but I can't look after you. I'm never in one place for any length of time and you're still a nipper even if you think you're a grown woman.'

'You can't tell me what to do.'

'I've got to make sure you're looked after, kid. You can't go back to the marshes and that's for certain.'

'Can't I stay with you? I could keep house and look after you.'

'As I just said, I'm away most of the time and I couldn't leave you on your own in London.'

'I'd go back to the village if I had anywhere to stay. Davey and the young ones will be missing me, and I was filling in at the school until Mr Wills returned after his riding accident.'

'Who would have thought that the little scrap I bundled up in my overcoat on that bitter cold Christmas morning would turn out to be a teacher? I never noticed that you'd grown up, kid.'

'I'm not a kid any more and I wish you would stop calling me that.' She came to a sudden halt, staring at a dirt-encrusted street sign. 'I know this place. It's Vinegar Yard. This is where I used to live when I was a little child. Ma used to scrub floors in the theatre.'

He patted her hand as it lay on his sleeve. 'You've had a hard life. I'm going to see if I can't make it a bit better from now on. Leave it to me, kid – sorry, I mean, Sarah.'

'That's much better,' she said with a nod of approval.

He grinned. 'Thinking of you as anything but a little girl running barefoot over the marshes is going to take some doing, but maybe this is my chance to do something that isn't entirely rotten.'

'You've always been good to me, Grey. And so was Elsie, in her own way. I'd like to know more about your family.'

'That can wait until we've eaten. I'm starving; I don't know about you.'

He refused to discuss the subject any further until they were settled at a table in the supper house and he had ordered two steak dinners and a bottle of claret, although Sarah protested that she had no appetite.

'What were you talking about earlier when you mentioned Elsie's brother?' She slipped off her cape as the warmth from the fire seeped into her bones. 'What has her family got to do with me?'

'Her brother, George, is an old skinflint but he's got a big house and a wife who likes to live in luxury. I thought he might be persuaded to take you on as a housemaid.' He held up his hand as she was about to protest. 'I know it's not what you might want, but I've got to be certain you're taken care of before I go off on my travels. You can't support yourself in London, and that's for certain.'

Sarah opened her mouth to argue but the waiter glided over to their table to fill their glasses and Grey raised his in a toast. 'To Elsie. God rest her soul.'

'Elsie.' Sarah sipped the wine, wrinkling her nose at the slightly sour taste but as the alcohol reached her empty stomach she experienced a warm glow that was not entirely unpleasant. 'I'll find work, Grey. I won't accept charity from Elsie's brother.'

He leaned back in his seat, eyeing her over the rim of his glass. 'And what would you do?'

She frowned and took another sip of wine. 'I've learned a lot helping Mr Wills. Maybe I could be a governess or a teacher. Nettie told me that Miss Parfitt works at a school near London Docks; I could go and see her and ask her advice.'

He put his glass down and reached across the table to lay his hand on hers. 'Go and see her by all means, but I'll still take you to meet my uncle George, just in case your schoolmistress friend can't help. I think Elsie would want me to do that at the very least.'

She drank more deeply this time. 'You're a good

man, Grey. In spite of what you say about yourself, you're a kind person and not a villain.'

He smiled, taking the glass from her hand. 'I think that's enough for now or you'll be tipsy and I'll have to carry you home.'

'But I'm beginning to like the stuff,' she said, giggling. 'It's quite nice really.'

The waiter returned with two steaming plates of food which he placed on the table in front of them. 'Will there be anything else, sir?' He jerked his head in Sarah's direction. 'Another bottle of wine perhaps?'

Grey fixed him with a hard stare. 'That will be all.'

The waiter hurried off, muttering something unintelligible.

'Eat up.' Grey refilled his own glass but shook his head when she reached for hers. 'I'm sorry, kid. I'm not used to young females who can't hold their liquor. I usually take more worldly women out to dine.'

Her head felt slightly muzzy and she stared at him, trying to digest this piece of information. 'Have you got a lady love, Grey?'

He grinned. 'I've had a few in my time, kid.'

'Please stop calling me that.'

'I will, but only if you eat all your supper, and I might even treat you to a slice of apple pie or some spotted Dick.'

Her stomach rumbled and she realised that she was very hungry. 'I haven't tasted food like this since I was living with the Arbuthnots. Mrs Burgess is a wonderful cook.'

'Maybe you ought to go there tomorrow after we've

been to Spital Square. I'm not leaving London until I see you well settled, and that's a promise I mean to keep. If all else fails maybe Mrs Arbuthnot will be in a position to take you in.'

The house in Spital Square was grander than anything that Sarah had ever seen. Set in the middle of an elegant Georgian terrace, the four-storey double-fronted building had an impressive Adam-style doorway with Ionic pilasters and trellis-patterned iron balconies at first-floor level. She had thought that the house in Wellclose Square was grand, but this imposing edifice surpassed all her expectations and she realised that Elsie's family must be very rich.

'Made their money in silk weaving,' Grey said as if reading her thoughts. 'George won't admit that their fortune came from trade, but that's the truth of the matter. He's a terrible snob and his wife Cecilia is even worse.' He rang the doorbell.

'Will they see us, do you think?'

'I'm not leaving here without speaking to my uncle. Anyway, he needs to know that his sister is dead. Someone has to tell him.'

The door was opened by a young maidservant who seemed flustered when Grey demanded to see her master. She disappeared into the hallway, closing the front door and keeping them waiting on the step for several minutes before reappearing and inviting them in. She showed them to a morning room at the back of the house and left without saying a word.

Sarah was suitably impressed by the size of the room

and the height of its ceiling with elaborate cornices and a central rose from which hung a crystal chandelier. A tall window swathed with crimson damask curtains overlooked a large garden surrounded by trees clad in their late autumn finery. Grey leaned against the fireplace, warming his hands over the blazing coals. 'We won't be here long,' he said, smiling grimly. 'George will be only too eager to get rid of me.'

'Even though you've come to give him the sad news that his sister has died?'

He nodded. 'Even so.'

The door opened before Sarah had a chance to question him further and a short, stocky man erupted into the room. He did not look pleased. 'What do you want, Tobias?'

Grey faced his uncle with a pleasant smile. 'And how are you, George? It's good to see you again.'

'I suppose you want money. That's the only reason you would cross my threshold.'

'As a matter of fact that is the case, but it isn't for myself.'

George turned his attention to Sarah, who had been standing quietly by the window. 'And who is the young person? Is she the reason for your request?'

'Indirectly, I suppose.' Grey crossed the floor to stand beside her. 'This young lady was Elsie's ward.'

'Elsie? What has my sister got to do with this? You know that we don't mention her name in this house.' George moved to the door and opened it. 'You had better leave before I say something I might later regret.'

'Elsie is dead, George.'

'Dead? How did she die? Is this one of your schemes to extort money from me?'

'Miss Fitch is dead, sir.' Sarah could keep silent no longer. She did not like Mr Fitch with his fat cheeks and mean eyes. She could see now why Elsie did not want anything to do with her family. 'There was a fire and Grey rescued her from the flames but she was badly burned. We brought her to London but the doctors couldn't save her.'

George stared at her, eyebrows raised. 'You have a lot to say for yourself, miss.'

'Elsie was kind to me. She took me in and taught me how to make medicines to heal the sick.'

George slumped down on the nearest chair, which creaked beneath his considerable weight. 'This is a shock indeed. I can't pretend that we were close, but she was my sister.'

'And as such deserves a decent burial,' Grey said quickly. 'She lies in the mortuary at the Charing Cross hospital, George. I've told them to contact an under-taker and make the necessary arrangements, but I haven't got the funds to cover the costs.'

'So you came to me.' George frowned, shaking his head. 'Why should I put myself out for the woman who disgraced our family?'

'Perhaps you would rather she ended up in a pauper's grave. That would not look good if it was reported in the newspapers.'

'You wouldn't!' George's eyes almost popped out of his head, reminding Sarah of a codfish that Davey had caught and given to Elsie in return for one of her potions.

'Would I not?' Grey held out his hand. 'Come on, Uncle George. What would it cost you to give the old girl a proper send-off? I don't expect a pageant and Elsie wouldn't have wanted anything like that, but surely you could stump up for a simple service and a headstone. She was your only surviving sister. My mother, God rest her soul, would be turning in her grave if she could see you now.'

'Elsie was always wild and irresponsible. I don't suppose she left a will.'

'I don't see that it matters since she had nothing to leave.'

George flushed and looked away. 'Your mother was the eldest and our grandfather was progressive in his thinking. He left the country estate to the two girls, even though it should by rights have come to me. I don't know how things stand now and I need to know if Elsie died intestate.'

'And if she did, I suppose the whole lot comes to you,' Grey said with an ironic smile. 'Has it occurred to you that I might inherit?'

'Don't be ridiculous. No one in their right mind would entrust a cat to your care.' George shot a sideways glance at Sarah. 'No offence meant, young lady.'

Sarah had lost the thread of this heated discussion and she shrugged her shoulders. 'It's got nothing to do with me.'

George leaned across the desk, fixing Grey with a hard stare. 'Did Elsie mention a will?'

'She did ask me to take a document to her solicitor, Bertram Moorcroft, but that was some time ago,' Grey said slowly. 'She didn't tell me what was in it, and I didn't ask. It was none of my business.'

'Moorcroft's brother handles my affairs.' George rose to his feet. 'I'll ask him to look into the matter. In the meantime you'd best send the bills to me, but don't expect me to invite all the poor relations to weep and wail over someone who disgraced the family name.'

Grey shook his hand. 'Thank you. Although I think you're being unfair to Elsie. As I see it she did a lot of good and asked very little in return.'

'I wouldn't know about that,' George said with an irritable shrug of his shoulders. 'I think our meeting is at an end, Tobias. I'm a busy man.'

'There is one other thing.'

'I knew it. You're in trouble and you want me to bail you out.'

'Not at all, but I feel responsible for Sarah. With Elsie gone the poor girl is all alone in the world.' Grey paused, as if waiting for his uncle to object, but George's lips were firmly closed.

'I can look after myself,' Sarah protested.

'Let me handle this,' Grey said in a low voice. He turned to George with a persuasive smile. 'I'll be perfectly frank with you. My style of living isn't suitable for the comfort and safety of a virtuous female, so knowing that you are a God-fearing man, I was hoping that you'd find her a position in your household.'

'Get out!' George gesticulated angrily. 'That's going too far, even for you, Tobias. My wife would never agree to such an arrangement. It simply wouldn't suit, and you have no right to put me in such a position.'

Sarah had heard and seen enough. 'I'd rather starve in the streets than work for a man like you, Mr Fitch. Elsie was worth ten of you . . .' She did not have time to finish her sentence as Grey whisked her out of the room and led her protesting loudly out of the house. 'Why did you do that?' she demanded as they reached the pavement.

'Making George angry was a mistake. In case you hadn't noticed it was only the threat of public humiliation that made him agree to pay for Elsie's funeral.' He raised his hand to hail a passing hansom cab. 'Anyway, I wouldn't want to leave you in his hands. I'd forgotten what a miserable toad he is. You deserve better, Sarah Scrase.' He handed her into the cab and leapt up beside her. 'Wellclose Square, cabby.'

She stared at him in surprise. 'You're coming with me?'

He leaned back against the worn leather squabs. 'As I told my uncle, I want to see you safely settled before I leave London. We all know what Trigg is capable of and he's not a man to make idle threats.'

'Why did you get tied up with him in the first place?'

'We met by pure mischance. I was up before the magistrate and Trigg was in court, I wasn't sure why, but he paid my fine and I wasn't in a position to argue. It was that or a spell in the clink.'

'What had you done?'

He grinned. 'Can't remember. Probably drunk and disorderly, or maybe it was a brawl, but Trigg saved me from going to jail and that put me in his debt.'

'Was that when you tried to kidnap me?'

'I'm ashamed to say it was.' Grey shook his head and his smile faded. 'Trigg told me some cock and bull story about you being his orphaned niece who'd been sold to the owner of the sugar mill. I'd no reason to disbelieve his story and I had no means of repaying him other than to go along with his demands.'

'But you must have realised that it was all lies when you took me the last time.'

'I did, but if I'd left you with Trigg he'd have found someone else to do his dirty work.'

'You could have taken me back to Wellclose Square.'

'And Trigg would have found out. He might have burned the house down as well as the manufactory.' He patted her hand. 'I knew that you'd be all right with Elsie.'

'And I was.' Sarah turned away so that he would not see the tears in her eyes. She had been fond of Elsie, and it did not seem fair that her family had disowned her because of her eccentric ways, or that she had lived in relative poverty while her brother enjoyed a life of wealth and privilege. Paying for his sister's funeral might salve his conscience but it would not make up for the years of callous indifference.

'We've arrived.' Grey stated the obvious as the cab pulled in at the kerb.

181

Sarah jumped at the sound of his voice. 'I was miles away.'

'I know.' He climbed down and held out his hand to assist her onto the pavement. 'How much, cabby?'

'That'll be one and six, please, guv.'

Grey tossed him a florin. 'Keep the change.'

'Ta very much, sir.' The cabby touched his cap and drove off.

'You're very flush all of a sudden,' Sarah said suspiciously.

'There's enough of Elsie's money left to keep us for a while and I've got some jobs lined up which will bring in a fair amount.'

'What sort of jobs?'

'A bit of trading here and there.' He brushed her cheek with the tips of his fingers. 'Don't look so worried. I won't end up in Newgate.'

'I should hope not, but does that mean I can stay with you?'

'Ring the doorbell. We'll see what the Arbuthnots have to offer before I make promises I can't keep.'

She mounted the steps and tugged at the bell pull. 'We could go back to Essex. I could find some rooms to rent in the village and I'm sure that Mr Wills would take me back as his assistant. You could find work locally.'

'Sarah, my dear girl, I have no skills other than my wits. I do a bit of buying and selling, most of it legal but sometimes it's a bit on the shady side, although I'm careful to steer clear of the law.'

'You could change. Anyone can improve their lot if they put their minds to it.'

'I suppose Elsie taught you that?'

'No. It was my ma.' She looked up as the door opened.

'Is it you, Sarah Scrase?'

'It is. May I come in?'

Dorcas stared at her in surprise and her face crumpled. 'You've come not a moment too soon.' She reached out to grab her by the hand, dragging her over the threshold. She was about to shut the door, but Sarah stopped her.

'He's with me.'

'Who is he?' Dorcas whispered. 'This ain't the time to bring a gentleman friend to the house, and he don't look the sort of chap you should be associating with.'

Grey took off his hat. 'We met before, Miss Dorcas. Mrs Arbuthnot will remember me, no doubt.'

'Yes, I recognise you now, but I still don't hold with your sort.' Dorcas stood back to let them in, but she turned her back on Grey. 'Come with me, Sarah. There's not much time.' She held her hand up as Grey was about to follow them upstairs. 'Not you. Wait here.'

Sarah shot him an apologetic look before hurrying after Dorcas who was already halfway up the staircase. 'What's wrong? Is someone ill?'

'You'll find out soon enough.' Dorcas hitched her skirts higher and raced up to the first landing, coming to a halt outside the room which Sarah remembered as the Arbuthnots' bedchamber.

'What's going on?' Sarah demanded breathlessly.

Placing her finger on her lips, Dorcas ushered her into the room and closed the door, but the click of the latch shattered the silence and heads turned. Sarah could not see their features clearly as the curtains were drawn across the windows and the only light came from a single candle which cast grotesque shifting shadows on the walls. The figures grouped at the bedside were vague shapes, some kneeling and some standing. 'Who lies there?' Sarah's hand shook as she released it from Dorcas's firm grasp, and she was suddenly afraid.

Chapter Eleven

A familiar figure came towards her and Sarah rushed into Nettie's arms. 'Is it the master? Am I too late?'

'He's been asking for you. His mind is wandering and he thinks that you and me are still living here like the old days.'

Sarah's eyes had adjusted to the gloom and she could see Mrs Arbuthnot kneeling at the bedside with her head bowed as if in prayer. Mrs Burgess was standing with her arm around Betty's shoulders and they were both snivelling quietly into their hankies. Pearl Parfitt gave her a sad smile. Sarah approached slowly, her eyes misting with unshed tears. Pearl moved swiftly to her side. 'Don't let him see you cry,' she said softly.

Sarah leaned over to touch Mr Arbuthnot's hand as it lay on the coverlet. 'I'm here, sir. It's me, Sarah.'

His face was ashen but his eyelids fluttered and his lips moved, although she could not hear what he was saying. Mrs Arbuthnot lifted her head. 'He knows it's you, dear. I'm very glad you came in time.'

'I didn't know he was so ill,' Sarah murmured.

Nettie gave her a reassuring hug. 'Come away now, nipper.'

'But I want to say goodbye properly.'

Mrs Arbuthnot dabbed her eyes with her hanky. 'It's

too late, child. He's gone.' She buried her head in her arms and her shoulders heaved.

Betty uttered a howl and Mrs Burgess led her hurriedly from the room, followed by Miss Parfitt, who held her hand out to Sarah and Nettie. 'Come along, girls,' she said in a low voice. 'Dorcas will look after her mistress.'

Grey was waiting for them in the entrance hall and he looked up. 'Are you all right, Sarah?'

Pearl eyed him warily. 'Is this gentleman with you, dear?'

At any other time Sarah might have thought it funny to hear Grey described as a gentleman, but, having witnessed the death of two people who had been close to her in as many days, she was too upset to see the humour in anything. She moved swiftly to his side and clutched Grey's hand. 'This man saved me from Trigg.'

Miss Parfitt's lovely face broke into a genuine smile of delight. 'Then I am very happy to make your acquaintance, Mr er . . .'

He bowed from the waist. 'Tobias Grey, ma'am.'

Sarah could see that he was impressed by Miss Parfitt, and who could blame him for such a natural reaction to charm and beauty. Even in her black bombazine gown, with her luxuriant dark locks secured in a severe bun at the nape of her neck, she was a lovely young woman who would turn any male head. 'This is Miss Parfitt. I told you all about her,' Sarah said, although she suspected that Grey had not heard a word she uttered.

186

'I'm afraid you have come on a sad occasion,' Pearl said with a gentle smile. 'Won't you join us in the dining room, Mr Grey? It's the only reception room not given over to the commercial gentlemen who lodge here.'

'Thank you, Miss Parfitt, but I don't want to intrude.'

'The master is dead,' Sarah said, gulping back a sob. 'I don't know if he knew it was me.'

'He did,' Nettie said stoutly. 'I'm sure he knew and was glad that you'd come home.'

Pearl ushered Grey into the dining room. 'Come along, girls. I'm sure you need some refreshments after your journey across London.'

Nettie caught Sarah by the wrist. 'Where was you? I waited for ages outside the apothecary's shop, and got some very odd looks and several lewd offers for me pains.'

'I'm so sorry, Nettie. Miss Fitch died yesterday afternoon and I had to go to Spital Square with Grey.'

'That's a bit of a smart place for the likes of us, isn't it?'

'I'll explain later.'

'Well, you might have dropped in at the theatre on your way.'

'Don't be difficult, Nettie. It was early morning and I didn't think you would be there.'

'Probably not, but you could have stopped by and left a note or something.' Nettie took off her bonnet. 'Bloody thing. It might look just the ticket but the feathers slap me in the face every time I move me head.' She tossed it onto the table beside Grey's

187

battered top hat. 'Don't be a slave to fashion, young Sarah. It ain't always worth the discomfort.'

Nettie's comic expression made Sarah smile in spite of the sadness in her heart, and she followed her into the dining room. 'I've missed you so much.'

'Well, I suppose I've missed you too, nipper. But don't ever keep me waiting again. I'm making a name for meself in the theatre and I can't be seen hanging around on street corners. It don't do nothing for me prestige.'

Grey held out his hand. 'So you're Nettie. I've heard a lot about you over the years.'

She angled her head, fluttering her long eyelashes. 'Have you now? Well, I thought you was an ogre, but I can see now that I was wrong.' She turned to Sarah, digging her in the ribs. 'No wonder you was happy in the countryside. He's all right.'

'Shut up,' Sarah hissed. 'It isn't like that.'

'No?' Nettie did not look convinced. 'He's a good-looking cove and I wouldn't say no if he wanted to take me out for a slap-up dinner in a pie and eel shop.'

Pearl sent her a warning look. 'This is a serious occasion, Nettie. A little less levity, please.'

Nettie had the grace to look ashamed. 'Sorry, miss. I was forgetting.'

'I know it's hard, but we must think of poor Sophia,' Pearl said gently. 'She'll need all our love and support in the days to come.'

'It's a sad day,' Grey said solemnly.

Pearl nodded and her brown eyes filled with tears. 'Mr Arbuthnot passed away peacefully, but it still came as a shock. We truly thought that he was on the road to recovery.'

Grey raised his hand as if he were about to pat her on the shoulder, but let it fall again. 'I'm truly sorry, miss. He was a good man.'

'He was indeed.' Mrs Arbuthnot walked into the room, looking round at their crestfallen faces with an attempt at a smile. 'I'm trying to convince myself that he's gone to a better place. My poor dear James was not a man to enjoy being an invalid, and he's never been the same since that terrible fire.'

Grey held out a chair. 'Won't you sit down, ma'am?'

She regarded him with a dazed expression in her red-rimmed eyes. 'I'm sorry, young man. I seem to remember your face but I can't recall when we last met or in what circumstances.'

'I came to see you after Sarah went missing, Mrs Arbuthnot. I was the fellow who abducted her and I confessed my part in the sorry business.' Grey helped her to take a seat. 'You were very kind and understanding, but that only made it worse. I knew I'd done a wicked deed, and I've been trying to atone for it ever since.'

Sarah stepped forward. 'You mustn't blame him, ma'am. Grey was kind to me from the start. He took me to his aunt and she looked after me.' She gulped back fresh tears. 'Miss Elsie was a good woman, no matter what anyone says about her. She died yesterday and now we've lost the master too. It makes me very sad.'

Mrs Arbuthnot took out her hanky and mopped her

streaming eyes. 'I'm sorry to hear that, Sarah dear. We must all try to be brave, but I can't quite believe that James has gone. We've been together for twenty-three years, and I don't know how I'll manage without him.'

Pearl moved closer to her and laid a sympathetic hand on her shoulder. 'We're all here to support you, Sophia.' She turned to Nettie. 'Go downstairs and see what's happening in the kitchen. A cup of tea is what's needed here.'

'Or a tot of brandy,' Nettie muttered, scowling.

Sarah eyed her anxiously. She was quick to recognise the ominous pout and the rebellious look in Nettie's eyes, and it was clear that the almost famous actress thought it beneath her to run errands. 'I'll go, Miss Parfitt,' she said hastily. She was about to leave the room when Dorcas entered carrying a tray laden with tea and cake, which she set carefully on the mahogany dining table. She picked up the teapot and poured the beverage into dainty bone-china cups and added a splash of milk.

'Have you done as I asked?' Mrs Arbuthnot said wearily.

'Yes, ma'am. I've sent Betty to fetch Mrs Puckle, the laying-out nurse. She'll come directly providing she isn't attending a confinement.'

'I don't want her to touch him if she's in liquor, Dorcas.'

'Certainly not, ma'am. I'll make sure she's stone cold sober before she does her business.' Dorcas beckoned to Sarah. 'Make yourself useful, my girl. Pass the tea and cake round.'

Only too pleased to keep her hands occupied, Sarah did as she was told, and she had to smile at the sight of Grey standing stiffly to attention as he attempted to balance a fragile cup and saucer in one large hand and a plate of seed cake in the other. She motioned to the empty chair beside Miss Parfitt. 'I'd sit down if I were you,' she whispered.

He glanced at Pearl who smiled up at him. 'Please take a seat, Mr Grey.'

'Thank you, ma'am.' He put the plate in Sarah's outstretched hand. 'You have it, Sarah. I'm not hungry.'

She passed it to Nettie who had already demolished hers and was looking round for a second helping. 'Ta, ducky. I haven't lost my appetite.' She shot an apologetic glance in Mrs Arbuthnot's direction. 'Begging your pardon, missis, but I ain't had nothing to eat since last evening.'

Mrs Arbuthnot managed a weak smile. 'That's all right, Nettie. We must try to carry on as normal, even if it is going to be extremely difficult.'

Sarah longed to give her a hug, but she did not dare overstep the bounds of convention. Servants must always keep their place, even at moments like this. 'Would you like some more tea, ma'am?'

'No, thank you, Sarah.' Mrs Arbuthnot glanced at the clock on the mantelshelf. 'Is that the time?'

Dorcas took the empty cup from her. 'No, ma'am. I stopped all the clocks. Mrs Burgess said I should.'

'Quite so. I feel that my life has stopped too.'

Pearl and Dorcas exchanged anxious glances. 'Perhaps you ought to rest, Sophia?' Pearl said softly.

'Let me help you, ma'am.' Dorcas was about to help her mistress to her feet when the doorbell rang and its sound echoed through the silent house. She bobbed a curtsey. 'I'll go and see who it is, ma'am. It might be Mrs Puckle.'

Grey cleared his throat. 'We should be moving on, Mrs Arbuthnot,' he said awkwardly. 'I hate to bother you at a time like this, but I had hoped that Sarah might remain here until I've found more suitable lodgings.'

She clutched her hand to her forehead. 'My poor mind has gone quite blank, and I can't seem to think about the future, but Sarah may stay if she wants to.'

Pearl turned to him with a sympathetic smile. 'Where are you residing at the moment, Mr Grey?'

'I have a room in Wych Street, but it's not a safe place for a young girl.'

'I'm quite all right there,' Sarah said stoutly.

'And I've got lodgings nearby,' Nettie added through a mouthful of cake. 'If it's good enough for me and the girls, then I don't see why it's not right for Sarah. She's not a child.'

'Is there something you're not telling us, Mr Grey?' Pearl's cheeks paled and her voice was barely a whisper.

'I'm afraid that Trigg is still a threat, ma'am. I wouldn't mention this in such circumstances but I know he bears a grudge against this house and Sarah in particular. He's already threatened her with violence.'

Mrs Arbuthnot was suddenly alert. 'Are you still having dealings with that villain, Mr Grey?'

'I'm sorry to say that I did some business with him recently which I sincerely regret, and I have to go away for a while. I don't want to leave Sarah on her own in my lodgings.'

'I see, and this is made even more difficult because your aunt, Miss Fitch, is no longer with us.'

'Exactly so, ma'am.'

A slow smile creased Mrs Arbuthnot's face. 'Then it is very simple, Mr Grey. Sarah must come here and live with us.' She turned to her, holding out her hand. 'Would you like that, my dear? I'm sure that Dorcas could find work for you. Taking care of commercial gentlemen is quite demanding, and no matter what the circumstances we have to pay the bills.'

Sarah grasped her hand. 'I would like that, ma'am. But I would also like to go back to the village to let my friends see that I am safe and well.' She sent a pleading glance to Pearl. 'I was taking classes in the school while the schoolmaster was absent after a riding accident. I want to be a teacher like you, miss.'

'I'm sure that's very laudable,' Pearl said seriously. 'But you're still very young, my dear. You have plenty of time to study, and if Mrs Arbuthnot is agreeable you can come and help me in class as well as doing your work in the house.'

'It all sounds a bit dull to me,' Nettie whispered. 'You could share with me and the girls. I'm sure we could find you a space to sleep, even if it's on the floor. Maybe you could get work in the theatre. The boss is always looking for cleaning women who don't steal or fall down blind drunk.'

Grey rose to his feet. 'I'm afraid I must leave now, Mrs Arbuthnot. I have to make the arrangements for Elsie's funeral.'

'Of course. I understand, Mr Grey.' Mrs Arbuthnot rose somewhat unsteadily to her feet and held out her hand. 'Sarah can remain here with us for as long as she likes.'

'You're very kind, ma'am.' Grey glanced over his shoulder and smiled at Pearl. 'And thanks to you too, Miss Parfitt. I know that Sarah is in good hands.'

She dropped her gaze and a faint blush stained her cheeks. 'Not at all, Mr Grey. It's a pleasure to have her back with us.'

Sarah stared from one to the other. Everyone was making arrangements for her as if she were still a child. 'Grey.' She ran after him as he hurried from the room. 'Don't I get to choose what happens to me?'

'Don't make a scene, kid. Can't you see that they're upset enough?'

'And I am too. Mr Arbuthnot was like a father to me, but I've been away from here for a long time. I've led a different life and I don't belong here any more. I want to go home.'

'You can't go back to the village, Sarah. Where would you live? And how would you support yourself?'

'I could stay with Davey and the children. They need me.'

'That wouldn't do. Davey Hawkes is a man now, not a boy. It wouldn't be right for you to live with him in that tiny cottage.'

She recoiled as if he had slapped her face. 'That's a horrible thing to say.'

'It's only what everyone in the village would think, and you wouldn't be able to work at the school.'

'But that's silly.'

'Is it?' He cupped her cheek in his hand, shaking his head. 'Think about it, Sarah. Grow up and see the world for what it is.' He snatched his hat off the hall table where he had left it and rammed it on his head. 'I'll sort out the funeral arrangements and let you know when it will be. Ladies do not usually attend an interment, but if you really want to say goodbye to Elsie I'm willing to take you.'

'Yes, please,' Sarah said, struggling with the overwhelming desire to sob on his shoulder. 'I want to be there.'

'All right, but you must stay here in the meantime, and for heaven's sake keep an eye out for Trigg. He's bound to hear that his old enemy has died, but I don't think he'll let matters rest there.'

'I know, but I'm not scared of him when I'm with you. Please take me with you.' She would have followed him into the street but Nettie had come up behind her and she grabbed her round the waist.

'Let him go, Sarah.'

'He lives in a pigsty when he's on his own. He needs someone to look after him.'

'That's his choice, ducky. He's a grown man and a good-looker too. I reckon he could have any woman he pleased, if he put his mind to it.'

'I don't think of him in that way.'

'Come off it, Sarah Scrase. You're a female, ain't you?' Nettie closed the door and leaned against it, grinning widely. 'I bet you fancy him just as much as I do.'

'That's not true.'

'Liar. You're kidding yourself, my girl. But it doesn't make much difference in my opinion, because your Tobias has only got eyes for a certain Miss Perfect, and who's to blame him?'

'Do you think so?'

Nettie tapped the side of her nose. 'I know so. I been around much more than you, my little country mouse. I've had a few admirers and I seen the way they look at a girl when they're smitten. Tobias will be back before you know it, even if he only comes on the off chance of seeing our dear Pearl.'

Sarah shook her head. 'I don't know what's happening to me, Nettie. Everything was going along so well, apart from Mr Wills giving me funny looks and dropping hints, but now everything's changed. I don't know what to do for the best.'

'It's not as if you've got a lot of choice. You can come with me and hope the girls don't scratch your eyes out for being prettier than them, or you can stay here and help Mrs Arbuthnot keep a roof over her head. It's up to you.' She grabbed her bonnet. 'As for me, I'm going to share a cab back to Wych Street with your man. Never let it be said that Nettie Bean let an opportunity slip through her fingers.' She wrenched the front door open and ran outside, slamming it behind her.

* * *

196

Sarah had little choice other than to remain in Wellclose Square at least until Elsie's funeral, but it was a house in deep mourning. All the clocks had been stopped at the time of Mr Arbuthnot's passing; the curtains were drawn and the mirrors covered with black cloth.

Franz Beckman had paid them a visit the moment he heard the news of his former employer's demise and was ready to help in any way he could, which Dorcas said was a gift from God as she could not shift furniture and it was muscle they needed now and not sympathy. At Mrs Arbuthnot's request Franz and a couple of his fellow sugar bakers had carried the coffin downstairs and placed it on a bier in the parlour. A constant stream of people came to pay their last respects and well-wishers left little notes of sympathy for the bereaved widow. Sarah placed them on a salver in the entrance hall, but Mrs Arbuthnot was too upset to look at them and spent much of her time in her darkened room.

On her first night back in Wellclose Square Sarah was given her old bed but she now shared the room with Dorcas. The commercial travellers occupied all the other bedrooms and that evening they took their supper in the dining room, eating their meal in respectful silence. Sarah helped to serve them and to clear the table when they had finished, but everything seemed strange and she was missing Elsie more than she had thought possible. Her thoughts kept returning to the village and she wondered how Davey and the children were getting on without her. She doubted whether Mary would be able to cope with the twins without her help. Lemuel and Jonah were nine-year-olds with minds of their own and were quite a handful. Sarah went to sleep that night listening to Dorcas snoring and thinking about the little family she had left behind.

Next morning she helped serve breakfast and one of the older gentlemen gave her a threepenny bit as a tip when he left, saying that he would look forward to staying in Wellclose Square on his next trip to London. Some of the commercial travellers would be returning that night, but Dorcas said that most of them would be moving on to other towns and cities. It seemed a callous disregard for Mrs Arbuthnot's feelings to take strangers into the house with the funeral only a couple of days away, but when Sarah mentioned her misgivings to Dorcas her immediate reaction was to shrug her thin shoulders. 'The money from the paying guests will keep a roof over our heads, Sarah. We've got to be practical,' she said firmly.

Below stairs they tried to maintain their normal routine but a pall of sadness hung over the house. Pearl came every day after school, sometimes accompanied by Franz, or he would appear soon after she arrived, and Sarah realised that this was no coincidence. Cook confirmed her suspicions that the sugar baker was sweet on Miss Parfitt, even though she gave him little encouragement. According to Mrs Burgess it was Dorcas who had a fondness for Franz and she had recently given poor Wally his marching orders. Cook was openly critical of the way in which Dorcas had treated her faithful swain, but Dorcas was unrepentant.

'One day Franz will open his eyes and see that Miss Perfect don't fancy him,' she said in answer to Cook's criticism. 'He's the man for me and I don't care who knows it.'

'Well he's not interested in you, my girl.' Cook folded her lips into a tight line, which was a sure indication that she disapproved of such talk.

Sarah kept out of the argument, not wanting to take sides. She did not know whom to pity the most in this tangle of hearts, but she would not allow anyone to criticise Miss Parfitt who did not go out of her way to attract the attentions of the lovelorn master sugar baker other than by being her gentle, sweet-natured self. If there was anyone whom Sarah would like to emulate it was Pearl, but she knew she would never be as clever or as beautiful as her idol.

In the days that followed Mrs Arbuthnot insisted on sleeping in the four-poster that she and her late husband had occupied, even though Dorcas suggested that they might rent the room to paying guests. Sophia Arbuthnot replied tearfully that she could not bear to have strangers occupying the bed where her husband had breathed his last, and she refused to have the sheets changed declaring that the scent of him lingered and she would not have it washed away.

On the morning of the funeral Dorcas and Cook were becoming even more concerned for Mrs Arbuthnot's state of mind. 'Some widows go off their heads with grief,' Dorcas said when they were enjoying a cup of tea in the kitchen after the lodgers had finished breakfast and left for work.

'Some have been known to turn their faces to the wall and die of a broken heart,' Cook added gloomily.

Betty covered her face with her apron and started to wail.

'Stop that, you silly girl,' Cook said crossly. 'Do you want me to take the wooden spoon to you, Betty?'

Sarah had been sitting quietly at the table but she leapt to her feet and went over to console Betty. 'Don't shout at her,' she cried angrily. 'She's upset.'

'So are we all.' Dorcas rose to her feet. 'I'm going upstairs to see if the mistress is ready. She insists on going to the funeral even though the doctor has advised her against it.' She cast a deprecating glance at Betty as she mounted the stairs. 'Stop her making that noise, Sarah. We don't want the mistress to hear.'

Sarah put her arms around Betty and rocked her like a baby.

Cook poured more tea into her cup. 'I dunno,' she muttered. 'A three-pound funeral is not the way to send off an important man like the master. I remember funerals where there were four or even six black horses pulling the hearse, which was glass-sided to show off the oak coffin draped in crimson velvet. There'd be attendants with silk hat bands, dozens of followers and at least two mutes. Those were the days.'

Sarah wiped Betty's eyes with a corner of her apron. 'Would you like a biscuit and a glass of warm milk?'

Betty nodded wordlessly as she tried to control her sobs.

Cook looked up at the board above the door as one of the bells jangled on its spring. 'Oh Lord. It's the front door. Dorcas can't answer it; you'd best go, Sarah. It's probably Miss Pearl, or it might even be the undertaker with the hearse and mourning coach, and none of us quite ready, for I won't let the mistress go on her own.'

Sarah gave Betty a biscuit, and satisfied that this had had the desired effect she hurried up the narrow staircase to the entrance hall. She straightened her mobcap and went to open the door, but it was not the undertaker who stood on the front step. Her hand flew to her mouth in dismay.

Chapter Twelve

'I had a feeling I might find you here, girlie.' Trigg put his foot over the threshold as she attempted to slam the door. 'Now that ain't friendly, is it, my dear?' His grey eyes glittered like chips of ice as he pushed past her.

'Get out,' Sarah shouted, quite forgetting that she was in a house of mourning where no one spoke above a whisper. 'The master is being buried today. Show some respect.'

He stopped, looking around with a critical eye. 'Hmm, not bad in its way, but a bit old-fashioned.'

'Get out of here now, or I'll run to the watch house and fetch a constable. You can't walk in as if you own the place.'

'But I do, girlie. Go if you want, but the law is on my side.'

Sarah tugged at his sleeve. 'I'm asking you nicely, please leave. Mrs Arbuthnot has enough to bear on a day like today.'

'What is all this commotion?' Mrs Arbuthnot appeared at the top of the stairs, a wraithlike figure in widow's weeds. She descended slowly, and her heavy crepe veil billowed around her like a black sail taking up the wind. 'What is this man doing in my house, Sarah?'

'It's my house now, lady,' Trigg said with a triumphant smile. 'All mine.'

Sarah ran to the foot of the stairs. 'Let me go for the constable, ma'am. I'll have him arrested for breaking and entering.'

Trigg threw back his head and roared with laughter. 'That's a good 'un, girlie. For a start I walked in without touching nothing other than the lion's head doorknocker, and second, I own this drum.'

Mrs Arbuthnot swayed on her feet. 'What is he saying, Sarah?' She tottered down the last two steps and Sarah helped her to a chair.

'Sit down, ma'am. I'll go for help.'

'Stay where you are.' Trigg's false smile was replaced by a snarl. 'I'll deal with you later, Sal Scratch. This is between me and the woman.' He moved closer, bending over Mrs Arbuthnot. 'I bought the lease on this property and now I own it.'

'But my husband purchased the house when we married.'

'And he mortgaged when he needed to rebuild the mill, but the venture failed miserably, leaving him even further in debt.'

Mrs Arbuthnot raised a trembling hand to her forehead. 'I – I don't know anything about that.'

'Leave her alone, you brute,' Sarah cried, beating him with her clenched fists.

He threw her to the ground. 'That's for a start, girl. Cross me again and see what you'll get. It won't be pretty.'

'Leave my house, you dreadful man.' Mrs Arbuthnot

rose to her feet. 'I won't have this abominable behaviour under my roof.'

He raised his hand as if to slap her, and then seemed to think better of it as he dropped it to his side with a hoarse chuckle. 'You've got a bit of spirit, woman, but it won't do you no good. Like I said before, the law is on my side and I want you out of here by the end of the week. I can't say fairer than that.' He shot a scornful glance at Sarah as she scrambled to her feet. 'You haven't seen the last of me. I'll have you, girl. One way or another you'll repay me for all the trouble you've caused me.'

'You're a wicked man and I'm not afraid to tell you so to your face.' Sarah turned to Mrs Arbuthnot who had collapsed onto the chair, burying her face in her hands as sobs racked her body. 'Don't upset yourself, ma'am.'

Dorcas burst through the green baize door brandishing a broomstick. 'We heard shouting from below stairs. What's he done to you, missis?'

Trigg lunged at her, snatched the broom and snapped it in two over his knee as if it were a twig. 'I've changed me mind,' he said, curling his lip. 'I don't want a pack of screeching women in my house. However, I'm a reasonable man and I'll allow you to stay until tomorrow, but I want you out of here by noon, otherwise I'll send the bailiffs in and have you evicted. Let's see how you like living on the street.' He marched towards the front door, opening it to find Franz about to raise the doorknocker. 'They're all yours, sugar baker.'

Franz stood aside with a bemused look on his face. 'Was that the workhouse master?'

Dorcas had been fanning Mrs Arbuthnot with her apron but she stopped the moment she saw Franz and ran to him. 'It was Trigg, and a real brute he is too. He terrified us poor women and we had no one to protect us until you arrived on the doorstep like a knight in shining armour.'

He did not seem to notice her as his attention was fixed on Mrs Arbuthnot. 'What did that man want? What has he been saying to upset you, ma'am?'

Mrs Arbuthnot's head lolled to one side and Dorcas uttered a shriek. 'He's killed her, that's what he's done.'

Sarah felt for a pulse as Elsie had shown her many times. 'It's all right, she's just fainted. It's that terrible man Trigg's doing. He's turning us out of the house, Mr Beckman. He says he's bought it and we must all leave by midday tomorrow.'

'The bastard!' Franz flushed to the roots of his hair. 'Begging your pardon, ladies. But it's hard to believe anyone could treat a grieving widow in such a manner.'

Dorcas flashed him a smile. 'I like a proper gent, and that's what you are, Franz.'

'Thank you, Miss Dorcas, but I don't like to see women bullied by the likes of him.'

Mrs Arbuthnot moaned and her eyelids fluttered. 'Has he gone?'

Sarah held her hand. 'Yes, ma'am.'

'The carriage will be here soon. I must be ready.' She attempted to rise but Dorcas restrained her with a gentle hand. 'Stay there for a moment, missis. We'll let you know when it arrives.' She turned to Sarah. 'Keep an eye on her and I'll fetch a tot of brandy. The poor thing needs something to revive her.'

Franz backed towards the doorway. 'I'll go outside and wait for the undertaker. Miss Pearl will be here soon; she'll know what to do.'

'I don't need no schoolmistress to tell me my duty, thank you, Mr Beckman.' Dorcas marched off with an indignant twitch of her shoulders.

'What did I say?' Franz asked, frowning.

'Nothing,' Sarah said hastily. 'We're all upset. I just wish that Grey were here. He'd know what to do about Mr Trigg.'

Franz shook his head. 'This is a bad day. Frau Arbuthnot should not go to the funeral. She should be looked after in her home and allowed to grieve in peace. That man has no right to throw her out on the streets.'

'No,' Sarah said sadly. 'He's a brute. It's all wrong and it's my fault. If Mr Arbuthnot hadn't taken pity on me all those years ago none of this would have happened. He might still be alive and you'd have your job at the sugar mill. Perhaps I am the devil's daughter after all.'

The church of St George in the East was packed with mourners who filed silently into the churchyard for the interment, and stood with heads bowed as James Arbuthnot's coffin was lowered into the ground. Mrs Arbuthnot had maintained a dignified presence throughout but as the handfuls of earth were scattered onto the coffin she collapsed in tears and Franz carried her to the waiting carriage. Sarah and Dorcas had accompanied her, leaving Mrs Burgess, Pearl and Betty at home to prepare the funeral feast. The remaining gentlemen lodgers had contributed generously to the cost of the food, and to a man had expressed their regret on losing their accommodation in such a fine house.

Sarah glanced anxiously at the faces in the crowd as she and Dorcas followed Franz out of the cemetery. She could not understand why Grey had not contacted her as he had promised. It was almost a week since Elsie died but there had been no word from him. She was about to follow Dorcas into the funeral carriage when she spotted Trigg standing on the pavement a little way from the church gates. Anger banished fear and she strode up to him. 'Are you satisfied? Can't you see how the poor lady is suffering?'

He shrugged his shoulders and bared his rotten teeth in a grin. 'I don't know the meaning of the word pity. No one helped me and the missis when we was cast out onto the streets. Let's see how you and the widow like it.'

'You won't win. We'll manage somehow.'

'Well don't expect your fancy man to save you this time, girlie.' Trigg was about to walk away but she caught him by the sleeve.

'What do you mean? What have you done to him?'

'I done nothing. The law caught up with him at last and he's in Whitecross Street prison.'

'In prison.'

'That's right, sweetheart.'

'But isn't that the debtors' jail?'

'Right again.'

'He paid you what he owed.'

'Can you prove that, girlie?'

The breath seemed to have been sucked from her lungs. She stared at him in horror. 'Why? Why would you do that to him?'

'Because it pleases me to see him suffer. He'll be an old man by the time he gets out, unless someone can stump up the reddy, and that won't be Mr Arbuthnot or his widow. He's dead and she's headed for the workhouse, as are you, girlie. Without Tobias Grey and his family to protect you, that's where you'll end up, and one of these days you're going to come crawling to me on your bended knees, begging me to take you in. I look forward to that, Sal Scratch. If you think you've been in hell, you ain't seen nothing yet.' He turned away and strolled off, whistling a popular tune.

Sarah could not move. Her feet seemed to be glued to the pavement and her limbs were too heavy to move. She did not want to believe it, but she knew in her heart that Trigg was telling the truth. He had plotted their downfall and now it was complete.

'Hey, Sarah. Come on. We're waiting for you.' Dorcas stuck her head out of the carriage window, beckoning furiously.

As if the weather had taken a turn to add to the gloom of a funeral, it had begun to rain. Runnels of inky water traced the outline of her fingers and fell like dark tears onto the paving stones as the black dye leached from the gown that Nettie had given her. Her best bonnet had suffered the same fate and she could feel rainwater dripping from the brim to trickle down her cheeks, but a ruined outfit was the least of her worries as Trigg's harsh words came back to her. 'The law caught up with him and he's in Whitecross Street prison.' But it was nothing to do with justice, she thought bitterly. This was revenge, pure and simple. Trigg had lied, and she had not a shred of proof that he had received Elsie's money in payment of the debt.

Dorcas leapt out of the carriage and ran to her side. 'What's up? Why are you standing in the rain like a booby? Your face is all streaky and you look like a chimney sweep. I'd split me sides laughing if it was at any other time.'

Sarah clutched her hand. 'Didn't you see Trigg? He came here to gloat.'

'All the more reason to get in the carriage and go home.'

'But it isn't our home now, Dorcas. We've only got until morning and then we must leave. We'll be homeless, and even worse, that dreadful creature has lied to the police and told them that Grey still owes him money. He's in prison and I don't know what to do.'

'That's not our problem, love.' Dorcas squeezed her fingers. 'C'mon. We're both getting soaked and the dye is running something chronic.'

Sarah snatched her hand free. 'You go. I'll come later but I've got to try and help Grey. I'm going to see his uncle in Spital Square. Maybe I can persuade him to pay the debt.'

'It's not your business. Being homeless is your business, Sarah.'

'And Grey is the only one who might be able to help us find somewhere to live. Who else is there?'

Dorcas threw up her hands. 'It's a wild goose chase if you ask me, but I can see that your mind is set on it.'

'I must do this, but I'll come home as soon as it's done.'

'Go on then, and good luck. You'll need it.' Dorcas turned on her heel and raced back to the carriage.

Doing her best to ignore the downpour and the amused glances from passers-by, Sarah started walking in the direction of Spital Square.

It was late morning by the time she arrived at her destination. She was soaked to the skin but she barely noticed the discomfort. She rang the bell and waited anxiously.

The door opened and a male servant gave her a cursory glance. 'Tradesmen's entrance.' He was about to close it again but using her last spurt of energy she sprang forward, throwing her weight against it. The footman staggered backwards into the entrance hall. 'Hey, what d'you think you're a-doing of, miss? This is a respectable house.'

'I want to see Mr Fitch,' Sarah said boldly. 'It's an urgent family matter so don't waste time arguing with me.'

He blinked several times, opening and closing his mouth as if at a loss for words. Sarah pushed home her advantage. 'Please tell him that Miss Sarah Scrase is here and it's very important that I speak to him about his nephew, Mr Tobias Grey. You might as well do as I say, because I'm not leaving without seeing him.'

'Wait here.' He pointed to a carved oak hall chair. 'Sit down and don't move.' He walked off, leaving her alone in the entrance hall that had been designed to impress. She had barely noticed her surroundings during her last visit to the house and it was only now that she realised that the Fitch family must be extremely wealthy. She gazed in awe at the ornate plasterwork on the cornices and the crystal chandeliers hanging from the ceiling. Even on such a dull day their dancing prisms reflected the light from tall windows draped with velvet curtains. The scent of the beeswax and lavender polish that some poor little slavey had lavished on the rosewood hall tables mingled with the perfume of hothouse flowers spilling from strategically placed urns and vases. Surely Grey's uncle would not begrudge the comparatively small amount that would settle the debt when he had all this?

The footman reappeared, making her jump. 'Mr Fitch is busy, miss. He can't see you today.'

'Can he not?' She leapt to her feet. 'We'll see about that.' She dodged his attempt to stop her and despite his protests she burst into the reception room to find George Fitch deep in conversation with a grey-haired gentleman. 'What's going on, Dobson?' George demanded angrily. 'I told you that Mr Moorcroft and I had business to discuss and we weren't to be disturbed.'

The footman cleared his throat nervously. 'I'm sorry, sir. I told the young person that you did not wish to see her, but she wouldn't take no for an answer.'

'So I see.' George glared at Sarah. 'What is the meaning of this outrageous behaviour?'

'I'm sorry, sir,' Sarah said breathlessly. 'But I had to speak to you. It's a matter of life and death.'

'Perhaps I'd better leave you to sort this out.' Mr Moorcroft rose from his seat. 'We can continue this at a more convenient time.'

'Sit down, Martin. You're here now so we might as well continue.' George dismissed the footman with a wave of his hand. 'I'll handle this, Dobson.' He waited until the door closed before turning to Sarah with an ominous frown. 'You have one minute to state your case.'

Sarah clasped her hands tightly behind her back. She was shaking inwardly but she was not going to let it show. She took a deep breath and looked him in the eye. 'Your nephew, Tobias, has been falsely accused of owing money to a man who is a villain. It's not true. I know that Grey paid Trigg and it's a pack of lies, but he's in Whitecross Street debtors' jail and he needs your help, sir.'

George subsided onto his chair. 'This is nothing new. Tobias has been in trouble ever since he ran away from home at the age of thirteen.'

Moorcroft stared at him in obvious surprise. 'Surely you don't mean to let him languish in prison?'

'Maybe it's what he needs to bring him to his senses, Martin. He has a wild streak as did poor Elsie, and look where it led her.'

'Your sister was a sad case, but you're a rich man, George. Couldn't you do something for the unfortunate young fellow?'

'Please listen to the gentleman, sir,' Sarah cried passionately. 'Grey doesn't deserve to be locked up in that dreadful place.'

Moorcroft's serious expression softened into something like a smile. 'He has a good advocate in this young woman.'

'Tobias has always had a way with females, especially young and naïve girls like this creature.' George leaned towards Sarah, his brows drawn into a frown. 'You have said your piece and the answer is no.'

'Please . . .'

'I said no, and I meant no. Tobias got himself mixed up with criminals and it is up to him to pay the price. Now go away and don't bother me again. You're nearer to the bell pull than I am, Martin. Will you please ring for Dobson?'

Moorcroft rose from his seat. 'I'm leaving now myself, but there is still the business of Elsie's will. My brother sent it to you, I believe.'

'I haven't had a chance to look at it yet,' George said vaguely. 'It's here somewhere and I'll examine it in my own time.'

'Very well, but it's just possible she might have left something to her nephew which would help him now. We can find our own way out. Don't bother Dobson.'

'I don't pay the servants' wages so that my lawyer can do their work for them. Ring the bell for Dobson, Martin.'

'It's really not necessary. I have to be in court at three o'clock and I need to call in at my office on the way.' Moorcroft beckoned to Sarah. 'Come along. I'll see you safely off the premises.'

There seemed to be no option other than to follow him. Sarah shot a wary glance at George Fitch as she left the room, but his features seemed to have turned to stone and she realised that nothing she could say would move him.

Dobson was standing stiffly to attention outside the door but he leapt into action and snatched Moorcroft's hat and cane from a side table.

'Thank you, Dobson.' Moorcroft accepted them with a nod of his head. 'I'd be obliged if you'd summon a cab.' He turned to Sarah with a sympathetic smile. 'You're very wet, my dear. You must allow me to see you safely home.'

'I can't do that, sir. It's a long way to Wellclose Square.'

'Did you walk here in spite of the weather?'

'I'm using to walking, sir.'

He glanced outside, shaking his head. 'It's still raining heavily. I insist on taking you home, child. You'll catch your death of cold and I don't want that on my conscience.'

Dobson hurried into the hall. 'The cab's here, sir.'

'Thank you, Dobson.' Moorcroft ushered Sarah out of the house and handed her into the cab. She was beginning to shiver and the full enormity of the situation was just beginning to dawn on her as she settled herself in the corner of the hansom.

'Wellclose Square, cabby,' Moorcroft said as he climbed in and sat down beside her. 'Tell me about yourself, Miss – I don't even know your name.'

'Sarah Scrase, sir.'

'And how old are you, Sarah?'

She clutched the side of the cab as it lurched forward. 'I'm sixteen, sir, nearly seventeen.'

'How did you come to know Tobias? I don't mean to cross-examine you, my dear, but I need to know a little about your situation if I'm to be of any help to you.'

'Why would you want to do that, sir? I'm nothing to you.'

'I'm a lawyer and I like to think I'm a fair man. I knew Tobias when he was a boy and I'm very sorry to hear that he has fallen in with the wrong people.'

'He hasn't,' Sarah said angrily. 'At least, not in the way you mean. He's a good man and he saved me from Mr Trigg, the workhouse master. He took me to Miss Elsie and she looked after me until . . .' She broke off, unable to speak of Elsie's sad end.

'Tell me how it all came about. I might be able to help.'

Sarah launched into a brief account of how she came to be in the workhouse and how the Arbuthnots had taken her in. She told him about Trigg's brutal treatment and how he had plotted Mr Arbuthnot's downfall, which had eventually led to his death, and how Trigg's final act of revenge would be the eviction of Mrs Arbuthnot from her home in Wellclose Square.

He listened intently. 'The man is evil and should be brought to justice,' he said at length.

'It was lucky for me that he chose Grey to do his dirty work. If he hadn't taken me to Miss Elsie I might have ended up in the river.'

He sighed. 'I knew her when she was young. She was quite extraordinary and very beautiful.'

Sarah looked up, startled by this revelation. 'Was she?'

'Yes, indeed she was. She had many admirers but sadly she gave her heart to the wrong man.'

'Were you in love with her, sir?'

'We were close for a while but I was an impecunious law student at the time and she fell in love with a fortune hunter.'

'But she never married.'

'The bounder jilted her. I believe that the family bought him off, although I have no proof. He left the country and to my knowledge has never returned. Poor Elsie was heartbroken and then she discovered that she was . . .' He broke off, staring out of the window. 'It's ancient history now.'

'You can't stop there, Mr Moorcroft. I lived with Elsie for six years or more, and she never spoke of her past life. She devoted herself to healing the sick and helping people. She was a good woman, even if she did behave oddly. Some people said she was a witch, but that wasn't true.'

He chuckled, shaking his head. 'Of course it wasn't. Elsie was just different from the rest of us. She believed in being free and living the life she chose instead of bowing to convention.'

'So what happened when the man she loved ran off?'

'She left London.'

'I can't believe that she ran away simply because a man didn't want to marry her.'

'It wasn't as simple as that, and it was a long time ago. Her family disowned her.'

'Why would they be so cruel? It wasn't her fault.'

He was not looking at her, and for a moment she thought he was going to ignore her question. He turned his head slowly and looked her in the eye. 'I think perhaps you are old enough to be told the truth.'

Chapter Thirteen

'I would really like to know, sir. I've no idea where I would have ended up if it hadn't been for Elsie.'

'Can I trust you to be discreet and keep this to yourself?'

'Yes, sir.'

'Elsie was only nineteen when she gave birth to an illegitimate child. She was ill for a long time afterwards, hovering between life and death, but she was young and strong and eventually she recovered. I don't know what happened to the baby, or even if it lived.'

'Poor Elsie. How terrible for her.'

'It was hushed up at the time, and shortly afterwards Elsie left home. Her family disowned her.'

'Grey didn't. He did business for her in London. He stood by her.'

'I could have done more for her and I always regret that I didn't, but I had my studies and then for many years I was a junior solicitor in Lincoln's Inn. Now I am a successful lawyer in practice with my brother Bertram. We were both at the graveside when Elsie was interred. She was still a young woman – it's tragic.'

'Young?' Sarah stared at him in surprise. 'But I thought she was old.'

'Everyone over twenty-five seems old at your age, my dear. But Elsie should have had many more years ahead of her.'

'I miss her so much. She could never take the place of my mother, but I think she did her best.'

'What will you do now, Sarah?'

'I don't know. If Grey was here he wouldn't see us turned out on the streets. He has a room in Wych Street, but I couldn't take a lady like Mrs Arbuthnot to live in a place like that. She was good to me in the past, and I can't simply abandon her.'

He was silent for a moment, staring straight ahead as the hansom cab lurched its way through the crowded streets. Suddenly, to Sarah's surprise, he tapped on the roof with his cane. 'Whitecross Street prison, please, cabby.'

'Right you are, guv.'

Moorcroft settled back against the leather squabs. 'I'm taking you to see Tobias. It's just possible he might be able to suggest something that would help.'

Sarah clasped her hands together with a cry of delight. 'Oh, I'd be so grateful, sir. I just want to be sure that he's all right, but you don't have to bother yourself. I mean, an important gentleman like you must be very busy.'

'There are some advantages to being a man of the law, and you wouldn't be allowed in on your own. I might be able to get you in, but it will take some subterfuge.'

Sarah frowned. 'I'm not sure what that means, sir. But I'll do anything you tell me to.'

The turnkey was reluctant at first but Moorcroft managed to convince him that Grey was his client and that Sarah was Grey's sister, and a generous tip smoothed the way. Sarah was forced to cover her mouth and nose with her hands as the stench of unwashed bodies and excrement filled the seemingly endless corridors lined with locked doors and closed grilles. She tried to shut her ears to the animal-like sounds of human beings in deep distress, but the prison was like her worst imaginings of hell.

They were shown into a small, bleak room with a barred window high up in one wall. The only furnishings were a deal table and two hardwood chairs. The unrelieved greyness was made worse by the chill rising from the flagstone floor.

'Five minutes, sir,' the turnkey said grimly. 'You are allowed five minutes to speak to your client and then you must leave.' He left them without waiting for an answer.

Sarah heard the key grate in the lock and she shot a startled glance at Moorcroft. 'He locked us in.'

'That's quite usual, my dear. I wouldn't normally bring a young person to a place like this.'

'It's worse than I ever imagined.'

'There are sixty men to a ward here,' he said solemnly. 'They are locked in for sixteen hours a day and have to pay for everything they receive, from soap and towels to their meals.'

'And if they can't pay?'

He shrugged his shoulders. 'We will make sure that Tobias does not fall into that category and I will do everything I can to secure his release. If what you say about this man Trigg is true, then it is he who should languish in jail.'

'I can hear footsteps,' Sarah said, clutching his hand. 'He's coming.' She held her breath as the door opened and would have rushed forward to greet Grey if Moorcroft had not restrained her.

'No touching,' the turnkey said, thrusting Grey into the room.

His hands were cuffed behind his back and his clothes were rumpled and filthy. His eyes shone at the sight of her but his initial look of pleasure was dimmed by a frown. 'Why are you here, kid? This is no place for a young girl.' He glared at Moorcroft. 'Is this your doing, Martin?'

'Grey,' Sarah whispered. 'Don't be cross. Mr Moorcroft has been very kind.' She forced herself to smile but she wanted to cry at the sight of his unshaven face and dishevelled appearance.

The turnkey folded his arms across his broad chest. 'Five minutes.'

Moorcroft put his hand in his pocket. 'Five minutes in private.' He pressed some coins into the turnkey's palm. 'And that will cover any necessities that my client needs, including food for the next few days.'

Judging by the man's face, Sarah could only guess

that Moorcroft had been extremely generous. She waited until the door closed on the warder. 'Mr Moorcroft is going to help you.' She attempted to hug him but Grey backed away.

'Don't get too near me. I'm not fit to be touched by anyone. I haven't had a wash since I was locked up and I'm running with fleas and lice.'

Moorcroft pulled up a chair. 'And you haven't had much to eat by the look of you, Tobias. Sit down and listen to me. We've only got a very short time together.'

'I don't know how Sarah found you, Moorcroft. But I'm very grateful for what you just did. I'll repay you somehow.'

Moorcroft acknowledged this with a curt nod. 'Take a seat, Sarah. You speak first but be brief.'

'Trigg has bought the house and he's evicting us all tomorrow,' she said with a break in her voice. 'We've nowhere to go, and I could only think of your room in Wych Street.'

'I only rented it by the month, and that's up tomorrow or the next day, but my things are still there.' Grey turned to Moorcroft with a glimmer of hope in his eyes. 'I still own Boxer and the cart. I was going to send word to you with instructions to sell everything so that I could get out of here, although it grieves me to pay that bastard Trigg twice.'

'You're my client now, Tobias. May I give you some advice?'

'Anything would be more than welcome.'

'My brother drew up Elsie's will. I haven't read the document but I think George assumes that the estate will now pass to him, but that isn't necessarily the case.'

'Elsie had nothing other than the cottage on the marshes, and that burned to the ground,' Sarah said with a sigh. 'She had nothing to leave.'

Moorcroft shook his head. 'That's not quite true. My brother and I have handled the family's legal affairs for many years and I know that they owned an estate close to the village of Blackwood. Elsie spent some time there as a child.'

'As did I,' Grey said with a hint of a smile. 'It's many years since I was there but I remember it as being a lovely old house, filled with secret places and enormous grounds. I always assumed it would go to my uncle.'

'Precisely so,' Moorcroft said, nodding. 'But according to my brother that is not the case. It was left to your late mother, Charlotte, and her younger sister Elsie. I imagine that is why Miss Fitch chose to live in the wilds of Essex.'

'She never spoke about her family,' Sarah said doubtfully. 'And she never said anything about owning a big house.'

'When Charlotte inherited her portion of the estate it automatically became the property of her husband, Henry Grey, but on their demise the entire estate reverted to Elsie. I know that for certain because I handled Henry Grey's affairs. It was well known that he did not get on with his brother-in-law, George Fitch, and he made certain that George did not inherit.'

Grey stared at him in astonishment. 'Why would

she live in a wooden cottage when she owned the old house? It doesn't make sense.'

Moorcroft's lips twitched. 'Knowing Elsie as I did, I'd say it was her last rebellion against her family and the society that shunned her all those years ago.'

'I'm sorry,' Sarah said, frowning. 'But I don't see how this helps Grey.'

'Tobias was the only relative who stood by her and it's just possible that Elsie might have left Blackwood to him.'

'We weren't that close, Martin,' Grey said wearily. 'Even if it were true I need money now, and I can't afford to pay for your services – or your brother's, for that matter.'

'We'll worry about that later.' Moorcroft took a gold half-hunter from his waistcoat pocket. 'We have little time left, but if you want me to act on your behalf then I'd be happy to do so. I will be handing George's affairs over to my brother because I don't feel that I can represent him any longer. I have yet to apprise him of my intention, but that's another matter.'

'Do anything you can to get me out of this place.' Grey tugged ineffectually at his bonds. 'And please do something for Sarah.' His lips twisted into a wry smile. 'As you can see, my hands are tied.'

She laid her hand on his shoulder. 'Don't worry about me.'

'But I do, kid. I can't help feeling responsible for you.' He sent a pleading look to Moorcroft. 'Find her somewhere safe to live. Trigg is a dangerous man and he's got his eye on her. He'll stop at nothing.'

'I'll be all right, and we'll get you out of here,' Sarah said with an attempt at a smile. 'I promise.'

'I can hear footsteps. I think our time is up.' Moorcroft placed his arm around her shoulders. 'I'll take care of everything, Tobias. I did nothing to help Elsie when she was alive and this will be my way of making amends. It's the least I can do.'

The turnkey appeared in the doorway. 'Time's up. Back to the ward, mister.'

Grey's brave attempt at a smile made Sarah want to cry, but she made a conscious attempt to look cheerful as he was led away. She did not speak until they were safely outside the gates. 'How will we help him, Mr Moorcroft? He shouldn't have to pay more money to Trigg. It's just not fair.'

'Indeed it's not, but that would be for a court to decide. The most pressing matter at the moment is to get Tobias out of jail. I'll speak to Mr Fitch again, although I don't hold out much hope, and I'll have a word with my brother. The Court of Probate Act of 1857 decreed that all wills must be sent for probate, thus avoiding long and costly disputes in Chancery. I think it quite possible that Tobias is her principal beneficiary and that in itself will help him out of his present difficulties, but what are we to do for you?'

'I could return to Blackwood, sir. I have good friends there who would take me in, but I can't abandon Mrs Arbuthnot. The poor lady has suffered terribly on my account. Her husband might be alive today if it weren't for me.' She gulped and swallowed, giving way to the tears that she had been desperately trying to hold back.

Moorcroft took a spotless white handkerchief from his pocket. 'Take this and dry your eyes, my dear. Don't give way to despair just yet. I must return to my office, but you'll be hearing from me either this evening or first thing in the morning. I'll send you back to Wellclose Square in a cab.'

'I think I should go to Wych Street first, sir. I must get Grey's things and make sure that Boxer is being cared for properly. He'll need his horse and cart when he comes out of prison.'

Moorcroft raised his hand to hail a cab. 'That can wait until tomorrow. Leave matters with me today and go back to your friends before they start worrying about you.' He waited until the hansom drew to a halt. 'Take this young lady to Wellclose Square, please, cabby.' He pressed some coins into the man's outstretched hand. 'See her safely to the house.'

'You took your time,' Nettie said, wiping her sticky fingers on her apron. 'I just finished the last scrap of cake, but there weren't much left anyway. You'd think the mourners hadn't eaten nothing for weeks. They fell on the grub like bleeding gannets.'

Sarah gazed at the empty plates on the dining table and her stomach rumbled. 'It's all right. I'm not hungry.' She moved aside as Dorcas bustled past her carrying a pile of crockery.

'Where've you been, young Sarah? It wasn't very respectful of you to waltz off like that so soon after the poor master was laid to rest.'

226

'I'm sorry, Dorcas. I was hoping to find us somewhere to go tomorrow.'

'Well you needn't have bothered. We're not leaving here. We're going to lock the doors and Franz has promised to bring some of the sugar bakers to stand outside and fend off Trigg and his bullies. Let's see who comes out on top then.' Dorcas marched out of the room with the light of battle in her eyes.

'She's not right in the head,' Nettie said as the door closed. 'Trigg will send the bailiffs in and then the missis will lose everything. It'll finish her off, mark my words.'

Sarah slumped down on one of the mahogany dining chairs. 'I tried my best, really I did. I went to see Mr Fitch and he all but threw me out of the house, and then his solicitor, a nice man called Moorcroft, took me to see Grey in prison.'

'He never did?' Nettie's green eyes widened in astonishment. 'So that's where you've been all day?'

'Yes. But we didn't get very far. I saw Grey and he looked awful. I don't think he'd eaten for days and he certainly hadn't washed, and him so particular about his personal cleanliness.'

'We've got more to worry about than whether or not your bloke's had a wash,' Nettie said, wiping her fingers on a napkin. 'Anyway, I've done me bit for the mistress and now I've got to get back to the theatre. We've got a show tonight.'

Sarah thought quickly. 'I'll come with you.'

'You'd be safer staying here where the others can keep an eye on you.'

'I don't care what Mr Moorcroft said. I'm going to make sure that Boxer is being looked after and then I'll go to the lodgings and pack up Grey's things.'

'You really are sweet on that chap, aren't you?'

'Don't be daft, Nettie. He's like a brother to me. I told you that.'

'I can't stand around arguing, but you'd better let Mrs Burgess know where you're going this time. She was worried sick when you took off like that.'

'All right, I will. Wait for me, Nettie. I won't be long.' Sarah hurried off to tell Cook and found her sitting by the range with her cap askew and her cheeks suspiciously red. She greeted her with a tipsy smile. 'So there you are, love. We was wondering where you'd got to.'

Betty looked up from the stone sink. 'Have you come to help us, Sarah? Me hands is red raw from washing all those dishes.'

Dorcas stopped piling dirty plates onto the wooden draining board, turning to Sarah with an angry scowl. 'You should be doing this, my girl. You need to pay for your bed and board.'

'I'm sorry, Dorcas. But I've been trying to find us somewhere to go when Trigg evicts us tomorrow.'

'He won't,' Dorcas said flatly. 'We're going to lock ourselves in. Franz will save us.'

'He won't be able to stop the bailiffs from coming in. Whether we like it or not, Trigg's the legal owner and he's got rights.'

Cook hiccuped loudly. 'Pour me another sherry wine, Dorcas. I need something to keep me spirits up.'

Dorcas snatched the bottle from the table and put it on the mantelshelf out of Cook's reach. 'You've imbibed enough today, Mrs Burgess. You should have a nap and sleep it off.'

'I never had no sherry wine,' Betty moaned, splashing greasy water onto the floor.

'You're daft enough when you're sober,' Dorcas said acidly. 'Lord help us if you was swipey. Get on with the washing up, or you'll feel the back of my hand.'

Sarah made a hasty exit.

Nettie was staring into the mirror adjusting her colourful bonnet decorated with ostrich feathers. She gave Sarah a sheepish grin. 'Sorry, but I can't stand mourning garb. It don't do nothing for me.'

'You wore it to the funeral and that's what matters.' Sarah opened the front door half expecting to see Trigg standing on the step, but there was only a pigeon strutting about pecking up crumbs left by the mourners. 'Come on, Nettie. Stop titivating or we'll never get there.'

Nettie flounced out of the house. 'We'll have to walk to Cable Street to catch an omnibus. A cab ride would be nice but I ain't got the necessary, have you?'

Sarah shook her head. She had just enough money to pay her bus fare, and that would leave her with tuppence for a baked potato and a cup of tea which would be her supper. 'At least it's stopped raining,' she said, glancing up at the streaks of blue sky in between the pot-bellied clouds. 'I don't think I could stand being soaked twice in a day.'

Nettie started off along the street swinging her

reticule and tossing her head so that the plumes on her bonnet waved like pennants in the breeze. 'You should try for a job in the theatre. You could sell programmes or show people to their seats. I'm sure I could persuade the manager to take you on. He's a personal friend of mine.' She waltzed off with Sarah hurrying to keep pace.

They parted outside the theatre and Sarah went straight to the mews where Boxer was housed in a dilapidated stable along with several other work horses. It was obvious that some of the owners shared the accommodation, as there were piles of grubby blankets in the stalls and oddments of tattered clothing. Meals must have been eaten and discarded as there were rat droppings everywhere, and the smell of horse dung laced with ammonia caught the back of her throat, making her retch.

Boxer whinnied in greeting and rubbed his head against her shoulder, pushing her against the wall as if pleading with her to take him from such a dreadful place. His water bucket was empty and there was no hay in the manger. Sarah was horrified and she knew that Grey would be furious if he found out that the stableman had neglected his duties despite payment in advance.

There was no one about to help her but on further exploration she found bales of hay and straw in the loft, which must have been intended as feed and bedding for the animals. It was obvious from the state of the stables below that the stall had not been mucked out for days and the horses had remained unfed. Perhaps the stableman intended to make a profit by selling the bales, or maybe the owners had not paid for the upkeep of their beasts. Whatever the reason she was disgusted to find Boxer existing in such dire conditions.

She heaved a couple of bales down the rickety wooden steps and, looping her skirts above her ankles, she began mucking out the stall. By the time she had finished she was hot, tired and hungry but at least Boxer was well cared for. She gave generous amounts of hay to the other hungry animals before leaving. 'I'll be back first thing in the morning,' she whispered, giving Boxer a final pat. His lustrous brown eyes gleamed as though he had understood and he pawed the ground, whickering softly.

It was growing dark by the time she reached Wych Street, having stopped to purchase a baked potato and a cup of tea from a street vendor before making her way to the lodging house. She did not relish the thought of a night alone in the cold, dark room, but she was too exhausted to contemplate walking to Wellclose Square, even though the thought of a warm bed and a hot meal was tempting. She had blisters on her heels that had burst and were throbbing painfully and her whole body ached. She let herself into the building and crept along the passageway to the room at the back of the house, but as she drew closer she saw a thin shred of light beneath the closed door. She could hear movement inside the room. For a moment she thought that Grey had been released from prison and had returned, but even as she placed her hand on the doorknob she felt the hairs standing up on the back of her neck. She hesitated, cocking her head on one side at the sound of heavy footsteps as if someone was walking towards the door. She turned and ran.

That night she slept on the straw beside Boxer, and despite the drunken snores of the stableman and the vagrants who crept in from the cold she did not wake up until dawn. She slipped the horse collar over Boxer's head and led him out into the yard, taking care not to disturb the other occupants. She had a quick wash in ice-cold water at the pump before tackling the difficult task of harnessing Boxer to the cart. She had never tried this on her own, but Boxer was a patient animal and eventually, after several failed attempts, she succeeded in putting him between the shafts.

The streets were coming alive as people went about their daily business and the road was crowded with horse-drawn vehicles, market stalls and pedestrians taking their lives in their hands by scurrying from one side to the other. She was shouted at by costermongers, cabbies and carters as she drove through the city, but somehow she managed to arrive in Wellclose Square without mishap, although she had learned a few new swear words on the way. Her legs were shaking as she climbed down from the driver's seat but she stopped to pat Boxer and praise him for his efforts. He nuzzled her hand and she rewarded him with a nosebag filled with hay. 'Good boy,' she said, giving him a final pat. 'You've done well.'

She glanced up and down the street to make sure

that neither Trigg nor his ruffians were loitering nearby, and seeing no one more suspicious than a nanny pushing a perambulator into the gardens, she was about to go down the area steps when the front door opened and Moorcroft appeared on the top step. 'Where have you been, Sarah?' he asked anxiously. 'Dorcas tells me that you didn't return last night.'

She was suddenly conscious of her dishevelled appearance. Her mourning gown was creased and stained where the rainwater had left pale streaks in the black dye. She had put on her bonnet without the benefit of a mirror and her hair hung loose about her shoulders. She knew she must look a sight and she felt the blood rush to her cheeks. 'There was someone in Grey's room, and I was afraid it might be Trigg, so I slept in the stables with Boxer.'

'I warned you against such an action, Sarah.' His stern gaze softened. 'Come inside, my dear. You look exhausted.' He turned to Dorcas, who was standing in the hallway regarding Sarah with her lips folded into a thin line of disapproval. 'Perhaps we could have some tea and toast in the parlour, please, Dorcas. I want to speak to Sarah.'

'Certainly, sir.' She stared pointedly at Sarah's crumpled clothing. 'You'd best go upstairs and tidy yourself before the mistress sees you. We may be locked in the house but there's no need to let our standards drop.'

Sarah glanced anxiously at Moorcroft but he nodded his approval. 'I'll wait for you in the parlour, my dear.'

'Don't loiter,' Dorcas muttered, taking Sarah by the shoulders and propelling her towards the staircase.

Sarah changed into the black linsey-woolsey skirt and white cambric blouse that had once belonged to Dorcas but were now too small for her, although she insisted that they had shrunk in the wash. She brushed her hair and secured it in a coil at the nape of her neck. The garments were shabby but at least they were clean and did not smell of the stables and she did not have the time to worry about her looks. Satisfied that she could do no more, she ran downstairs, slowing her pace as she reached the parlour where she found Moorcroft sitting by the fire.

He looked up and smiled. 'Come and sit down, Sarah.'

She settled in the chair on the opposite side of the hearth. 'I know you told me to leave it until today, but I went to fetch the horse and cart, sir. The servants think they can stay here no matter what, but I thought if we go now we could take some of Mrs Arbuthnot's things.'

'I agree, Sarah. Trigg might have purchased the property but that doesn't entitle him to the contents, which presumably belong to Mrs Arbuthnot.'

'I think so, sir.'

'I wanted to speak to the good lady, but Dorcas tells me that she is indisposed and it's not surprising, given the circumstances.'

'She is very upset, sir.'

'Understandably so.'

'You have something to tell me, Mr Moorcroft. Is it good news? Have you raised the money to get Grey out of prison?'

'Don't worry about that, Sarah. It's all in hand.' He leaned towards her, lowering his voice. 'This is a delicate matter and one that I must stress must be kept strictly between us. I don't want Mrs Arbuthnot to be bothered with the knowledge I am going to impart to you.'

'I can keep a secret, sir.'

'What I am about to tell you is strictly against my principles as a lawyer, but I want to help you and the good lady who has been so cruelly cheated of her home.'

Sensing that they were not alone, Sarah turned her head and saw Mrs Arbuthnot standing in the doorway. 'Who are you, sir? And what is it that you are afraid to say to my face?'

Moorcroft rose to his feet. 'I beg your pardon, madam. I was informed that you were indisposed and unable to see me.'

'I am quite well, thank you,' Mrs Arbuthnot said coldly. 'And I want to know what is going on. Why are you all whispering behind my back? I'm not a child.'

'It's my doing, ma'am.' Sarah leapt to her feet. 'Mr Moorcroft is a solicitor. We met by chance yesterday and he has been trying to help us.'

'I am still the mistress in this house, Sarah. I decide who should handle my affairs, and I don't think I should trust a man who admits to putting aside his principles.'

Moorcroft bowed his head. 'I apologise for any offence my actions may have caused, but I hate injustice

235

and it's obvious that you have been badly done by. If you will just hear me out maybe I can convince you that I am sincere in my wish to help.'

With obvious reluctance, Sophia Arbuthnot took a seat. 'I'm listening.'

Moorcroft was about to speak when Dorcas burst into the room. 'You got to come right away, madam. They're hammering on the door like they mean to break it down. I dunno what to do.'

Chapter Fourteen

Dorcas put her lips to the keyhole. 'Go away, you brutes. Leave us alone.'

'Open up or we'll call the police. This property belongs to Mr Thaddeus Trigg.'

Sarah covered her mouth with her hand to stifle a hysterical giggle. 'Thaddeus,' she whispered.

Dorcas nudged her in the ribs. 'Shut up. It's not funny.'

Mrs Arbuthnot had come up behind them. She tapped Dorcas on the shoulder. 'Out of the way, Dorcas. I'll deal with this.'

'Don't open the door, ma'am,' Dorcas said urgently. 'They'll attack us poor defenceless females.'

'Nonsense,' Mrs Arbuthnot said, pushing her aside. 'I want to see the title deeds in Trigg's name before I let him take my home. That's right, isn't it, Mr Moorcroft?'

'I would certainly say so, ma'am. But these men are not used to dealing with ladies like you. Would you allow me to speak to them?'

The hammering on the door increased and she backed away. 'Perhaps it might help. But I won't leave until it's absolutely necessary. I refuse to be bullied, Mr Moorcroft.'

'You are very brave, ma'am.' He turned to Dorcas. 'Keep the door closed. I'll go out though the tradesmen's entrance. They won't be expecting that.'

'I'll show you the way, sir.' Dorcas fled in the direction of the back stairs and Moorcroft followed at a slower pace.

Sarah gazed anxiously at Mrs Arbuthnot. 'Come and sit down, ma'am. Leave it to Mr Moorcroft. I'm sure he'll make them see sense.'

'Thank you, my dear. I will sit down. It's been a very trying time, but I won't give in to grief or hysteria. My dear husband protected me from everything during his lifetime but I am stronger than he gave me credit for.'

'I'm sure you are, ma'am.' Sarah led her unprotesting to the parlour and seated her by the fire. 'Would you like a cup of tea?'

'Thank you. That would be nice.' Mrs Arbuthnot sat back in the chair and closed her eyes. 'I dare not imagine what will happen to us all if we have to leave this house.'

Sarah hesitated in the doorway. 'Have you any relatives you could depend upon, ma'am?'

'No one, Sarah. All dead and gone, every last one of them.'

'You have me, ma'am. You took me in when I was a nipper and I'll stand by you.'

'You are a good girl and you deserve a better life than one of servitude.'

'I'll fetch the tea. You rest there and let Mr Moorcroft sort things out. He's a good man.' Sarah closed the door softly behind her as she left the room. The hammering

238

had ceased and the house was suddenly and eerily silent. She made her way down the back stairs to the kitchen.

Cook was standing by the area door brandishing a copper-bottomed saucepan and Dorcas stood behind her with a rolling pin in her hand. Betty was curled up on the floor with a blanket over her head but no one seemed to notice. Sarah went over to her and lifted her to her feet. 'It's all right, Betty. No one is going to harm you.'

'Bad men, miss. There are bad men out there and they hurt girls. They do nasty things to them and beat them if they cry. I knows it for certain.'

'Mr Moorcroft will send them away. He's a lawyer and he won't let them do anything to hurt you.'

'If you say so, miss.'

'Good girl. Sit quietly in the corner and I'll give you a piece of cake.'

'Don't pander to her,' Dorcas said crossly. 'She'll do anything for something sweet. She's not such a fool as she makes out.'

Betty began to sniffle and Cook stepped outside into the area, banging the saucepan with a wooden spoon. 'I'll soon sort 'em out.'

'No!' Sarah and Dorcas cried in unison as they dragged her into the relative safety of the kitchen and slammed the door.

'Leave it to Mr Moorcroft,' Sarah said breathlessly. 'He's got the law on his side and he knows what to say.' She cocked her head on one side. 'It's gone quiet out there.'

Moments later they saw Moorcroft descending the area steps. Sarah ran to open the door. 'Have they gone, sir?'

He entered the kitchen, pausing to wipe beads of sweat from his brow. 'I managed to convince them that we needed to see proof of ownership. It buys us a little time, that's all.'

Cook uttered a low moan. 'Where will I find another position at my age? I'll end up in the workhouse with the idiot girl.'

Taking her by the shoulders Dorcas gave her a sharp shake. 'Stop that, or you'll start Betty off again. None of us are going to come out of this smelling of roses. I should have married Wally and not set me cap at the sugar baker. I'll end up an old maid, doomed to spend the rest of me life in service.'

'None of this is her fault, Dorcas.' Sarah slipped between them and helped Cook to her chair by the range. 'Let Mr Moorcroft have his say. He's trying to help.'

'I'll do my best,' Moorcroft said warily. 'But please don't give way to despair yet, ladies. I'm going to speak to Mrs Arbuthnot and see what we can do.' He beckoned to Sarah. 'Come with me, my dear. And bring the sal volatile if you have any to hand.'

Dorcas reached up to take a small brown bottle from the dresser. 'A whiff of this would bring anyone round unless they was dead.' She plucked her shawl from a peg near the door. 'I'm going to get help.'

Moorcroft frowned. 'The police won't be able to interfere in a civil case unless there is violence.'

She wrapped the shawl around her head. 'Who said anything about the cops? Franz and his mates will see off Trigg's bullies.' She was out of the door and tearing up the area steps before anyone could stop her.

'I was hoping to settle this without resorting to violence,' Moorcroft said with a sigh. 'Let's hope that firebrand doesn't start a riot.'

Upstairs in the parlour Moorcroft stood with his back to the fire, gazing anxiously at Mrs Arbuthnot. 'I've bought us some time, ma'am. But your maid has gone to fetch help, and I'm afraid that this could turn nasty.'

She raised her eyes to his face and her bottom lip quivered. 'Do you think that Trigg was telling the truth?'

'Is it true that your husband remortgaged the property, Mrs Arbuthnot?'

She looked away. 'Yes, I'm afraid he did. James was desperate to raise the funds in order to rebuild the sugar mill but it all went wrong. The money was lost and my poor husband was so ill that I hadn't the heart to tell him.'

'You've known about this for some time?'

'Yes,' she said in a low voice. 'I tried to make ends meet by taking in commercial travellers and then I had to sell or pawn anything that was of value. I kept up the payments for as long as I could, but there were doctors' bills and so many expenses. I'm not a business woman, Mr Moorcroft.' Her voice broke on a sob. 'But I did my best.'

Sarah laid her hand on her shoulder. 'You've been very brave, ma'am.'

'Quite heroic,' Moorcroft said, clearing his throat. 'But now I know more of your circumstances I think we should face the inevitable.'

'You mean that I'll lose my home.' Mrs Arbuthnot's face crumpled and tears rolled unchecked down her cheeks.

'I'll do anything I can to help, ma'am. Please don't cry.' Sarah looked around the room, realising for the first time that the shelves were bare of ornaments. The ormolu clock that had once graced the mantelshelf with a garniture of two matching candelabra had also disappeared, and there were faded patches on the walls where oil paintings of rural scenes had once hung. She sent a pleading glance to Moorcroft. 'What can we do?'

'The first thing must be to find alternative accommodation,' he said slowly. 'And it would be wise to remove as many of your possessions as possible, Mrs Arbuthnot. I'm afraid that the arrival of the bailiffs is a definite possibility if you still owe money.'

'I don't know if Cook has paid the tradesmen,' she said, holding her hanky to her streaming eyes. 'I'm not very good at handling money or keeping the household accounts. I've been leaving it to her.'

Moorcroft drew Sarah aside. 'I think you ought to start packing Mrs Arbuthnot's personal effects and anything of value that you can find. She may have to leave in rather a hurry.'

Sarah nodded wordlessly. She knew that it made sense to be prepared to evacuate the house but she did not know where to begin. Leaving Moorcroft to comfort Mrs Arbuthnot, she went downstairs hoping that Dorcas might have returned, but she found Cook collapsed in her chair with the sherry bottle held to her lips. Betty eyed her warily as she cowered in the corner, stuffing the remains of the cake into her mouth.

Sarah could see that neither of them was going to be much help and she was about to go upstairs and begin packing when she saw Dorcas and Franz coming down the steps. She ran to open the door. 'Well?'

Flushed and breathless Dorcas smiled triumphantly. 'Franz is going to help. Tell her what you told me, Franz.'

He entered the kitchen, dragging off his cap. 'There's an empty house in Elbow Lane. I know it because I walk that way when I call for Miss Parfitt at the school. One of the sugar bakers bought the place for his aged parents, but they died last year and he wants to sell it.'

'Hold on, Franz,' Dorcas said angrily. 'You never said nothing about buying the house. The mistress is all but bankrupt.'

'I've been saving my earnings for some time and I intend to purchase the property, but I don't want to live there until I have a wife to make a home for me.'

Dorcas blushed rosily. 'Oh, Franz. Have you anyone in mind?'

'That's for me to know. I won't speak up until I'm ready and in the meantime I would gladly let Mrs Arbuthnot live there until she finds somewhere better.

243

It is in a poor state and I would not charge rent. An empty house is not good.'

Dorcas's mouth turned down at the corners and her eyes narrowed. 'You're not thinking of proposing to the schoolteacher, are you? She thinks she's a cut above you, Franz Beckman.'

'Again, that is for me to know.' He turned to Sarah. 'Will you take me to the mistress? I would like to speak to her personally.'

'I'm the head parlourmaid,' Dorcas said, pushing Sarah out of the way. 'She's not even employed here, and all our troubles are due to her in the first place. If Mr Arbuthnot hadn't taken her and that flighty carrot-headed girl from the workhouse, none of this would have happened. I would have been a married woman and Cook wouldn't have a tendency to take nips of the cooking sherry when things go wrong.' Dorcas sent a warning look to Sarah as if daring her to argue, and tossing her head she flounced up the stairs. 'Come on, Franz. Don't stand there gawping like a fish on a slab. The bailiffs could turn up at any moment.'

He paused at the foot of the stairs, glancing over his shoulder with a hint of a grin. 'And she wonders why she is still unmarried.'

The decision was made and Sarah suspected that it was Moorcroft who had persuaded Mrs Arbuthnot that there was no alternative but to leave as quickly as possible. Cook was sobered up with cups of strong coffee. She was still slightly groggy and unsteady on her feet but she rallied sufficiently to help Betty pack up the kitchen utensils and the crockery, together with any foodstuffs they found in the larder. Franz had sent for some of his fellow workers, who carried everything to the waiting cart. Dorcas and Sarah concentrated on the rest of the house and the first load was sent off to Elbow Lane with Franz on the driver's seat and his mate Heinrich at his side.

Pale-faced but seemingly resigned Mrs Arbuthnot went to her room to sort out what she intended to take to her new home, leaving Sarah and Dorcas to accomplish the rest of the packing. They decided between them that the large furniture would have to be left behind but they would need beds, bedding and anything else that they could pile onto the cart.

It was mid-afternoon and Franz, accompanied by Dorcas and Betty, had just driven off with the fourth and last load when Trigg arrived with the bailiffs and a mob of tough-looking individuals. They seemed mildly disappointed to discover that there were only women and a middle-aged solicitor in the house, and that the occupants were not going to put up a fight.

Moorcroft examined the documents and acknowledged their validity. With her head held high Sophia Arbuthnot walked out of her home and Moorcroft handed the keys to Trigg. Sarah was glad to see that some of the men had the grace to look shame-faced as the dignified widow walked past them. The bailiffs moved on and even Trigg seemed to be more subdued than normal, but that did not prevent him from seizing

Sarah by the arm and pressing his face close to hers. 'You'll keep, girlie. But don't think I've done with you.'

Moorcroft stepped in between them. 'I hope you're not threatening my client, sir.'

Trigg backed away. 'Of course I ain't, guv. Just passing the time of day with a sweet young thing what used to be my ward all those years ago.'

Sarah was tempted to ignore him, but concern for Grey overrode commonsense. 'Isn't it enough for you that you've robbed an innocent woman of her home, Mr Trigg? Why don't you act like a gentleman and drop the charges against Tobias Grey? He's done nothing to you.'

'He crossed me, girl. I never forgets and I never forgives. I ain't finished with him by a long chalk.'

'Come away, Sarah,' Moorcroft said, tucking her hand in the crook of his arm. 'Don't waste words on a man of his ilk.'

'Look down on me, would you, squire?' Trigg took a menacing step towards him. 'We'll see who comes out on top, and it won't be you, lawyer.'

The house in Elbow Lane was squashed between two warehouses like the jam in a sandwich. Sarah accompanied Franz with the last load of possessions from Wellclose Square, while Mrs Arbuthnot and Moorcroft followed in a hansom cab and Cook together with her precious copper pots and pans travelled in a growler.

Sarah climbed down from the cart, peering up at a tiny patch of blue just visible above the rooftops. The dark canyons between the manufactories and industrial buildings seemed to linger in a state of perpetual twilight. The ground shook beneath her feet as carts and drays thundered past laden with barrels, sacks and crates. The docks were just a street away and the shouts of stevedores, warehousemen and porters competed with the sound of the flapping of sails and the creak of wooden masts as sailing ships prepared to enter the docks. Unfamiliar odours emanated from the buildings; tobacco, molasses and roasting coffee beans struggled to overpower the stench of the Shadwell Basin and the festering mud on the foreshore. She felt as though she had entered another world, far different from the peace and quiet of the salt marshes as they slumbered beneath acres of open sky.

'Here,' Franz said, leaping off the driver's seat. 'Take the lightest things into the house. I'll bring the rest.'

She smiled. 'You're a gent, Franz.'

'I'm used to heavy work.' He stroked Boxer's muzzle. 'You're due for a rest, I think.'

Sarah heaved two baskets of food from the back of the cart. 'Are there any stables round here? Boxer belongs to my friend, and this conveyance is his livelihood.'

'There's the yard at the refinery. The cart will be safe there and there are several horses in the stables. One more won't make much difference.'

'Thank you, Franz. I don't know what we'd have done without you today.'

'Miss Pearl would want me to help you. I do it for her.'

She nodded. Everyone loved Pearl and she could

understand why Franz was smitten, but she could not help wondering if Miss Parfitt felt the same or what went on beneath her calm exterior. As far as Sarah could tell her wonderful Miss Perfect went through life like a silver swan gliding over a glassy lake, serene and unruffled by the world around her. How wonderful, Sarah thought, to be untouched by the turbulent emotions experienced by ordinary mortals.

The front door was open and she stepped into the narrow entrance hall, almost tripping over a box of books that someone had left in the middle of the floor. 'Dorcas,' she called. 'Where are you?'

A door to her right opened and Dorcas stuck her head out. 'I'm trying to light the fire and the bloody thing keeps going out. Come and give me a hand.'

Sarah put the baskets on top of the box and took off her bonnet and shawl. 'What can I do?'

Dorcas thrust a pair of bellows into her hands. 'Get the damn thing going. We've tried to make the place as homely as possible for the mistress. Miss Parfitt says that first impressions are the most important and we all know what a terrible wrench it must be for madam to leave the house she went to as a young bride.'

Sarah took the bellows and went down on her knees in front of the grate. She worked them vigorously. 'It's not too bad,' she said, trying to ignore the peeling wallpaper, chipped paintwork and patches of damp creeping up the walls.

Dorcas grabbed a broom and began sweeping the floor. 'Looks like they kept pigs in the kitchen,' she muttered. 'And why there's sawdust on the floor in the front parlour beats me.' She swept the dust into the hall. 'Lay the rugs down when you've seen to the fire,' she said over her shoulder. 'At least the poor lady will have somewhere decent to sit this evening. Miss Parfitt's seeing to her bedroom with the help of that Heinrich fellow. I can hardly understand a word he says but he's willing enough if you can make him understand what you want.'

Sarah concentrated on the task in hand and after a few minutes the flames took hold, producing a welcome blaze. She would have liked to sit there and enjoy the warmth, but there was still work to do and she rose to her feet. Having laid the rugs on the floor and set the furniture straight she took a moment to look round to see if there were any finishing touches that would make Mrs Arbuthnot feel more at home. The small house in a poor area was undoubtedly a come-down from Wellclose Square, but it was better than living on the streets and quite palatial compared to Miss Fitch's humble abode on the marshes. Satisfied that she could do no more, Sarah went to retrieve the baskets from the hall.

Dorcas swept the last of the dust into the street. 'No one will notice a bit more rubbish on top of what's already there,' she said with a grim smile. 'Come with me, and I'll show you the rest of the ground floor.' She bustled on ahead. 'That will have to do as the dining room,' she said, thrusting a door open so that Sarah could peer inside a small, dark room that smelled of damp and dry rot. Dorcas closed the door with a sigh. 'God alone knows what Mrs Burgess will say when she sees her kitchen, and Betty will have to sleep in the washhouse or the outside privy, but don't say nothing to her about it. I've set her to cleaning the range and she's not happy.' She led the way to the room in question where they found Betty sobbing quietly as she attempted to scrape the rust off the range. It was quite obvious that no one had cleaned it for a very long time, let alone applied a coat of blacklead.

Sarah rolled up her sleeves. 'I'll give you a hand, Betty. We'll need to get a fire going as soon as possible or it'll be bread and cheese for supper.'

'There's a pie and eel shop round the corner in the High Street,' Dorcas said, licking her lips. 'I like a bit of eel pie and liquor with some mashed taters.'

'I doubt if Mrs Arbuthnot would agree.' Sarah dipped a scrubbing brush in a bucket of cold water. 'But I don't think we're going to get this thing working today. Did you pack the blacklead, Dorcas?'

'Of course I did, but don't ask me which box it's in.' Dorcas started to unpack the baskets. She held up a bottle of mushroom ketchup. 'I don't think Cook will need this for a few days.' She opened a cupboard and began emptying the contents of the basket onto the shelves. 'You should have seen the state the larder was in when I arrived. I wouldn't have believed it if I hadn't seen it with me own eyes. There was cockroaches the size of mice. I'm not joking, Sarah. I never seen the like. And mouse droppings – the floor was thick with them. Mrs Burgess would've had a fit if she'd seen it. If I could get my hands on that man Trigg, I'd wring his fat neck.' She stopped talking and cocked her head on one side. 'I think they've arrived. Now we're for it. Cook will have hysterics. Hide the cooking sherry.' She rushed from the room.

Sarah smiled to herself as she heard Dorcas welcoming Mrs Arbuthnot to her new home as if it were a palace and not a shabby three-storey dwelling that had probably been on the site since the time of Good Queen Bess. Moments later Cook sidled into the kitchen, clutching her hanky to her nose and mouth. 'Is this where I'm supposed to work?' she demanded with a cry of anguish. 'It's little bigger than a scullery.'

Betty clambered to her feet. 'Can we go home now, Cook? Me hands is red raw from scrubbing this old monster.'

'Be quiet, you silly girl,' Cook said, sinking down onto a chair. 'How am I supposed to make meals on that ancient range? I doubt if it's had a fire in it this century.'

'It's not so bad, Cook,' Sarah said hastily. 'We've got the worst of the rust off it and when it's been black-leaded it'll come up a treat, although it might need the chimney sweep before we can light the fire.'

Cook buried her face in her hands. 'I can't even boil a kettle. What have we come to?'

Dorcas rushed into the room. 'Stop that, Cook. They can hear you in the front parlour and Mr Moorcroft says we mustn't upset the mistress. She's the one who's come down in the world. I daresay that you and I have seen worse than this in our time.'

'I have,' Betty volunteered. 'I remember when . . .'

'Shut up,' Dorcas said angrily. 'We don't care what

251

you can or can't recall, my girl. Go outside to the pump and fill the kettle with water. We can heat it on a trivet by the fire in the front room. At least we can make a pot of tea and there's one of Cook's ginger cakes in the tin, if Betty hasn't been there before us.'

'I'm afraid to go out the back,' Betty said, clutching the kettle in her hands. 'There's rats like bulldogs out there and cats like tigers.'

'Nonsense.' Sarah guided her towards the back door. 'We'll go together and you'll see that the rats are no bigger than the ones in Wellclose Square.'

Outside there were two small brick buildings. One, Sarah discovered, was a tiny washhouse and the other housed a privy, which consisted of a bucket placed beneath a wooden seat. The yard was enclosed by a high brick wall with a gate leading into a service alley for the dustman and the night soil collector. There did not seem to be a pump but Sarah found one hidden beneath a stack of wooden floorboards that someone had been chopping up for firewood. She worked the handle and after a few spurts of rust and slime the water flowed freely. 'There, Betty. Look at that. Nice clean water.'

'Probably comes from the docks,' Betty muttered as she filled the kettle.

Sarah thought she was probably right but she did not want to discourage her. If Betty got an idea stuck in her head it was almost impossible to make her see sense, and if she told Mrs Burgess that their water was tainted it would be the final straw. She guided Betty back to the kitchen and Dorcas snatched the kettle from her. 'You took your time. I'll see to the tea. Betty, you must finish cleaning the range and Sarah you can go and help Miss Parfitt make up the beds.' She hurried from the room, bristling with efficiency.

'You'd think she was the mistress of the house,' Cook grumbled, shaking her head. 'This is a bad day. A very bad day indeed.'

Sarah patted her on the shoulder. 'At least we've got a roof over our heads, no thanks to that brute Trigg. Is it all right if I go and help Miss Parfitt, or do you want me to carry on unpacking the kitchen things?'

'You're a good girl, Sarah. There's no point getting the cooking utensils out when I've got nothing to cook on. You go upstairs and help Miss Parfitt. We'll all be glad to lay our heads on our pillows tonight.'

'Where will I sleep, Cook?' Betty asked nervously.

Cook gave her a withering look. 'Get on with your work, you silly girl.'

Sarah left them with Betty muttering beneath her breath and Cook searching the larder, presumably hoping to find the cooking sherry amongst the jars of ketchup, jam and pickles. She was about to mount the stairs when Moorcroft emerged from the front room. 'Sarah, wait a moment. Can I have a word?'

'Yes, sir. Of course.'

'I visited Spital Square first thing this morning to make enquiries about Elsie's will.'

'Did she leave everything to Grey? Will he be able to pay Trigg and get out of prison?'

'The document seems to have gone astray. Bertram's

clerk delivered it to Spital Square, as requested, but now it's missing.'

'Oh, no. That's awful.'

'I'm afraid there's worse to come. I don't like to speak ill of a man whom I've counted as a friend for many years, but George Fitch seems determined to ruin his nephew. He is now saying that Tobias took the will from his desk when you and he visited the house.'

'That's not true,' Sarah cried angrily. 'I was with him all the time and he didn't take anything.'

'George also said that certain valuable items had been stolen from him that day, and he's determined to press charges. Neither you nor I could state for certain that this is untrue, and if he carries out his threat I'm afraid Tobias could go to prison for a very long time.'

Chapter Fifteen

'Grey didn't take anything from the house. He never left my sight.'

'And would you be prepared to swear that in court?'

'Of course I would.'

'I believe that Tobias is innocent, and because of that I've taken an enormous risk.' Moorcroft closed the parlour door. 'I don't want anyone to hear this but you, Sarah.'

'I won't tell anyone, sir.'

'I've used my own money to pay the debt and have Tobias released, but if George Fitch does press charges I'm afraid he could find himself back in prison.'

Sarah stared at him in horror. 'This can't be happening. Why would Mr Fitch be so cruel to his own nephew?'

'Where money and property are concerned people become greedy and ruthless. I know George only too well.'

'Why are you doing all this, sir? It doesn't make sense for you to risk your reputation to save someone you barely know.'

'I was more than fond of Elsie.' His pale cheeks flooded with colour and he turned his head away. 'I told you that we were close for a while, but I did not tell you the whole truth. In fact, I was desperately in love with her, but I'm afraid I abandoned her in her hour of need.'

'You told me that she had been jilted by her lover.'

'That part was true. She was in love with someone else, but, as I said before, he was only interested in her money. When he discovered that she was with child and had been disowned by her family he left and was never seen again.'

'Poor Elsie. It's all so sad.'

'I begged her to marry me, but she refused. I should have pursued her and pleaded with her, but I was piqued to think that she had given her heart to someone else and I was ambitious. If I'm to be brutally honest I would have to say that I was embarrassed by her unconventional way of living, and I doubted whether she was a proper wife for an aspiring lawyer.'

'Were you the father of her child, Mr Moorcroft?'

'She denied it, and I'm ashamed to say that I was somewhat relieved. I'll never discover the truth now.'

'That's very sad, sir.'

'If I'd had a son or a daughter I might not have grown into such a selfish, self-centred old bachelor.'

'I don't think you're being fair to yourself.'

'Do you not?' He smiled. 'Anyway, to answer your question, I can see a lot of Elsie in Tobias and that's why I feel compelled to do everything in my power to help him. I know how easy it is for men to slip into a life of crime, especially when they become involved with ruthless villains like Trigg.'

Sarah thought for a moment, but she was still

puzzled. 'I can understand that, but you're risking everything. It doesn't seem fair.'

A slow smile eased the lines of worry from his brow. 'Elsie must have been very fond of you, Sarah. She was not the sort of person to bother with people she didn't like, but she took you in and raised you as if you were the child she had lost.'

Sarah recalled the backbreaking work she had been obliged to do, chopping wood for the fire and hefting buckets of water from the stream. She would not describe the living conditions in the cabin as being those provided by a kindly parent, unless sleeping on bare boards and surviving on vegetable soup was now considered to be the ideal method of child rearing. But Moorcroft obviously wanted to believe well of Elsie and she nodded her head. 'Elsie was good to me in her own way, sir. And Tobias saved my life.'

'It's obvious that he has a fondness for you, and I'm sure it's mutual.'

'I'd do anything for him, sir.'

'Anything? Even if it places you outside the law?'

'Yes, sir. Anything.'

'Then come with me now, Sarah. I'll explain everything on the way.'

'But what will I tell Mrs Arbuthnot?'

His frown deepened. 'The poor lady has been through so much recently. Let me talk to her and I'll do my utmost to explain matters and put her mind at ease. Do you trust me, Sarah?'

She nodded vigorously. 'Of course I do, sir.'

'Then get your bonnet and shawl and wait for me

outside in the street. I've sent the sugar baker to find me a cab.'

Minutes later they were on their way to Whitecross Street. 'I've told Mrs Arbuthnot all she needs to know.' Moorcroft examined his pocket watch with a satisfied nod. 'We'll be in good time, even allowing for the traffic.'

'What are we going to do, sir?'

'I've arranged to meet Tobias in a tavern close to the prison. My clerk, Joliffe, has been instructed to provide everything he needs.'

'I'm sorry, sir. I don't understand.'

'Tobias must leave the country. I don't know why George couldn't settle matters in a civilised manner, but he seems determined to ruin his nephew. Whatever lies behind the false accusations the only answer is for Tobias to live abroad until we can prove his innocence and that isn't going to be easy. I've told George that I can no longer represent him, and that hasn't gone down well.'

'How can I help?'

'The moment a warrant for Tobias's re-arrest is issued the police will be on the lookout for him. It won't be safe to book passage on any ship leaving London, but a fishing boat leaving an Essex harbour is unlikely to excite much attention. Do I make myself clear?'

Sarah nodded slowly. 'You want me to take him to . . .'

Moorcroft laid his finger on her lips. 'Don't mention names of places or people you might contact. I'm still a man of the law and the less I know the better. But I hear that Belgium is a nice place with friendly people, or even France.'

'I have no money, Mr Moorcroft. How will we pay our way?'

'Joliffe will take care of that, but I'm not suggesting that you should go abroad. Just ensure that the person we're talking about finds a safe passage out of the country, and then you'll be free to return to London, if you so wish.'

'I don't know what I'll do, sir. I have to earn my living and Mrs Arbuthnot can't afford to keep me or pay my wages. It's going to be very hard for her to manage on her own.'

'I might be able to help the good lady.'

'Would you, sir?'

'I admire the way she's coped with everything, and she has spirit. I'm a lonely old bachelor, Sarah. I would benefit enormously from some feminine company. It will be my pleasure to see that Mrs Arbuthnot wants for nothing.'

There was little left to say and Sarah was becoming increasingly nervous as the cab rattled over the cobblestones on its tortuous way to Whitecross Street. The cabby drew his horse to a halt outside the Green Man and Still public house, and having paid the fare Moorcroft ushered Sarah into the taproom. Through a haze of tobacco smoke she spotted Grey seated at a table in the company of a bald-headed man.

'There's Joliffe,' Moorcroft said, edging his way

towards them. He pulled up a chair and motioned Sarah to take a seat. 'Is it all arranged?'

Joliffe nodded vigorously. 'Yes, sir. We've discussed everything.'

Grey reached out to grasp Sarah's hand. 'If you don't want to be mixed up in this I'll quite understand.'

She squeezed his fingers, forcing her lips into a smile. 'I'll do anything to help. It's just not fair that you're being treated like this.'

'You've handed over the monies, Joliffe?' Moorcroft said in a low voice.

'Yes, sir.'

'And you've arranged the necessary transport?'

'I have, sir. The person is known to me and will take them to their destination, no questions asked. Discretion guaranteed.'

'You've done well,' Grey murmured. 'Thank you.'

'My pleasure, sir.' Joliffe rose to his feet. 'The carriage is waiting in Fore Street, close to Three Dagger Court. I suggest that you make haste as my contact informs me that the former client has already taken the matter further.'

Moorcroft frowned. 'As I feared. Then there's no time to lose. You'd best be on your way.'

'I agree.' Grey leapt to his feet. 'Are you sure about this, Sarah?'

'Of course,' she said firmly. 'Let's go.'

'Joliffe and I will leave first,' Moorcroft said, glancing over his shoulder. 'Good luck and rest assured that I'll do my best to sort matters out while you're away.'

'I'm more than grateful.' Grey shook his hand.

Moorcroft turned to Sarah. 'When you return to London go straight to Elbow Lane. I will contact you there but don't on any account come to my chambers.'

'No, sir. I'll do as you say. But could I ask you a favour?'

'Of course, but be quick. You really should be on your way.'

'Would you be kind enough to send a message to Nettie Bean at the Olympic Theatre, letting her know that I'm all right and I'll be in touch as soon as I'm able.'

He nodded. 'I'll see that it's done.'

She watched him walk away with a sinking feeling in the pit of her stomach. Now they were well and truly on their own. She turned to Grey. 'What are we going to do?'

He slipped his arm around her waist. 'Just try to look natural. There's no need to be scared. I won't let any harm come to you, nipper. We're old mates, aren't we?'

His smile was infectious and she felt a surge of confidence. 'Very old mates. We'll be all right.'

The carriage was waiting as Joliffe had said at the entrance of the aptly named Three Daggers Court, which looked as disreputable as its name. Grey made himself known to the driver whose identity was carefully concealed by a muffler wrapped around the lower half of his face. 'Don't hang about, mate.' His fingers tightened on the handle of the horsewhip. 'We're too close to the clink for comfort and there's a police station round the corner in Moor Lane.'

'You've been given instructions as to the destination.'

With a grunt and a nod of assent, the driver flicked his whip and Grey practically threw Sarah into the carriage and leapt in after her. 'It seems as though we're doomed to flee London together, kid. Only this time you're saving me.'

'I can't believe that this is happening,' she said, clutching the seat as the carriage lurched into motion. 'Why would your cousin treat you so badly, Grey? What could he hope to gain by having you locked up?'

'He never liked me much, but I can only think it must have something to do with Elsie's will. She never told me what was in it and I didn't ask. I didn't think she had anything to leave apart from that leaky old hut, and why would she want me to have it anyway?'

'Perhaps she left your grandparents' house to you.'

'If she inherited Blackwood House, why on earth did she choose to stay in that hovel? It doesn't make sense.'

'Maybe not, but she loved the freedom of living on the marshes where she could do as she pleased. Some people said she was a witch, but she wasn't anything of the sort. She was a healer and her medicines really worked. I'd love to carry on her work, but I know it's impossible.'

'It wouldn't be easy, but I think you could do anything you put your mind to.' Grey settled back against the squabs, closing his eyes. 'I haven't had much sleep since I was shut up in that place. Listening to sixty men coughing and snoring doesn't make for a restful night.' Within minutes he was sound asleep, but it took Sarah a long time to relax. She gazed out of the window as the vehicle trundled through the city streets where poverty rubbed shoulders with wealth, and virtue struggled to overcome vice. Eventually, lulled by the rhythmic pounding of the horses' hooves and the drumming of cartwheels on cobblestones, she too fell asleep.

They arrived on the outskirts of Blackwood early next morning, having stopped to change horses at an inn halfway along the route. Sarah would have given anything to curl up in a warm bed, but she was only too well aware that time was not on their side. The police might be searching for Grey and they could not afford to take chances. She had slept fitfully after that, waking every time the carriage wheels hit a pothole, and then sinking into a world of vivid dreams that turned into nightmares. It was a relief to open her eyes when the vehicle finally drew to a halt.

Grey opened his eyes and stretched. 'Haven't slept like that for ages.'

'You're lucky,' Sarah said crossly. 'I'm black and blue from being tossed about in this contraption. Your cart was more comfortable.'

He was suddenly alert. 'What happened to Boxer? You didn't leave him in the stables, did you?'

'Of course not. He's being taken care of, but that's the least of your worries. Now we've got to hope that we catch Davey before he puts to sea.'

The driver wrenched the door open. 'Where to now, guv?'

'We can't just drive down the main street,' Sarah said hastily. 'It's a small village and anything out of the ordinary would set tongues wagging.'

'I know exactly where we are.' Grey stepped out of the carriage, looking round with a satisfied smile. 'I used to go fishing near here when I was a boy.'

'How does that help?' Sarah demanded. She was cold, stiff and hungry and not in the mood to listen to childhood reminiscences.

'We'll walk from here, Sarah. It isn't far.'

'You don't know where we're going,' she protested as he swung her to the ground.

'That's where you're wrong. I know just the place.' He turned to the driver, who was about to climb back onto the box. 'What do I owe you?'

'I was paid in advance and very handsomely too. You must have a price on your head, mate. Good luck is all I can say.' He tipped his cap and drove off, leaving them in the country lane with no habitation in sight.

'It's about a mile to the village,' Sarah said, sighing. 'He could have taken us a bit further. I want to catch Davey before he sets sail for the fishing grounds.'

'It's a chance we'll have to take.' Grey took her

by the hand. 'We might have to wait days for a safe passage, but at least we'll have a roof over our heads.'

There seemed little point in arguing, but she had been pinning her hopes on seeing Davey and the children and now she would have to wait a little longer. 'You need to get away quickly. I'm not sure I trust the man who brought us here to keep his mouth shut, especially if your uncle offers a reward.'

Grey's eyes danced with amusement. 'I don't think I'm worth anything to George. He just wants me out of the way.'

'I don't know why you're laughing. It's not funny.'

'You'll feel better when you've had something to eat,' he said cheerfully. 'There's a farm nearby.'

'I know that. I went there once with Elsie when she took medicine for the farmer's wife.'

'Then I'm sure they'll be pleased to see you.'

She held out her hand. 'I haven't any money.'

'I'll come in with you.'

'Are you mad? These people know me but if they see me with a stranger it will be all round the village before you can blink.'

'Be careful then.' He took a leather pouch from his pocket and gave it to her. 'Don't tell them anything.'

'Wait here. I'll be as quick as I can.' She opened the gate and started off along the track that led to the farmhouse. As she drew nearer she saw the farmer's young daughter feeding the hens. Maud had been one of her pupils in the school and she felt a surge of pleasure at the sight of a familiar face. She waved her hand. 'Maud, it's me. Miss Scrase.'

The child stared at her for a moment and then she dropped the plate of scraps and fled. Sarah followed her to the farmhouse door. 'It's me, Maud. There's no need to be afraid.'

'It's a ghost, Ma,' Maud cried, running to bury her head in her mother's skirts. 'Miss has come back from the dead.'

Sarah hesitated in the doorway. In the old days she would have received a warm greeting but the farmer's wife picked the child up and backed away. 'It's all right, Mrs Bonney. I'm no ghost. It's me, Sarah Scrase. I used to teach Maud in school.'

'But you was burned to death in the fire along with the witch.'

'Miss Elsie wasn't a witch. She gave you medicine when you fell ill and she cured one of your cows when it went dry.'

'So you ain't dead then?'

'No, ma'am. I'm very much alive, but I'm sorry to say that Miss Elsie died of her injuries.'

Mrs Bonney crossed herself. 'I don't know where heathens go when they pass on, but God rest her soul, anyway.' She gave her daughter a gentle push. 'Stop being silly, Maud. Go and finish feeding the hens.'

'She looks like a ghost,' Maud said as she sidled past Sarah and ran out into the yard.

'I must look a sight,' Sarah said, her hand flying to her hair, which hung loose around her shoulders. 'I've had a long journey, and I wondered if I could buy some eggs and perhaps you could spare a loaf of bread. Miss Elsie always said you were the best cook in Blackwood.'

Mrs Bonney puffed out her chest. 'I've heard it said often, Miss Scrase. Of course I can let you have anything you need.' She stared at Sarah's shabby clothes. 'You can pay, I suppose.'

Sarah took the purse from her pocket, giving it a shake. 'Yes, indeed.'

'Come into the house and I'll see what I can find.'

In the farmhouse kitchen Mrs Bonney took a loaf from the cooling rack and wrapped it in a piece of butter muslin. 'So where will you stay, miss? There's nothing left of Miss Elsie's place but a pile of ash and charred wood.'

'I'll find somewhere in the village. I doubt if I'll be staying very long, but I wanted to look up old friends.'

'Everyone thinks you died in the flames,' Mrs Bonney said, sorting eggs into a rush basket. 'Will you have some butter and a piece of cheese?'

'Yes, that would be nice, thank you.'

'The Hawkes children was very upset, and young Davey was beside himself by all accounts.'

'But I sent him a note, telling him that I'd gone to London.'

'I don't know nothing about that, miss. But you'd best be careful if you're intending to go into the village. Some folks might drop down dead with fright if they think you've come back to haunt the place.'

Sarah paid for the produce but her thoughts were elsewhere as she left the farm and hurried off to find

Grey. She could only imagine how Davey must be feeling if he had not received her brief letter explaining her sudden departure. It had never occurred to her that people would assume that both she and Elsie had been consumed by the flames. She was out of breath and angry when she rejoined Grey.

'What's the matter?' he demanded, frowning. 'Have you been crying?'

'You didn't send it, did you?'

He stared at her open-mouthed. 'What are you talking about?'

'Young Maud thought I was a ghost. Everyone in Blackwood assumes that Elsie and I were killed in the fire. I gave you a note to send to Davey.' His guilty expression confirmed her suspicions. 'Tobias Grey. How could you?'

He took the basket from her. 'I gave it to a boy and tipped him a penny to deliver the note. I can't help it if he didn't carry out my instructions.' He walked on. 'It's too late to do anything about it now.'

She ran after him. 'But they all think I'm dead. How am I to contact Davey if I can't be seen without causing a stir?'

'We'll think of something. The most important thing now is to get off the road before someone sees us.' He hurried onwards and she had to run to keep up with him.

'I wish you'd tell me where we're going.'

'Have you ever been to Blackwood House?'

'Of course not,' she said breathlessly. 'But I know

where it is. Everyone in the village knows about the haunted yew tree tunnel that surrounds the house.'

'That's the story that was put about to keep people away.' He stopped outside a pair of rusty wrought-iron gates. 'It obviously worked.' He tugged at a bell pull. 'Let's see if Parker is still here.'

'Who is he?'

'He used to be the gatekeeper. He got me out of scrapes no end of times when I was a boy, but he must be getting on a bit now. I don't even know if he was kept on after my grandparents passed away.'

'Your family owns all this?'

'Grandfather chose to leave Spitalfields and live in the country. My mother, George and Elsie grew up here and I visited quite often when I was a child. Elsie was a lot younger than my mother. She was only eleven when I was born and she used to boss me around, but I didn't mind too much because she taught me to fish and to climb trees and she had a tame fox that she had reared from a cub. Then she went away and I didn't see her again until I was a grown man. I heard the whispers about her in the servants' hall, but I never took much notice of them.' His voice broke and he turned away, wiping his sleeve across his eyes. 'She didn't deserve to die like that.'

'I'm sure her spirit is still here,' Sarah murmured, peering through the gates at the avenue of overgrown trees, some of which had fallen across the drive and been left to rot. 'What's that?' She pointed at a tangle of dark green foliage above which she could just make out the upper storey of a building cloaked in ivy.

'The yew tree tunnel,' Grey said with a wry twist of his lips. 'It's supposed to be over seven hundred years old, planted when the house was built by a Knight Templar returning from the Holy Land, although I think that's just a story.' He rattled the gates and flakes of rust showered down on them. He tugged at the padlock and chain. 'It doesn't look as though Parker survived,' he said, bending down to pick up a large piece of stone. The lock succumbed to one sharp tap and the gates screamed on their hinges as he pushed them open. 'Welcome to Blackwood House.' He closed the gates behind them and replaced the chain so that it appeared intact. 'Come along, Sarah. We can stay here for a day or two. I can assure you that no one will bother us.'

They made their way along the leaf-strewn carriage sweep, dodging fallen tree trunks and kicking aside broken branches. As Sarah had seen from the road, the yew tree tunnel began at the end of the drive and twisted in a serpentine fashion around the side of the house. The gnarled old trees were in desperate need of pruning, and it would have taken a brave person to negotiate the narrow gap beneath their intertwined branches unless armed with shears and a hacksaw. Even so, the sight of it sent a shiver down her spine and she was relieved when Grey took the gravel path that led to the back of the house.

They came to a paved area pockmarked with weeds, and beyond a stone balustrade was a wilderness of tall grasses. 'That was once a croquet lawn,' Grey said, following her line of vision. 'And what looks like a jungle was the shrubbery where I used to hide from Elsie.'

'I wish I'd known her then,' Sarah said, staring at the tangled mass of vegetation with a practised eye. The stone urns that once must have been filled with flowering plants were now strangled with bindweed, but she could see many of the plants and herbs that Elsie had used in her potions. She recognised cleavers, a common enough weed that rampaged unchecked and was the basis of many of Elsie's favoured remedies for everything from eczema to insomnia. 'It's a shame she's not here now. She would have loved all this.'

'You're the only person, apart from her, who would look at all this and see something other than gross negligence.'

Sarah rested the basket on top of the balustrade. 'She taught me well.'

'And if I fell ill I'm sure I'd be grateful for a garden filled with weeds, and a budding apothecary to cure me.' Grey glanced up at the louring clouds. 'It looks like rain. We'd best find a way in.' He tried the door, and to Sarah's amazement it opened. He stepped inside. 'Come on. I promise you that the ghosts are friendly.'

The sky had darkened suddenly and large spots of rain splattered onto the paving stones. Sarah snatched up the basket and hurried after him. The moment she entered the room she felt the hairs standing up on the back of her neck. The air was thick with mustiness and the smell of decay. The furniture was shrouded in dust sheets and silence hung in a pall over the sleeping

271

house. If there were ghosts, she thought nervously, they were in hiding, but she felt a tangible presence and it had nothing to do with the fact that she was standing close to Grey. The scent of the outdoors clung to him, but there was the pervading odour of an unwashed human body in the room.

She felt Grey stiffen and she felt instinctively for his hand. She wanted to run but she found that she could not move and then, without warning, a figure sprang from the gloom, yelling like a banshee and brandishing an axe.

Chapter Sixteen

Grey stood his ground. 'Parker, is that you?'

The axe fell to the floor and the sound reverberated round the room, bouncing off the walls and causing flakes of plaster to rain down from the ceiling. 'Who is it?'

Grey took a step forward. 'It's Toby Grey, Parker. You remember me.'

'Master Toby? You was just a boy when I last saw you.'

'You're right. I haven't been near the place for ten years or more, but now I've come home.' Grey moved swiftly to shake Parker's hand. 'I didn't know you were still here, but it's good to see you.'

'I thought you was a robber, sir,' Parker said apologetically.

'Is there any chance of something to drink? The young lady and myself have been travelling since yesterday.'

'That's not Miss Elsie.'

Sarah stepped forward. 'My name is Sarah and I was Miss Elsie's ward.'

He stared at her as if attempting to assimilate this information. 'I haven't seen her for a long time. She used to bring me vittles, but she stopped coming a while ago. You aren't going to turn me out, are you? She told me that everything would be all right.'

'And so it will,' Grey said, picking up the axe and placing it out of Parker's reach. 'I can see that you've done a good job in looking after the house, but it's a big place for you to manage on your own.'

'I done me best, sir.' Parker made a move towards the door. 'I'll light a fire in the morning room if you'd like to take the young lady there, and I'll bring you some tea.'

'Better still,' Grey said gently, 'we'll have tea in the kitchen.' He followed Parker, pausing in the doorway to beckon to Sarah.

She hurried to his side. 'The old man's mind is wandering,' she whispered. 'You'll have to tell him about Elsie.'

'Not yet. It might be too much for him to take in. I don't know if it's simply his imagination playing tricks or whether Elsie did keep him supplied with his day to day needs. Did she ever mention the house or her visits to see Parker?'

She shook her head. 'No, she didn't. Neither did you, for that matter. All these years I've thought that you were poor and that's why you fell in with Trigg.'

'It's quite true that I was desperate for money. My father was a gambler and he left nothing but debts.'

'And you naturally turned to a life of crime.'

He ushered her into the kitchen. 'It didn't happen like that. I tried to earn an honest living, but then I began to take risks and you know the rest.'

'There's just enough tea to make a brew,' Parker said

triumphantly. 'But as to food, I'm afraid there's only nettle soup. I've been living off that for days while I waited for Miss Elsie to come with provisions.'

Sarah placed the rush basket on the table. 'You'll eat well tonight, Mr Parker.'

'You mean that Miss Elsie hasn't forgotten me?'

Sarah was about to tell him the truth but Grey was frowning at her and shaking his head. 'Yes, that's right. You could say that this comes from Miss Elsie.' She glanced around the large empty kitchen which once would have bustled with activity. She had no idea how many servants would have been employed in a house of these proportions, but she could see from the size of the range and the battery of copper pots and pans that there must have been a significant number of women cooking, cleaning and attending to all the needs of the wealthy Fitch family. Mrs Burgess would think herself queen of all she surveyed if she had a kitchen such as this and a full complement of staff to organise.

'It was quite splendid in its time,' Grey said, apparently reading her thoughts. 'But its glory days are long past.'

'You never said a truer word, Master Toby.' Parker had been riddling the embers in the range to little effect and he rested the poker with an exasperated sigh. 'It's difficult keeping the fire going with only green wood for fuel. I remember when we had coal aplenty and the log store filled to capacity.' His hands began to shake and he dropped the poker.

Grey hurried to his side. 'I'll do that, Parker.' He helped him to a chair. 'Sit down, old chap. You'll feel better when you've got some food inside you. I'll see what I can do with the fire and then we can have that cup of tea.'

'And all I need is a knife and some plates.' Sarah emptied the contents of the basket onto the table. 'And then we'll eat.'

They left Parker dozing by the fire, replete after a meal of tea, bread and cheese. Grey led the way through a maze of narrow corridors until they came to the entrance hall. A heavily carved oak staircase led to the first floor and beneath a layer of dust the floorboards glowed with the patina of many years of dedicated polishing by housemaids long departed. As in the drawing room the furniture was shrouded in holland covers, giving the old house the appearance of being inhabited by ghostly spectres. Dust motes filled the air, dancing and glinting in the feeble rays of sunshine that penetrated the grimy windowpanes.

'Why did you bring me here, Grey?' Sarah demanded anxiously. 'Hiding away isn't going to solve anything.'

'I know, but it can only be temporary. If I know George he'll have the police looking for me at this very moment, and eventually they'll come here.'

'Then I must go into the village right away. I have to see Davey and put things right and then he'll help me get you on a boat bound for the Continent.'

'Wait until dark. I'll go with you as far as the church.'

Illuminated by moonlight, the church was silhouetted darkly against the night sky. Grey had insisted on accompanying Sarah but she stopped by the lychgate. 'Wait here for me.'

'If you're not back within the hour I'll come looking for you,' he said in a low voice.

'Just keep out of sight,' she whispered. 'I'll be as quick as I can, but please don't follow me. I know almost everyone in the village and I'll be quite safe.'

'All right, but be careful.'

'Don't worry about me.' She walked away, wrapping her shawl around her head so that she merged into the shadows. Her pulse began to race as she hurried along the main street. The school and the blacksmith's forge were shuttered and silent and the warm glow of firelight and tallow lamps shone from uncurtained windows, but for some inexplicable reason she felt like a stranger as she made her way to the cottage. She was suddenly nervous as she raised her hand to knock on the door, but then she remembered that it was never locked, and taking a deep breath she lifted the latch and stepped inside.

The sight that met her eyes brought a lump to her throat. Mary, Lemuel and Jonah were seated round the table with their heads bent over a book, but at the sound of the door opening Mary looked up. Her face paled and she leapt to her feet uttering a shriek of fright. Jonah pointed a shaking finger at Sarah. 'Ghost,' he cried, reaching out to hold his sister's hand. 'Don't let her get me, Mary.'

Lemuel jumped up and advanced on Sarah with his small hands fisted. 'Get out of here, evil spirit.'

Sarah stood her ground. 'I'm not a ghost or an evil spirit. It's me, Sarah. I've come home.'

Mary was the first to recover. She moved slowly towards her. 'B-but you died in the fire. Everyone said so. The vicar held a service of remembrance for you and Miss Elsie, even though we all knew she was a heathen.'

'I sent a note,' Sarah said, fighting back tears. 'I'm so sorry if you didn't receive it, but I was certain you knew that I was safe and well.'

Mary's pale face assumed a mask of indifference. 'We've been thinking you were dead and gone for nearly three weeks. Why did you go away? Why didn't you come here and let us all see that you was alive?'

'I still say she's a ghost,' Jonah said, hiding behind his sister. 'Pinch her, Lem. See if she's real.'

Lemuel darted forward and pinched Sarah's forearm, making her squeal. 'She's real,' he said, backing away.

Sarah rubbed the sore spot. 'I hope you're satisfied, boys. That hurt.'

'You should be ashamed of yourself,' Mary said angrily.

'Don't blame him.' Sarah smiled as she pulled her sleeve down to cover the red mark.

'I didn't mean Lemmy. It's you who are in the wrong.' Mary's pretty lips hardened into an unsympathetic line. 'You nearly broke our Davey's heart. He's been off his food ever since you got burned to a crisp in the fire, and won't hardly speak to no one. It's all your fault, Sarah Scrase.'

Sarah pulled up a stool and sat down. 'I couldn't help what happened, Mary. You must hear me out.'

'There's no excuse for running off like that,' she said, frowning.

'There might be if you'd just listen to what I have to say.' Sarah was angry now. She had slept little on the journey from London and she was exhausted as well as overwrought. 'Miss Elsie suffered terrible burns. She might have died in the fire if it hadn't been for a brave man who saved her from the burning building. We took her to a hospital in London, but it was too late and she died of her injuries.'

'She was a witch,' Jonah muttered beneath his breath but just loud enough for Sarah to hear.

'She was a healer and she took care of your father,' Sarah said firmly. 'You all know that, so don't talk nonsense, Jonah Hawkes.'

Jonah's face crumpled at her sharp tone and she was instantly ashamed of her quick temper. They were all too young to understand. 'Miss Elsie was a good woman,' she added in a gentler tone. 'But she was different from the rest of us, Jonah. That doesn't mean she was bad or that she was a witch. She used her knowledge to cure sick people.'

Jonah did not look convinced and he went to join his brother, who had retreated to the hearth and was squatting on the packed earth floor eyeing her suspiciously.

Mary's expression softened just a little. 'Well, I suppose that's right, but why did you stay away so long? How are you going to explain that to Davey?'

'Explain what to Davey?'

Sarah spun round to see Davey standing in the doorway. He stared at her in disbelief. 'Sarah?'

She held out her hands. 'It's me, Davey. I'm not a ghost. I was just trying to explain things to the children.'

He closed the door with such violence that the house shook. 'You let us think you died in the fire and then you turn up out of the blue.' He planted his feet apart, folding his arms across his broad chest. 'And we're supposed to pretend that it's all right. Is that it?'

'I sent you a note.'

'Well I never got no note. Everyone said that you'd perished in the flames and I had no reason to suppose different.'

'I'm so sorry.'

'You've had plenty of time to send word since then. Where've you been all this time?'

His frosty gaze sent shivers down her spine and she looked away. 'In London. We took Miss Elsie to hospital but they couldn't save her.'

'Who took you to London? Was it that villain who forced you to live with the mad woman?'

'Don't say things like that, Davey.' She met his hostile gaze with a frown. 'I won't let you speak to me like this. I thought you'd be pleased to see me and I'm sorry you thought I was dead, but I had to do everything I could for Elsie.' She made for the door but he barred her way.

'You put me through hell,' he growled, taking her

by the shoulders. 'What am I supposed to think? Did you run off with your fancy man?'

'Stop it, Davey.' Mary stamped her foot. 'Don't be mean to Sarah. Can't you see she's trying to explain what happened?'

'Be quiet, Mary. This is between Sarah and me.' Davey turned to his brothers, scowling. 'And you two should be in bed. Don't sit there gawping.'

Lemuel and Jonah scrambled to their feet and went to sit on the wooden bed at the back of the room, watching them wide-eyed.

'Leave them alone. It's me you're angry with, not them.' Sarah pulled free from his grasp. 'I'm sick of saying sorry, and Grey isn't my fancy man. He saved Elsie from the fire and his hands were too badly burned for him to drive, so I did. We took her to London but it was no use. She died in hospital.'

'Why didn't you come home then?'

She was quick to hear the note of uncertainty in his voice and she laid her hand on his arm. 'I wanted to, Davey. But things happened and it was complicated.' Her voice broke on a sob. 'I don't want to talk about it now. Perhaps I'd better go.' She made a move to walk past him but he reached out and caught her by the hand.

Mary hurried to her side. 'You must be hungry, Sarah. There's enough soup left in the pot for both of you.'

'Thank you, Mary, but I had supper at Blackwood House. That's where I'm staying until things are sorted.'

'Blackwood House?' Davey stared at her in amazement. 'That old place? It's been empty for years.'

'And it's haunted,' Lemuel said in a loud voice. 'No one goes there. The yew tree tunnel eats people.'

'And spits out their bones,' Jonah added gleefully. 'It's the truth.'

'Get into bed and stop being silly.' Mary snatched their nightshirts from the back of a chair. 'I don't want to hear another word from either of you.' She tossed the garments at them. 'Don't make me come over there, boys. I'm getting cross now.'

Davey drew Sarah aside, lowering his voice. 'There's something you're not telling me. What is it?'

'It's complicated. Grey's family own Blackwood House and his uncle has falsely accused him of theft. Now the police are after him, and he must leave the country as soon as possible, which means finding a ship that will take him to the Continent.'

'Which is why you've come to me, I suppose.' Davey's tone was not encouraging.

'You're the only chance he has of getting out of the country. He's innocent, Davey. I wouldn't ask you to do this for him if he was guilty.'

'Why should I? He's brought you nothing but trouble.'

She raised her hand and then let it fall to her side. 'I thought you were my friend.'

'And I thought we had an understanding, Sarah Scrase. I thought that one day I'd go down on bended knee and ask you to marry me, but it seems I've been a fool. First of all it was the schoolmaster who was ogling you like a lovesick old goat and then you go off with that criminal. I wouldn't lift a finger to save his neck.'

Sarah backed towards the door. 'You're a stupid, jealous fool, Davey Hawkes. I never made any promises to you.'

'And now you've found someone you like better. It wouldn't be because he might own the big house some day, unless his neck gets stretched by the hangman's noose? I thought better of you.'

'That's not true and it's not fair.' She wrenched the door open. 'I'll never ask you for anything again as long as I live.' She slammed out of the cottage with Mary's sobs ringing in her ears.

She was halfway down the main street when Davey caught up with her. 'Wait, please.'

She continued walking. 'Leave me alone.'

'No, please stop a moment.' He caught her by the hand and drew her to a halt. 'I'm sorry. Seeing you like that was a shock. I hardly knew what I was saying.'

'You made your feelings perfectly clear. I was stupid to think that you'd want to help.'

'I'm the one who was stupid. I can't begin to tell you how I've been feeling these past few weeks, but I had no call to speak to you like that.'

'I did send you a note, Davey. I would have come sooner if I hadn't got caught up in everything that was going on in London. But I really thought you knew I was safe.'

'I'll do anything you ask,' he said, lifting her hand to his cheek. 'Just tell me what needs to be done.'

'Grey has to leave the country. If you can't take him I thought you might know someone who can.' He hesitated and she thought that he was going to refuse. 'But if you don't want to get involved I can hardly blame you,' she added hastily. 'It's not your problem, Davey.'

'You're wrong,' he said slowly. 'If it makes you unhappy it becomes my problem. We've been through hard times before, Sarah. I know someone who might be willing to help, for a price.'

She thought quickly. There was still money left in the leather pouch, although she did not know how much. 'That shouldn't be a problem. What do I have to do?'

'Nothing. Give me a day or two and I'll let you know.'

She stood on tiptoe to kiss his cheek. 'Ta, Davey. I knew you wouldn't let me down. Now I must go. Grey's waiting for me in the churchyard.' She attempted to wrest her hand from his grasp but he tightened his hold.

'Are you sure there's nothing going on between you?'

'He's years older than me, Davey. I've never thought of him as anything other than a friend.'

Davey uttered a derisive snort. 'That wouldn't stop him fancying you. You're an innocent, Sarah.'

'I can look after myself and I trust Grey. He's been good to me and I don't want anything to happen to him. Promise me that you'll do everything you can to get him to safety.'

He raised her hand to his lips and brushed it with a kiss before letting her go. 'I promise. Now go and find him. I'll wait here until I see you safely on your way.'

'Thank you, Davey. I'll never forget this.' She turned and ran towards the churchyard, waving to Grey who was waiting in the shelter of the lychgate.

Time would have hung heavily while Sarah waited for news from Davey had it not been for exploring Blackwood House, and its overgrown grounds. When she saw the yew tree tunnel in daylight she could quite understand how the rumours concerning it had arisen. Neglected and left untrimmed the green boughs intertwined and twisted into strange shapes that had all but obliterated the passage between them. But when all was said and done they were just ancient trees that someone had planted many centuries ago in order to create a sheltered approach to the formal garden at the rear of the building. Perhaps the toxic berries that the trees produced had something to do with its macabre reputation, but whatever had started the rumour was patently absurd.

Sarah wandered on through the lost gardens of Blackwood House finding something new and interesting at every turn. Half-hidden pathways led to a tumbledown gazebo or a weed-choked lily pond, and at the bottom of what once must have been a croquet lawn she discovered a long-forgotten summerhouse. The windowpanes were cracked and the roof leaked, but the wooden table and chairs inside must once have been the setting for afternoon teas enjoyed by ladies and gentlemen of leisure.

She could only be glad that Parker had not chopped the furniture up for firewood, which seemed to be his main occupation. He roamed the grounds armed with an axe and hacked at fallen branches to fuel the kitchen range and set snares for rabbits, which ended up in the pot. Behind the red-brick walls of the kitchen garden Sarah discovered vegetable beds which he had done his best to tend, but they too were weed-strewn and the wildlife seemed to have benefited from their produce more than Parker himself.

A greenhouse occupied the length of one wall, and although it was dilapidated she found evidence of planting, which confirmed her suspicion that Elsie had been growing some of the rarer specimens for use in her herbal remedies. She could not wait to discuss her find with Grey, but when she returned to the house she found him in the drawing room covered from head to toe in soot.

'What are you doing?' she demanded, trying not to laugh.

He blinked and shook his head. 'I was trying to light the bloody fire, and there was a fall of soot.'

She struggled to keep a straight face. 'I can see that.'

He shook his head and black specks flew in all directions. 'We might be here for days and I can't spend another night sitting in the kitchen with Parker snoring his head off by the fire. I thought we'd be more comfortable in here.'

'I hope we won't be here that long. It's too dangerous.'

He plucked a dust sheet off one of the chairs and wiped his face. 'I want pleasant memories of the old house when I'm in exile.'

'Don't put it like that. It sounds so final.'

'I can't see myself being able to return in the near future. George wants me out of the way and he's not going to relent. He's not that type of man.'

'Elsie would turn in her grave if she knew how her brother was treating you.'

'Poor Elsie. I wish I could have done more for her. It was a miserable end for someone who spent a good part of her life healing others.'

'Maybe she left the house to you, Grey. If Mr Moorcroft finds her will, you might be the rightful owner.'

He shrugged his shoulders. 'That won't do me much good if I'm arrested the moment I put a foot on English soil.' He frowned. 'But if that should be the case, Sarah, I want you to live here and look after the old place until it's safe for me to return. I doubt if it will happen that way, but I'd be happier knowing that you had a roof over your head.'

'But I have no money, Grey. I'll have to find work somewhere and even if I could get a job as a schoolteacher I wouldn't be able to afford the upkeep of a house like this.'

'There should be an income from farms and cottages on the estate, but I suppose George has been keeping that for himself. He certainly hasn't spent it on the property.' Grey stared helplessly at the heap of soot on the hearth, topped with an empty bird's nest and a pile of dead leaves. 'What a mess.'

'I'll clean it up,' Sarah said firmly. 'Go and stick your head under the pump in the stable yard, and perhaps you can find a change of clothes in one of the bedchambers. The house seems to have been abandoned with everything just as it was when your grandparents passed away.'

'You might take your own advice,' Grey said, grinning. 'You look as though you've been dragged through a hedge backwards.'

She glanced ruefully at her mud-spattered skirt and the tear where it had snagged on a bramble. 'There's a huge clothes press in the room where I slept last night, but wouldn't it be stealing if I took something for myself?'

'You can't steal from dead people.' Grey made for the door. 'My mother was about your size and I daresay she might have left some garments here, although they'll be a bit old-fashioned and probably motheaten.'

This made Sarah laugh. 'Do you remember the clothes I wore when I was with Elsie? We had to take whatever cast-offs people swapped for her pills and potions. I'm not fussy.' She followed him out of the room and made her way upstairs, where she spent an hour sorting through the outdated but surprisingly wearable garments carelessly abandoned by people who did not know the meaning of poverty. In the end she selected a grey gown in a fine woollen material with a slightly yellowed lace collar and pagoda sleeves. No doubt Grey's fashion-conscious mother would have made the garment ever more up to the minute by adding separate undersleeves in lace or broderie anglaise, but she was unlikely to have done anything more arduous than ply her needle or entertain her friends with afternoon tea in the summerhouse.

That evening, over a supper of stew that Sarah had prepared using produce from the garden and Parker's contribution of a pair of rabbits, skinned and neatly butchered, she told Grey about her finds in the walled garden. 'Elsie cultivated herbs in the greenhouse and she visited regularly to bring food to Parker. I wonder why she never mentioned it?'

'I don't know. Perhaps it was her way of cocking a snook at the family who disowned her. We'll never know now.'

She pushed her plate away, resting her elbows on the table. 'If it had been my house I wouldn't have let it go to rack and ruin. I'd look after it and bring it back to life. I can't bear to see the grounds strangled by weeds, and the house longing for someone to take it in hand. A lot of hard work and a bit of polish would work wonders.'

Grey stared at her, eyebrows raised. 'I can't see it myself.'

'I feel as though I've lived here all my life. Isn't that strange?' She turned with a start at the sound of tapping on the drawing room window. 'There's someone out there, Grey.'

He leapt to his feet and crossed the floor to fling the casement open. 'Who's there?'

'It's me, Davey Hawkes. Let me in.'

'Go to the front entrance.' Grey closed the window

and made for the door. 'I'll let him in, Sarah. You stay here in the warm.'

She rose from the table and went to stand by the fireplace where a log fire burned brightly thanks to Grey's efforts that morning. She waited anxiously, hoping that Davey might have good news.

He followed Grey into the room and came to a halt, taking in his surroundings. 'Why do you need me when you own all this? I'd have thought a man of property could buy his way out of trouble.'

'It's not mine,' Grey said, taking the leather pouch from his pocket and laying it on the table. 'This is all the money I've got in the world. I don't know if it's enough to buy me a safe passage.'

'That depends.' Davey picked up the pouch and weighed it in his hand.

'Grey is a good friend,' Sarah said hastily. 'You'd do it for next to nothing, wouldn't you, Davey?'

He shook his head. 'My boat isn't sturdy enough for a Channel crossing, but I've got contacts. Free traders who'll do anything for the right amount of cash.'

'Do you mean smugglers?' She stared at him in horror. 'Surely you aren't mixed up with people like that?'

'How d'you think we survive when the fish don't run or the weather is too bad to put out to sea? We have to have an insurance against hard times, and much of it is stored in the crypt beneath the church.'

'Do you mean that the vicar knows what's going on?'

He threw back his head and laughed. 'Aye, and the

squire and the schoolmaster too. Don't tell me you didn't know what went on here.'

'Are you saying that my grandparents were aware of this free trading business?' Grey demanded, giving him a searching look. 'Have you any proof of that?'

'The secret passage from your cellars to the church wasn't put there for the glory of God.'

'Well I'm damned,' Grey said, chuckling. 'And the family accused me of being the black sheep. I wonder if my uncle George is party to the illicit trade.'

Sarah looked from one to the other in amazement. 'I don't know whether to laugh or cry. You're talking about respectable people acting like criminals, risking imprisonment or even the death penalty.'

Davey turned to her grinning. 'If all the folks who'd had dealing with the free traders were found out there wouldn't be enough jails to hold them.'

'I'm sure Elsie didn't take part in such goings on,' Sarah said emphatically. 'She wouldn't.'

'I don't know,' Grey said, frowning. 'All I can say is that the deals I did for her were all above board.'

'We're getting away from the point.' Davey stowed the purse in his pocket. 'I didn't come here tonight to talk about smuggling.'

'Then say what you've got to say and be done with it,' Grey said impatiently.

Sarah stared at him in dismay. 'Don't talk to Davey like that. He's trying to help.'

'I'm sorry, Hawkes. It's just that the longer I'm here the more dangerous it becomes, especially for Sarah.'

Davey's jaw hardened. 'You should have thought of that before you dragged her into this.'

'Stop it, the pair of you.' Sarah glared at each of them in turn. 'You're behaving like schoolboys.'

'I came to tell you that the weather's taken a turn for the worse, and it'll be a few days before you can get away.'

'What will we do in the meantime?' Sarah turned to Grey with an anxious frown. 'What if the police come here looking for you?'

'We'll have to deal with that if and when it happens.'

Davey made a move towards the door. 'It might be a good idea to find the secret passage. The coppers aren't going to look for you in the church.'

Sarah beamed at him. 'That's the best idea yet. Let's go right away.'

Chapter Seventeen

In the wavering lantern light, the cellars of Blackwood House were filled with eerie echoes and dark corners. The cloying smell of damp lingered in the stale air and it was several degrees cooler here than in the rest of the house. Sarah shivered and wrapped her shawl around her shoulders, keeping close to Davey as they followed Grey. He stopped in the middle of the second chamber, holding the lamp high above his head so that it cast its beam around the dank cavern. 'I can't see anything that resembles a doorway,' he said, peering into the gloom. 'Can you?'

Davey knelt down to examine an uneven flagstone. 'They must have dug the tunnel but it's well hidden.'

'Maybe they filled it in,' Sarah suggested. 'Perhaps your grandparents had a change of heart, Grey.'

'What's going on here?'

They spun round to see Parker standing behind them.

'We've been told there's a secret passage leading to the church,' Grey said calmly. 'Do you know anything about it?'

A sly expression crossed Parker's wizened features and he dropped his gaze. 'I don't know nothing.'

'And I don't believe you.' Grey faced him squarely. 'Come on, man. We're all on the same side.'

Parker shot him a sideways glance. 'How do I know you ain't working for the excise men, Master Toby? You ain't been what I'd call a regular visitor to Blackwood House.'

'That's true, but I'll be straight with you, old chap. I've suffered hard times since my parents died and I've been on the wrong side of the law many a time, but now the police are after me for a crime I didn't commit.'

'I'm glad to hear that you've turned over a new leaf, Master Toby. You and Miss Elsie were both wild 'uns when you was young, but there was no real badness in either of you.'

'Parker, that's neither here nor there. Do you know where the entrance of the passage is? It's a simple enough question.'

'Of course I do, Master Toby. I been along it enough times in days gone by.' Parker hobbled over to a rack of wine bins on the far wall. Sarah could not see quite how he accomplished it but the wooden shelves swung gently away to reveal a small door. Parker took a bunch of keys from his pocket and put one in the lock. It turned soundlessly and the door opened.

'Well, I'm damned. It was there all the time and we didn't spot it.' Grey strode across the floor and ducked through the narrow opening. Sarah made to follow him but Davey held her back.

'Perhaps you'd best wait here with Parker.'

She shook free from his restraining hand. 'You go ahead, but I'm right behind you. I'm not missing this for anything.'

He grinned, touching her cheek with the tips of his fingers. 'You're a plucky girl, Sarah.'

She gave him a push towards the doorway. 'So you've forgiven me for not dying?'

'Almost, but not quite. Don't ever do that to me again.' He took her by the hand and led her into the narrow passageway.

It seemed to go on for miles. The air was dank and water seeped through the brick walls, dripping onto the packed earth floor and turning it into mud. The light from Grey's lantern dipped and bobbed in the distance and Sarah had to quicken her pace to keep up with Davey's long strides. Her heart was racing and every nerve ending tingled with suppressed excitement. She was finding it increasingly hard to breathe as she struggled against the fear of being in such a confined space, but eventually they reached the far end and Grey opened the heavy oak door which led into the crypt. She gulped deep breaths of air that was somewhat fresher beneath the vaulted ceiling but tainted with the odour of must and disuse.

Grey stood in the middle of the stone chamber filled with kegs and wooden crates. 'So this is how my ancestors made their money,' he said, grinning. 'And I believed it came from silk weaving.' He bent down to examine a keg. 'This isn't communion wine.'

'It'll be brandy all the way from France.' Davey picked up a small crate. 'And this is probably silk.'

'Are you part of this, Davey?' Sarah stared at him in amazement.

'I don't go over to the Continent if that's what you

mean. I do a bit of ferrying and it helps to feed the little 'uns, but I've never been down here before.' He made his way to the door leading into the church. 'Bring the lantern over, there's a good fellow. I can't see a thing.' Grey moved to his side and held the lantern high while Davey tried the latch. The metal-studded door swung open on well-oiled hinges. 'It's obviously been used recently,' he said triumphantly.

'Davey, wait a minute.' Sarah barred his exit. 'Be careful. You've got the nippers to consider. Perhaps I could visit the cottage one evening after dark to make sure they're all right.'

He shook his head. 'You mustn't risk it, Sarah. If you were seen it would be all round the village in next to no time.'

'But I want to stay in Blackwood,' she said slowly. 'I've been giving it a lot of thought and there's nothing for me in London. I haven't had a good enough education to be a governess but Mr Wills might take me on again at the school.'

'We can talk about that when all this is settled.' Davey turned to Grey with an anxious frown. 'I'm counting on you to keep her out of harm's way.'

'I'll do my best,' Grey said, grinning. 'But Sarah's got a will of her own.'

'I know that very well.'

Sarah gave him a reluctant smile. 'You will be careful, won't you, Davey?'

'Of course I will.' Davey dropped a kiss on her forehead. 'I've got to go now, but I'll be back as soon as I get word from the ship's master.'

'I knew I could rely on you, Davey. Thank you for helping us.'

Grey shook him by the hand. 'I thank you too, Hawkes. I'm in your debt.'

'Just look after Sarah for me and I'll do what I can for you.' Davey gave Sarah a quick hug before sprinting up the steps.

'Take care of yourself,' she whispered as he disappeared into the dark maw of the eerily silent church.

Grey closed the door and they were alone. 'You're very fond of that fellow, aren't you, Sarah?'

'We grew up together. He's like a brother to me.'

'I don't think he sees it that way.'

'We took it for granted that we'd wed one day,' she said with a sigh. 'But that was before all this happened. I'm not sure that I'd be content to be a fisherman's wife, especially now I know that he has dealings with smugglers.'

His lips twisted into a wry smile. 'You mean free traders.'

'It doesn't matter what name you give them, they're outside the law and I want none of it.'

'My future seems to depend on men who operate on the wrong side of the law.' Grey felt along the wall for the entrance to the secret passage. 'Come on, Sarah. Let's go home.' He sprang the hidden lock and the door opened as if by magic and he led the way back along the narrow passageway. Sarah followed him with the word *home* ringing in her ears. She had never had a proper home since she left Vinegar Yard as a child. Elsie's cottage had been somewhere to shelter from the elements but she had not felt any affection for the place, nor had she any desire to return to the marshes. Blackwood House was completely different. Even in its uncared-for state it had opened its arms and enfolded her within its walls. She realised suddenly that it would be a wrench to leave, knowing that it would slip back into neglect and decay. She had attempted to clean the rooms that they had been using, although it would take an army of charwomen to do it justice, but she had seen the beauty that lay beneath the dust and grime. The house called out for her to rescue it and she had heard its cry. For the first time in her life she had felt that this was where she truly belonged.

She kept her eyes fixed on the light from Grey's lantern as she hurried after him. 'Don't go so fast.'

They reached the cellar to find Parker waiting for them. 'So now you know everything,' he said grimly. 'The trade goes on.'

Grey took him by the arm, propelling him up the stairs to the ground floor of the house. 'Is my uncle involved, Parker? I must know.'

'Leave me be, Master Toby. I'm an old man.'

'That's no excuse. Tell me what's been going on all these years while the house has been empty.'

'Very well, sir. But come to the kitchen where it's warm. I'm chilled to the bone.' Parker shuffled his way towards the back of the house. 'I need a drop of brandy.'

'Smuggled, no doubt.'

'We all have to live, Master Toby. What else was I to do but follow the master's instructions?'

Grey hurried after him. 'With my aunt's will missing

I don't see how George Fitch can claim to be the new master. There's something not quite right about all this.'

'I dunno about all that, Master Toby. I'm just repeating what I've been told.' Parker opened the kitchen door and a gust of cold air blustered through ill-fitting window frames, rattling doors and causing dust sheets to move as if lifted by unseen hands. 'I knew there was a storm coming. I could feel it in me bones.' He went to the larder and brought out a small keg, placing it on the table.

Sarah watched in silence as he filled three wine glasses with the amber liquid. The warmth of the kitchen wrapped her in a cocoon of comfort, but outside the wind was soughing and howling like a soul in distress. She understood now what Davey meant when he had said the weather would keep the boats on shore for the next few days. She accepted a glass of brandy and sipped the strong liquor, choking as its fumes caught the back of her throat.

Grey pulled up a chair and motioned her to sit down. He perched on the edge of the table. 'Now then, Parker. Tell me everything that's happened since my grandparents passed away.'

Parker swallowed a mouthful of the spirit. 'Mr George came down from London for the funeral and he says that the estate belongs to him now. He sacks all the staff, except me. I thought I was to go as well but he takes me aside. Parker, he says, I want you to be caretaker but I've no intention of living here myself.'

'That seems strange,' Sarah said slowly. 'Why would he keep on a residence if he had no intention of using it?'

Grey tossed back his drink. 'Isn't it obvious? My respectable, upstanding uncle intended to continue the family tradition of free trading. With the silk weaving industry ruined by cheap foreign imports he had found an easier and more profitable way of funding his lavish way of life.'

'And he obviously knew that Blackwood House was supposed to be haunted,' Sarah said, taking another tentative sip of brandy and finding it more pleasant this time. 'So the locals kept their distance.'

'And the secret passage enabled the goods to be transported without any questions being asked.' Grey turned to Parker. 'And what exactly was your part in all this?'

'I had to show the messengers where to collect the goods and they loaded their wagons in the dead of night, and that was the end of it as far as I was concerned.'

'They didn't give you any money?'

'None at all, Master Toby. As far as I can make out their dealings was with the agent in London.'

Grey refilled his glass. 'I don't know who that would be. I haven't had anything to do with the running of the house, and I don't think Elsie was involved in all this.'

The brandy was making Sarah feel pleasantly muzzy and the warmth from the log fire made her sleepy. She gathered her thoughts with difficulty. 'So when will they come for the next load, Parker? There were a lot of barrels, kegs and crates in the crypt.'

Grey's eyes widened. 'By God, you're right, Sarah. I was thinking along the lines of this trade being something that occurred in the past, but it's going on now, right under our noses.' He turned to Parker. 'When do you expect the men to call again?'

Parker held out his empty glass. 'Another tot would help me to remember, master.'

'Think, man. It's vital that I know. If George discovers that I'm here, all will be lost.'

Parker ran his hand through his thinning hair. 'Soon, master. I never know exactly when they're going to turn up, but it should be very soon.'

Despite the heat from the fire and the warmth of the spirit in her stomach, Sarah shivered. 'Let's hope the storm is over quickly, Grey. You must get away at the first opportunity.'

The wind raged all that night and rain lashed the windowpanes in Sarah's room, keeping her awake into the small hours before she fell into an exhausted sleep. She was awakened by an ear-splitting crash and she snapped into a sitting position. It was light outside but as she stared sleepily at the window she could see twigs and dead leaves pressed against the glass. She leapt out of bed and on closer inspection she saw that an oak tree had been uprooted by the gale and the lower part had crashed down onto the yew tunnel while the topmost branches had come to rest against the side wall of the house. She dressed hastily and hurried downstairs to the kitchen where she found Grey and Parker deep in conversation. They looked up as she entered the room.

'I saw that a tree had come down,' she said anxiously. 'Is there much damage?'

'That yew tree tunnel is cursed,' Parker said solemnly. 'The yew is the tree of death. Mark my words.'

'That's superstitious nonsense.' Grey slipped on his overcoat. 'I'm going outside to take a look. You'd best come with me, Parker.'

Sarah glanced out of the window at the storm-swept stable yard. Wooden pails had been tossed about like children's toys and part of the coach house roof had been ripped apart by the force of the wind. 'There won't be any ships setting sail today,' she murmured as Grey and Parker disappeared into the scullery. She was tempted to follow them outside and view the damage for herself, but she decided that it would be futile. There would be time to inspect the gardens and the grounds when the storm abated, and she busied herself preparing a simple breakfast of tea and toast, using up the stale bread. She would have to pay a visit to the farm to get fresh supplies of butter, milk and eggs but that too would have to wait until the weather improved.

Her hand shook as she filled the kettle and placed it on the hob. She was used to the wild weather that swept the east coast in winter, but this storm was different and she had a feeling of foreboding. Perhaps it was the revelations of last evening and the know-ledge that Blackwood House was immersed in the dark secrets of the smuggling rings. Or maybe her irritation of nerves was due to the danger that threatened Grey and her own uncertain future.

Grey and Parker returned within minutes; they were wet and bedraggled but convinced that the house had not suffered any structural damage. The yew tree tunnel, despite its dire reputation, had saved the bricks and mortar by taking the full force of the fallen tree. Sarah made tea and toasted the bread, which they ate with a scraping of butter, and afterwards she took a pile of dusters and a jar of beeswax furniture polish that she had found at the back of a cupboard and set about cleaning the drawing room. The physical labour took her mind off Grey's predicament and she comforted herself with the thought that the inclement weather might hamper the police in their search.

By mid-afternoon the weather was showing signs of improvement and Sarah put on her cape and bonnet, hooked a wicker basket over her arm and set off for the farm, refusing Grey's offer to accompany her. She knew that by venturing outside the gates she risked being seen, but they were in desperate need of supplies, and she trusted Mrs Bonney to be discreet. She had a few shillings in her purse that Grey had given her before he handed the rest of Elsie's money to Davey, and she would have to spend it wisely. Quite what she would do after Grey had left the country she did not know, but that would depend largely on whether she could find employment in the village. She could do nothing until Grey was safe from harm.

She received a friendly greeting this time at the farm, and was soon on her way home with a basketful of produce. A fitful sun peeped through threatening cumulus clouds as she made her way back to Blackwood House. She could smell the salt tang in the air and the countryside looked as if it had been scoured clean by the raging winds and rain. The last of the leaves had been stripped from the deciduous trees and their bare branches fanned out, filtering the sunlight like black lace. She quickened her pace as she walked along the wooded lane leading to the house, and as she approached the entrance to the carriage sweep she realised that the gates were wide open. They had been closed when she left and the feeling that something was desperately wrong made her break into a run.

There were ruts in the piles of dead leaves on the drive leading up to the house and hoof prints in the mud. A heavy horse had been driven at some speed and without any thought to the damage it might cause. The trail led round to the stable yard and as she turned the corner of the house she could see a large farm wagon with a shire horse harnessed between the shafts, feeding from its nosebag. She put her basket down and crept towards the scullery door, keeping close to the wall in the hope that she would remain unseen. She ducked behind a rain barrel as she saw a man emerge from the scullery staggering beneath the weight of a wooden keg, which he hefted into the waiting vehicle. He returned to the house cursing volubly and was met in the doorway by a second man carrying a wooden crate. 'Here, mate. Shove this in the cart, will you?'

'Do it yourself, you lazy bugger.'

They began to argue and Sarah thought a fight was about to break out when another man erupted from the scullery roaring expletives at the top of his voice. She froze, hardly daring to breathe.

Trigg seized the larger of the two men by the collar and gave him a hearty push that sent him stumbling against the door post. 'Shut your bloody trap, you fool. We're taking a chance doing this in broad daylight without you two letting the whole world know we're here.'

Muttering but obviously too scared of their boss to argue, the men hurried into the scullery, leaving Trigg on his own in the yard.

Sarah clamped her hand over her mouth, hardly daring to breathe. She was shocked to see him here in a place she had thought of as a safe haven, but it came as no surprise that he was involved with the smugglers. She willed him to go back inside the house but he was walking round the wagon and seemed to be checking the contents. She prayed silently that he would not look her way. The rain barrel afforded a minimum of concealment and if he moved a couple of inches to his left and turned his head, he would almost certainly see her. She stood poised for flight and then, as if sensing her presence, he looked round. Sick with fear she took a step backwards and knocked over a spade that had been propped up against the wall.

Trigg spotted her and his jaw dropped, his mouth a gaping black hole in his pale face. Sarah fled.

She raced round the side of the house but she was hampered by her long skirts and she could hear his heavy tread as he narrowed the gap between them. She hurled herself into the damp embrace of the yew tree tunnel. Even as she did so she realised that she had made an error of judgement. She had had a vague idea that he would not follow her and that she could hide in its dark green foliage, but she had forgotten that it was partially blocked. She ran, ducking her head beneath the low-hanging branches. Trigg was shouting at her, ordering her to stop, but she continued to run until she came to the fallen oak.

'I've got you now, you little whore.'

Trigg's triumphant cry made her even more desperate to escape. She could see daylight above her where the tree trunk had smashed through the tightly knit branches of the yew, and she realised that there was a gap beneath the branches just narrow enough for a small person to squeeze through. She threw herself to the ground, landing on a soft bed of dried leaves and seed cones, and she wriggled on her stomach, pushing her way through to the other side. She was about to scramble to her feet when her left ankle was grabbed in a vice-like grip.

'Got you, you bitch.' Trigg's voice was muffled but triumphant. He tugged mercilessly, but fear gave her strength and with a mighty kick she managed to free herself from his grasp. She heard him swearing as she headed for the end of the tunnel.

Pausing for a moment to catch her breath she could hear Trigg crashing about as he tried to fight his way through the knotted branches, and a sudden and terrifying thought occurred to her. Was it a coincidence that Trigg was involved with this end of the smuggling ring? And did Grey know more about it than he cared to admit? Suspicions clouded her mind. She could not believe that Grey would knowingly put her in danger, but he had worked for Trigg in the past and she was beginning to wonder if he had told her everything. She took several deep breaths, telling herself that she was being ridiculous. Grey had been her friend and saviour since she was a child. He hated Trigg and all he stood for. Grey had turned his back on a life of crime.

She held on to that thought as she made her way through the shrubbery to the back of the house. She entered through the half-glassed doors that led into the drawing room and tiptoed across the floor to open the door which led into the entrance hall. She could hear angry voices as Trigg's men clattered through the house. 'This is the last one, mate.'

'Aye, thank God. I'm ready for a drop of ale and a bite to eat. That's if the old bugger will give us leave to stop on the way back to London.' Their voices died away and Sarah knew it was only a matter of time before they found their boss struggling to free himself from the yew tree tunnel. She went straight to the kitchen where she found Grey and Parker slumped on the floor, bound and helpless.

'Sarah. Thank God you're safe.'

Grey's relief was patent and her suspicions were allayed in an instant. She rushed over to the table and seized a knife to cut his bonds. 'Trigg saw me,' she said breathlessly. 'He got stuck in the yew tree tunnel and I only just got away from him.'

He leapt to his feet, rubbing his chafed wrists. 'He caught us unawares. Parker was expecting the men to collect the goods.'

'I never seen the big fellow afore.' Parker glanced down at his bound wrists. 'I'd be grateful for the use of the knife, miss.'

Sarah gave Grey a searching look. 'So you didn't know that Trigg was involved with the smugglers?'

'No, of course I didn't. I've done some crooked deals but I'd never involve my family in them. It seems that my uncle George has no such scruples. He must have suspected that I might come here and he's sent Trigg to find me.'

'That explains a lot.' Sarah knelt down to release Parker. 'Are you all right?' she asked anxiously, noting his pallor and trembling hands.

'Aye, miss. It's nothing, but a drop of brandy would go down nicely.'

She helped him to stand and guided him to a chair. 'Just rest for a moment and I'll see what I can do.' She turned to Grey. 'What do we do about Trigg?'

He snatched the knife from her hand. 'Leave him to me.'

'What are you going to do?' she cried, catching him by the sleeve. 'He's bigger and stronger than you. He'll kill you.'

'He's hell bent on taking me back to London and handing me over to the police, but he's a wanted man too. I'm going to send him packing.' Grey shook her hand off and headed for the scullery. 'Stay inside, Sarah. I don't want you getting hurt.'

Chapter Eighteen

She raced after him. 'Stop. Please don't go out there. You're outnumbered and you'll come off worst.'

Deaf to her pleas Grey strode through the stable yard, where the men were preparing to drive off. One of them called out, warning Grey not to approach Trigg who was likely to tear him limb from limb, but Grey did not look back. He walked on purposefully, shouting Trigg's name and challenging him to take on someone his own size. Sarah ran after him but she could tell by the determined set of his shoulders and the stubborn line of his jaw that any attempt to intervene would be futile. She came to a halt as Trigg emerged from the poisonous embrace of the yew trees brandishing a pistol. He levelled it at Grey. 'I'm taking you back to London, cully. Your uncle George has offered a reward for your capture. It seems that you've been a bad boy, Toby.'

Grey's knuckles whitened as he tightened his grip on the knife. 'Think again, Trigg. You're not taking me anywhere.'

Trigg cocked the pistol. 'My friend here says different.'

Sarah held her breath. Trigg's attention was fixed on Grey but she sensed that one false move on her part might have fatal consequences.

The wagon approached slowly with one of the men handling the reins and the other at the horse's head with a steadying hand on its bridle. 'Shoot him and be done with it, guv.'

'Drive on,' Trigg snarled. 'Wait for me at the bottom of the drive.' He signalled to the man on foot. 'Grab him, Samson. He's worth more alive than dead.'

'No!' Sarah cried as Samson rushed at Grey. At the same moment the driver flicked the horsewhip and the animal broke into a lumbering trot. The heavily laden wagon rumbled through the puddles, spraying muddy water over everyone as it trundled past.

'Get away from me.' Grey struggled violently as Samson seized him from behind, pinning his arms to his sides, and Trigg took the opportunity to charge at him, roaring like an angry bull.

Sarah ran towards them but she stopped suddenly, covering her mouth with her hands as an agonised cry rang out. A murder of crows rose noisily into the sky from the bare branches of the beech trees that surrounded the grounds. And then there was silence.

'Grey,' Sarah murmured, moving closer.

Samson released him but it was Trigg who crumpled to the ground. Grey stepped aside, staring at his bloody hand.

'You killed him, mate.' Samson backed away.

'He fell on the knife,' Grey said dully.

'It wasn't your fault.' Sarah turned on Samson. 'You were holding him. If you'd kept out of it none of this would have happened.'

Grey knelt down beside the prostrate figure on the

ground. A pool of blood stained the muddy puddle crimson. 'He's dead.'

'It weren't me holding the chiv. You're the one who'll swing for it, guv.'

Sarah rounded on him in a fury. 'I saw it all – you're to blame. Trigg would have killed him and you told him to shoot.'

'I'm getting out of here. I don't want nothing to do with it.' Samson broke into a run, chasing after the wagon as it disappeared into the distance.

'You can't get away with it that easily,' Sarah called after him. She knelt down beside Grey. 'What are we going to do?'

He shook his head. 'I don't know.'

She heard footsteps and glancing over her shoulder she uttered a sigh of relief when she saw Parker hurrying towards them. He came to a halt, staring dispassionately at Trigg's inanimate body. 'He's no loss to anyone.'

Sarah jumped to her feet. 'We must get rid of the body, Parker. No one knows he's here apart from those men and they can't say anything without incriminating themselves.'

Parker helped Grey to his feet. 'We'll hide him in amongst the yews until dark. We can't do anything in broad daylight, master.'

'Yes, of course,' Grey said dazedly. 'Go indoors, Sarah. We'll see to this.'

'What are you going to do with him?' She stared in horror at the body of the man who had been responsible for so many evil deeds in his lifetime, but whose

311

existence had been snuffed out in a moment. Even in death he posed a threat.

'I don't know.' Grey shook his head. 'I've never killed anyone before.'

'It wasn't your fault. I saw it all.'

Parker took Trigg by the feet. 'Come on, Master Toby. Help me get him out of sight.'

'I'll wash the blood away,' Sarah said firmly. 'Do what he says, Grey. I'll see to the rest,' She went to the stable yard and filled a bucket with water from the rain barrel. Grey and Parker had moved the body to the cover of the yew trees by the time she returned, and it took several trips before she was satisfied that no trace of Trigg's blood was left at the scene. She put the bucket back where she had found it and went to retrieve the basket of food. Trigg might be dead but they were very much alive and when the shock of what had happened wore off she knew that both Grey and Parker would be ready for a meal. As for herself, she could still see Trigg's staring but lifeless eyes and the ugly twist of his lips that remained even in death. The sickly metallic smell of his blood lingered in her nostrils and she doubted if she would ever want to eat again.

She returned to the house and found Grey seated at the kitchen table, sipping brandy. He looked up as she entered the room. Parker half rose to his feet but she motioned him to sit. 'It's all right, Parker. Don't get up on my account.'

Grey raised his head with an attempt at a smile which did not quite work. 'Thank you, Sarah.'

She put the basket on the table. 'I didn't do much.'

'You were very brave. Most young ladies would have had a fit of the vapours if they'd witnessed something like that.'

She smiled. 'I'm a child of the workhouse, Grey. I watched my mother die. I don't think anything could be worse than that, and all the bad things that have happened to me were caused by Trigg. I can't mourn a man like him.'

Parker raised his glass. 'Let him rot in hell. That's what I say.'

'Have a tot of brandy, Sarah.' Grey pushed the bottle across the table. 'You look as though you need it.'

She shook her head. 'I'll make myself a cup of tea. I need to keep a clear head and so do you if you're to find a way to dispose of the body.' She went to the range where the kettle simmered on the hob and was about to make the tea when she heard a movement in the scullery. Grey leapt to his feet as the door opened.

'Davey.' Sarah rushed forward to throw her arms around him. 'Thank goodness it's you.'

He held her at arm's length. 'What's going on? There's a knife in the sink with blood on the blade.'

'Hell and damnation. I should have seen to that first.' Grey pushed past him and disappeared into the scullery.

'It was Trigg's blood,' Sarah whispered. 'He's dead, Davey.'

He stared at her, frowning. 'You'd better tell me everything.'

She opened her mouth to tell him but the words stuck in her throat and she turned away. 'I was making a pot of tea. Would you like some, Davey?' She went to pick up the kettle but her hand was shaking uncontrollably and boiling water splashed onto the fire, hissing and spitting as it hit the burning logs.

'Sit down and tell me what's happened.' Davey pulled up a chair. 'I'll make the tea.'

'It were an accident, boy,' Parker said grimly. 'It weren't meant to happen like it did.'

Grey walked into the kitchen and tossed the knife onto the table. 'He attacked me,' he said tersely. 'He fell on the blade.'

'It wasn't your fault,' Sarah cried passionately.

'No one's going to believe that.' Grey sat down, holding his head in his hands. 'I wanted to kill him, but that doesn't mean to say that I'd have gone through with it.'

'He's no great loss, if you ask me.' Parker stood up, swaying slightly. 'I've got things to do, master.' He went out through the scullery and the back door slammed against the lintel as he closed it behind him.

'Can you trust him?' Davey set the teapot on the table in front of Sarah. 'Where d'you keep the cups?'

She pointed to the oak dresser. 'Grey must leave the country as soon as possible, Davey.'

He fetched a cup and saucer and passed them to her. 'That's why I've come here in daylight. We need to move quickly, Grey. The ship's master will take you but he's sailing within the hour. He needs to leave the country in a bit of a hurry.'

Grey shook his head. 'I can't go now. What happens if the police come here and start poking around?

Someone is sure to report Trigg as missing and there were two witnesses. They'll say it was me if only to save their own skins.'

'All the more reason for you to go now,' Sarah said earnestly.

'But there's still the matter of a dead body. I can't leave that to you and Parker. Trigg was a big man.'

Davey leaned both hands on the table. 'Look, mate, I don't care what happens to you but I don't want Sarah mixed up in a murder, and you're putting her in danger by staying. Let's get you away safely and I'll return after dark and help Parker to do what's necessary.'

'He's right, Grey. You must go now.' Sarah rose to her feet and went round the table to give him a hug. 'Please do as Davey says. It's your only chance.'

He stood up slowly, wrapping his arms around her. 'Take care of yourself, kid.'

Davey tapped him on the shoulder. 'We're running out of time.'

Grey released Sarah, dashing his hands across his eyes. 'You will look after her for me, won't you?'

'I will.' Davey nodded his head. 'Hurry up. The ship will sail with or without you.'

Minutes later Sarah stood on the carriage sweep watching Davey drive the horse and cart through the gates of Blackwood House. Grey was concealed beneath a tarpaulin, sharing the space with empty but smelly fish boxes. She waved even though neither of them could see her, and she stood motionless until it was out of sight and the sound of the horse's hooves had faded into the distance.

Grey was leaving the country and might never return. He had played a large part in her life and there had been long periods of separation, but she had always known that he would turn up eventually. She had come to depend upon him and now he had gone from her life, possibly forever. Trigg's untimely death had put the final seal on Grey's fate and the irony of the situation was not lost on her. She walked slowly back towards the house, skirting the yew tree tunnel and trying not to think of the corpse that lay within its dark embrace.

She did not go indoors immediately and, needing time to think, she took a walk in the gardens. She knew that she would have to face the future sooner rather than later. She must decide whether to return to London or to remain in Blackwood and make a life for herself. Her childish dreams of marrying Davey and living happily ever after seemed irrelevant now and had simply been wishful thinking. Trigg might be dead but his evil lived on and sooner or later someone would come looking for him. She dared not even consider the consequences if his mutilated remains were found.

She waited all afternoon to hear from Davey and when darkness fell she was beginning to think that something had gone drastically wrong. She did not want to sit in the drawing room on her own that evening and she kept Parker company in the kitchen, but it was obvious that he too was becoming anxious as he kept glancing at the clock above the mantelshelf. 'We ought to be doing something about the body, miss,' he said, rising from his usual seat by the range. 'If I was a younger man I'd do it by myself, but he were a big chap and I don't think I've got the strength to drag him far.'

'Davey promised to help.'

'Well, he ain't here, is he? Maybe the lad forgot.'

'He wouldn't do that. Not Davey.'

'Then something's happened to prevent him. I don't like the look of it, miss.'

She stood up, reaching for her shawl. 'I'll have to go to the village, Parker.'

'It ain't safe for you to be seen.'

'I'll take the secret passage to the church. Davey's cottage isn't too far from there and it's pitch dark outside. There's no moon.'

'All right,' he said grudgingly. 'I'll see you safe down the tunnel and I'll wait for you, but we'll have to be on the lookout for the smugglers. There are those amongst them that would slit your throat as soon as look at you, or worse.'

She left Parker seated on a tomb in the crypt and set off along the deserted main street. A dog barked at her but no one bothered to investigate and she arrived at the Hawkeses' cottage without incident. She knocked on the door and when there was no reply she lifted the latch.

Mary was seated in the rocking chair by the fire, darning a sock. She leapt up as Sarah entered, and her quick smile turned into a frown. 'Oh, it's you. I thought it was Davey.'

'He hasn't come home?'

Mary laid her finger on her lips. 'Shh. Keep your voice down. The boys have only just fallen asleep.'

'I'm worried about Davey. He should have returned hours ago.'

'He's risking everything to help you and your London friend. The excise men won't care if he's guilty or innocent if they catch him with the free traders.'

'Then we must hope that hasn't happened. I don't blame you for being angry with me, Mary. But none of this was my doing.'

'I was pleased that you'd come back to us, but it's all gone wrong. You brought that man to Blackwood and you got Davey involved in your problems. I wish you'd stayed in London.'

'You and I used to be friends, Mary. I'm still the same girl I was back then, and you know I wouldn't do anything to hurt Davey or you and the boys. I love you all.'

Mary's eyes filled with tears. 'You was good to us when Pa died. You used to sing me to sleep and give me a cuddle when I fell over and hurt myself.'

'And Grey looked after me when I was a little girl. It's not his fault that he's in trouble, and I've got to do all I can for him, Mary. You do understand, don't you?'

Mary nodded mutely.

'I'm as worried about Davey as you are, and that's why I came here this evening. I was hoping he might have come home.'

'I know something's wrong. I felt like this when Pa was lost at sea. I couldn't bear it if Davey was drownded too.'

'Where would the ship have sailed from?' Sarah struggled to contain feelings of panic. Tiredness had crept up when she relaxed in the warmth of the fire. Try as she might to put the nightmarish events of the day from her mind they now came flooding back with frightening clarity, and she began to tremble. 'Would they have gone to the Ferryboat Inn? Or did they set sail from one of the deeper creeks?'

Mary's bottom lip began to quiver. 'I dunno and that's God's honest truth. Davey never lets on. He says the least we know the better.'

'Then I'll start at the inn.'

'Let me come with you.'

'You can't leave the boys on their own.'

'But I want to do something.'

'You must be here in case Davey returns. He'd be out of his mind with worry if he came home and you were missing. You wouldn't want that, would you?'

'No. But . . .'

'I'm leaving now, and I'll find him if it's the last thing I ever do. You can help by keeping the fire going and having some supper ready for Davey. Will you do that, Mary?'

'I suppose so.'

Sarah left before Mary could raise any further objections. She slipped out of the cottage, heading towards the creek and the pub frequented by sailors, smugglers and excise men alike.

'Don't know anything about it, duck,' the landlord said, drawing a pint of ale from a barrel behind the bar. 'All sorts of craft come and go from here. I'm too busy to take much notice.'

The men gathered around the fire turned away and resumed their conversation. They had stopped talking to stare when Sarah walked into the taproom and the silence had been unnerving. The smoky atmosphere was thick with the smell of stale beer, tobacco and the hint of tar and fish oil that clung to the hands and clothes of men who worked the sea for a living. 'But you must know Davey Hawkes,' Sarah insisted. 'Alfred Hawkes' son.'

The landlord glanced around the bar. He leaned across the counter. 'Keep your voice down, miss. You never know who's listening.'

'But you do know Davey.'

'What's your business with the lad?'

'He didn't go home tonight and I'm worried about him.'

He pushed a tankard of ale along the bar to a rough-looking individual wearing a fisherman's smock. 'This young lady wants some information, Moses. Have that on the house, mate.' He lowered his voice. 'Take her outside and tell her what you know.'

Moses snatched up the tankard and took a swig of beer. He wiped his lips on the back of his hand. 'What's it worth?'

Sarah put her hand in her pocket and took out the change from her purchases at the farm. She laid the coppers on the counter. 'That should buy you another pint, mister.'

'Just going outside for a piss.' Moses ambled out

of the bar and a gust of salt-laden east wind shredded the smoky air.

'Best give him a moment, miss,' the landlord said, grinning. 'He weren't joking. Moses has got the manners of a farmyard beast and he smells like a goat, but you can believe what he tells you.'

Sarah waited for a few more seconds before going outside, where she found Moses standing by the chain ferry, gazing across the creek. He appeared to have tidied himself up after responding to the call of nature, and she approached him cautiously. 'Mr Moses.'

'I saw it all,' he said, staring into the distance.

'What did you see?'

'The ship had sailed and the two of 'em set after it in young Davey's boat. That's the last I saw of them.'

She breathed a sigh of relief. 'I thought you were going to say that they came to grief.'

He glanced at her over his shoulder and she noticed that he had one blue eye and one brown, like a wall-eyed dog. 'They might've or they might not. Can't say for certain, but the tide was running fast and furious and the wind weren't in their favour. And the stranger stepped on board left foot first.' He shuddered and pushed past her as he hurried back to the pub.

'What does that mean?' Sarah hurried after him.

'Bad luck.' He stopped in the doorway, turning to her with his blue eye glittering and his brown eye half closed. 'Very bad luck.' He barged into the pub, slamming the door in her face.

* * *

She chose her words carefully as she attempted to comfort Mary. 'Davey knows what he's doing. He's been sailing these waters since he was even younger than you.'

Mary wiped her eyes on the sleeve of her worn and much-darned print frock. 'He shouldn't have gone to sea so soon after the storm. There'll be a huge swell and waves higher than the church spire. I've heard my pa speak of such things.'

'You mustn't worry, Mary. Davey won't do anything to risk the boat or their lives.'

'Do you know how many of the village men have been drowned even though they never took chances?' Mary demanded angrily. 'There's hardly a family here that hasn't lost someone to the sea, including ours.'

'There's nothing we can do but hope and pray,' Sarah said softly. 'I'm as anxious as you are, but we've got to be brave.'

'It's easy for you to say, living in the big house. But how am I supposed to feed us and pay the rent without the money that Davey brings in? I could probably find work at the squire's house, but who would look after the boys?'

Sarah shifted uneasily in her seat. 'Davey will be back soon. You've got to believe that, Mary.'

'But what if he ain't? It'll be the workhouse for us if anything's happened to him.'

'No.' Sarah leapt to her feet. 'I won't let that happen, and I refuse to believe that anything has gone wrong with Davey's boat. He knows what he's doing and he'll be back before you know it.' She made a move towards the door but Mary barred her way, folding her arms across her chest.

'So you're going to leave us again, are you? You're going back to Blackwood House and you'll forget all about us.'

'That isn't fair,' Sarah cried passionately. 'I never forgot you and I'll do everything I can to help you now, but I haven't got any money. I'm as poor as you are.'

'What about them toffs in London you spoke about? They can't be short of a bob or two.'

'They aren't rich, Mary, and they don't owe me anything. I'm not their problem and I've got to find a way to earn my living.'

'Then come and live with us,' Mary said earnestly. 'Stay here tonight and keep me company until Davey comes home.'

'I would if I could, but Parker is waiting for me.' Sarah gave her a hug and moved her gently out of the way. 'I'll be back first thing tomorrow morning. That's a promise.'

'I'll wait up all night,' Mary said with a stubborn lift of her small chin. 'I'll keep the fire burning for Davey and leave the kettle on the trivet so I can make him a cup of tea the moment he walks through the door.'

Sarah blew her a kiss. 'You're a good girl. I don't know what he'd do without you.' She felt her throat constrict as she left the tiny cottage and emerged into the cold night air. Tears that she had been holding back spilled down her cheeks as she hurried towards the church, where she hoped that Parker would be waiting for her. The last thing she wanted was to negotiate the eerie tunnel on her own. Her feet felt as leaden as her spirit as she faced the fact that Davey and Grey had a perilous journey ahead of them. She had tried to be positive with Mary but she knew only too well the dangers of the sea and the fragility of a small fishing boat when faced with the might of the wind and waves. She sighed with relief when she found Parker asleep on the stone tomb with a pipe of baccy clasped in his bony hand.

They walked back through the tunnel in silence, but when they were safe in the kitchen of Blackwood House Parker brought up the subject of the body in the yew tree tunnel. 'I'll have to dispose of it, miss,' he said wearily. 'It'll start to smell something terrible if it's left too long, and with young Hawkes still at sea there's no one else I'd trust to keep their mouth shut.'

'What will you do with him, Parker?'

'I'll wait till first light and then I'll do the necessary. You needn't worry about it, miss. Leave it to me.'

Sarah had to put her trust in Parker, and next morning when she somewhat nervously went to examine the site, all traces of Trigg had disappeared.

The next few days passed in an agony of waiting for news of Davey and Grey, but hope was beginning to fade and although Sarah did her best to keep the children's spirits up, she too was beginning to fear the worst. It had become impossible to keep her presence in the village a secret, and after the first shock that people had expressed on seeing her alive and well, she was accepted back into the community as though nothing had happened. She was saddened to learn that Elsie's demise had passed largely unnoticed, but she realised that very few people had known her well enough to mourn her loss, and Elsie's hermit-like existence had alienated her from the rest of the population. They had been pleased to accept her ministrations when they were sick, but they had regarded her more as an itinerant pedlar than a trusted apothecary.

Sarah spent the best part of each day with the children, and although everyone in the village knew the reason for Davey's sudden disappearance, no one mentioned the fact that he was helping a known criminal to escape and questions were never asked. The people of Blackwood knew how to protect their own, and when Sarah arrived at the cottage each morning she found small packages on the doorstep left by unseen hands – a loaf of bread, a piece of cheese, a box of herring or a meat pie. The gifts of food helped to eke out the few pennies that Mary had left in the old sock which she hung on the beam above the chimneypiece.

Sarah dug vegetables in the walled garden and cut cabbages. There were plenty of windfalls in the orchard and she collected the ones that had not been consumed by birds, wasps or field mice, and she took baskets of fruit and root vegetables to help feed the children, but winter was coming and there was no money to pay the rent on the Hawkeses' cottage.

She paid a call on Mr Wills at the schoolhouse but the reception she received was off-handed and he turned down her offer of help as he had taken on Bertha Smallgood, the vicar's youngest daughter, who had attended a Church of England school in Colchester and had excellent qualifications. His cold demeanour was enough to convince Sarah that he had not forgiven her for repulsing his clumsy advances or for her sudden and unexplained departure. She was aware of the smug glances that Bertha gave her as she left the schoolhouse, and it was safe to assume that this was now Mr Wills' firm favourite. She said as much to Mary when she arrived at the cottage.

'Everyone knows that Bertha's set her cap at old Wills,' Mary said, pursing her lips. 'Who else is going to marry the vicar's ugly youngest daughter?'

Sarah chuckled in spite of everything. 'You're so worldly wise, but I still think of you as a little girl.'

'I'm eleven. Almost a woman.'

Struggling to keep a straight face, Sarah nodded in agreement. 'Yes, indeed you are.' She turned with a start as the door flew open and Lemuel barged into the room followed by Jonah. 'What are you boys doing here?' she demanded. 'You were in school just now.'

'They've found it,' Lemuel gasped, clutching his side as he struggled to catch his breath.

'Davey's boat,' Jonah added tearfully. 'Washed up on the shore. Mast's snapped in two and both oars are missing.'

Chapter Nineteen

The wrecked boat had been found but no bodies had been washed ashore. Sarah could only hope that this was a good sign, but Parker was not optimistic. 'Sometimes they never surface,' he said gloomily. 'Or else they appear further up the coast. It doesn't mean a thing, miss.'

As the days dragged on it seemed that Parker was right. The vicar had visited the cottage to offer comfort to Mary and the boys, but she refused to believe that Davey was dead. Sarah was not so certain. She tried to be positive but she feared that they had perished beneath the waves. The strange thing was that she felt nothing. She could not grieve and her heart felt like a stone, weighing heavily inside her. She wanted to scream and shout but it was physically impossible. There were no more tears to shed and her emotions were numbed. She doubted if she would ever feel anything again. She thought about returning to London, but she could not abandon the children. She must find work, but there was nothing for her in the village. It was this dilemma that occupied her mind as she trudged through the first snowfall of early winter, making her way to the cottage.

She arrived to find Mary in tears, clutching a piece

of paper in her hands. 'Is it news of Davey?' Sarah snatched it from her. Her hand shook as she realised that it was a notice to quit the cottage.

'No,' Mary said, sniffing. 'It's the rent. I haven't been able to pay it since he was lost at sea.'

'Don't say that.' Sarah spoke more sharply than she had meant to. 'I'm sorry, Mary. I didn't mean to sound harsh, but you mustn't give up hope.'

'There's no money left,' Mary said dully. 'It'll be the workhouse for us.'

'Nonsense. I won't let that happen.'

Mary gazed at her with the eyes of a much older woman. 'You can't help us, Sarah. You're as hard up as we are.'

'Perhaps your landlord will give you more time to raise the money.' Sarah paced the dirt floor, wringing her hands. 'If I could find work I could do something to help. Perhaps the squire would take me on as a housemaid.'

Mary slumped down on the rocking chair. 'I went there yesterday, but the housekeeper said they don't need anyone. I asked the vicar, and he said the same.'

Sarah came to a halt, smiling as an idea came to her. 'There's the boat. Someone might want to buy it, even though the mast is broken and there's a hole in the hull. It could fetch enough to keep the landlord happy for a week or two.'

Mary glanced at the fireplace. 'It's been keeping us warm since the weather took a turn for the worse.'

Horrified, Sarah stared at the flames licking up the

chimney. 'You've been chopping up Davey's boat for firewood?'

Mary nodded, casting her eyes down as if anticipating a scolding. 'Parts of it, yes, I have.'

It might have been funny had it not been so serious. Sarah slipped her arm around Mary's skinny shoulders. 'I could have sent Parker with a barrowload of logs if you'd told me what you were doing. Now if Davey returns . . .'

Mary pushed her away. 'Stop saying that. You know very well that he's drownded and so is your friend Grey. They won't be coming back. Not ever.'

'You don't know that for certain,' Sarah said gently. 'None of us can know what the future holds. They might have been picked up by a passing boat. We mustn't stop hoping.'

'That's easy for you to say. Sooner or later you'll go away and leave us. Me and the boys have got to find a way to keep out of the workhouse.'

The logic of this was inescapable and Sarah was trying to think of an answer when someone pounded on the front door. Mary leapt to her feet and ran to open it. 'Who are you?' Her childish voice cracked with fear.

'I'm here to collect the rent.'

Sarah spun round to see a large woman whose ample frame seemed to fill the doorway. Her back was to the light and her face was in shadow but there was something frighteningly familiar about her. She stepped into the small room, overpowering it with her formidable presence. 'Well, well. Look who we have here. It's Sal

Scratch, the devil's daughter. You're all grown up now, but I'd know you anywhere.'

Sarah's worst nightmares seemed to crowd in on her as she stared at Mrs Trigg. Momentarily lost for words, she gulped and swallowed hard.

'Cat got your tongue, dearie?'

'What do you want?' Sarah demanded, controlling her voice with difficulty.

'The rent that's owed. That's what I come for.' Mrs Trigg seized Mary by the scruff of her neck and shook her. 'Don't give me no excuses, little girl. I could snap your neck with one hand.'

'Leave her alone.' Sarah dragged Mary away from her. 'Don't bully the child.'

Mrs Trigg moved a step closer, her eyes narrowed to slits. 'Keep out of this, Sal Scratch. I dunno how you come to be involved with this family but they're a parcel of wasters. Trigg's man has tried to get the rent from them but it's always the same hard luck story. Well, I'm not a soft touch, as you know to your cost.'

'You don't own this cottage.' Sarah faced up to her, even though every instinct told her to back away. 'What right have you got to come here demanding money?'

'We're agents for the landowner,' Mrs Trigg said, curling her lip. 'Mr Fitch puts his trust in Trigg and me and we get the job done to his satisfaction. Not that it's any of your business.'

'George Fitch owns this cottage?'

'Mr Fitch to you, girl.' Mrs Trigg allowed her gaze to wander round the humble interior. 'I'd pull the place down if it was mine, but that doesn't give the kid the right to withhold what's due.'

'My brother's dead,' Mary cried passionately. 'He was drownded and now we got no money, so go away, you old bat. I got nothing for you.'

'You'll regret calling me names.' Mrs Trigg shot a malicious glance at Mary. 'I'm sending the bailiffs in and you'll be out on the street. That includes you too, Sal Scratch.'

'I know Mr Fitch,' Sarah said bravely. 'I'll go and see him and tell him all about you. Let's see who ends up on the streets.'

With a mighty swipe of her large hand Mrs Trigg caught Sarah a blow on the side of her head that sent her stumbling to the ground. 'I heard that you'd run away with that villain Tobias Grey. The police are looking for him, and so is Trigg.'

'Grey was lost at sea with Davey,' Sarah muttered as she attempted to get up.

Mary helped her to her feet. 'Go away, you wicked woman. Sarah's been caring for us like a mother.'

Mrs Trigg drew back her neck in the manner of a snake about to strike. 'Her mother was a whore who died in the workhouse and Sal Scratch will end up the same way.' She made for the door and flung it open. 'I'll be back tomorrow with the bailiffs, so either have the money ready or be prepared to sleep in the gutter where you belong.'

'What right have you to do this, Mrs Trigg?' Sarah demanded angrily.

'My old man's been away on business for weeks and

I took over with Mr Fitch's blessing. He knows a good woman when he sees one, but I'm going to find Trigg, and he'll sort you out, Sal Scratch, so don't look at me like that. He'll have you begging for mercy and I'll sit back and watch while these little rats are thrown out on the street.' She left without bothering to close the door and a powdering of snowflakes fluttered into the room.

'She can't do that, can she?' Wide-eyed and trembling, Mary searched Sarah's face for an answer.

'I'm afraid she can.' Sarah hurried to the door and closed it. 'It's not safe for you here, Mary. Where are the boys?'

'In school, of course.'

Sarah glanced round the sparsely furnished room. 'There's only one thing for it. You must come with me to Blackwood House. Pack up your things and we'll leave as soon as they come home for their dinner.'

'But we can't go to that place. They say it's haunted and the yew tree tunnel eats people and spits out their bones.'

'That's nonsense. It's a lovely old house and you'll be safe there until Davey returns.'

'But he's not going to come back, is he?' Mary's voice broke on a sob. 'He's never coming home.'

Sarah gave her a hug. 'I don't know, and that's the truth, but he'd want you and the boys to be safe. That means coming with me to Blackwood House. I'm not taking no for an answer.'

The children were in the kitchen gobbling bowlfuls of rabbit stew as if their lives depended upon it while

Parker looked on with a disapproving frown. He drew Sarah aside. 'This won't do, miss. We can't have them living here and getting into everything. The master wouldn't allow it.'

'Mr Fitch won't find out unless you tell him,' Sarah said in a low voice. 'They're homeless thanks to him.'

'And they lost their brother because of Master Toby.'

'That's not fair, Parker.'

'I'll lose my living if the master finds out that I've allowed you to stay here and the brats as well.' He shot them a covert glance. 'What if they finds out about the stuff in the cellar? I can't keep my eye on all three of them and neither can you.'

'It's only temporary. If I can find the money for their rent they can go home.'

He leaned towards her, lowering his voice. 'And if the other thing comes to light.' He tapped the side of his nose. 'What if someone comes looking for a certain person?'

'You buried the evidence.'

'Not exactly.'

'What do you mean by that, Parker?'

'Like I said before, I'm not as young as I was. I didn't have the strength to move the article in question on my own, so I had to leave it where it was.' He glanced over his shoulder to see if the children were listening, but they were intent on finishing their meal. 'I covered it with branches and bracken and left it to nature to do the rest.'

She stared at him aghast. 'But that's asking for trouble. His men are bound to tell Mrs Trigg what happened. What would we do if she came knocking on the door and demanding to know the truth?'

As if on cue, one of the bells on the servants' board began to jingle. It lurched to and fro on its spring and they stared at it in disbelief. 'God save us,' Parker whispered. 'It's his ghost.'

'Nonsense,' Sarah said in a low voice. She gave him a gentle shove towards the doorway. 'It's the doorbell. We've got a visitor, Parker. Best go and see who's there.'

He shook his head. 'Not me. It'll be him, come to tear our hearts out.'

Lemuel jumped to his feet. 'Who's going to tear your heart out, Parker?'

'Sit down and finish your dinner,' Mary said firmly.

Jonah abandoned his meal and went to stand beside his brother. 'Let's go and see who's at the door. I ain't afeared.'

Sarah shooed them back to their seats. 'It's not a ghost and no one need be afraid. I'll go and see who it is. Now sit down and finish your dinner.'

It was bitterly cold in the entrance hall and whoever was standing on the step outside was now hammering on the knocker. Sarah wrenched the door open and came face to face with an irate Mrs Trigg. Snowflakes clung to the ostrich feathers adorning her hat and settled like lace on her three-tiered cape. Her mouth dropped open as she stared at Sarah. 'What the bloody hell are you doing here?'

'I might ask the same of you,' Sarah said, hoping that she sounded more confident than she was feeling.

'You cheeky little bitch.' Mrs Trigg pushed past

her. 'This house belongs to Mr Fitch and you're trespassing.'

Glancing outside Sarah could see Mrs Trigg's coachman huddled up on the driver's seat of the barouche. She beckoned to him. 'Come in. You'll freeze to death out there.'

'Leave him be,' Mrs Trigg snapped. 'He's paid to do his job.'

The driver tipped his hat to Sarah and hunched down beneath his many-caped greatcoat so that only his nose was visible beneath the brim of his hat. Sarah closed the door. 'That was a bit harsh, even for you, Mrs Trigg.'

'You haven't changed, Sal Scratch. Trigg shouldn't have spared the rod in your case.'

Sarah drew herself up to her full height. 'He didn't as I recall. Anyway, what right have you to come barging in here?'

'I told you before. Me and Trigg are Mr Fitch's agents. I've come looking for my old man who was supposed to come here and collect . . .' She gave Sarah a penetrating glance as if calculating how much she knew. 'He came to collect items belonging to the master.'

'I suppose you mean the contraband left here by the smugglers. I think the excise men would be very interested in that piece of information.'

'And the police might want to question you about the disappearance of the criminal Tobias Grey. He's the only one who would have brought you here, so where is he now? I'll warrant he's hiding here somewhere.' Mrs Trigg looked round as if expecting to see Grey materialise from beneath a dust sheet.

'I told you yesterday that he was lost at sea.'

'More's the pity, if that's true. I'd have liked to collect the bounty on his head, but that's not my main concern. My old man must have come here as planned because the goods have arrived in the warehouse, but I ain't seen hide nor hair of him.' She picked up a Chinese vase and examined it as if assessing its value. 'Not that that's out of the way. Trigg goes off on his jaunts and turns up when he's a mind to, but he's been away longer than normal this time. You wouldn't know anything about it, would you?' She put the vase down, glaring at Sarah.

'No. Why should I?'

'Don't take that tone with me, girl. It's a simple question: have you or have you not seen my husband recently?'

Sarah thought quickly. 'He was here some time ago when they collected the merchandise, but the men left and he went with them.'

'You're sure of that, are you?'

'Quite sure.'

'And if I was to look round this old mansion, am I right in thinking I'd find the nippers from the fisherman's cottage? The ones what owes Mr Fitch a month's rent?'

'Would you rather see them freezing to death in the snow?'

'I'm just doing my job. You're not supposed to be here and neither are they. I want to see Parker.'

Sarah could see that it was useless to argue. 'Very well.' She crossed the hall to open the drawing room door. 'If you'll wait in here I'll send him to you.'

'Hoity toity,' Mrs Trigg sneered. 'You didn't learn them manners in the workhouse.'

'The Arbuthnots showed me how decent people live. They were good people and your husband ruined them.'

Mrs Trigg marched into the drawing room. 'Send Parker to me now.'

Having made the children promise to stay out of sight in the kitchen, Sarah hovered outside the drawing room attempting to catch snippets of the mainly one-sided conversation between Mrs Trigg and Parker. His monosyllabic answers were gruff and to the point but Mrs Trigg ranted on and on, trying to extort more information from him. Having stood as much as she could bear Sarah burst into the room. 'He's told you everything he knows. Leave him alone.'

Mrs Trigg bore down on Sarah like a fury. 'Don't speak to me like that, you little whore. I think you both know more than you're telling me.'

Sarah faced up to her even though she was inwardly quaking. 'Why don't you ask the men who do your dirty work?'

'I sacked them for being drunk and lazy, but I'll get to the bottom of this.' Mrs Trigg glanced out of the window. 'Just look at the bloody weather. I'd better get going while the roads are still passable, but when I report to Mr Fitch I'll tell him what's going on here.' She fixed Sarah with a basilisk stare. 'You won't be so cocksure when you're living on the streets and selling your body for a couple of pennies to spend on blue ruin.' She snatched up her reticule and opened it, taking out a small purse which she tossed to Parker. 'That's your wages from the master. It'll be the last you get so don't spend it all at once.' She flounced out of the room, slamming the door behind her.

Sarah ran to the window and saw the coachman clamber stiffly to the ground. She could only imagine what he must be thinking as he opened the carriage door for Mrs Trigg and waited while she settled her bulk in the luxurious interior. He resumed his seat on the box and the pair of matched greys moved off slowly with their hooves slipping on the icy crust of the new-fallen snow. 'She's gone,' Sarah said, breathing a sigh of relief. 'At least she didn't snoop around.' She turned to Parker. 'You're certain that the body is well hidden, aren't you? It won't suddenly appear and give the game away?'

'No fear of that. When Master Toby returns we'll be able to bury the corpse where no one will ever find it.' Parker weighed the purse in his hand. 'You'd best take this and get in some supplies before we're completely cut off by the snow. Take them damn kids with you and let them work off their high spirits.'

Sarah took the money and tucked it into her pocket. 'You're right. We might be snowed in for days.'

'We can't keep the children here, you know,' Parker said as she was about to leave the room. 'She'll tell the master about you and the nippers and that'll be the end of it. You'll have to find somewhere else to live.'

338

She stared at him aghast. 'But you don't mind us being here, do you, Parker?'

A slow smile deepened his wrinkles into furrows. 'Bless you, no. It's done me a power of good having young company. Maybe we should have murdered the old faggot and buried her alongside her man.'

'Don't tempt me,' Sarah said with a wan smile. 'She made my life a misery when I was in the workhouse. I thought I was rid of her, but no such luck.' She went to find the children.

There was no sign of a thaw and although the sun shone in the daytime the temperature dropped at night and the ground froze. More snow fell and drifts piled up at the side of the house and half buried the yew tree tunnel. Parker took the boys out daily and they helped him saw fallen branches into logs, piling them on an old sled they had found in the coach house and dragging them back to the shelter of the stable block. Sarah had often watched Mrs Burgess making pastry and kneading bread dough, and when she discovered a book containing the former cook's recipes she decided to experiment. Her first attempts at making bread turned out something halfway between a brick and a ship's biscuit, but she persevered and soon the delicious aroma of baking filled the kitchen and filtered into the depths of the house.

Marooned by the weather they settled into a daily routine, and Sarah had the satisfaction of seeing Mary regain some of her childhood as she played hide and seek with her brothers. Their laughter seemed to bring the old house back to life and Parker began to warm to their presence, although he liked to grumble and complain that he had not had a day's peace since the children arrived to plague him. The weather had temporarily put a stop to the free traders' activities and it also prevented any further visitations from Mrs Trigg. They were able to enjoy the preparations for Christmas without fear of eviction and Sarah found herself wishing that they could stay like this forever. Without Grey and Davey the outside world held little attraction for her.

On Christmas Eve Parker went into the grounds to cut a fir tree, and although he insisted that the boys were unruly brats who needed a firm hand and a good hiding, he suffered them to follow him providing they kept their distance and did as they were told. They returned, pink-cheeked and smiling, carrying armfuls of holly and ivy with Parker bringing up the rear, dragging a large pine tree. They set it up in the drawing room and Sarah led an expedition to the attics where they found a wooden chest filled with glass baubles. Adding to the excitement Jonah stumbled across another box containing lead soldiers and a wooden Noah's ark complete with animals. Sarah sent the boys downstairs with the decorations and with Mary's help she sorted out the toys that would make ideal Christmas presents. They must, she thought, have belonged to Grey and Elsie and sadly they would not need them again, nor would they be passing them on to their own children. Her eyes misted with tears, but she turned away so that Mary would not see that she was upset by this glimpse into the childhood of two people who had meant so much to her.

'I didn't think there would be anything to give the boys for Christmas, but we'll wrap these up and put them under the tree.'

Mary glanced enviously at a wax-faced doll dressed in a cotton-print gown and a lace-trimmed bonnet. 'She's beautiful. I never had a dolly.'

Sarah put the lid on the box. 'Neither did I, but maybe Father Christmas will be kind to you this year, Mary.'

'It would be stealing,' Mary whispered. 'I mean, that lovely thing belongs to whoever owns the house. They might want it for their nippers.'

'We'll see.' Sarah stood up, dusting cobwebs from her hair. 'It must be years since anyone came up here. It's a treasure trove.' She held the candle higher and in its wavering beam she could see a wooden rocking horse with a white mane and a crimson velvet saddle. Shrouded in a yellowing cloth she could just make out a doll's house, although it took a stretch of imagination to picture Elsie playing with something like that, or maybe it had belonged to Grey's mother. Sarah could see them in her mind's eye, two little girls playing with their toys in the nursery. She could hear their childish laughter, and for the first time since Elsie died she felt close to her. She passed the candlestick to Mary. 'I'll carry the box if you'll light the way.'

When the children were safely in bed, Sarah sent Parker upstairs to the attic to bring down the doll's house and the doll that Mary had admired that morning. The boys were too big for the rocking horse and it was with regret that she left it in the cold dark attic with only spiders, mice and bats for company.

She sat by the fire in the drawing room, wrapping the presents for the boys in sheets of brown paper that she had found in one of the many kitchen cupboards. Outside the snow was falling steadily and it was likely that the roads were now completely impassable. They were safe for a while and the house seemed to wrap her in its warm embrace. She was certain that the dour expressions on the family portraits had mellowed a little and were smiling with approval. She would never understand why Elsie had chosen to live in poverty on the marsh instead of occupying her ancestral home, although it was obvious that she had spent a lot of time in the walled garden cultivating the herbs she needed for her medicines. Even so, she had turned her back on the way of life to which she had been born, and she had been a rebel until the last.

Sarah stared dreamily into the dancing orange and yellow flames as they licked up the chimney. She was convinced that Fitch had something to do with the disappearance of Elsie's will. In its absence it seemed likely that he would be the sole beneficiary and if Grey had perished at sea there would be no one to contest his claim to the estate. Fitch was an absentee landlord and involved in free trade. He was as much a villain as Trigg but somehow he had managed to keep one step ahead of the legal system.

Sarah jumped as the door opened and she covered the present she had been wrapping with the folds of her skirt, but it was only Parker, staggering beneath the weight of the wooden doll's house.

'I dunno why you're spoiling them kids,' he said, placing it on a table by the window. They'll spend the rest of their lives in the workhouse if Mr Fitch has his way, and I'll probably end up there too.'

'Nonsense. He can't afford to lose you, Parker. You know too much about him. One word from you and he'd end up in prison, which is where he belongs.'

Parker took the doll from inside his jacket and laid it on a cushion. 'I remember Miss Elsie playing with this when she was a little girl.'

Sarah shot him a curious glance. 'Really? I can't imagine Elsie playing with dolls.'

'Oh yes, miss. The doll's house was hers too. Miss Charlotte joined in sometimes but she was always the flighty one.' He plucked a cobweb from its roof. 'Miss Charlotte loved pretty things and she was her father's darling. She was a sunny little thing and everyone loved her. We was all heartbroken when she died so young.'

'What happened, Parker? Was she ill?'

He shook his head. 'She was just setting off for a ride when a fox ran out of the yew tree tunnel and she was thrown from her horse. She lay there like a broken flower, so young and beautiful and not a mark on her. You'd think she was sleeping, but Master Toby was only five and he was walking in the grounds with his nanny. He was the first to reach his ma and he clung to her crying and begging her to wake up.'

'That's so sad,' Sarah murmured, biting back tears.

343

She tried hard to picture Grey as a small boy and failed. 'He must have loved his mother very much.'

'We all did, miss.' Parker cleared his throat and turned away. 'It were tragic. The old master never got over it and Miss Elsie was heartbroken. She was never the same after that.'

'It must have been a terrible time.'

'Miss Charlotte's husband never got over it. He gambled away his fortune and took to the bottle. He died a couple of years later and Master Toby was sent off to school, but he came here in his holidays. It's no wonder he got in with the wrong crowd.'

'He's a good man at heart.' On the verge of tears, Sarah made an attempt at a smile. 'I mean, he was a good man, who had taken the wrong path.' Setting aside the half-wrapped present she rose to her feet. 'I refuse to believe that he and Davey are dead, Parker. I think I'd know it if anything dreadful had happened to them.'

He gave her a pitying look. 'Believe what you will, miss. But their boat was wrecked. They wouldn't have lasted long in them seas.' He ambled from the room, leaving her alone with her thoughts.

She clenched her hands at her sides, glaring at the portrait of Grey's sombre-faced grandfather. 'You could have done something more for your grandson,' she said angrily. 'You were the head of the family but you didn't stand by Elsie and it seems you didn't lift a finger to stop Grey from getting into bad company, and look how your son George turned out. He's not a credit to the family name.' She glanced round the wainscoted room, most of which was in deep shadow, and she smiled. 'How you would laugh if you could see me now, Grey. Here I am on Christmas Eve, talking to your long-dead grandfather.' She pulled a face. 'And Davey would say I was a mad woman.' She gathered up the presents and placed them under the tree. At least the children would have a good Christmas. What would happen in the future remained to be seen.

The snow continued to fall in the days that followed and froze into a solid mass, making the roads impassable. When their meagre supplies ran out Sarah was forced to use the secret passage in order to reach the village, but it was becoming increasingly difficult to purchase even the most basic essentials. She bartered logs for flour, salt cod, herring and occasionally a pat of butter or a wedge of cheese that some hardy soul had trudged through the snowdrifts to purchase from one of the outlying farms.

Late one afternoon at the end of January, she was returning home from one of her forays to the village with half a dozen eggs in her basket together with a small bag of flour and a lump of salt cod, which would feed them for a day or two if she eked out the rations. She entered the church and took a few moments to say a brief prayer, before lighting a candle and going down the steps to the crypt. She had made this journey at least twice a week and was no longer afraid of the darkness or the creepy atmosphere below ground, but this time it was different. As she reached the bottom of the stairs she thought she heard a movement behind the closed door. She hesitated, cocking her head on one side and listening, but there was silence. Thinking it was her imagination playing tricks on her she opened the door, but as she stepped inside a draught of cold air extinguished her candle and someone seized her in a grasp that knocked the air from her lungs.

Chapter Twenty

'Don't make a sound.' The voice was deep and gruff and the arms that held her were merciless. 'Give us some light, Joe.'

She heard the scrape of a vesta being struck and she was momentarily dazzled by its glow. 'Who are you?' she demanded angrily. 'Let me go.'

'This must be the one, Fred.' The man called Joe, a scruffy individual with a crooked nose, lit a candle and held it closer, peering into her face. 'He said as how she was a plucky little thing.'

Released without warning Sarah stumbled and would have fallen if he had not steadied her. 'Who are you?' she demanded angrily. 'What are you doing here?'

'I'd have thought you could work that out for yourself, duck.' Fred, a muscular fellow with a toothless grin, jerked his head at the piles of contraband. 'Trade's been slack these past weeks, but you might say we're back in business now.'

Looking round she could see that they had been busy. Kegs, crates and bolts of cloth were stacked neatly around the room. 'Aren't you taking a terrible risk by coming here in broad daylight?'

Joe perched on the edge of a tomb. 'The excise men

can't get about for the snow,' he said, chuckling. 'It makes our lives a lot easier so long as the natives don't peach on us.'

'And most of them are involved in one way or another,' Fred said with a careless shrug of his shoulders. 'They're all at it, from the vicar and the schoolmaster to the chap who owns the big house, and that's where you come in, missy.'

'I've nothing to do with it,' Sarah said hastily. 'I know it goes on, but . . .'

'Knowing is as good as doing, according to the law.' Joe took an expensive-looking half-hunter from his pocket and examined it. 'Tide will be on the turn shortly, Fred. Best be going.'

Sarah clutched Fred's sleeve as he was about to open the door. 'Wait a minute. You can't just walk away without telling me who you were talking about. Who said I was plucky and how did you know who I am?'

He gave her a cursory glance. 'Young fellow by the name of Davey. We pulled him and his mate out of the sea a few weeks ago.'

'They're alive?' Her breath hitched in her throat and the words came out in a barely audible whisper. 'Tell me, please.'

'They was half dead but still breathing when I last saw them.'

'Where are they now? Please tell me.'

Joe pushed past them to open the door. 'We left them in safe hands. C'mon, let's go, mate.' He mounted the steps. 'I'll sail on me own if you don't get a move on, cully.'

Sarah barred their way. 'Where I can find them?'

'We left them in a village near Calais. They'll be well cared for so long as they can pay their way.'

Sarah thought quickly. 'Do they need money?'

'Everybody always needs money.' Fred sidestepped her and was about to leave but she caught him by the coat tails.

'Wait a moment. Will you take me to them?' The words spilled from her lips before she had time to think.

'It'll cost you.'

'I don't care. Where are they exactly?'

He rattled off a French name. 'It'll cost you more than you've got, I daresay.'

'If I can raise the money will you take me to them?'

He stared at her, frowning. 'Are you serious?'

'Yes, I am. When will you be back?'

'Come on, Fred.' Joe's impatient voice floated down from the inner sanctum of the apse. 'We'll miss the bloody tide.'

'We'll be back a week today with a bit of luck. If not you'll have to find your own way. Keep a lookout for us.' Fred disappeared into the dark interior of the church, leaving Sarah with the stub of a candle to light her way back to the house. She closed the door and leaned against it as she fought to control her erratic breathing. She did not know whether to laugh or cry. They were alive and that was all that mattered. It was all the incentive she needed to risk the perilous sea journey. She retrieved her basket, which she had dropped in her fright, and found that miraculously the

349

eggs had survived in their bed of straw and not a single one was broken. It must be a good omen. She made her way back to the house.

She found Parker chopping wood in the log store and told him of her encounter with the smugglers. He listened intently. 'Well now,' he said, bringing the axe down on a log and splitting it in two. 'That's good news in one way and bad in another.'

She stared at him in surprise. 'I thought you'd be delighted to know that Master Toby is alive and well.'

'And I am, miss. But there's a haul of contraband to be collected and stowed away until the roads are passable.'

'Yes, I understand that.'

'And that means that the she-devil herself will be back with her men to collect the merchandise.'

'I suppose so, but I hope to be in France by then.'

'And how will you raise the money?'

She shook her head. 'I haven't worked that out yet.'

'And in the meantime we've got a dead body frozen like an icicle in the yew tree tunnel. We couldn't move it even if we'd got a team of strong men, but when the thaw sets in . . .' Parker's voice trailed off and he fixed Sarah with a meaningful gaze. 'D'you see what I mean?'

'Yes,' she said slowly. 'I do, and we've got the children to consider now. If I go to France who will look after them?'

'Don't look at me. I'm no nursery maid.'

'They can't go back to the cottage. Mrs Trigg has let it to someone else. Old Mrs Scranton told me so when

I bought eggs from her. She said that one of the fishing families has taken it for their newly married son and daughter-in-law. The children couldn't go back even if they wanted to.'

'It'll be the workhouse then,' Parker said gloomily. 'The master won't stand for no nonsense, especially with that woman bending his ear.'

'I won't let it happen. I'll get help.'

Parker raised a shaggy eyebrow. 'The only one who can help is him up there.' He pointed at the sky with its iron-clad clouds threatening yet more heavy snowfalls.

'Mr Moorcroft,' Sarah said, wondering why she had not thought of him before. 'He's a kind gentleman and he's rich. If I can get to London I know he'll help me.'

Once again Parker pointed skywards. 'It's going to snow again.'

'There must be an answer.' She thought hard. 'What about the railway? I've never been on a train but I've seen the great iron monsters steaming out of the London stations, belching smoke and spitting sparks. Where's the nearest station, Parker?'

'That'd be Maldon, but you've still got to get there, and the roads are blocked with drifts.'

Sarah thought for a moment. 'But I could get there by boat. I just need to find a fisherman who's willing to take me.'

'And what will you do for money?'

'There's a small fortune in contraband waiting to be collected by Trigg's men, or I suppose I should say Mrs Trigg's men now.'

'Aye, that's true, and I'd best start bringing it back to the house.'

'You're missing the point, Parker. What if it never reached the cellars here? What would the landlord of the Ferryboat Inn pay for a keg or two of finest cognac? Wouldn't the squire's wife love to have a gown made of pure silk at half the price it would cost if purchased in Spitalfields?'

He scratched his head, staring at her as if she was speaking in a foreign tongue. 'But it belongs to the master. He's paid for it in advance.'

'He can hardly report the theft to the police,' Sarah said, chuckling. 'How can things get any worse? We've got a dead man on our hands and you stand to lose your job and your home simply because you gave us shelter. Mr Moorcroft will know what to do and he might be able to prove that Master Toby is the rightful owner of Blackwood House and not his uncle. Help me to do this, Parker. Please.'

It was arranged. Parker had delivered two kegs of brandy to the Ferryboat Inn, and, after a bit of hard bargaining, Moses Cable had agreed to take Sarah to Maldon in his boat.

They set sail at first light. The sea was reasonably calm for the time of year, or so Moses informed Sarah as he trimmed the sail. 'If the wind don't pick up we'll have to row,' he said, chewing on a plug of tobacco and spitting a stream of juice into the water.

Sarah huddled in the bows and said nothing. The smell of fish guts seemed to have permeated every

352

inch of the small craft and she was feeling distinctly queasy.

'I'm wasting good fishing time by doing this,' Moses grumbled. 'The herring are running and I'm losing money by taking you to Maldon.'

'You're being paid,' she said, stung into a response. 'And you're helping to save Davey's life. Surely that means something to you.'

His blue eye glared at her while his brown eye focused on the sail. 'I got to make a living,' he muttered. 'Start baling out: the sea's getting up a bit.' He tossed a pannikin at her.

By the time they reached the calmer waters of the River Blackwater Sarah was feeling cold and wretched. When she stepped ashore her legs felt like jelly and her stomach was still churning from the effects of seasickness, but she paid Moses for his services and thanked him, trying not to sound too relieved that they were parting. He tipped his cap and put a fresh twist of tobacco into his mouth before pushing his boat away from the jetty and picking up the oars.

Sarah set off on foot for the station. It was hard going on the tightly packed snow and even harder if she stepped off the path into the drifts at the side of the road, but she arrived at the railway station at midday and bought a ticket for Bishopsgate.

'The next train will leave at half-past two,' the man in the ticket office said, examining his pocket watch. 'There's a fire in the waiting room.' He peered through the glass partition. 'You look a bit peaky, miss. Are you all right?'

'Yes, thank you.'

He continued to stare. 'You look as though you could do with a nice hot cup of tea.'

She was hungry and thirsty but she needed to be careful with her money. She smiled vaguely and nodded. 'I think I'll just go and sit in the waiting room.'

A gust of wind spiked with hard pellets of sleety snow almost blew her over as she made her way along the platform and she took shelter in the waiting room. A coal fire blazed up the chimney and she settled down on a wooden bench, warming her hands and feet on the hearth. She had been there for less than five minutes when the ticket clerk brought her a cup of strong, sweet tea and two jam tarts on a plate. 'The missis baked these this morning. She always makes too many for us.' He handed her the cup and saucer and balanced the plate precariously on the narrow mantelshelf. 'She can't get used to the fact that our nippers have grown up and left home. There's always a piece of cake or a slice of pie going begging in our house.'

Sarah sipped the tea. 'That's very kind of her. Thank you.'

'Not at all, miss. Just leave the crockery there when you've finished. I'll collect it later.' He went to the door but he hesitated, turning to her with a concerned look. 'The train should be on time, but it depends on the weather up the line.'

'I understand.' She took a jam tart and bit into it. 'Please thank your wife. This is delicious.'

He puffed out his chest. 'My Maggie is a fine cook. She used to work in a big house before we was wed.

I'll pass on your message, miss.' He glanced out of the window as a man in a top hat strode past. 'There's the station master. I'd best get back to my post.'

The train was ten minutes late, but at least it arrived. For a while Sarah had been afraid that the service would be cancelled due to the weather, but gradually the waiting room filled with people and the platform was crowded when the train pulled into the station. She found a seat in a third-class compartment and settled down for the journey to London, cramped between a travelling salesman who kept taking furtive nips from a flask which smelled strongly of gin, and a large woman with a wicker basket on her lap containing two live and extremely vocal chickens.

It was dark when the train arrived at its final destination and Sarah was stiff, tired and extremely hungry. It was, she thought, too late to go to Mr Moorcroft's office, and she decided to go straight to Mrs Arbuthnot's house in Elbow Lane. She toyed with the idea of walking in order to save money but when she saw the slushy state of the pavements and discovered that it had started to snow again, she hailed a cab.

It seemed strange to be back in the hustle and bustle of the city with its gaslit streets and tall buildings, but by the time they reached Shadwell and the cabby drew his horse to a halt Sarah was beginning to feel at home again. She paid the cabby, but as she knocked on the door she was suddenly nervous and unsure of her welcome. She waited, shivering in the cold night air as she listened for sounds of life within, and was rewarded by the pitter-patter of footsteps on the tiled floor. The door opened and it was Nettie who stood there with a look of astonishment on her face. 'Gawd above, it's you!' She grabbed Sarah by the hand and dragged her over the threshold.

Hugged in a suffocating embrace, Sarah could scarcely breathe. 'What are you doing here, Nettie?'

'I could say the same to you.'

'It's a long story, but why aren't you in the theatre?'

'The show closed. I'm what we professionals call resting.'

'You mean you're out of work.'

'I'm looking for a better part. I ain't going to be in the chorus all me life, girl. Anyway, I came here on the off-chance that Mrs Arbuthnot might know someone who needed help in the house and I've been here ever since.' She held Sarah at arm's length. 'You look terrible. What's been going on? Cook told me that you'd gone off on some wild goose chase with that bloke of yours. Wanted by the police, so Dorcas says.'

Sarah took off her bonnet and cape. 'I'll tell you everything but first I ought to see Mrs Arbuthnot and ask her if I can stay here for a few days.'

'She's in the parlour with Mr Moorcroft.' Nettie nudged Sarah in the ribs and winked. 'I think there's romance in the air.'

'Really?' Sarah could hardly believe such a thing. 'They're a bit old for romance.'

'Don't let Mr M hear you talking like that. He's been ever so kind to me. He's the one who persuaded the missis to let me stay and he's promised to introduce me to a chap who's casting a new musical comedy. I could be a leading lady before you know it.' Nettie skipped along the narrow hallway and burst into the parlour without knocking. 'Look who's turned up on the doorstep.'

Mrs Arbuthnot was seated in a chair by the fire but she rose to her feet when she saw Sarah, and held out her arms. 'My dear girl, how glad I am to see you. Martin told me where you'd gone and why, but that didn't stop me worrying about you.'

Mr Moorcroft had been sitting in the chair on the opposite side of the fireplace and he raised himself, giving her a searching look. 'How are things, Sarah? Is all well?'

Overwhelmed by her welcome and overcome with exhaustion after her long journey, Sarah could not speak. She hugged Mrs Arbuthnot, breathing in the familiar scent of lavender, tuberose and patchouli that reminded her of their first meeting when she was a frightened child fresh from the horrors of the workhouse. 'I need help,' she murmured.

'Oh dear.' Mrs Arbuthnot sank down on her chair, fanning herself with her hand. 'What's happened, Sarah? It's not that dreadful man you were trying to save, is it?'

'What's up?' Nettie asked anxiously. 'Has he been ill-treating you, nipper?'

Sarah shook her head. 'No, of course not. It's nothing like that.'

Moorcroft cleared his throat. 'Nettie, my dear, would you be so kind as to fetch a glass of port wine for Sarah, and something to eat. She looks as though she needs sustenance.'

'Yes, of course.' Nettie backed towards the doorway. 'But what's going on, Sarah?'

'Wine, please.' Moorcroft sent her a warning look and Nettie scuttled from the room. He turned to Sarah, smiling. 'That girl is a law unto herself, and she needs a firm hand, but she's a breath of fresh air.'

'Never mind her, Martin,' Mrs Arbuthnot said firmly. 'I want to hear what Sarah has to say and what led her to brave a long journey in this awful weather.'

'Grey killed a man.' There was no way to dress up the facts and Sarah was too tired to dissemble. 'It wasn't his fault,' she added hastily, seeing the shocked look on their faces. 'Trigg attacked him and he fell on the knife, but he died all the same.'

Mrs Arbuthnot clapped her hands. 'Serves him right. That man ruined us and he was responsible for what happened to my poor James. I'm glad he's dead.'

Moorcroft frowned. 'Even so, it doesn't look good for Tobias. Where is he now, Sarah?'

'That's just it. He's in France.' Sarah paused as Nettie rushed into the room carrying a tray which she deposited on a sofa table.

'Stop,' she cried dramatically. 'Don't utter another word, Sarah. I want to hear it all from the beginning.'

In between sips of the wine, which warmed her stomach and made her feel pleasantly relaxed, Sarah told them everything down to the last detail.

'Smugglers.' Nettie's eyes shone with excitement. 'How wonderful. Were they big and bold and handsome?'

Sarah smiled. 'No, actually both of them were quite

short and not particularly good-looking. And if we're talking about Moses, he's ancient and he has one blue eye and one brown eye. It's not romantic or exciting, Nettie. In fact it's all quite sordid and frightening, especially knowing that I've left the children in a den of thieves with only Parker to look after them.'

'The poor dears,' Mrs Arbuthnot cried, covering her face with her hands. 'Poor motherless little things.'

'You mustn't upset yourself, Sophia,' Moorcroft said calmly. 'I'm sure that young Mary is a very capable child. Isn't that so, Sarah?'

'Yes, indeed.' Sarah swallowed a mouthful of cake. 'She's a good girl, but I do worry about them. That's why I must get to France as soon as possible so that I can bring Davey back to look after them, and that's where I was hoping you'd be able to help me, Mr Moorcroft.'

'Yes, Martin, you must do something.' Mrs Arbuthnot sent him a pleading look. 'You will help, won't you?'

He was silent for a moment, regarding Sarah intently. 'You said that a certain person's remains have yet to be interred.'

'Yes, and that worries me too.'

'We could sell the body to a hospital,' Nettie suggested. 'No questions asked.'

'I think it's too late for that.' Moorcroft stood up and began pacing the floor, his hands clasped tightly behind his back. 'In my professional capacity I would have to report this matter to the police, but in the present circumstances I will act merely as a concerned friend.'

'I should hope so, Martin.' Mrs Arbuthnot nodded

with approval. 'Tobias has suffered enough at the hands of that villain Trigg. It may not be justice as far as the law is concerned, but as Mr Dickens put it, "the law is a ass – a idiot". I do so love the story of Oliver Twist.'

Moorcroft smiled indulgently. 'I'm sure that many would agree, Sophia, but this is real life and I must think of a way round this particular problem.'

'And I desperately need to get to France, sir.' Sarah gulped the last of the wine. 'I want to get Davey home as soon as possible and I must make certain that Grey is all right.'

'I can fund your journey,' Moorcroft said slowly. 'But you will travel by the normal route. That means taking the train to Dover and the packet to Calais. I'll make the necessary bookings first thing in the morning.'

'And I'm coming with you.' Nettie fluttered her eyelashes at Moorcroft. 'Please say that I can, sir.'

'Yes, Martin.' Mrs Arbuthnot reached out to touch his hand. 'I think that's an excellent idea. I wouldn't like to think of Sarah travelling to the Continent on her own.'

'Of course Nettie must accompany her.' He raised her hand to his lips in a gallant gesture. 'I must leave now, Sophia. But I'll return tomorrow with the necessary travel documents.'

She stood up, still clutching his hand. 'Won't you stay for dinner, Martin?'

'Not tonight, my dear. I still have some work to do at the office.' He turned to Sarah. 'You must get some

360

rest before you set off on your travels, and don't worry. I'll arrange everything.'

Nettie waited until they had left the room and as soon as the door closed she threw herself down on a chair beside Sarah. 'D'you see what I mean? They're so sweet together.'

A wave of tiredness washed over Sarah and she found she could hardly keep her eyes open. 'I'm glad for both of them,' she murmured. 'Mrs Arbuthnot is such a lovely lady and Mr Moorcroft is a real gentleman.'

'He's been kindness itself to me. He says I remind him of someone he once knew, but I can't imagine that he'd have known anyone who'd allow their baby to end up in the workhouse. Anyway, you and me are going on a big adventure. I never been further than Limehouse so you got a head start on me.' She jumped to her feet. 'Let's go to the kitchen. Cook and Dorcas are itching to find out what's been going on and Betty wants to see you too.' She grabbed Sarah by the hand and pulled her to her feet. 'Come on. Don't fall asleep.' She looked her up and down with a critical eye. 'Where on earth did you get that frock? That style went out twenty years ago. Never mind, I'm sure I've got something that will fit you.'

The packet boat pitched and tossed mid-Channel and Sarah hung over the side, wanting to die. Nettie tried to persuade her to go below, but Sarah could not move. In the end Nettie produced a boat cloak that she had somehow managed to procure, although she refused to say how, and wrapped it round Sarah, assuring her that her torment would be over soon and that once ashore she would feel fine again.

It was dark when they docked in Calais but Sarah had no idea of the time. She had slept for the last four hours of the crossing, and although she was reluctant to admit that Nettie had been right, she started to feel better the moment she stepped onto dry land. It was then she discovered that, during the voyage while she had been indisposed, Nettie had found someone who could speak English who was willing to interpret for them when they landed in France. It was no surprise to Sarah that this person was young, male and good-looking, and it was his cloak that had kept the chill from Sarah while she was unwell. The Frenchman was charming and Nettie flirted outrageously with him over supper at the inn, which he not only recommended but coincidentally was where he was also putting up for the night. Next morning he was waiting to escort them to their destination, the village a few miles to the west of the town as named by one of the men who had pulled Davey and Grey from the sea.

'Are you sure this is a good idea?' Sarah said in a whisper as Nettie sent her latest conquest to see if the vehicle he had hired on their behalf had arrived.

'Can you speak the lingo?'

'No, of course not.'

'Then how are we to find your blokes if we can't communicate with the natives?'

'But what if he gets the wrong idea, Nettie? He might think you're easy. You've been playing up to him ever since we arrived.'

'Gaston's all right. Anyway, it's just a bit of fun. Don't be so prissy.'

Sarah bit her lip. The most important thing was to find Grey and Davey, but a small warning voice in her head was making her feel uncomfortable in handsome Gaston's presence. Nettie might think that he had fallen for her charms in a gentlemanly way, but Sarah was not so sure. 'What's his business, Nettie? Why is he going out of his way for us?'

Nettie's lips formed a moue. 'Why wouldn't he do something to help a damsel in distress?'

'Because you aren't a damsel in distress, and you seem to think that you're the heroine of one of your stage plays. Why was he on the packet from England to France in the first place? If he's a businessman I would have thought he'd be too busy to bother with us.'

Nettie elbowed her in the ribs. 'Shh. He's coming. Stop acting like a governess and enjoy the thrill of doing something new and exciting.' She waltzed off to join Gaston with her coppery curls bobbing and her gold earrings catching the light as the sun's rays flooded through the open door. 'Hurry up, Sarah,' she called over her shoulder as she linked her hand in the crook of Gaston's arm. 'The carriage is waiting and we're paying by the hour. Do you want to find your friends, or not?'

Chapter Twenty-One

Nettie and Gaston kept up a lively exchange during the one-hour carriage ride through narrow country lanes. The vehicle bumped over potholes with the occasional jolt that almost threw them off their seats when the wooden wheels caught in ruts.

Sarah huddled against the squabs, trying to ignore the smell of sweat laced with garlic and the patches where Macassar oil had stained the leather. Her thoughts were with Grey and Davey as she stared out of the window at the winter landscape of bare trees, and the dark earth where ploughed fields waited for the touch of spring warmth to bring them back to life.

'Where are your friends staying?'

She looked up to find Gaston staring at her. His lips were smiling which belied the calculating look in his eyes. She shook her head. 'I don't know.'

'No matter. There cannot be many Englishmen in the village who are hiding from the law.'

'Who said they were hiding?' Sarah demanded, glaring at Nettie. 'What have you told him?'

Nettie giggled nervously. 'I said their boat had gone down in a storm, that's all.'

'And you two ladies are going to bring them home,'

Gaston said smoothly. 'Or perhaps just one of them will be returning with you.'

'Perhaps,' Sarah said stonily.

'And I will make enquiries when we arrive.' Gaston turned his head to look out of the window. 'We will be there very soon, I think.'

Minutes later the carriage drew to a halt and Gaston leapt out first. He helped Nettie to alight and proffered his hand to Sarah, but she climbed down without his assistance. Despite his pleasant manner she did not trust him. He did not seem put out by the rebuff and after a few words with the driver he turned to them with a smile. 'We will start at the inn. This is always the best place to ask questions.' He raised an eyebrow. 'Does that suit you, Mademoiselle Sarah?'

'I don't want to keep you from your business,' she said coldly. 'I'm sure we can manage from now on, but thank you for your assistance.'

His smile seemed to be permanently attached to his face. 'But I have come this far with you beautiful young ladies. It would be ungallant to abandon you now.' He patted Nettie's hand as it rested on his sleeve.

'That's very kind of you, Gaston,' she said, sending a warning glance to Sarah. 'We're very grateful.'

Sarah could not disagree without appearing churlish and reluctantly she followed them to the inn. 'We'll wait outside,' she said, grabbing Nettie by the hand before she could follow Gaston into the building.

'What's the matter with you?' Nettie hissed. 'He's gone out of his way to help us and you're behaving as if he's a spy or something.' She frowned. 'No. Surely you can't think that?'

'I don't trust him,' Sarah said in a low voice. 'I know you like him and you think he likes you, but I can't help wondering why he's going out of his way to help a couple of strangers.'

'He does like me,' Nettie said, pouting. 'It's just possible that he's doing it because he's a gent.'

'Is that so? What if George Fitch sent him to find out where Grey is? Your French gent could be a policeman for all we know, or a private detective.'

'But that's silly.'

'Is it? Well, we'll see, but I don't want him poking his elegant nose into what doesn't concern him.'

'I think you're being unreasonable.' Nettie glanced over her shoulder. 'Here he comes. We won't be able to find your mates without him, so for God's sake stop scowling and smile.'

'All right, but don't encourage him.' Sarah shivered as a cold wind tugged at her bonnet and a bank of dark clouds obliterated the sun. She could not raise a smile no matter how hard she tried. 'Any news, Gaston?' She made an effort to sound casual, but inwardly her pulses were racing and her palms were damp with sweat. If Gaston Fournier was in George Fitch's pay all her efforts to save Grey would come to nothing. If he was a policeman the end result would be the same. She crossed her fingers.

'Indeed, yes,' he said, beaming. 'There are two Englishmen staying on a farm nearby. I can take you there.'

'You are so kind, Gaston.' Nettie fluttered her lashes and took his arm in a possessive gesture that was not lost on Sarah.

'You mustn't waste any more of your valuable time on us,' she said hastily. 'I'm sure you must be eager to go about your business, Gaston. If you give us directions I'm sure we can find our way.'

His expression was urbane and gave nothing away. 'I wouldn't hear of it. We've come this far together and I want to see you safely reunited with your friends before I leave.'

Nettie smirked and Sarah seethed inwardly, but there was little she could do without appearing rude and ungrateful. 'Is it far?'

'It's quite near, but it looks like rain and we'd better hurry.' Gaston started forward at a brisk pace with Nettie making efforts to match his strides. There was nothing Sarah could do other than follow them. The narrow lane threaded its way between pastures where cows grazed and orchards filled with serried rows of dormant fruit trees. It had begun to rain as they reached the stone farmhouse, which was surrounded by a cluster of single-storey outbuildings. Once again Gaston asked them to remain in the shelter of the tiled porch while he went inside to make enquiries.

'I don't like this,' Sarah murmured, wrapping her arms around her chilled body. 'We don't know what he's saying to these people.'

'It wouldn't help if we were in there with him.' Nettie looked around, wrinkling her nose. 'This place stinks. I hope your mates aren't being kept in the pigsty.'

Sarah opened her mouth to retort but Gaston emerged at that moment with a smug grin that made her want to slap him. He either did not understand the seriousness of the situation or he was congratulating himself on his success. She waited for him to speak.

'The gentlemen in question are in the barn,' he said, pointing at one of the outbuildings. 'The farmer says we may visit them.'

'I would rather go in alone,' Sarah said firmly. 'I can't thank you enough for what you've done for us, Gaston. But I want to do this on my own.'

For once Nettie seemed to be on her side as she nodded in agreement. 'That's right. If they're feeling poorly they won't thank us for barging in. Let me know if there's anything I can do, Sarah.'

Gaston frowned. 'I might be able to help.'

Nettie laid her hand on his arm. 'I would kill for a cup of tea, Gaston.'

'We're in France now, chérie.' He smiled indulgently. 'I think the farmer's wife might be persuaded to give us some coffee.'

'Then let's go inside out of the rain. It's ruining me best hat,' Nettie said, dragging him into the kitchen.

Sarah could hear her speaking slowly and loudly to the farmer's wife as if by enunciating clearly she could make the woman understand English. Smiling to herself, she hurried through the rain and entered the barn. The smell of cow dung and urine-soaked straw caught the back of her throat making her retch, but she did her best to ignore it as she waited until her eyes had become accustomed to the gloom. The cows tethered in stalls looked at her with large, baleful eyes, swishing their tails and lowing. She hurried past them, and at the far end of the barn she could just make out two figures lying on piles of empty sacks. She moved closer and her heart did an uncomfortable leap in her chest when she saw Grey, pale-faced and either unconscious or in a deep sleep. Propped up against the wall, Davey was staring at her in disbelief. His head was roughly bandaged and one arm was tied up in a makeshift sling. 'Sarah?'

She fell onto her knees beside him. 'Are you all right?' It seemed like a silly question but she could think of nothing better to say. She wanted to hug him and sob with relief but she could see by the colour of his skin and the lacklustre look in his eyes that he was unwell.

'My arm's broken,' he said dully. 'And I've got a terrible headache – had it for days now. I don't know how long we've been here but it feels like forever.'

She laid her hand on his brow and breathed a sigh of relief as she felt his cool skin beneath her fingers. 'You haven't got a fever, but you should be in a proper bed. This place is no good for you.' She turned her attention to Grey, but a cursory examination revealed that he was burning up with fever, and he did not respond to the sound of his name.

'He's been like that since we were brought ashore,' Davey murmured. 'He's in a bad way, but to be honest I thought we were both goners when the mast broke and the boat capsized.'

'Don't talk,' Sarah said urgently. 'Save your strength. I'm going to get you out of here. We'll soon have you on your feet again.' She stood up, gazing at them with a mixture of relief and anxiety. At least they had survived, but Grey was a sick man. Davey raised his uninjured hand. 'Don't go, Sarah.'

'I have to make arrangements to get you both out of here, but I'll be back as soon as I can.' She hurried from the barn, struggling to hold back tears of desperation. It was easy to make promises, but keeping them was another matter.

She found Nettie and Gaston in the farmhouse kitchen sipping coffee from china bowls. The farmer sat in a chair by the fire with his feet on the brass rail of the range. A cigarette drooped from the corner of his mouth and the odd-smelling tobacco smoke that she had noticed at the inn wreathed his bald head. He seemed unperturbed by their sudden arrival but his wife had the flustered look of a woman whose daily routine had been disturbed by the influx of foreigners requiring sustenance. She glanced nervously at Gaston who spoke to her in rapid French. He turned to Sarah. 'I asked her if you could have some coffee. It's excellent.'

'It's rather bitter,' Nettie said in a low voice. 'But I don't like to ask for cream and sugar in case I offend her. She seems a bit put out.'

The farmer's wife poured thick brown liquid into a bowl, which she passed to Sarah with a hint of a smile.

'Thank you, ma'am. Very kind, I'm sure.' Sarah sipped the scalding coffee and burned her tongue but she nodded and smiled, not wishing to appear ungrateful or rude. These people had sheltered Grey and Davey, even though they had housed them in the cattle shed without proper bedding or medical

370

attention, but at least they had kept them alive and for that she was thankful. The bowl was burning her fingers and she put it down on the table. 'Gaston, I'm afraid I must ask your help once again.'

'I thought you might.' His dark eyes met hers with a steady look. 'You want your friends moved to a hospital?'

'No, not that, but perhaps I could rent a cottage where I could nurse them back to health. I think I have enough money.'

'That is not a problem. I can give you what you need.'

'Who are you?' Sarah demanded. 'You're not simply a kind stranger who took pity on us. I think someone sent you to spy on us. Was it George Fitch?'

'Sarah!' Nettie's shocked voice echoed round the kitchen and the farmer's wife moved closer to her husband, clutching his hand.

Gaston rose slowly to his feet. 'You're right, but I'm not a spy. I am a lawyer and my services were engaged by Martin Moorcroft. I was to assist you in any way I saw fit, but you were not supposed to find out.'

'Mr Moorcroft paid you to keep an eye on us?' Sarah stared at him in amazement. 'Why didn't you tell me that in the first place?'

'Would you have accepted my advice?' Gaston chuckled and the farmer's wife relaxed visibly.

'I don't know,' Sarah said truthfully. 'I hope I would.'

'No, you wouldn't.' Nettie gurgled with laughter. 'You was always a stubborn piece, Sarah Scrase. You wouldn't give in to nothing and no one. Mr Moorcroft has got your number, darling.'

Sarah smiled reluctantly. 'Maybe, but I wish he'd

told me what he was doing. I was thinking all sorts of things about you, Gaston.'

'All of them wrong,' he said with an expressive shrug. 'I am here to help and the first thing I must do is to ask these good people if they know of an empty property round here. 'Have I your permission to do so?'

Sarah nodded wordlessly but Nettie clapped her hands. 'I said all along that he was a toff. I should have guessed that dear old Moorcroft had something to do with it. He's a darling. I love him.'

'He is a good man and a true friend,' Gaston said seriously. He turned to the farmer, speaking in his native tongue, and was answered with much gesticulation and a flow of words that left Sarah feeling breathless but none the wiser. She looked to Gaston to translate.

'There is a house on the far side of the village. He says it has been empty for quite some time but the rent will be cheap. He's given me the landlord's name and address.'

The cottage in the woods was a perfect hideaway for a person on the run from the police, or so Nettie declared, striking a dramatic pose. Gaston laughed at her antics but Sarah was eager to inspect the interior and she could hardly contain her impatience as she waited for Gaston to pull away some of the creeper that clambered over the porch and partially obscured the front door. He wrenched away the trailing fronds and turned the key in the lock. The door opened with a groan of protest and Nettie covered her mouth and nose with her hand. 'It smells,' she said in a muffled voice. 'Something must have died in there, or someone.' She giggled nervously and hung back as Sarah followed Gaston into the building.

'It's a dead bird. It must have fallen down the chimney and become trapped.' He bent down to pick it up by one of its clawed feet.

'Take it away,' Nettie screamed in genuine horror. 'It's a bad omen: it means a death in the family.'

'That's just superstition,' Sarah said, suppressing a shudder as Gaston took the stinking corpse outside. She made an effort to ignore the lingering smell of corruption as she looked round the large room with its bare stone walls and low, beamed ceiling. The flagstone floor was littered with dead leaves, feathers and soot from the fireplace which must have fallen down the chimney during the bird's frantic and futile fight for survival.

'It's a mess,' Nettie said, wrinkling her nose. 'And it's too small. You can't bring them here.'

Sarah was already halfway up the narrow staircase which led to the first floor. 'It's better than the cattle shed where they are now.' She paused as she reached the tiny landing. 'Come and have a look. There are two rooms up here.' She went into the smaller of the two, which was empty of furniture apart from an iron bedstead. The feather mattress had burst at the seams and was leaking its contents onto the bare floorboards. The walls were whitewashed and a small window overlooked the neglected front garden. She could hear Nettie's light footsteps on the stairs and she took a quick look at the back bedroom, which was slightly larger and contained two crudely fashioned wooden beds.

'I hope you don't expect me to sleep here,' Nettie said, looking pointedly at the grey mantle of cobwebs that festooned the beams. 'I've got used to better things and I'm not going back to the bad old days in the workhouse where we were four or five to a bed.'

'It's just a temporary measure until Grey and Davey are well again and we can return home.'

Nettie shook her head. 'Your mate Grey won't be going home though, will he? If he's wanted by the police it'll be a long time before he can set foot on English soil without getting himself arrested.'

'Mr Moorcroft will clear his name,' Sarah said stoutly. 'He'll prove that George Fitch was lying.'

'But there's the small matter of a body and two witnesses to a murder; or three if you count yourself.'

'Keep your voice down.' Sarah went to the door to check on Gaston's whereabouts. She could hear him moving about downstairs and she turned to Nettie, laying a warning finger on her lips. 'It was self defence. Parker will dispose of the evidence.'

'I hope you're right, I really do, but I can't stay here, Sarah.' Nettie headed for the stairs, pausing at the top to pick up her long skirts. 'I've got to get back to London and look for work. If Moorcroft keeps his promise I could be auditioned for a part in a musical comedy. I don't care how small it is, I just want to get out of the chorus.' She negotiated the steep steps with Sarah close on her heels.

'I can't stop you and I'm grateful that you came this

far, but I'll miss your company.' Sarah came to a halt, staring in astonishment at Gaston who had found a broom and was sweeping the floor. 'You don't have to do that.'

He leaned on the handle. 'I thought I'd make a start. You want to get your friends here as soon as possible, don't you?'

'Of course.'

He thrust the broom into Nettie's hands. 'You may take over now. I'm going back to the village to find the owner of this desirable residence.' He closed her fingers around the wooden handle. 'I'm sure you've done this before, chérie. You'll soon remember how it goes.' He winked at Sarah. 'You will need a few things to make the house habitable. Will you leave it to me?'

She nodded her head. 'I don't know how we would have managed without you, Gaston.'

'The excellent Mr Moorcroft will no doubt be pleased to hear you say so.' He moved swiftly to the door and opened it. 'I'll be back as quickly as I can.' He went outside, closing it behind him.

Nettie threw the broom down with an exclamation of disgust. 'Well, what a cheek. Who does he think he's talking to? I'm not a skivvy.'

Sarah picked it up. 'No, but someone has to do it. Perhaps your ladyship would like to clean the grate, or if that's too much to ask maybe you'd like to fetch some wood for the fire. I'm going to get Grey and Davey over here by nightfall if it kills me and you too, Nettie Bean.'

Still grumbling, Nettie went outside while Sarah

finished sweeping the floor. She was cleaning out the grate when Nettie returned, dumping an armful of firewood on the floor and complaining volubly that she had a splinter in her finger. She perched on the deep window seat, sucking the afflicted digit.

Gaston returned a couple of hours later, driving a cart laden with a deal table and four chairs, a couple of straw-filled palliasses, some second-hand bed linen and a supply of food that would feed a large family for a month. While he was absent Sarah had lit the fire, drawn water from the well she discovered at the back of the house, and had mopped the floors in all the rooms. Nettie had been put in charge of brushing away the cobwebs, but a large black spider had landed on her head and that had been the end of her contribution to the housework.

Sarah helped Gaston unload the cart and sent Nettie upstairs to make the beds, hoping that she could manage a simple task without further mishap. Gaston manhandled the deal table into the house and set it down in the middle of the floor. 'That is the last of it. You will be quite comfortable here for as long as you need to stay.'

'I'm sorry I suspected you of being a spy,' Sarah said shyly. 'You've been so good to us, Gaston.'

'You were right to be suspicious. I was not just a helpful stranger.'

She smiled. 'You were too good to be true.'

'That is how I am. Very good.' He laughed and his dark eyes danced with humour. 'But I can report back to Mr Moorcroft that you are safe and will remain so until it is time for you to return to England.'

'You're going away?'

'I will help you to bring the injured men to this place, and then I regret I will have to leave you. I will spend the night at the village inn, but I must get the packet boat to Dover tomorrow as I have business to conduct in London.'

'Then take me with you.' Nettie came hurtling down the stairs. 'I'm not going to stay here a moment longer than necessary.' She met Sarah's surprised look with a defiant toss of her head. 'I'm sorry, but I can't face a night in this cottage. It's cursed for a start and anyway I have to be back in London. I told you that, Sarah. Don't gaze at me with your big sad eyes. I came with you, didn't I? I've helped you to find your man.'

Gaston touched Sarah lightly on the shoulder. 'I suggest that we leave now to get your friends from the barn. It will be dark in a couple of hours and I think it's going to rain again soon.' He glanced at Nettie. 'There's room in the cart for you too, or would you rather stay here?'

She grabbed her cape and bonnet from the window seat. 'You're not leaving me alone in this creepy hovel. I'm coming now and you can book me a room at the inn for tonight.'

'But you haven't any money,' Sarah said pointedly. 'You can't expect Gaston to pay for you.'

Nettie slipped her cape around her shoulders and jammed her bonnet onto her head, fighting her unruly curls as they tried to make their escape. 'He's paid for all this, or rather Moorcroft has, and he'll reimburse Gaston without question.' She tied the ribbons under her chin, looking round with a sigh. 'Whoever heard of a house with no mirrors? Is this on straight?'

'You look lovely,' Sarah said, giving her a gentle shove towards the doorway. She struggled into her mantle and snatched up her bonnet on her way out of the cottage. She allowed Nettie to sit next to Gaston on the driver's seat and she climbed into the back of the cart. It was not the most comfortable way to travel but she clung to the sides as the vehicle lurched and swayed, throwing up sprays of muddy water as the wheels stuck in ruts and the horse struggled to pull it free. Her first concern was to get Grey and Davey to safety, but Nettie's words echoed in her mind, creating a feeling of unrest. She had not stopped to question Moorcroft's reasons for helping them, assuming that he acted out of the goodness of his heart and his innate sense of justice, but Nettie's casual assumption that he would pay for everything without question had made Sarah wonder how she would ever repay him.

Twilight was rapidly dissolving into all-enveloping darkness and it was growing colder by the minute. It was a relief to see the distant twinkle of lights from the village and smoke from chimneys spiralling into the night sky. The scent of burning apple wood and a hint of something savoury wafted from an open doorway on a beam of candlelight and then disappeared as the door closed. Sarah felt her stomach growling with hunger, and she realised that she had had nothing to eat since a breakfast of coffee and croissants at the inn that morning.

'Let's get this over quickly,' Nettie said as Gaston drew the horse to a halt outside the barn. 'I'm cold and I'm hungry.'

He climbed down to the ground, saying nothing, but Sarah clambered from the back of the cart finding it difficult to curb her impatience. 'Don't you ever think of anyone but yourself, Nettie?'

Nettie held her arms out to Gaston and he helped her to alight. She shook out her skirts. 'I was only saying how I feel. I'm sure you're cold and hungry too, but you keep quiet about it.'

Gaston took a lamp from the footwell and lit it with a vesta. 'Just imagine that you are an angel of mercy, ma petite. This is the part you have to play for now.'

'I never thought of it like that,' Nettie said gleefully. 'I could be like Miss Nightingale at Scutari. Perhaps someone will write a play about her one day and I could play the part. What do you think, Sarah?'

'I think you'd make a wonderful Florence Nightingale.' Sarah took the lamp from Gaston and thrust it into Nettie's hands. 'There you are, Florence. Now can we please do what we came to do?' She marched into the barn.

Two hours later they had successfully transported the injured men to the cottage. Gaston had carried Grey upstairs and with help from Sarah had stripped him of his filthy garments and dressed him in an old nightshirt purchased from the farmer at an exorbitant price. Sarah was worried about the fever that racked Grey's emaciated body, but there was little she could do other than bathe him with a damp cloth and give him small sips of water.

She went downstairs to say goodbye to Nettie and Gaston, who were about to leave for the inn and would, no doubt, enjoy a delicious hot meal and a comfortable bed. She tried not to feel envious or resentful, telling herself that Nettie was within her rights to return home. She need not have come but had done so in a spirit of friendship and for that Sarah was grateful. She hugged Nettie and kissed her cheek. 'Good luck with your audition. I hope you get the part.'

Nettie's brow creased in a frown. 'I feel bad leaving you like this. I'll stay if you want me to.'

Sarah did want her to stay, very much, but she knew how much Nettie's career meant to her, and she was not going to stand in her way. The long shadow of the workhouse reached out to them even now, and Nettie had known no other life until Mr Arbuthnot had come to their rescue. Sarah forced her lips into a smile. 'I'll miss you, of course, but I've got Davey to help look after Grey. We'll be fine, so you mustn't worry.'

Nettie clutched her hand. 'I don't like leaving you in this cursed place.'

'I'll be quite all right,' Sarah murmured, hoping that she sounded more positive than she was feeling.

'Hurry up, Nettie.' Gaston opened the front door and a gust of wind hurled dead leaves into the kitchen. He held on to his hat. 'We'll miss our dinner if we don't go now. Are you coming with me or not?'

Chapter Twenty-Two

'I'll take care of Sarah,' Davey said, rising from his seat at the table. 'A one-armed man is better than none.'

Nettie hesitated for a moment. 'Make sure you do, or you'll have me to answer to.' She hurried to Gaston's side, pausing to give Sarah an apologetic smile. 'I'm sorry, love. I must go, but please don't stay in this godforsaken place a moment longer than necessary.'

The door closed on them and Sarah felt suddenly nervous. She was in a foreign country where she neither spoke nor understood the language. She had two sick men to bring back to health and one of them was a fugitive.

'We'll be all right,' Davey said as if reading her thoughts. 'Luckily I've got a thick skull so that crack on the head didn't bash my brains out, and my arm will heal in time.'

Sarah began unpacking the hamper of food that Gaston had brought earlier that day. 'It's Grey I'm worried about. How long has he been like this?' She took out a loaf and a large pat of butter wrapped in a cabbage leaf.

'A week,' Davey said vaguely. 'Maybe longer. I was unconscious for several days and when I came to my senses we were in the barn with the cattle. The farmer and his wife brought me food and water but I had no idea of time and I couldn't understand a word they said. I could hardly believe it when you appeared. I thought I must have died and that you were an angel.'

A wry smile twisted her lips. 'According to the people who ran the workhouse I'm the devil's daughter.' She delved once again into the basket and brought out a round, odorous cheese. 'I hope this tastes better than it smells. If I wasn't so hungry I don't think I'd even try it.'

'I had that almost every day at the farm. It's quite good when you get used to it.'

'I'm not sure I believe you.' She sighed heavily. 'I'm sorry I got you involved in this, Davey. You might have died in that storm and now we're stuck here eating cheese that smells like dirty socks.'

'We'll get by,' he said, smiling. 'To tell the truth I'm glad to have you on my own without Tobias sticking his oar in, or that Gaston fellow acting as if he owned the place. What's he to you, anyway?'

'That's a tale in itself.' She put a hunk of bread on a plate with a generous portion of the cheese and passed it to him. 'Eat first and we'll talk later over a cup of coffee. I'd give anything for a cup of tea, but they don't seem to drink tea in this part of the world. I used to watch Cook when she brewed coffee for the Arbuthnots, so I know how it's done.'

Alone in her saggy feather bed with draughts whistling through cracks in the windowpanes and the wind soughing in the trees like a spirit in torment, Sarah lay wide awake and troubled. From the room next door she could hear Davey's rhythmic breathing and Grey's fevered ramblings. She found herself wishing that Nettie had stayed, but it would have been selfish to deny her the chance of achieving the fame and fortune she had always craved. Eventually she sank into a fitful sleep haunted by visions of Trigg's spectre rising from the branches of the yew trees to seek vengeance for his untimely death. He was advancing on her with his skeletal hands outstretched, fingers clawed and his tattered clothing flapping around fleshless bones. He was shaking her and she cried out in horror.

'Wake up, Sarah. It's me, Davey.'

She opened her eyes and tried to sit up, still half asleep, but he pressed her gently back against the pillows. 'You were dreaming,' he said gently. 'But I need you to come quick. Tobias has taken a turn for the worse.'

She was wide awake now and she leapt out of bed. 'What's the matter with him?'

'I dunno. He's a funny colour and his breathing is sketchy. I saw my pa suffer this way when he was taken poorly.'

'Oh, God. No.' Sarah hurried into the back bedroom and bent over Grey, feeling his forehead. 'He's feverish. I wish I had some of the medicines that Miss Elsie used to make, but I have a horrible feeling he's gone beyond that.' She straightened up. 'We need help.'

Davey laid his hand on her shoulder. 'I'll go to the village and see if I can find a doctor.'

She shook her head. 'No, Davey. You should be resting and anyway you don't speak French, and neither do I. I'm going to run to the inn and see if I can catch Gaston before he leaves for Calais.' She made for the door. 'Stay with him and bathe him with cold water. Try to bring his temperature down.'

Within minutes she was dressed, wrapped in her cape and tying her bonnet ribbons beneath her chin. She left the cottage and headed for the village. It was light now and a heavy frost had dusted the countryside with silver. A pale sun turned ice particles into diamond necklaces tossed carelessly over twigs and bare branches, but she was in no mood to appreciate the beauty of a winter's day. Her breath curled around her head as she ran, taking care to avoid the cast-iron ruts in the frozen mud and leaping over the potholes.

She arrived at the inn and paused for a moment in order to catch her breath. The door was ajar and she went inside to find the landlord, swaddled in a long white apron. He was busy wiping the tabletops but he stopped, eyeing her suspiciously, and addressed her in rapid French. She had no idea what he was saying and she tried to communicate with sign language, but he stared at her as though she was quite mad. 'Gaston Fournier,' she shouted. 'I wish to speak to him.'

'Ah! Monsieur Fournier.' He nodded his head and then shook it, pointing to the doorway, gesticulating and gabbling at her in a foreign tongue.

The truth dawned upon her slowly. The man was trying to tell her that she was too late. Gaston and Nettie had gone. But she could not give up now. Grey's life depended upon her. 'Doctor,' she said in desperation. 'My friend needs a doctor. He needs medicine.'

'*Un médecin*.' The landlord grinned. '*Docteur*.'

'Yes. We need a doctor.'

His smile faded and he shook his head. *'Non.'* He turned his back on her.

She left the taproom, wondering what to do. It was obvious that there was no doctor in the village, but without medical help Grey would be lucky to survive. It was not so long ago that they had made the dash from Blackwood to London in the hope of saving Miss Elsie, only now it was Grey's life that was hanging by a thread. Sarah knew enough about medicine to realise that lung fever was invariably fatal, but Grey was a young man and physically strong.

She started walking, planning to retrace her steps and return to the cottage. She could only hope and pray for some divine intervention that might save his life. She came to a sudden halt as she reached the village church, and a vision of Miss Parfitt reading the lesson in the workhouse chapel came forcibly to mind. She would have given anything at that moment to see her former teacher and ask for her advice. Closing her eyes, she could hear Miss Parfitt's gentle tones and she seemed to be telling her to go into the holy place and pray. Never particularly religious and raised by Miss Elsie, whose pagan rituals had coloured their daily lives, Sarah entered the stone building.

She stood in front of the altar, pressing her hands together as she had when saying her prayers as a small child. She could feel the cold rising through the stone floor and there was the familiar smell of musty hymnals and dampness that she associated with the church in Blackwood, but there were also the less familiar odours of hot wax from the votive candles placed before a statue of the Virgin Mary, and the heady fragrance of incense.

The silence was tangible but the creak of door hinges followed by swift footsteps on the aisle made her spin round. A priest wearing an ankle-length soutane and a black biretta was hurrying towards her and she felt suddenly guilty. 'I – I'm sorry, Father,' she stammered. 'I shouldn't have come in without permission.'

He smiled. 'You are English.'

She bit back tears of relief. Here at last was someone who understood what she was saying. 'I need your help, Father.'

'You have come to see the Englishmen?' He motioned her to take a seat. 'This is a small village. News travels fast.'

'One of them is very ill. He needs a doctor.'

'We have no doctor in this village.'

'Then I have no choice. I must take him home to England.' She realised even as she uttered the words that this would be a risky procedure, but she could not leave Grey to die in a foreign land. The priest was silent, watching her closely. She thought quickly. 'I want to hire a carriage to take us to Calais, Father. Can you help?'

'Have you money, my child?'

She jingled the gold coins in her reticule. 'I can pay.' She glanced at the offertory and took a coin from her bag, placing it in the collection plate. She noticed that the priest did not refuse her gift. 'Will you help me, Father?'

'I think it can be arranged, my child.'

* * *

She ran all the way back to the cottage. The priest had agreed to make the necessary arrangements and she felt light-headed with relief. It was only when she walked into the bedroom and found Davey sitting at Grey's bedside that she realised the full implications of taking her old friend back to England. If Trigg's body had been discovered he would be facing a trial for murder.

Davey looked up expectantly. 'Did you find a doctor?'

'There isn't one in the village and I was too late to catch Gaston. He'd already left the inn by the time I arrived.'

'Tobias is in a bad way.'

Sarah perched on the edge of the bed, taking Grey's limp hand and clasping it as if she could pass some of her own life force into him by touch alone. 'I met a priest who speaks English,' she said slowly. 'I gave him money to hire a vehicle to take us to Calais, Davey. We're taking him home.'

His eyes narrowed. 'Is it worth the risk? Mightn't he get better if we care for him here?'

'I can't cure this. He needs proper medical attention.'

'But he could face the hangman's noose if we take him home.'

'And he'll almost certainly die here if he doesn't get proper medical attention. I've just about enough money left to get us back to England. I couldn't afford to put him in a hospital here, but if we can get him home I know Mr Moorcroft will help. The Fitch family is worth a fortune and if Grey has inherited Blackwood House he's a rich man in his own right. I think we have to take the risk.'

'What does this chap mean to you, Sarah?'

Startled, she looked Davey in the eye. 'What sort of question is that?'

'You've gone to such lengths on his behalf, and he's been lurking in the background ever since I've known you.'

'That's silly. Grey's been like an older brother to me. He could have abandoned me but he saved my life, and I'll always be in his debt.'

Davey leaned towards her, his expression unusually serious. 'He abducted you, Sarah. He did it on Trigg's orders but he was the one who stole you away from the people who loved you. He might have had a fit of conscience but he didn't do the right thing and return you to the Arbuthnots. He took you to live with that crazy woman and you were just a kid.'

'You're forgetting one thing, Davey. If Grey hadn't left me with Miss Elsie I would never have met you.'

'And that would have been a tragedy because I love you, Sarah. I've always loved you since we was nippers, but I'm just a fisherman and the man lying in this bed was born into the gentry. He's not a villain like Trigg, he's a rebel like Miss Elsie, but at the bottom of it they're a different breed from us, Sarah. You and me are cut from the same cloth.'

She rose swiftly to her feet. 'Davey, I don't know what you're talking about. It doesn't matter how I feel about Grey or even you at this moment. Whatever happens I'm not going to let him die in this miserable cottage, far from home.'

He pushed back his chair and stood up. 'I can see you've made up your mind, no matter what I say.'

'The most important thing is for Grey to have proper medical attention and to get you home to Mary and the boys.' She was quick to see the flicker of doubt in his eyes as she mentioned his family and she pressed home her point. 'There's something I haven't told you, but you'll find out sooner or later.'

'What is it? Tell me, for God's sake.'

'I didn't mention it before because you were ill, but Mary and the children were evicted. She couldn't pay the rent and Mrs Trigg, acting for the landlord who happens to be George Fitch, threw them out and put another tenant in your house.'

'The bastard. Where are they now? What's happened to them?'

'They're safe and well. I took them to Blackwood House and Parker is looking after them, but if Mrs Trigg finds out she'll tell George Fitch, and the poor little things will be homeless again. They need you, Davey.'

'You took care of them for me. I won't forget that.'

Grey moaned and his eyelids fluttered. He peered up at Sarah and there was a flash of recognition in his eyes. 'Sarah?' His voice was barely a whisper.

She clasped his hand. 'Don't try to talk. I'm here and I won't leave you.'

Something like a sigh escaped his lips and his head lolled to one side. For a terrible moment Sarah thought that it was the end, but leaning over him she could feel his breath soft against her cheek. She straightened up with a determined lift of her chin. 'We must get him to Calais before nightfall. I don't fancy his chances if we stay here a day longer.'

'Someone's coming.' Davey stood up to look out of the window. 'I think your priest has done his best, but we won't be travelling in style,' he said, chuckling.

She stood up and hurried to his side. 'It's not funny, Davey,' she said, gazing in dismay at the farm wagon below. The ancient carthorse looked as though it was ready for the knacker's yard and the driver could have been any age from sixty to ninety. The priest climbed down and made his way up the path to the front door.

'Don't you dare make a joke of this,' Sarah said angrily. 'Stay here and I'll let him in.' She left the room and ran downstairs to open the front door

The priest brushed past her and stood in the middle of the room, gazing around with a critical eye. 'It's a decent enough place,' he said slowly. 'It would make a good home, but the people in the village will not come here.'

A shiver ran down Sarah's spine as she remembered the dead bird and Nettie's dire foreboding. 'Why not, Father?'

He shrugged his shoulders. 'It is how do you say in English?' He frowned thoughtfully. 'Ah yes, superstition. There was talk of witchcraft but that was long ago.'

She was about to question him further when Davey appeared at the top of the stairs. 'I need help to get

Tobias out of bed. I can carry him over my good shoulder but I can't lift him on my own.'

'I have done enough. I have to go now.' The priest made for the door. 'God go with you, my child.' He left the cottage and Sarah had to run to catch up with him. 'The purse, Father. You forgot to give it back to me.'

'The driver has been paid.' He put his hand in his pocket and drew out the depleted leather pouch. 'You should leave quickly. Word has got round that you are living in this cursed place and the villagers are angry. Who knows what they will do.' He strode off with his robes flapping around him and his sandals making slapping sounds on the frozen ground.

Sarah weighed the pouch in her hand and sighed. It was obvious that the driver had received a generous sum of money for his trouble, but he was huddled on the driving seat like a malignant goblin, staring straight ahead. She had been planning to ask for his assistance but one look at his surly profile was enough to make her change her mind.

She hurried back to the cottage and went upstairs to join Davey in the sick room. 'We must leave right away.'

Davey gave her a searching look. 'What's happened?'

'I'll explain later, but I can't help feeling we should have left with Gaston. It's my fault that we're in this mess.'

'Stop blaming yourself,' Davey said firmly. 'You should be proud of what you've done. You came to a foreign country to find us and that was brave. You're a heroine.'

She blinked back tears, overwhelmed by this unexpected praise. 'That's silly.'

He put his good arm around her waist and gave her a hug. 'We'll manage and we'll get through this together. We'll be back home in no time at all.'

Their progress was painfully slow and the light was fading by the time they arrived in Calais. Grey's condition was giving Sarah cause for great concern. He was alternately burning up with fever or shivering convulsively. They found an inn near the harbour which could only offer them one room, but the need to make Grey comfortable outweighed all other considerations.

Davey insisted on going to the packet boat office to book tickets for the first sailing next day, and Sarah put Grey to bed in the room that they were all to share that night. Her attempts to communicate with the landlord and beg him to send for a doctor had failed miserably, but had caused much merriment amongst the locals in the bar, and in the end she gave up and purchased a bottle of cognac. She added a generous tot to a cup of warm milk and after a few sips Grey fell into a deep sleep.

Later that evening Sarah and Davey ate their supper at a small table in the bar. They ordered pot au feu, which turned out to be a savoury beef stew, and shared a bottle of rough red wine. When they returned to their room Davey took the chair by the fire. 'I can sleep anywhere,' he said, eyeing the bed with a rueful grin. 'I've thought about sharing a bed with you, Sarah. But not with a third party lying between us.'

'Don't say things like that.'

'Why not? It's true. We used to talk about getting married when we grew up. That's the way a husband and wife behave.'

She turned away, unable to meet his amused gaze. 'I don't know what they do. No one ever told me.' She shot him a sideways glance. 'Miss Elsie never spoke about men in that way.'

Davey lowered himself into the chair. 'You must have some idea.'

'Not really.' She perched on the edge of the bed, taking off her boots. 'Have you ever taken a woman to bed, Davey?'

'I'm a bit drunk, but not so tipsy that I'd admit to something like that, even if it was true. Which I'm not saying it is.'

'So you haven't?'

'Get some rest, Sarah. We'll have a long day ahead of us tomorrow.' He yawned and leaned back, grimacing as the chair creaked ominously. 'I'm not talking about personal things with him lying there. Maybe one day we might continue with this conversation, but not now.' He closed his eyes. 'Goodnight, my brave, lovely girl.'

She lay down on the bed next to Grey with Davey's words ringing in her ears, but exhaustion combined with two glasses of strong French wine had her falling, falling, falling into the welcome oblivion of a dreamless sleep.

The sea was choppy but Davey had used a large part of their dwindling supply of money to pay for a cabin. It was small and stuffy and the lingering smell of vomit was making Sarah feel queasy as she sat beside the bunk where Grey tossed and turned feverishly. His lips moved ceaselessly but she could barely make sense of his mumblings. She bathed his forehead and fed him sips of water, but there was little else she could do. Davey spent most of his time on deck but he brought her cups of tea and hunks of soggy gingerbread, insisting that she must keep up her strength.

The journey back to Dover seemed to take twice as long as the outward voyage, but when Davey returned to the cabin and urged her to come up on deck and enjoy the sight of the white cliffs of Dover she did not hesitate. She stood beside him on the salt-stained, windswept deck and he placed his arm around her shoulders, steadying her as the vessel yawed slightly in preparation for entering the harbour. 'That's a good sight, isn't it?'

The cliffs stood out ghostly white against the darkening sky, but her initial relief at the sight of them was tempered by her anxiety for Grey. 'Yes, it is, and I'm glad to be home, but I've been wondering what to do for the best when we go ashore. It'll be dark soon and Grey has to see a doctor, but there's not much money left and I need to see Moorcroft urgently. He's the only one who can help us, but Grey is too ill to travel further.'

'Then we'll find a lodging house for you and Tobias and I'll get the train to London.'

'To London?' She stared at him in surprise. 'But you've never been there. You wouldn't know where to go.'

'I've got a tongue in my head, sweetheart. I'm not a helpless boy who's scared of the big city. Just tell me where to find your friend Moorcroft and I'll seek him out.'

'You'd do that for Grey?'

'No, Sarah. I'll do it for you because I know you care about him. Now tell me what to do when I reach London.'

'All right,' she said slowly. 'If you're sure about this, you'll most likely find Mr Moorcroft at Mrs Arbuthnot's home in Elbow Lane, or at least she would know how to contact him. Nettie might be there too. But I should be the one to go to London, not you.'

'I'm no good at nursing sick people. Tobias needs you, Sarah. Let me do this thing and prove to you that I'm not just a bone-headed fisherman who doesn't know his arse from his elbow.'

'Oh, Davey, I never thought that.'

'I'm just as good a man as your London friends, even if I don't have their town polish. I can do anything I set my mind to. It just happens that fishing is my trade.'

'And I wouldn't want to change you. I don't know where you're getting these wild ideas. It must be the bump on the head making you say such things.'

His lips curved into a humorous grin. 'I think the bump on the head brought me to my senses.' A sudden movement of the deck threw them closer together and he drew her to him, holding her in a close embrace and taking her mouth in a kiss that sent sweet sensations rippling through her veins. She parted her lips with a sigh and kissed him back. Passion robbed her of reason and the world around them had ceased to exist. The taste and scent of him overwhelmed her and she clung to him, wanting more, her whole body aflame with desire, but he released her suddenly and she was left shivering with shock. She stared at him, stunned by the sudden change in their relationship. It seemed that in a single moment their childish attachment had deepened into something stronger and more physical. She realised that they had crossed an invisible line, and she was glad. She waited for him to say something but he turned away. 'We'll be landing soon,' he said gruffly.

The boat slid towards the harbour wall and the crew began rushing around tossing ropes ashore and preparing to disembark their passengers and cargo.

'We'd best go below and get Tobias ready to go ashore,' Davey said in a matter-of-fact voice that startled her. Her world had been turned upside down by that unexpected and achingly sweet embrace, but for him it seemed that nothing had changed.

'Yes, of course.' She headed for the companionway that led below decks to the cabins. She could hear his footsteps behind her and she reached out to hold his hand. His warm grasp comforted and reassured her. Together, she thought, they could do anything.

They found a lodging house close to the docks. The landlady, a burly woman who introduced herself as Mrs Kenny, widow, looked as though she could wrestle a drunken sailor to the ground should the need arise.

She looked askance at Grey and demanded to know whether he had anything catching. Sarah assured her that he was suffering from an illness caused by near drowning and the woman, whose husband had apparently been lost at sea some years previously, agreed to let them have two rooms for the night but only after she had been paid in advance.

She counted the coins carefully. 'I'll send my youngest for the doctor. You can't be too careful when it comes to people who've been abroad.' She fixed Davey with a hard stare. 'I don't want no hanky-panky, mind. This is a respectable boarding house. Now get that young fellow up to bed before my other guests see him.'

The rooms were small and basic but they were clean and the bedding smelt of starch and the frosty outdoors. With Davey's help Sarah managed to get Grey undressed and into bed before the doctor arrived.

'I must go now,' Davey said in a low voice. 'I'll be back as soon as I can.'

Sarah reached up to brush his cheek with a kiss. 'You do know what to do when you reach London, don't you?'

'Don't worry about me. I can take care of myself.' He hesitated, gazing into her eyes, and for a moment she thought that he was going to take her in his arms, but the door burst open and the landlady erupted into the room.

'The doctor's here. Just in time if you want my opinion.'

Chapter Twenty-Three

The doctor straightened up, turning to Sarah with a serious expression on his lean features. 'Your companion is a very sick man.'

'Yes, doctor. I was afraid you might say that. Will he be all right?'

He frowned. 'His lungs are very congested, and there is nothing I can do other than make him comfortable. The rest is in the hands of the Lord.' He opened his bag and took out a small brown bottle. 'You are familiar with laudanum?'

'Yes, doctor.'

'Give him a few of drops in a little water if he becomes restless. I'll come again tomorrow morning. My fee for this visit is half a crown, if you please.'

Sarah handed him the money. 'Is there any hope, doctor?'

'We must always hope for the best, my dear.' He gazed at her over the top of his steel-rimmed spectacles and his eyes were kind. 'But perhaps a prayer or two would not go amiss.' He patted her on the shoulder as he left the room.

'It's nothing catching, is it, doctor?' Mrs Kenny's anxious voice was raised above the sound of a man and woman shouting at each other in a nearby room. 'She said it weren't, but they come off the packet boat and you never know what diseases people bring from foreign parts. He could have the bloody plague for all I know.'

The rest of the conversation was lost as the doctor closed the door behind him. Sarah moved to the bedside. Grey's complexion was ashen and beads of perspiration stood out on his forehead. His breathing was laboured and his fingers plucked at the coarse cotton sheeting. She dipped a cloth in the washbowl and wrung it out. 'You will get better, Grey,' she said, gently mopping his brow. 'The doctor doesn't know everything. I didn't go all the way to France to let you die in a Dover boarding house.'

It was impossible to gauge whether or not he had heard and understood her words, but she willed him to get well. If he could not fight then she would fight for him. Grey had risked his life to save Miss Elsie and he had gone against Trigg in order to protect her when she was too young to stand up for herself. She settled down for a long night's vigil at his bedside.

She awakened to find someone stroking her hair as it spilled over the coverlet, and she raised her head, realising with a start that she had fallen asleep. The pale iridescent light of dawn filtered through the small windowpanes and she could hear sounds of movement in the rooms on the top floor. As the last vestiges of sleep cleared from her brain she realised that Grey was looking directly at her. The feverish, unfocused look in his eyes had been replaced with the hint of a smile. She laid her hand on his hardly daring to believe that he had passed the crisis. 'How do you feel?'

'Strange,' he said gruffly. 'Thirsty.'

'Of course.' She stood up, ignoring the cramps in her muscles as she went to the washstand to fetch him a drink of water. She returned to the bed and propped him up on his pillows, holding the cup to his lips while he sipped.

'Enough. Thank you.' He raised his hand feebly and then let it fall back on the bed.

'Are you in pain? The doctor left laudanum for you if you needed it.'

He shook his head. 'I want to keep a clear head. There's something important I must tell you.'

'It can wait.' She sat down again, taking his hand in hers. 'You need to rest and regain your strength.'

'I haven't got long. You must listen to what I have to say.' He struggled to catch his breath.

'Don't talk like that. You're on the mend . . .' Her voice trailed off as she realised that he had spoken the truth. She could feel him slipping away from her second by second. She leaned closer. 'Don't try to talk. The doctor will be here soon.'

'Listen to me.' His voice was little more than a whisper. 'I've done many wrong things, Sarah. I want to atone before it's too late.'

She tightened her grasp on his hand. 'You will get well and all this will be forgotten.'

He was silent for a moment, fighting for each rasping breath. 'Elsie had a child.'

'Moorcroft told me all about it, but the baby died.'

'No, she didn't. George had the infant taken to the workhouse. She was raised in St Giles, just like you.

Trigg blurted it out one night when he was the worse for drink.'

'But that's terrible.' For a moment she wondered if it was the fever that had affected his mind, but the intensity of his gaze convinced her that he was speaking the truth. 'Elsie thought her baby was dead.'

'I told her on her deathbed that her child lived.' He took a deep, shuddering breath and his cheeks paled to ashen.

'Don't tire yourself.' Sarah chafed his cold hands in an attempt to revive him. 'Don't say any more. You must rest now.'

'I have to tell you everything,' he said urgently. 'Trigg discovered the baby girl's true identity and he black-mailed George.'

'You told me once that Trigg paid your fine in court, but I could never understand why he would do something like that. It wasn't like him to be generous.'

'He'd seen me at the house in Spital Square and he knew I was related to the Fitch family. He spotted a chance to make even more money from my uncle by threatening to expose me as a petty crook, and when that failed he made me work for him until the debt was repaid with interest. I was a fool to get involved . . .' He broke off, struggling for breath as he fell back on the pillow.

'You mustn't worry about anything, Grey. You must concentrate on getting well again. Moorcroft will see to it that justice is done.'

'It's too late for me, Sarah. I'm done for.'

'You mustn't say things like that.'

'The truth weighs heavily on my conscience. I should have told Elsie that her child lived as soon as I found out, but I didn't because I was a coward. I didn't want her to know that I was involved with a criminal like Trigg.'

'None of that matters now, Grey.'

'Yes, it does. I want to die with a clear conscience. You must find her daughter and make sure she's all right.'

'I'll try but it won't be easy. How old would she be now?'

'A year or two older than you.'

'Do you remember her name?'

Grey's eyes opened wider and he gripped her hand so hard that she cried out with pain. His lips formed a word but she could not hear what he was trying to tell her. 'What are you saying?'

'Nan . . .' The word escaped from his lips like a sigh and his head fell to one side. His eyes were closed as if he had fallen into a peaceful sleep.

'Grey. Speak to me.' Sarah laid her head on his chest, listening in vain for a heartbeat. 'No . . .' She buried her face in her arms and sobbed.

'I can't have a dead body in one of my best rooms.' Mrs Kenny stood arms akimbo, glaring at Sarah. 'It's bad for business. I'll send my boy for the undertaker.'

'No.' Sarah dashed her hand across her eyes. 'I must take him home.'

Mrs Kenny raised an eyebrow. 'And where is that, may I ask?'

'I don't think it's any of your business. My friend will be here soon and then we'll make arrangements.'

A flicker of doubt crossed Mrs Kenny's face. 'Well he'd better hurry because I want you out of here by tonight. Anyway, it's best if you leave under the cover of darkness. I don't want the neighbours to see a corpse being carted out of the house.' She turned on her heel and marched out of the room.

Sarah remained at the bedside, keeping a vigil over Grey's body as it lay cold and still beneath the sheet. Even though she knew he had gone from her, she still found it hard to believe that he could have succumbed to a simple fever when he had survived shipwreck and near drowning, but the sea had claimed his life as surely as if he had been swallowed up by the waves. It seemed that she had only to love someone and they were taken from her. The Thames had robbed her of her father, and she had watched her mother die in the squalid surroundings of the workhouse labour ward. Elsie had survived the fire only to succumb to her injuries and now Grey was dead. He had been a fallible human being and had fallen into a life of crime, but she had always felt safe in his company, and there was no one who could fill the gap his passing had left in her heart and in her life.

She wept until she could cry no more, and she must have fallen asleep as she was awakened by the sound of voices and footsteps outside her room. The door opened and she snapped upright in her chair, blinking as her eyes grew accustomed to candlelight.

'Sarah, my dear. We've just heard the sad news.'

'Mr Moorcroft.' She rose stiffly to her feet and flung herself into his arms. 'You came.'

'Of course I did, Sarah. When I heard Davey's account of your trials nothing would keep me from you.'

She glanced over his shoulder and saw Davey standing beside Mrs Kenny. He hurried to her side. 'I'm so sorry,' he said softly.

'Grey's gone,' Sarah murmured, choking back a sob. 'He died this morning.'

'And I want the corpse out of here,' Mrs Kenny said firmly. 'This is a respectable lodging house and I've got my reputation to think of. There's nothing that will put customers off more than a death in one of the letting rooms.'

Moorcroft turned on her, glowering. 'While I appreciate your concern, my good woman, I can assure you that we will take all the necessary steps. Now if you want to be of assistance I suggest you send for a laying-out nurse and an undertaker.'

'No.' Sarah clasped his hand. 'I want Grey taken home to Blackwood. I don't want to leave him here where no one knew him.'

Davey slipped his arm around her waist, giving her a comforting hug. 'I'm sure it can be arranged.'

Moorcroft nodded. 'Of course. And I'm sure that Mrs Kenny will see that my instructions are carried out.'

'Yes, sir.' Mrs Kenny backed away. 'I'll see to it now.'

Moorcroft waited until the door closed on her. 'Dreadful woman. I wouldn't spend the night here if

404

she gave me bed and board for nothing.' He turned to Sarah with an encouraging smile. 'You look exhausted, my dear. We'll wait until the undertaker arrives and then we'll set off.'

'We're travelling overnight?' Sarah looked from one to the other. 'But you must be tired after coming all the way from London.'

'I've booked rooms at the hotel not far from here,' Moorcroft said, glancing round the room with a look of distaste. 'We'll catch the London train in the morning and break our journey there. Sophia is eager to see you and so is Nettie.'

'What happened about her audition?'

'She's got a part in Boucicault's latest play at the Lyceum,' Davey said enthusiastically. 'I've forgotten what it's called but she can't talk about anything else.'

'Perhaps this isn't the right time to talk about it,' Moorcroft said softly.

'I'm glad for her,' Sarah said dully. 'But at the moment I can't really think straight.'

Moorcroft took Davey aside. 'It's the living we must take care of now, my boy. I want you to take Sarah to the hotel and order dinner for all three of us. I'll settle matters here and follow on as soon as I can.'

Sarah pulled back the sheet and dropped a kiss on Grey's forehead. 'I'll take you to Blackwood. You're going home, Tobias Grey.'

They arrived in Elbow Lane in the early afternoon. The events of the previous day were a blur in Sarah's mind, but after a good night's sleep in a comfortable bed she was feeling more able to cope with what lay ahead. Mrs Arbuthnot was sincere in her welcome, and below stairs in the warmth of the kitchen Sarah had an eager audience in Cook, Dorcas and Betty, who wanted to hear every detail of her trip to France and bombarded her with questions. She was plied with tea and seed cake and each of them in turn begged her to remain in London.

'You don't want to go back to that draughty old house in the wilds of Essex,' Cook said, refilling Sarah's teacup for the second time. 'We've got room for you here now that young Nettie's living in digs nearer the theatre. Dorcas and me have got tickets for her first night. I can't wait to see her on stage.'

Dorcas offered her another slice of cake. 'I've made it up with Wally and we'll be getting married soon, Sarah. I'm sure that the mistress would take you on in my place.'

Betty shuffled across the floor to sit by Sarah's side. 'I'd like you to stay. I misses you something terrible.' She shot a resentful glance at Dorcas. 'She slaps me round the lughole for nothing. Bad-tempered bitch.'

'Language, Betty,' Cook said, frowning. 'Dorcas has every right to discipline you when you do wrong.'

Betty huddled up against Sarah's knee. 'I'd like to live in that house in the country. Can I come with you?'

Sarah stroked Betty's lank mousey hair back from her forehead. 'Not today, love. I'm not sure what I'll be doing. I think the house belongs to Mr Fitch now, and he won't want me there.'

'What about that handsome young chap who came

to fetch Mr Moorcroft?' Dorcas said, eyeing Sarah curiously. 'There's a romance in the air if I'm not mistaken.'

'You hear wedding bells everywhere.' Cook chuckled and all her chins wobbled. 'Ever since Miss Parfitt and Franz announced their engagement there's been wedding fever in this house, Sarah. You're lucky you've missed it all.'

'Miss Parfitt is going to be married?'

'In a few weeks' time,' Dorcas said smugly. 'But Wally and me will beat her to it. You'll come to our wedding, won't you?'

'Of course,' Sarah said, smiling dazedly. 'It's a lot to take in at once, but I'll be here if I can. The trouble is that I don't know what's happening to Davey and his brothers and sister. I have to go back to Blackwood for Grey's funeral and Davey needs to find a new home for himself and the children.' She rose to her feet, gently freeing her skirt from Betty's clutching fingers. 'You be a good girl now, Betty, and I'll see you again very soon.'

Cook's mouth turned down at the corners. 'Think about what I said, Sarah. There's a job here when Dorcas goes. You could do worse and I'm sure that the mistress will agree to take you on.'

'Thank you all for being so kind.' Sarah turned away to hide the tears that had sprung to her eyes. She did not want to disgrace herself by crying in front of them, nor did she want to upset Betty who would almost certainly join in and start howling. 'I'd best go upstairs before they come looking for me.'

She found Davey and Moorcroft in the parlour conversing earnestly with Mrs Arbuthnot.

'I'm just leaving,' Moorcroft said, turning to Sarah with a tired smile. 'It's been a long day but it's not over yet. I'm going straight to Spital Square to see George Fitch. He is the next of kin and must be notified.'

'I'm coming with you.' Sarah met his surprised look with a steady gaze. 'I think he hid Elsie's will because he knew that she'd left the house to Grey.'

'That's a serious accusation,' Moorcroft said slowly. 'Can you prove it?'

'Of course not, but he's capable of anything. Did Davey tell you that Fitch has been dealing with the free traders? That's why he allowed the rumours of Blackwood House being haunted to circulate and frighten off visitors. He didn't want anyone to discover the secret passage that leads to the church crypt, and the regular cargoes of contraband that find their way to Blackwood's cellars.'

Moorcroft's eyebrows almost disappeared into his hairline. 'Is this true?'

'It's true, sir.' Davey nodded emphatically. 'I'll bear witness to that and I can name a dozen or more people who'll testify against Fitch.'

'What does all this mean, Martin?' Mrs Arbuthnot looked from one to the other. 'It sounds very serious.'

'It changes everything,' Moorcroft said, running his hand through his grizzled hair. 'I need to speak to my former client right away, and you should accompany me, Sarah.'

'Me too, sir.' Davey moved swiftly to Sarah's side. 'I'll have a few words to say to Mr Fitch.'

'No, my boy. I think it best if you return to your

village. You must go to Blackwood House and make sure that your sister and brothers are all right. If George has sent Mrs Trigg to evict them they could be in serious trouble.'

Sarah caught Davey's eye and shook her head. She knew that he was thinking of the body caught up in the embrace of the yew tree tunnel. The thaw must have set in by now, and unless Parker had managed to dispose of the corpse it would be decomposing. 'Yes, Davey,' she said, fixing him with a meaningful stare. 'Please go to Blackwood and make sure that everything is all right. Parker isn't the most forgiving or patient of men and your brothers can be very lively. The children need you.'

'Yes, of course.' He hesitated. 'But there's a question of funds. I'm sorry, Mr Moorcroft, but I'll have to ask if I may borrow the train fare. I'll repay you as soon as I'm able to.'

Moorcroft put his hand in his pocket and took out a handful of coins. 'This should be enough to keep you and your family for a while. You won't be able to go fishing until your broken bones mend.'

'Thank you, sir. I'm indebted to you.' Davey's cheeks flushed and he looked away.

Sarah could feel his embarrassment and she linked her hand through his arm. 'Don't worry. We'll get through this somehow, Davey. I'll follow you to Blackwood as soon as I can. I've a funeral to arrange and I know that Grey would want to be buried in the family plot. That's something else I want to discuss with Mr Fitch.'

* * *

George Fitch sat behind his large desk, steepling his fingers. 'Well, Martin, what have you to say? I'm a busy man and I don't have time to spare on trivialities.'

'The first thing I have to do is to tell you that your nephew, Tobias Grey, passed away after a short illness.'

George's jaw dropped as he digested this piece of news. 'So he's escaped the law after all. I always knew he was a slippery character.'

'That's not fair,' Sarah cried angrily. 'You placed false charges against him. Grey didn't do anything wrong.'

'What's she doing here, Martin? My agent, Mrs Trigg, told me that this little troublemaker was trespassing on my property.'

'I came because Grey wanted to be buried in the family plot,' Sarah said without giving Moorcroft a chance to respond. 'And it was Grey who took me to Blackwood House, so I wasn't trespassing as you put it. He had as much right as anyone to be there. In fact, it was probably left to him in Elsie's will, the document that has so mysteriously disappeared.'

George slammed his hands down on the tooled leather top of his desk. 'You can't prove anything. The whole estate belongs to me now.'

'So you admit that you are responsible for the property?' Moorcroft betrayed nothing by his expression or tone of voice.

'Of course,' George said firmly. 'I am the legal owner, and I've sent my agent to evict those who have no right to be in my property.'

'Does that include the smugglers?' The words

tumbled from her lips before Sarah could stop herself.

George leapt to his feet. 'Get out of my house. I won't have you making such preposterous accusations against me. Martin, you're my lawyer, I want to sue her for slander.'

'I gave up that onerous task some time ago as you will recall, Mr Fitch,' Moorcroft said calmly. 'There are witnesses who will testify in court that Blackwood House has been used to store contraband for many years, and that there is a secret passage leading to the crypt of the village church.'

'Utter nonsense,' George spluttered. 'And if anyone has been using the house in my absence then it's Parker who is to blame. I don't know anything about it.'

'But you've just told us that Mrs Trigg is your agent,' Sarah said smoothly. 'And she organises the collection of the smuggled goods and their transport to your warehouse in London.'

'Then she is the criminal. I trusted that woman to do my business for me and this is how she repays me. My depot is filled with Spitalfields silk, ready for export to the Americas. I don't deal in contraband.' George began pacing the floor in an agitated manner that was not lost on Sarah.

'Then it won't worry you that the revenue men are at this moment on their way to examine the contents of your warehouse,' Moorcroft said, rising to his feet. 'I notified them before I came here this morning. They will also search Blackwood House and its cellars, but if you have nothing to hide then you need not worry.'

George's face reddened and his eyes bulged. 'Get out of here and take that little trollop with you. You shouldn't believe a word she says. She's a little whore who thought she could get her hands on the estate by sleeping with my nephew because he told her that he would inherit Blackwood when Elsie died. I wouldn't be surprised if they murdered my sister so that they could get their hands on her money.'

Sarah flew at him, fingers clawed. Taking him by surprise, she raked her nails down his cheek. Uttering an oath, he gave her a mighty shove that sent her tumbling to the floor. He clutched his hand to his bleeding face. 'Get her out of here, Moorcroft, or I'll send for a constable to arrest her for assault on my person.'

Moorcroft helped Sarah to rise. 'You deserved that, Fitch. And I don't think you'll press charges because you won't want the police involved. You're already in a great deal of trouble. I suggest you hire a solicitor who is less particular in his choice of clients than I am.' He took Sarah by the arm. 'We're leaving.'

Outside in the square Moorcroft hailed a hansom cab. 'We've started something now,' he said as he climbed in after Sarah. 'I've known George for many years and he'll stop at nothing to get his own way.'

'But he's guilty. He's been dealing in contraband for years, and there's something else.' She stared straight ahead, unable to look him in the face. 'It's something that Grey told me with his dying breath.'

'What is it, Sarah? You can tell me anything.'

'I know I can, sir. But this affects you personally, or I think it does.'

'Go on.'

'He told me that Elsie's baby was a girl and that she didn't die at birth. George Fitch had her taken to the St Giles workhouse and abandoned her there.' She shot him a sideways glance and was alarmed to see his jaw muscle tighten and the glint of tears in his eyes. 'I'm sorry, but it might be good news, sir. She might still be living in London.'

'I can't believe that even George would give up his own flesh and blood to be reared in such appalling circumstances,' he said dazedly. 'It would have broken Elsie's heart had she ever discovered the truth.'

'Grey told her on her deathbed, but I'm certain that she would have been happy to know that her child lived,' Sarah said softly. 'It's possible that you might have a daughter.'

He took a large white cotton handkerchief from his pocket and blew his nose. 'It's not very likely, Sarah, and even if she survived the workhouse she could be anywhere in the country.' He stowed his hanky away, adopting a brisk attitude. 'Now we must work quickly. George can't afford to let matters lie. We should go to Blackwood House immediately.'

'I agree. That man has a lot to answer for.'

'Indeed he does. I've already notified the police in London, but if George gets there first he'll destroy all the physical evidence, and Mrs Trigg will back him up because she stands to lose everything including her freedom.'

'I'm afraid for the children.'

'We'll stop at my lodgings and I'll collect a change

of linen, and then we'll go on to Elbow Lane and put Sophia in the picture. I don't want her worrying herself sick over what might happen to me. I mean us. She's very fond of you, Sarah.'

'I'm coming with you.' Mrs Arbuthnot faced them with a martial glint in her eyes. 'I'm not missing this for anything, Martin, so you can just wait while I pack a few things and then I'll be ready to leave.'

'But my dear Sophia, this might prove to be dangerous. George isn't a man to toy with, and there is a lot at stake here.'

'Do you think I'm afraid?' Mrs Arbuthnot drew herself up to her full height. 'If George Fitch is involved with that dreadful Trigg woman I have a score to settle with them both. My poor James was ruined by her husband and I daresay she knew all about it and egged him on. I want them both punished.'

Sarah could see that Moorcroft was at a loss. 'But things might turn nasty, Mrs Arbuthnot. The yew tree tunnel holds a terrible secret.'

Chapter Twenty-Four

Despite Sarah's forebodings all was quiet when they finally arrived at Blackwood House. 'It's a fine place,' Moorcroft said as he helped Mrs Arbuthnot alight from the carriage that had transported them from Maldon station. 'No wonder you speak so highly of it, Sarah.'

She smiled vaguely. 'I hope everything is all right.'

'Lead the way, my dear,' Mrs Arbuthnot said, shaking the creases from her wide skirts. 'We'll follow on.'

Sarah left Moorcroft arguing about the fare with the driver who had apparently almost doubled the price he originally quoted. She picked up her skirts and walked briskly along the gravel path that ran alongside the yew tree tunnel. Her heart was racing as she peered into the thick branches, but if Trigg was still entwined within its deep green depths there was no outward sign of his presence. She quickened her pace at the sound of childish voices and ran into the stable yard to find the boys playing ball, and Mary pegging clothes on a makeshift washing line. It was a pleasing domestic scene utterly at odds with the mayhem she had been imagining all the way from London.

Mary dropped the small garment she was about to hang out and ran towards her with a cry of delight. 'You're home. I'm so glad to see you.'

Jonah and Lemuel stopped in the middle of their game and crowded round them. 'Did you bring us anything?' Jonah demanded with a cheeky grin.

'Shame on you,' Mary said, giving him a playful slap. 'Where are your manners?'

Sarah smiled. 'I've brought a very kind lady and gentleman to see you, and Mrs Arbuthnot's cook sent a whole basket of nice things to eat, including cake.'

'Cake?' Lemuel's eyes shone with expectation. 'Where is it?'

'What sort of cake?' Jonah demanded, licking his lips. 'I can't remember the last time we had cake.'

'Run as fast as you can to the carriage sweep and help them with their luggage,' Sarah said, laughing. 'Show them to the drawing room and we'll be in directly.' They had run off before the last word left her lips. She turned to Mary, shaking her head. 'What a pair of rogues.'

Mary's blue eyes darkened and her mouth drooped at the corners. 'Davey told us what happened to Grey, and although I didn't really know him it made me cry a lot because he was your friend.'

Sarah gave her a hug. 'Thank you, Mary. I'm glad you've forgiven me for putting Davey in danger. He was very brave and he saved Grey's life.'

'But he died anyway.'

'Yes, but we did everything we could for him.' She hesitated, not quite knowing how to broach the subject. 'The undertakers were instructed to bring his coffin home . . .'

'It's in the parlour,' Mary said hastily. 'Me and the

boys won't go in there, but Davey says he's spoken to the vicar about the funeral. I dunno what they arranged.' She put the final peg on a small shirt and picked up the empty basket. 'Come inside and I'll make us a pot of tea. I expect you could do with one after travelling all the way from London.'

'That sounds wonderful, and I'm sure our visitors would be most grateful.'

'Who are they? It's not Mrs Trigg, that's for sure. I wouldn't describe her as a kind lady.'

'No, it's not Mrs Trigg. It's a gentleman called Mr Moorcroft and Mrs Arbuthnot, the lady who looked after me when I left the workhouse.' Sarah followed Mary into the scullery. 'They've come here to help us.'

'We don't need help now you're here.' Mary placed the empty washing basket on the draining board and went into the kitchen. 'Davey will be pleased to see you.'

'Where is he?' Sarah asked eagerly. The memory of his kiss had never been far from her thoughts since they parted in Dover, and her pulses raced at the mere mention of his name.

'He's gone shooting with Parker.' Mary bustled about, fetching cups and saucers from the dresser. 'Not that he can do much with one good arm, but he's been fidgety ever since he arrived home. Something's up, I know it.'

'It's nothing for you to worry about.' Sarah went to the larder to take the milk jug from the marble shelf. 'I see that you've managed to get supplies from the farm.'

'No, it's better than that. We've got a goat,' Mary said proudly. 'Parker swapped it for a keg of rum or brandy, I don't know which. We've had all sorts of things since you've been gone. Parker goes off at night to do the business and one day he came back with a goat. I'm learning to milk it but it's not as easy as it looks.'

'And you haven't had any visits from Trigg's men?'

Mary shook her head. 'No, but Parker's expecting them soon. The cellar should be piled high with stuff but he said there's not a lot left now. I hope there won't be trouble.'

Sarah digested this in silence. Everything was calm and peaceful at the moment, but it would not be long before George Fitch descended upon them, and it was only a matter of time before Mrs Trigg came searching once again for her errant husband.

Her hand shook as she laid the cups and saucers on a tray together with the jug of milk. 'I'll take this to the drawing room,' she said in an attempt to sound calm and matter of fact. 'If you'd like to bring the teapot, Mary, I'll introduce you to our guests.'

'Why do we need their help?' Mary demanded. 'We're all right as we are. I could stay here forever, or at least until Davey is able to go back to sea. I suppose he'll have to crew for one of the other fishermen until he can save enough to buy another boat.'

'Yes, I suppose so. Come along. You'll love Mrs Arbuthnot, she's the kindest person I've ever met.'

'We don't need no one else,' Mary muttered as she followed Sarah from the room. 'We're happy here and Parker's going to get some chickens next time he goes out trading. We'll have as many eggs as we can eat and maybe he'll get a pig as well.'

Sarah was sitting in the candlelit parlour keeping a vigil by the coffin when Davey entered the room. She rose swiftly to her feet. 'Thank goodness you've come,' she whispered. 'I've been waiting for you.'

'I've just been speaking to Mr Moorcroft. He told me to expect a visit from Fitch.' He held her at arm's length, anxiously scanning her face. 'Are you all right?'

'Not really.' She laid her hand on the polished oak surface of the coffin. 'I couldn't believe that Grey was gone at first, but now it's real and I know I'll never see him again.'

'You told me you didn't care for him in that way.'

She met his puzzled gaze with a vague smile. 'It's not as simple as that, Davey. He was my friend and protector. He has a special place in my heart.' She stroked the satiny patina of the wood. 'It's hard to explain, but there was never anything romantic between us. He was a lot older than me for one thing, and if he had feelings for any woman it wasn't me. I think he fell in love with Miss Parfitt the moment he saw her. I sensed it even though I was just a nipper.'

'He never mentioned her.'

'She only had eyes for Franz Beckman, the master sugar baker. In fact they're to be married soon and I doubt if she ever suspected how Grey felt about her. At least he's spared that heartbreak now.' She looked up at him and smiled. 'You almost gave your life to save him. I can't tell you how much that means to me.'

'I'd do anything for you, Sarah. Just tell me what you want and I'll do it.'

She slid her arms around his waist, looking deeply into his eyes. 'We'll need to be strong for everyone, Davey. All hell is going to break loose when Fitch arrives, especially if he brings Mrs Trigg with him. Mary told me that Parker has been selling off the contraband and we need to have the cellar filled with smuggled goods if we're to prove that Fitch is involved.'

He frowned. 'I hadn't thought of that. I've been away a long time so I don't know when the next shipment will arrive.'

'I think there's someone who might know – Moses, the wall-eyed fisherman who drinks at the Ferryboat Inn.'

'You're right. I'll go there tonight and see what I can get out of him.' He bent his head and gave her a lingering kiss on the lips.

'Don't, Davey.' She drew away from him. 'It's not that I don't like being kissed by you, but when you touch me I just can't think straight.'

A pleased smile curved his lips. 'That's the general idea.'

She wanted to laugh but it did not seem right in the circumstances. 'This isn't about us.'

'Of course it is, sweetheart.'

'No, it isn't, Davey. Can't you see that the future of Blackwood House and maybe the whole village is at stake here? George Fitch would see us all in the work-house rather than let us stay here, and we've nowhere else to go.'

'We'd manage, Sarah. You could marry me. I'd look after you.'

'You'll be hard pressed to support Mary and the boys, let alone a wife. We'll have to wait a long time before either of us can think of getting married.'

He took her hand and held it to his heart. 'Will you, though? Will you wait for me to make good?'

She was about to answer when the door opened and Lemuel burst into the room. 'Come quick. There's a carriage pulling up outside and it might be that bad woman looking for the dead man. Parker told me all about him being swallowed up by the yew tree tunnel. I always knew it was a bad place.'

'Don't say things like that,' Sarah said, taking him by the shoulders and shaking him. 'It's our secret. No one must know or we'll all be in terrible trouble.'

Lemuel's bottom lip trembled. 'I never meant to say the wrong thing.'

She hugged him to her. 'Of course you didn't, but remember what I've just told you.' She sent an agonised glance to Davey. 'This could be the start of it.'

He made for the door. 'I'm going to find Moses. I'll use the secret passage so that our visitor doesn't see me leave.'

'Be careful,' she called after him. 'Don't take risks, Davey. I don't want to lose you too.' She took Lemuel by the hand. 'Let's go and see who's calling on us so late in the day.'

They reached the front door just as Mary opened it and a stream of damp air flooded into the entrance hall, rattling doors and lifting the holland covers that remained draped over the furniture.

'Crikey, what a place.' Nettie stood in the doorway, staring round in wide-eyed astonishment. 'You never told me you'd been living in a bloody castle.'

Sarah flung her arms around her. 'Oh, Nettie. I'm so glad to see you, but why are you here? I thought you'd landed a big part in a play.'

'It's just a walk-on,' Nettie said casually. 'I'm not needed for a day or two and my digs were disgusting, so I went to Elbow Lane to see if I could stay there until I'd found something better.' She paused for breath and her eyes filled with tears. 'Dorcas told me what had happened. I'm so sorry about Tobias. He was a good bloke and I wanted to pay my respects.'

'I still can't believe that he's gone.' Sarah dashed a tear from her cheek and turned her attention to Mary and Lemuel, who were gaping at Nettie's colourful attire. 'This is my very good friend Nettie Bean. We've known each other since we were children.'

'How do?' Nettie said, extending a mittened hand to Mary. 'And what's your name, poppet?'

Mary bobbed a curtsey. 'It's Mary, miss. And this is me brother, Lemuel.'

'I ain't no one's poppet, lady.' Lemuel backed away, eyeing Nettie doubtfully. 'I got things to do.' He ran off in the direction of the kitchen.

'Don't take any notice of him,' Sarah said, chuckling. 'He probably thinks you've come to evict them from the house. We don't get many visitors here.'

Nettie wrinkled her nose. 'I'm not surprised. It's a bit gloomy, not to say spooky.'

'It's nothing of the kind.' Sarah linked her hand through Nettie's arm. 'Come into the drawing room and get warm. You're just in time for supper.'

They were seated round the kitchen table enjoying the ham and pickles provided by Mrs Arbuthnot when Davey burst into the room. 'I thought you'd gone to the inn to find Moses,' Sarah said anxiously. 'What happened?'

'There wasn't any need. When I reached the crypt I found it stacked with contraband. Parker and I have just finished moving it to the cellar, and I sent him to the village to warn everyone that the excise men will be raiding Blackwood House in the very near future.' He took his seat at the table opposite Moorcroft. 'That's right, wasn't it, guv? You tipped them off when you reported Fitch to the police.'

'I most certainly did, and they're probably on their way here as we speak. You've done well, Davey. Now all we have to do is to wait and see.'

'Will there be fighting?' Jonah's eyes shone with anticipation. 'Can I have a cutlass like a pirate?'

'And me,' Lemuel added excitedly. 'We can bury the dead bodies with the old man.'

'That's enough of that.' Sarah sent him a warning glance. 'It's his vivid imagination,' she added, noting Mrs Arbuthnot's anxious look. 'He gets carried away by it at times.'

'Yes,' Mary said emphatically. 'We never buried no one in the woods. It's just a story I told the boys.'

'That's some tale at bedtime,' Mrs Arbuthnot said, laughing. 'It would be enough to give the little fellows nightmares.'

Nettie speared a pickled onion with her fork. 'I'm glad I came. This is all very exciting. But I doubt if I'll get a wink of sleep tonight.' She glanced around with a theatrical shiver. 'Is this place haunted?'

'Certainly not.' Sarah frowned at Jonah who was obviously bursting to tell Nettie about the yew tree tunnel. 'That's the sort of tale that the older children used to frighten us with in the workhouse.'

Mrs Arbuthnot held her table napkin to her lips. 'Oh dear, you poor girls.'

Nettie gulped down a mouthful of food. 'Don't upset yourself, ma'am. We had a good laugh sometimes, didn't we, Sarah? Like the time when Mrs Trigg fell over dead drunk and we saw her drawers.'

Lemuel and Jonah almost fell off their seats giggling and Mary stared open-mouthed at Nettie. 'I'd get smacked for saying that,' she whispered.

'Ah, but I'm a grown-up and I'm too big to be slapped,' Nettie said, grinning mischievously. 'But I had me backside tanned no end of times by the Tickler when I was in the workhouse, and that weren't funny. If I had old Trigg here now I'd snap me fingers in his face and tell the old devil to go to hell.'

Moorcroft smiled benevolently. 'My dear, you're a tonic.'

'I think you ought to moderate your language in front of the little ones,' Mrs Arbuthnot said firmly, but Sarah noticed that her lips twitched and she exchanged

424

amused glances with Moorcroft. There was definitely something going on between them, Sarah decided, and that could only be a good thing. Two such nice people ought to get together and give each other mutual comfort, even if they were old.

'I never know when to keep me mouth shut,' Nettie said ruefully. 'It's what comes of not having a proper upbringing. I was dumped in the workhouse when I was just a few days old, or so Trigg liked to tell me. He used to say that even me own mother couldn't stand the sight of me because I had hair the colour of boiled carrots. Who would credit someone saying that to a nipper?'

'Do you know anything about your parents, my dear?' Mrs Arbuthnot was suddenly serious.

Nettie shrugged her shoulders. 'Not a thing, ma'am.'

'There's nothing wrong with copper-coloured hair,' Moorcroft said stoutly. 'I knew a young lady who had hair the very same colour as yours, Nettie, and she . . .' He broke off, staring at Nettie as if seeing her for the first time. 'How old are you, my dear?'

'I'm nearly nineteen, sir.'

Sarah's hand flew to cover her mouth as she uttered a gasp of surprise. Why had she not seen it before? The likeness was startling. She glanced at Moorcroft but he was concentrating all his attention on Nettie. 'Was your name given to the workhouse master when you were brought there as a baby?'

'I dunno, sir.' Nettie bit into a slice of bread, chewed and swallowed. 'What's up?' she demanded. 'Why are you all staring at me?'

'Because any information you have is vital,' Moorcroft said gently. 'Think hard, Nettie.'

She shrugged her shoulders and reached for another slice of meat. 'I've been living off cold pies and watercress for the last two days. I don't get me wages until the end of the month and I'm broke.' She glanced at Moorcroft and smiled. 'Sorry, you was asking about me real name. They told me it was Nanette, but they changed it to Nettie and they gave me the name Bean. I never knew why they chose that but I suppose it's as good as any.'

Moorcroft rose to his feet. 'If you'll excuse me, I would like to go outside and get some air.'

'Are you unwell, Martin?' Mrs Arbuthnot clutched her hand to her throat, eyeing him in alarm. 'Would you like me to accompany you?'

He laid his hand on her shoulder. 'Thank you, Sophia, but I have a lot to think about. I'll say goodnight, my dear.' He hurried from the room.

'What was all that about?' Nettie turned to Sarah with a puzzled look. 'Did I say something wrong?'

'No, of course not,' Sarah said hastily. 'It's been a long and tiring day and it's time that Jonah and Lemuel were in bed. You too, Mary.' She stood up to marshal the children out of the kitchen, giving Mary a chamber candlestick to light their way to bed. 'Tomorrow is going to be a very busy day,' she said when they protested. 'All sorts of exciting things will happen and I need you to be very brave.'

'Will you read us a story before we go to sleep?' Lemuel glanced nervously at the place where the stairs disappeared into the darkness. 'Are there really ghosts, Sarah?'

She bent down to drop a kiss on his curly head. 'Of course not. It's just a story put about by wicked Mr Fitch to keep people from discovering the secrets of Blackwood House. But tomorrow when the revenue men raid the cellars he'll find that his plan didn't work.'

'But we'll have to leave here, won't we?' Mary whispered. 'It's his house now and he'll throw us out.'

'I don't know what will happen, but we'll stick together even if we have to live in what's left of Davey's boat.' She kissed Mary on the cheek but Jonah backed away.

'I'm a big boy,' he muttered. 'Big boys don't get kissed.'

'That's where you're wrong, Joe.' Davey had come up behind them unnoticed. 'I think Sarah told you to go to bed. I'm going to count to ten and if you haven't got to the top of the stairs by then . . .' The boys raced on ahead with Mary following at a more dignified pace. Davey turned to Sarah with a wide smile. 'It works every time, but he was wrong about big boys not wanting to be kissed.'

She pushed him away, laughing. 'Not now, Davey. I've been thinking about your boat.'

He pulled a face. 'That's not very flattering, sweetheart.'

'Be serious for a moment. I was trying to cheer the children up and I said we could live in your boat. I don't mean we should do that, but what state is the hull in? Could it be repaired for you to take to sea?'

'Of course it could, but that would cost money which I haven't got. I was planning to sell what's left of the hulk. We'll need the money for rent if Fitch throws us out, which I'm sure will happen very soon.'

'But if you could get the money to fix your boat, that would be even better. You could go back to sea when your arm heals. You'd be able to earn a living.'

'Would you give up all this to marry a fisherman?'

'Blackwood House doesn't belong to me, Davey.'

'Would you settle for village life and the smell of fish?'

'I love you, Davey, but I want to continue Elsie's work. I've spent years learning about herbal cures and one day, when I'm older and more experienced, I'd like to set up a pharmacy.'

He stared at her, frowning. 'I didn't know you felt like that.'

'Would you stand in my way, or would you help me?' She reached out to hold his hand. 'I couldn't do it unless I had your support.'

'I wouldn't stop you doing anything you really wanted to do, my love.'

'Davey.' The sound of Parker's voice echoed off the wainscoting in the entrance hall as he came running towards them, his footsteps clattering loudly on the polished floorboards. 'They're here. Trigg's men have come to collect the goods.'

Chapter Twenty-Five

'I've locked them in,' Parker said breathlessly. 'I didn't know what else to do.'

'Are they here alone?' Sarah clutched Davey's arm. 'What do we do if Mrs Trigg and Fitch have come with them? They'll clear the place out and be gone before the revenue men arrive.'

'It's no good locking them in our cellar, Parker. They can get away down the secret tunnel.'

Parker bowed his head. 'I didn't think of that, son.'

'One of you must warn the vicar,' Sarah said urgently. 'Get him to lock the crypt door so that they can't get out that way.'

'I'll go.' Davey headed for the front door. 'I can run faster than you, Parker.'

'But I know a shortcut through the woods. I can get there in half the time and you're in no condition to go racing across country.' Parker strode across the hall and let himself out through the front door.

'You're still recovering from your injuries,' Sarah said severely. 'You have to be careful you don't hurt your arm again, Davey.'

'Don't fuss, girl.' He tempered his words with a

smile. 'We'd better warn the others and keep a watch in case Fitch decides to turn up before morning.'

Sarah slept little that night. She had had to share her bed with Nettie as all the habitable bedchambers were now occupied, and the rest were in such a state of dilapidation that it would take an army of cleaning women to make them fit for use. She had forgotten that Nettie talked in her sleep and when she pulled the coverlet off her for the umpteenth time Sarah had had enough. She got up, wrapped her shawl around her shoulders and went to sit in the chair by the window. The carriage sweep glittered with frost in the pale moonlight and the yew trees took on an even more sinister shape silhouetted as they were against the rime-encrusted lawn. A barn owl swooped past the window, graceful and deadly in its hunt for food, and the distant bark of a dog fox shattered the silence. She huddled in the chair, shivering in a chilly draught from the casement window, curling her bare feet under her in an attempt to keep them warm.

She must have dozed off, or else she was dreaming, but the sound of horses' hooves on the gravel was real enough and she was suddenly wide awake. Peering out of the window she saw that the grounds were suddenly alive with movement. In the pale green light of early dawn she saw men in uniform mustering in front of the house while others took charge of their mounts. Steam rose from the horses' coats and she could hear their snorts and whinnies mingling with the staccato bark of the officers' orders.

She leapt up and ran to the bed, shaking Nettie by

the shoulders. 'Wake up. The police are here and the revenue men too, unless I'm very much mistaken.'

'What? Go away, I'm asleep,' Nettie groaned, pulling the covers over her head. Sarah could see that it was useless to try to wake her. She dressed hastily and ran to Davey's room, hammering on the door and calling his name. Moments later he opened it, still wearing a night-shirt that had belonged to one of the former residents.

'What's the matter?'

'They've arrived. The police and revenue men are outside now.'

'We need to get our stories straight. I'll go downstairs to warn Parker, and you'd better rouse the others.' He closed the door without giving her a chance to argue.

Even before she had reached his room Moorcroft appeared in the corridor fully clothed. 'I heard them arrive,' he said tersely. 'I didn't disrobe last night as I had a feeling this would happen. Where's Davey?'

'He's getting dressed and then he's going downstairs to wake Parker.'

'I'll do that, and I suggest you assemble everyone else in the drawing room. We don't want to get in the way of the authorities.' He strode off towards the head of the stairs, leaving Sarah to knock on Mrs Arbuthnot's door. She had just roused her from her sleep when Mary came padding barefoot along the landing. Her blonde curls were tumbled about her head and in the half light she looked like a sleepy cherub. 'What's happening, Sarah?'

'The revenue men have come to catch the smugglers, so we must keep out of their way. Wake the boys and bring them down to the drawing room. We'll wait there.'

'All right. How exciting.' Mary danced off to fetch her brothers.

In spite of everything her enthusiasm brought a smile to Sarah's lips. To the children it was all a game, but only the adults would realise how high the stakes were.

'Sarah, dear. Would you come here and help me with my laces?' Mrs Arbuthnot called in a plaintive voice. 'I can't manage without Dorcas. It's very trying.'

Minutes later Sarah and Mrs Arbuthnot were descending the stairs when the sound of shouting and the pounding of footsteps made them falter. 'What's happening?' Mrs Arbuthnot whispered in Sarah's ear.

'It sounds like the Trigg woman. I'd know that voice anywhere.' Sarah hurtled down the remaining stairs and arrived in the entrance hall as Mrs Trigg forced her way between two burly constables.

'Don't you touch me,' she screamed. 'I'll have you know that I'm a respectable businesswoman. Mr Fitch will vouch for that.'

'She's a criminal,' Sarah cried, pointing a finger at Mrs Trigg whose feathered hat had fallen over one eye and the sleeve of her mantle was hanging in shreds as if someone had tried to restrain her and in the process had ripped the material. 'She's in with the smugglers. Just ask the men who are locked in the cellar.'

'They're nothing to do with me, you lying bitch.' Mrs Trigg lurched at her but the elder of the two constables seized her, pinning her arms to her sides.

'Now, now, madam,' he said sternly. 'Calm yourself and stop fighting. You'll come off the worst.'

She turned on him, baring her yellowed teeth in a

lupine snarl. 'I'll have you demoted to – to whatever is beneath your rank now. I have influential friends. Mr Fitch will be here directly and he'll put you in your place.'

'Is that so, madam? Then perhaps you'd best find somewhere to sit quietly and wait until he arrives.'

Sarah moved swiftly to fling the drawing-room door open. 'In here, constable. We'll keep an eye on her for you.'

Mrs Arbuthnot hurried to her side. 'Indeed we will. It will give me great pleasure to assist the law.'

'You're a stuck-up old cow.' Mrs Trigg spat on the floor. 'That's what I think of you, you sugar maker's whore.'

'That's enough of that, madam.' The police officer manhandled a protesting Mrs Trigg into the room. 'I'll leave this person to your care then, ladies.' He turned to his subordinate. 'Keep an eye on them, Barley. We've got enough on our hands today.'

'Yes, sir.' Barley saluted smartly as his superior walked away, passing Moorcroft who was coming from the direction of the kitchen.

'Your sergeant needs you, constable. He's having a bit of difficulty with two men he's apprehended in the cellar while the revenue men search for contraband.'

'I'm on my way, sir.' The constable hurried off and Moorcroft entered the drawing room, closing the door behind him.

'Just you wait until Mr Fitch arrives,' Mrs Trigg said mutinously. 'You'll suffer for this, Sal Scratch.'

Sarah clenched her hands at her sides, controlling her temper with a supreme effort. 'You're a wicked woman and you should be punished.'

'What a lot of boobies you are.' Mrs Trigg glared at each of them in turn. 'I could take you lot on with one hand tied behind my back, and I'll fetch you one if you come near me, old lady.'

Mrs Arbuthnot flew at her and, catching her unawares, gave Mrs Trigg a shove that sent her staggering against the wall. 'You killed my husband. You're an evil woman.'

Mrs Trigg curled her lip. 'And you're a fat old fool.'

'Don't speak to her like that,' Sarah cried angrily. 'You'll keep a civil tongue in your head while you're in this house.'

'It's Mr Fitch's house and he'll send the whole lot of you packing as soon as he gets here. It'll be the workhouse for you, Sal Scratch. It's where you came from and it's where you'll end up.'

'Not while I have a breath left in my body.' Mrs Arbuthnot yanked Mrs Trigg's hat down over her eyes with such force that one of the ostrich feathers came away in her hand. She threw it onto the embers in the grate where it sputtered and burst into flames. 'There! That's what I think of you, madam.'

Sarah stepped in between them as Mrs Trigg struggled to get her hat off and Mrs Arbuthnot squared up to her like a prize fighter. Lemuel and Jonah were jumping up and down, chanting 'Fight,' while Mary looked on open-mouthed.

'Stop it, both of you.' Sarah had to raise her voice in order to make herself heard and Constable Barley stepped in to restrain Mrs Arbuthnot, who was muttering about having an old score to settle.

'Now, now, ladies,' he said mildly. 'Let's behave with a bit of decorum, shall we?'

'She killed my husband,' Mrs Arbuthnot cried, fisting her small hands. 'She burned down our sugar mill and ruined us.'

'Oh, shut up and sit down, you stupid mare.' Mrs Trigg sank onto a chair, fanning herself with her ruined hat. 'I'm saying nothing until my boss gets here. He'll sort you out, just you wait and see.'

Sarah led Mrs Arbuthnot to the sofa and pressed her down onto the cushions. 'She's not worth it, ma'am. Don't stoop to her level.'

Jonah and Lemuel subsided onto the window seat, sighing with disappointment. 'They won't take my dolly away, will they, Sarah?' Mary asked anxiously. 'Or the doll's house.'

'No, of course not,' Sarah said with more conviction than she was feeling. The whole world seemed to have gone mad and nothing was certain. She was eager to find out what was happening, but she feared that a fight might break out between the widows if she left the room. If she had not seen it with her own eyes she would not have believed that mild, sweet-natured Sophia Arbuthnot could suddenly become a tigress driven by anger and the desire for revenge, whereas Mrs Trigg was undoubtedly a hell-cat who had been raised in the rookeries of St Giles where only the strongest and fittest survived. It was a frightening combination.

'A carriage has just pulled up outside,' Jonah cried excitedly. 'Can we go and see who it is, Sarah?'

'No, you may not,' she said firmly. 'We've been told to wait here and that's what we must do.'

'It'll be Fitch,' Mrs Trigg said, smirking. 'He'll put a stop to this, and then we'll see who comes off best.'

They did not have long to wait. George Fitch was apparently a match for the police and the revenue men as the door was flung open and he marched into the room, stopping to take in the scene with a scowl contorting his features. Mrs Trigg leapt up and ran to his side. 'I've been assaulted, sir. That old witch attacked me and ruined my best hat.'

He brushed her hand off his sleeve as if it were an irritating insect. 'Be quiet, woman. There are more important things than your damned hat.' He turned to Sarah and his expression was not encouraging. 'You are a meddling little baggage and I want you and your cronies out of here immediately. This is my house and you are trespassing.'

Sarah was about to argue but at that moment Moorcroft entered the room followed by a man who was a stranger to her.

'Bertram?' Fitch stared at him, eyebrows raised. 'What are you doing here?'

'I asked my brother to come here today,' Moorcroft said smoothly.

'You were my lawyer, Martin. I don't deal with the junior partner when there is this much at stake.'

'When will you accept the fact that I am no longer your solicitor, George? I've told you on two separate occasions that you must find another man to handle your affairs.'

Bertram Moorcroft shrugged off his overcoat and laid it neatly on the back of a chair together with his bowler hat and gloves. 'I've travelled all night to be here, Mr Fitch. I came because something important has come to light. A certain document has been found – namely, the will of your late sister, Elsie Fortunata Fitch.' He took a scroll of parchment from his coat pocket and waved it in the air.

'What? No, that's impossible.' The colour drained from Fitch's face.

'Is that because you knew where the will was hidden?' Bertram said icily. 'It was delivered into your safekeeping, and yet strangely enough it went missing.'

'My nephew Tobias stole it from my house. What you have there must be a forgery.'

'Tobias cannot speak for himself,' Martin Moorcroft said slowly. 'But he swore his innocence and I believed him. The will was never lost or even mislaid, was it, George? You destroyed it because you wanted the property for yourself.'

Fitch made for the door. 'I don't have to put up with these wild accusations. Whatever you have in your hand cannot be my sister's will. Now let me pass, officer. There are more important matters for me to attend to.'

Constable Barley barred his way. 'I have orders to keep you in here, sir. You may not pass.'

'This is preposterous. I'm being held prisoner in my own house.'

'But this is not your property.' Bertram unrolled the document. 'I can assure you that this is Elsie's last will and testament as dictated to a member of the staff at the Charing Cross hospital.'

Fitch's mouth hung open and his eyes bulged. Sarah thought he might fall down in an apoplectic fit at any moment, but he recovered himself enough to splutter and shake his head. 'Nonsense, I don't believe you. My sister was in no fit state to make another will.'

'Did you visit her in hospital, George?' Moorcroft's tone was sombre and he nodded when Fitch shook his head. 'I thought not. Continue, if you please, brother.'

Bertram held the scroll up for all to see. 'When I received this I had to make certain that it was valid, which is why there was a delay. However, probate has been granted and my brother and I are executors. We will see that Miss Fitch's wishes are carried out to the last letter.'

'I suppose she left the whole bloody lot to Tobias,' Fitch snarled. 'Well, he's dead and I'm his next of kin, so there shouldn't be a problem. Now if you'll excuse me I have to go and speak to the revenue officers. Someone, namely my caretaker, Parker, has been using my cellars for receiving and dealing in contraband. I want him arrested.'

'No!' Sarah protested angrily. 'That's a lie. Parker was only following your orders, Mr Fitch.'

'Don't take any notice of that stupid little trollop. She's in league with them. Now let me pass, my good man.'

Constable Barley blocked his way, staring straight ahead with an impassive expression. 'I'm sorry, sir. I'm just following orders.'

Fitch turned to Moorcroft. 'Martin, tell this man to let

me pass. I'm the master of the house, and I insist on being treated with the respect due to my station in life.'

'You don't own this property, Mr Fitch.' Bertram stepped between them. 'You may see for yourself that Miss Fitch's will is very simple. She left the house to Tobias for his lifetime, but if he should die the whole estate goes to her natural daughter, Nanette Fitch.'

'What are you talking about?' Fitch snarled. 'The child died soon after birth.'

'That's not so and you know it,' Bertram said calmly. 'When Tobias realised that she was dying he told her what he knew of the deception and gave her the news that her daughter was alive and well.'

'This is true,' Moorcroft added hastily. 'Tobias only discovered the truth when he became involved with Trigg and his wife, which I have reason to believe that you engineered, Mr Fitch, because it suited your purpose to involve your nephew with your under-world contacts. Tobias became your go-between in your dealings with the Triggs, who were only too happy to fence smuggled goods, and having become involved Tobias was unable to break the cycle.'

'This is all nonsense,' Fitch protested, looking round the room as if expecting to find support and failing miserably. 'This is a made-up story to discredit me.'

Moorcroft shook his head. 'Sarah was witness to a deathbed confession from Tobias Grey's own lips. We can only imagine how Elsie must have felt as she dictated her will to one of the nurses at the Charing Cross hospital.'

'But that will is invalid,' Fitch said triumphantly. 'She

439

wasn't in her right mind. The will in my possession is the legal document.'

'But that will is lost, Mr Fitch. You said it had been stolen.' Moorcroft exchanged meaningful glances with his brother.

'I-I was mistaken,' Fitch muttered. 'My man Dobson came across it only the other day. I meant to tell you, but with all this going on I became confused.'

Bertram nodded his head. 'That's very interesting, but Elsie's last will and testament was witnessed by two doctors at the Charing Cross hospital and she managed to sign it despite the severity of her injuries.'

'And that means,' Moorcroft added with a hint of a smile, 'that Nanette Fitch inherits the entire Blackwood estate.'

The room echoed with silence, broken by the sudden appearance of Nettie who pushed past the startled policeman. 'What's going on? All hell's broken loose in the kitchen. There are uniformed men all over the place and they've got two villains trussed up like turkeys and shouting their heads off. And who's this Nanette Fitch?'

Mrs Trigg rose to her feet. 'All this has nothing to do with me. I came because he asked me to,' she said, pointing a shaking finger at Fitch. 'And I want to know what they've done to my hubby. He's been missing for months and that's not like Trigg. I reckon they done him in for the money, the murdering swine.'

'Shut up, Trigg.' Fitch turned on her in a fury. 'Keep your stupid mouth shut, woman. Who cares about your husband anyway? He was a villain and a thug, and if he's met a sticky end it's only what he deserved.'

'Oh, you brute. You callous bugger. You was pleased enough to hire him to do your dirty work.' Mrs Trigg attempted to lunge at him but was held back by Constable Barley. 'He got me into this,' she shrieked. 'I was a respectable workhouse mistress until that man persuaded Trigg to turn to crime.'

'She's deranged,' Fitch said coldly. 'Arrest her, constable. She's the one who's guilty of fencing illegal goods. She's been using her job as my agent to steal from me and conceal her own nefarious deeds.'

Moorcroft laid his hand on Fitch's shoulder. 'As your former solicitor I would advise you not to say anything that would incriminate you further.'

'I've paid you a fortune to act on my behalf, Martin. I'm reinstating you as from now.'

'I was unaware of your criminal activities then, and it would be improper for me to act for you,' Moorcroft said icily. 'I'd advise you to seek legal advice from another law firm.'

'Just a minute, everyone,' Nettie said, holding up her hands. 'Will someone tell me what's going on? And who's this Nanette Fitch? I'm Nanette but I ain't no Fitch.'

Bertram shook his head. 'I don't think it concerns you, miss. The person in question is heir to this whole estate but she is at present unknown to us.'

'And that isn't you, girl,' Fitch snapped. 'This whole thing is ridiculous. Blackwood House belongs to me, and that woman is to blame for everything.' He pointed at Mrs Trigg. 'Arrest her now.'

She moved towards him, her eyes narrowed to slits. 'So you're washing your hands of me, are you, George?

You've landed me in trouble and now you're going to put the blame on Trigg and me.'

He looked her up and down. 'It's obvious to everyone here that you are as much a criminal as your husband, wherever he may be at this moment. You've been cheating me for years and no doubt creaming off rent money in the process.' He turned to Bertram, his eyes flashing dangerously. 'As to you, sir, that will is useless unless you find Elsie's illegitimate child, which you won't because she's dead. This whole thing is a farrago of lies. My sister was mad. Anyone will tell you that.'

'No, she wasn't.' Sarah had been standing quietly beside Mrs Arbuthnot but she could keep silent no longer. 'Elsie was as sane as you and I, maybe more so. She spent her whole life helping people and healing the sick.' She broke off, choked with tears.

'Fitch is a lying sod. He's the one who deserves to rot in jail.' Mrs Trigg turned to Bertram with an ingratiating smile. 'What you just said was true, mister. George Fitch took the baby from his sister and brought her to the workhouse. That's when we first got caught up in his wicked schemes. He told us that his sister had died in childbirth but her baby was born on the wrong side of the blanket, and he didn't want a little bastard disgracing the family name.' She grabbed Nettie by the arm and shoved her towards Fitch. 'This is your niece. I raised that sickly, mewling baby and I'm telling you that this is Nanette Fitch. We had to call her something, and when pressed you told us that her mother's dying wish was to name her Nanette after her grandmother. We registered her as Nanette Bean because

442

Fitch didn't want anyone to be able to trace her true identity.' She shook her fist at George. 'Ain't that a laugh? She owns your bloody house now, not you.'

Nettie pulled away from her. 'What are you saying, you mad woman? I'm still Nettie Bean. I'm an actress and I'm going to be famous. I don't want to be related to him. It can't be true.'

'I knew it,' Sarah cried triumphantly. 'Grey tried to tell me your name. It was the last word on his lips, and you are a lot like her, Nettie. I don't know why I didn't see it from the beginning.' Sarah rushed to Nettie's side and wrapped her in a warm embrace. 'Don't be upset, love. You're still you, no matter what it says on a bit of paper.'

Moorcroft beckoned to Constable Barley. 'I suggest you take this man and this woman into custody, officer. There are witnesses aplenty to uphold your version of events. My brother will come with you and explain matters to your superior officer.'

'Yes, sir.' Constable Barley saluted smartly and produced a set of handcuffs from his belt, which he proceeded to clip onto Fitch's wrist. He was about to do the same to Mrs Trigg but she drew herself up to her full height, thrusting out her bosom and fixing him with a defiant stare.

'I'll come quietly, constable. I'm the innocent party in all this.' She turned her head to give Sarah a vicious look. 'I'll get the cops to search the grounds. You won't get off easily, miss. I know that Trigg is here and when I find out what happened to him I promise you that you'll suffer for it.' She marched out of the room

443

followed closely by Fitch handcuffed to the police officer, with Bertram bringing up the rear.

The door swung shut behind them and an audible sigh of relief rippled round the room. 'Well!' Mrs Arbuthnot looked up at Moorcroft. 'Who would have thought it, Martin?'

He sat down beside her, taking her hand in his. 'It's quite breathtaking, my dear, but a happy outcome – at least, so far.'

She eyed him curiously. 'I'm not sure what you mean, Martin.'

He patted her hand. 'I'll explain in a moment.'

'Does this mean that she owns the house?' Lemuel jumped off the window seat and came to stand beside Nettie, tugging at her skirt. 'Are you going to let us stay here, miss?'

Mary hurried over to lay her hand on his shoulder. 'Leave the lady alone, Lemmy. She's a bit overcome with it all.'

Nettie wiped her eyes on her sleeve and sniffed. 'I'm fine, really I am, but it's been a shock, I'd admit that.'

Sarah passed her a clean handkerchief. 'But a good one for all that, Nettie.'

'I had a mother and we never knew each other. I don't even know what she looked like.'

'I knew her well and I loved her as you would have done, given half a chance.' Sarah grasped Nettie's hand, giving it a gentle squeeze. 'She was a wonderful person. She had red hair just like you, and she was funny and a bit wild, just like you. She didn't give a jot for convention . . .'

'Just like me,' Nettie said, smiling through her tears.

'At least you had her to take care of you. It could have been me that ended up living as you did and I would have been with my own mother. That's very strange.'

'And she would have loved you. She was fond of me but she never loved me, but I think you were always in her heart. She would have been so proud of you, Nettie.'

'And I'll work even harder,' Nettie said, dabbing her eyes with a lace hanky. 'I always said I'd be rich and famous and I will. You'll see.'

'You're already rich, Nettie. You own this lovely old house and the grounds, not to mention the income from the properties in the village.'

'Gawd almighty, I'm an heiress,' Nettie said, chuckling. 'I'm a rich woman and I don't need to tread the boards for nuppence a week.' She frowned. 'But I'll still keep on with my career. I won't always be a walk-on. I'll be a famous actress and an heiress at the same time. My ma will look down from heaven and cheer me on.'

'Of course she will, my dear.' Moorcroft cleared his throat. 'I knew your mother, Nettie. She was a fine woman, and there are things that you should know.'

Sarah's hand flew to her lips. All her instincts warned her that this was neither the time nor the place for further revelations. She caught Moorcroft's eye and shook her head. 'Perhaps later, sir.'

'I really would like to get everything out in the open,' he said, rising to his feet, but at that moment the door opened and Bertram rushed into the room.

'The truth has come out, Martin. They're searching for a body,' he said breathlessly. 'You'd better come quickly.'

Chapter Twenty-Six

Sarah was the first to reach the kitchen. Fitch remained handcuffed to Constable Barley and Mrs Trigg was seated at the table opposite the two men who had been witness to Trigg's demise. Sarah recognised them instantly and her heart sank. They were bound hand and foot, and she could tell from their grim expressions that they knew their days of freedom were at an end. They might decide to tell the truth or it could be a pack of lies if they thought that Mrs Trigg would stand by them. She looked for Davey and saw him standing at the back of the room being interrogated by two uniformed revenue men. Davey met her anxious glance with a barely perceptible shake of his head, as if warning her to say nothing, but there was a hint of a smile in his eyes that was for her alone and it gave her courage.

Nettie had followed her into the kitchen together with Moorcroft, Bertram and Mrs Arbuthnot, who had Lemuel and Jonah clinging to her hands. Mary moved swiftly to stand beside Sarah, giving her an encouraging smile. 'I'm with you,' she murmured. 'I won't let no one take you away from us.'

'Don't worry, Mary,' Sarah said with more confidence than she was feeling. 'Everything will be all right.'

'What's going on, officer?' Moorcroft demanded. 'I understand that you're looking for a body. Is that correct?'

The most senior police officer stepped forward. 'And who are you, sir?'

'My name is Martin Moorcroft and I am, or rather I was, Mr Fitch's solicitor.'

'I am Inspector Giles of the Metropolitan Police. Following information received we are investigating Mr Fitch's affairs.' He jerked his head in the direction of Trigg's men. 'We came to investigate a smuggling ring but this is now a case of murder. According to these men Mr Thaddeus Trigg met his end at the hands of one Tobias Grey.'

'That's not true.' Sarah could keep silent no longer. 'Trigg had a gun. I witnessed the whole thing. He was going to kill Grey: there was a struggle and he fell on the knife.'

Mrs Trigg let out a howl of anguish. 'Murdered.'

'It was self defence.' Sarah turned to Trigg's men. 'Tell them, please. You saw it all. Tobias Grey is dead now, but he was no murderer.'

The man who had intervened on that fatal day nodded his head. 'That's the truth, guv. She saw it all. Trigg was acting like a madman and he went in on the attack. What happened was an accident.'

'What were you doing at the time of the murder?' Inspector Giles fixed him with a gimlet stare. 'What was your business here?'

'We was only following orders to collect goods and transport them to Mr Fitch's warehouse in London. It weren't our business to ask where the stuff come from.' He turned to his mate. 'Ain't that so, Kelly?'

'That's the size of it.' Kelly cast a look of pure malice in Mrs Trigg's direction. 'She's as bad as her old man was. She gave the orders and she paid us for our trouble. We never asked no questions.'

Mrs Trigg leapt to her feet. 'They're both lying. I didn't know that the goods were contraband. I was just following instructions from my employer, Mr Fitch.' She pointed at George, shaking her finger at him. 'He's the villain, not my poor hubby, nor me. We was just dupes in the game he was playing.'

'The woman is lying,' Fitch said angrily. 'You surely don't believe her. She's from the criminal classes. You only have to look at her to see that.'

'I will have me say.' Mrs Trigg's voice rose a pitch or two. 'That devil thinks he can treat people how he likes because he's a toff, but he's no better than anyone here. He abandoned his own flesh and blood to the workhouse. That's her, over there – the carroty one with the skin the colour of whey. She's the real owner of this old pile of shit and much good it will do her.' She sank down on her seat as one of the constables made a move to restrain her. 'All right, son. I ain't going nowhere.'

'It's a pack of lies.' Fitch glared at Mrs Trigg as if he would like to throttle her. 'I'm a respectable businessman who's been taken advantage of by a gang leader and his woman.'

'That's enough, sir.' Inspector Giles stepped forward, holding up his hand. 'You'll have your chance to prove your innocence in court, but this is neither the time nor the place.' He turned to Constable Barley and his two subordinate officers. 'Take them to the Black Maria. This matter will be dealt with in the London courts.'

Fitch was still protesting his innocence as Constable Barley led him from the room.

'I ain't going nowhere with him,' Mrs Trigg said, folding her arms across her bosom. 'He'd slit me throat as soon as look at me, and I ain't leaving until I've seen the body. I won't believe that my Trigg is dead unless I see him with me own eyes.'

Inspector Giles shook his head. 'You're under arrest, madam. You have no choice in the matter. Take her away.'

'Mr Moorcroft, sir. Don't let them do this,' Mrs Trigg screamed as she tried to fight off the two young constables who tried to lift her to her feet. 'You're a man of the law. Do something.'

Nettie shook her head. 'You don't deserve anyone's sympathy. You and that evil husband of yours made our lives hell in the workhouse. Not just me and Sarah but all the hundreds of men, women and children who passed through your hands. You knew who I was but you kept me a prisoner until you sold me to Mr Arbuthnot. You didn't know it then, but that was the best thing that ever happened to me. Now I want you to pay for what you did to us, you wicked old witch. I hope you rot in prison for the rest of your miserable life.' She turned on her heel and ran from the kitchen.

'Go after her, Sarah,' Moorcroft said urgently. 'I'll look after things here.'

She hesitated, casting an anxious glance at Davey. 'You won't let them take Davey away will you, Mr Moorcroft? You know that he didn't do anything wrong, nor did Parker who was just following orders.'

'I'll do everything I can to stop that happening,' Moorcroft said with a reassuring smile.

'We'll leave the gentlemen to settle matters.' Mrs Arbuthnot shooed the children into the passageway. 'Go along, my dears. As soon as the kitchen is free we'll have some breakfast. I'm sure you must be starving.'

Sarah found Nettie in the small parlour where the children kept their toys. She was sitting on the floor, cuddling Mary's doll and rocking to and fro with tears running down her cheeks. Sarah knelt down beside her. 'Don't take on so, Nettie.'

'I don't know who I am now. I've got used to being just Nettie Bean, a nobody from nowhere, and now suddenly I'm someone else.'

'At least you know who your mother was, even if you never met her. She loved you always, and she proved it at the last when she changed her will in your favour. She wanted you to have what was rightfully yours.'

'I suppose so, but I'm still an orphan. I'll never know who my father was.'

Sarah looked up to see Moorcroft standing in the

450

doorway and she scrambled to her feet. 'I think Mr Moorcroft might be able to help you there, Nettie. I'll leave him to explain.'

Moorcroft ran his finger round the inside of his stiff shirt collar. 'I'm sure that Nettie won't mind if you stay, Sarah. You two have been friends for a very long time.'

Nettie brightened visibly. 'What's all this about? I do love a mystery.'

The timbre of her voice and the way Nettie held her head brought Elsie vividly to mind, and glancing at Moorcroft Sarah realised that he was experiencing something similar. He had the look of someone who had discovered something so utterly wonderful that he could scarcely believe his eyes. She smiled to herself as she left them to get to know each other, and went to find Davey.

Grey's funeral, no longer a secret affair, was conducted next morning and to Sarah's amazement the village church was packed with people wishing to pay their respects to someone they had known since he was a child. The churchyard was blanketed with snowdrops, a sea of white shimmering in the sunshine, and there was a breath of spring in the air. The mourners crowded round the grave to toss handfuls of soil onto the coffin in their final farewell to a member of the Fitch family, and Sarah realised suddenly that the strength of their feeling was as much for the dynasty as it was for Grey. People came up to her, holding her hand and telling her how much Elsie was missed, and they begged her to take over where Elsie had left off in her mission to heal the sick.

'You can't trust them fancy physicians,' Old Mother Perks said, shaking her hand. 'They take your money and stick leeches all over you, but that don't do no good for a bellyache or a sore throat. The sooner you set up again the better for all of us.' She hobbled away to join her family, who were nodding with approval.

'I never knew that you were so popular,' Nettie whispered.

'It wasn't me, it was Elsie. Your mother was a remarkable woman.' Sarah looked round at the expectant faces of the people she had known since she was a child. 'I think they're waiting for you to invite them back to the house. You represent the Fitch family now and it's quite a responsibility.'

'I'm scared, Sarah. I'm a stranger here. They don't know me and I certainly don't know them.' Nettie clutched her hand. 'What shall I do?'

Moorcroft moved to her side. 'Will you allow me to do the honours, my dear? I think that you ought to be introduced to your audience.'

A smile banished Nettie's worried frown. 'My audience. Of course, I hadn't thought of it that way. Go on then, Pa. Introduce our double act.'

Moorcroft stepped forward. 'Ladies and gentlemen, you've probably heard that this young lady is Elsie's daughter, and I'm proud to announce publicly that she is my daughter too. Sadly we have lost Elsie and Tobias, but their spirit lives on at Blackwood House and I hope you will follow us there now so that we may raise a glass to those who are no longer with us.' He held up his hand as a murmur of assent rippled round the congregation. 'And you all know Sarah, who learned everything she knows about herbal medicines from Elsie. She tells me that her dearest wish is to become even more proficient as a pharmacist so that she can come back and work amongst you when she is fully qualified. Knowing Sarah I don't think it will be long before she returns to Blackwood to continue Elsie's good work.'

A round of applause sent a clamour of rooks flying skywards from the tall elm trees that surrounded the church, protesting noisily.

Sarah felt the blood rush to her cheeks. 'You shouldn't have said that, sir. I have to earn my living. I can't afford to study for the examinations that will soon become compulsory before anyone can practise.'

'We'll talk about that later, Sarah.' He glanced over his shoulder. 'But in the meantime I suggest we lead the way back to the house. These people look in need of refreshment.'

'But Pa,' Nettie protested, tucking her hand in the crook of his arm, 'we haven't anything to give them. Not like Mr Arbuthnot's wake where Cook had been slaving away in the kitchen for a couple of days.'

'Why do you think that Sophia and Mary remained at home, my dear? Parker liberated a keg of brandy and one of sherry wine before Mrs Trigg's ruffians arrived at the house, and Sophia will have mastered the range by now and no doubt created some little fancies to feed the masses.' He beckoned to Davey who had been standing at a respectful distance. 'Come along, my boy. You and I have matters to discuss that will not wait.'

Davey fell into step beside them as they left the churchyard. 'Really, sir? I can't think what interest you might have in what happens to me and my family.'

'I already think of Sarah as my daughter and we had a long talk last night, after the police had taken the villains away.'

'And they didn't find the body,' Sarah added, smiling for the first time that day. 'Grey would be pleased about that if only he knew. Parker did a good job of covering his tracks.'

'But will Mrs Trigg let matters lie?' Davey opened the lychgate. 'She's not the sort to give up easily.'

Moorcroft stood aside to allow Nettie and Sarah to pass. 'That woman will almost certainly be sentenced to a long term of imprisonment. When she gets out she'll have to survive by her wits. I don't think she'll trouble us again.'

'And what about George Fitch?' Nettie asked anxiously. 'Do you think he'll contest Elsie's will?'

'I'm quite certain that he'll also spend a considerable time in prison, and his house in Spital Square is heavily mortgaged, I know that for a fact. I imagine that his wife will have to sell up and live modestly or return to her family. George won't have much to look forward to when he's released, and that's only if he survives life behind bars.'

'I almost feel sorry for him,' Sarah said, slipping her hand into Davey's as they walked side by side.

'Well, I don't. Even if he is my uncle I don't want anything to do with him.' Nettie smiled up at Moorcroft. 'We're going to be a proper family, aren't we, Pa?'

'Of course we are, my dear. And that's another thing I want to talk to you about, Nettie.'

'Really, Pa? What is it?'

Walking behind them, Sarah squeezed Davey's hand. 'I think I know what he's going to say.'

He gave her a smile that sent her heart fluttering inside her chest. 'I love you, you clever girl.'

She laid her finger on her lips. 'Shh. Not now.'

'Definitely later.'

'Yes, definitely.'

Nettie uttered a whoop of glee. 'Oh, you are a one, Pa. I should have seen it coming.' She stopped, turning to Sarah with a wide grin. 'He's going to ask Mrs Arbuthnot to marry him. What do you think of that?'

Later, when the guests had left, weaving their somewhat tipsy way home, Sarah and Nettie were in the kitchen amongst piles of dirty glasses and crockery. They had sent Mrs Arbuthnot to her room to rest after her labours, and Mary was keeping an eye on the score as the boys played a rather soggy game of cricket with Davey and Moorcroft on the lawn, which was now neatly cropped by the goat, although it had also munched on all the woody plants and shrubs within its reach.

'What do you really think about Moorcroft wanting to marry Mrs Arbuthnot?' Sarah asked as she poured boiling water into the teapot. 'Does it upset you to know that he's fallen in love?'

455

Nettie sat down at the table, making a space amongst the detritus left by the wake and resting her elbows on the wooden surface. 'No, not at all. He deserves to be happy after the life he's had. I'd be a mean bitch to deny him that, and I'm just glad to know that I've got a dad who cares about me. That won't change when he marries Sophia.'

'If she accepts him.' Sarah stirred the pot and left the tea to brew. She searched the dresser for clean cups. 'So will you live here and become lady of the manor?'

'It's all happened so quickly, Sarah. Yesterday I was just Nettie Bean with a walk-on part in a big London production, but now I'm Nanette Fitch, heiress to a bloody fortune and I'm responsible for this house and goodness knows how many acres of grounds. Worse still, half the village seems to think I'm a bigwig and they'll want me to wet-nurse them. That's not the life for me. I want excitement and glamour. I want to breathe in the smell of greasepaint and smoky old London with its overflowing sewers and rotten rubbish. I don't like fresh country air and the stink of cow shit.'

'You still want to be an actress?' Sarah could hardly believe her ears. This old house and its grounds and indeed the whole way of country living was, she realised now, her idea of heaven. She would always be a Londoner at heart, but if she could live and work in Blackwood she would be happy to return to the city for long visits. She poured the tea into two cracked and chipped cups that she found at the back of the shelf. 'Here's your tea.' She stared at Nettie, angling her head as a sudden thought struck her. 'I suppose your urgent wish to return to London wouldn't have anything to do with a handsome Frenchman, would it?'

Nettie's cheeks bloomed pink and she snatched the cup from Sarah's hand. 'I dunno who you mean.'

Sarah pulled up a chair and sat down. 'Come on, Nettie Bean. This is me you're talking to. I mean Gaston Fournier, of course. He lives and works in London, doesn't he?'

'I think so.' Nettie sipped her tea, refusing to look Sarah in the eye. 'Well, yes, as a matter of fact he does.'

'And you've seen him again?'

'He came to the theatre during rehearsals and we went for supper afterwards. Where's the harm in that?'

Sarah chuckled. 'You're blushing, Nettie. You like him, don't you? What happened during that trip home from France? Did you get to know him very well?'

'I dunno what you mean.' Nettie pushed the cup away and stood up. 'I'm going to find Parker. He can clear this lot up. I'm the lady of the house now.' She flounced out of the kitchen, leaving Sarah on her own amidst the chaos.

She finished her tea, rolled up her sleeves and went outside into the yard to fetch water from the pump.

'Here, let me do that.'

She turned with a start as Davey took the bucket from her. 'You'll have to work the handle,' he said ruefully. 'I feel like a cripple with a useless arm.'

She pumped valiantly and water splashed into the bucket. 'It will get better, and anyway you haven't got a boat at the moment so you can't go back to sea.'

'That's not exactly true,' he said mysteriously. 'Whoa, that's enough.'

She released the handle. 'What's not true?'

Davey carried the overflowing bucket into the scullery and emptied it into the sink. 'Is there any hot water in the boiler?'

She nodded. 'Yes, but I'll fetch it when you've told me what's going on. Why the mystery?'

'There's no mystery, my love. Mr Moorcroft had a chat with me while we were waiting for Jonah to find the ball that I'd lobbed into the shrubbery. Not bad for a one-armed batsman.'

'You're being deliberately annoying, Davey Hawkes. What did he say?'

'He's offered to lend me the money to fix the boat up, and I'm to repay him out of my earnings. I should be fit enough to take it to sea by the time the work is finished. Then I can ask you to marry me.' He frowned. 'What's the matter, Sarah? You don't look too pleased. Isn't that what you want?'

'Of course it is, but not yet. I told you that I want to qualify as a pharmacist so that I can continue the work that Elsie started and do it properly. I want to help people and they need me here in the village. Old Mrs Perks told me that today after the funeral, and it made my mind up for me. You do understand, don't you?'

'We've been here before, Sarah. I'm not sure that I do know what you want. Isn't being my wife going to be enough for you? It's what most women settle for.'

She leaned against the stone sink, wiping her hands on her apron. 'That's just it, Davey. I don't want to settle for anything. I'll never be happy to spend my days cooking, cleaning and washing clothes in the stream with the other village women.'

'You've been mixing with the toffs and it's given you ideas above your station. You don't want to marry a humble fisherman.'

She shook her head vehemently. 'No, that's not it at all, but I saw what poverty and hard physical labour did to my mother. I watched the life ebb from her body that was worn out with childbearing, and I vowed then that it wouldn't happen to me. Elsie showed me another way, Davey.'

'So you don't love me enough to marry me?'

'Of course I love you. I always have, since that first day on the seashore when you rescued me from the crab. I want to be your wife, but I don't see why I can't have both. If you will just give me time . . .'

He threw up his hands with an impatient sigh. 'How long do you want? A month, a year or even longer? We'll be old and grey before you make up your mind.'

She laid her hand on his arm. 'We're very young, Davey. I'm not sure how long it would take me to become qualified, but I've done my apprenticeship with Elsie. Would a year be too long? Do you love me enough to wait for a year?'

He hesitated, looking deeply into her eyes, and his expression softened. 'If you promise that you'll give me your answer a year from now, then I suppose I can wait.'

That evening after a supper of rabbit stew and an apple pie baked by Mrs Arbuthnot who was rediscovering the pleasure of cooking that she had learned as a young bride, the children were sent to bed and everyone else, with the exception of Parker who chose to go for a moonlight walk and smoke his briar pipe, gathered round the fire in the drawing room.

'I want you all to know that I'm going back to London on the first train tomorrow morning,' Nettie said firmly. 'I'll lose my part in the show if I don't turn up for rehearsals.'

Mrs Arbuthnot raised her delicate eyebrows. 'But my dear, don't you want to remain here and enjoy being the mistress of this wonderful house?'

Nettie shook her head. 'I've spoken to Pa about it and he agrees with me.' She looked to Moorcroft, who smiled benignly.

'Yes, Sophia. Nettie and I had a long chat before supper and she wants to follow her chosen career.'

'Yes, I understand that,' Mrs Arbuthnot said with a worried frown. 'But surely the stage is not the life for a young woman of substance?'

Moorcroft reached out to hold her hand. 'The theatrical world is becoming quite respectable and some young women have even married into the aristocracy.'

'And others have gone down a completely different path.' Sophia did not look convinced. She sighed. 'I suppose you will do precisely what you want to do, Nettie.'

'What about Davey and the children?' Sarah tossed another log on the fire, watching the sparks ignite the soot on the chimney back and wishing she could see into the future. 'What's going to happen to Blackwood House?'

Nettie shrugged her shoulders. 'They can stay here for as long as they like. Parker will carry on as usual. I don't see why anything should change.'

Moorcroft glanced at Mrs Arbuthnot and she nodded in response. 'We've already discussed this, Nettie. As I'm soon to be your stepmother I was hoping that you would allow me to stay on here.'

'You want to bury yourself in the country?' Nettie stared as her as if she had lost her senses. 'Are you sure, ma'am?'

'It would be wonderful to get away from Shadwell. I was born in the country, Nettie, and I suppose I'll always be a country woman at heart. I moved to London when I married James, but I've always longed for a different way of life.'

'And you, sir?' Sarah said, turning to Moorcroft. 'Do you plan to live here too? What about your law firm?'

Until this moment Bertram had remained slightly apart from those gathered round the fire, but he now rose to his feet and came to stand behind his brother's chair. 'I can answer that, Sarah. Martin has seen fit to make me the senior partner.'

'And I will remain in London until I am certain that everything is working as it should,' Moorcroft added, smiling. 'Then I will set up a practice in Maldon or Colchester. Sophia and I plan to marry as soon as my affairs are settled.' He covered her hand with his. 'We are at a stage in life when every moment counts. I see no reason for a long engagement.'

Nettie clapped her hands. 'And I'll visit you every now and then.' She turned to Sarah. 'And what about you? Are you and Davey going to tie the knot?'

Sarah flinched, uncomfortably aware that all eyes were upon her, including Davey's. She was about to speak but he silenced her with a tender smile. 'We've decided to wait for a year so that Sarah can complete her studies and take the examination set by the Society of Apothecaries.'

'That's right,' Sarah said eagerly. 'But I want to practise here in Blackwood.' Her smile faded. 'The only problem is that I will have to live in London and study at Bart's or the Middlesex hospital, if they'll accept me on their course. I've already done my apprenticeship with Elsie, so it shouldn't be a problem.'

'Then what is to prevent you?' Mrs Arbuthnot moved closer to Moorcroft. 'You know that I love you like a daughter, Sarah. Is there anything I can do to help?'

'I'll need to live somewhere, ma'am. I have no money and I'll have to find work to support myself.'

'I'll send you funds,' Davey said stoutly. 'As soon as my boat is seaworthy I'll be able to earn my own living.'

Mrs Arbuthnot held up her hand. 'It's simpler than that, Davey. Martin is going to move from Islington to my house in Elbow Lane. Sarah can keep him company and I suggest that you should live there too, Nettie. You are very young to live in digs where you might be subjected to all manner of temptations.'

Nettie pulled a face. 'I think I can look after myself, ma'am, but thank you all the same.'

'Very well, my dear, but the offer is open to you at any time.'

'And as your father I might have something to say about where and how you live, my girl.' Moorcroft's eyes shone with amusement and he blew her a kiss. 'You look so much like your mother when you pout, Nettie. But I intend to make certain that no one, not even my friend Gaston Fournier, takes advantage of you.'

Nettie's cheeks flamed scarlet. 'Oh, Pa!'

Chapter Twenty-Seven

Leaving Blackwood House and those she loved most in the world was harder than Sarah had anticipated, but she knew that she owed it to herself and to Elsie to finish her education and to qualify as an apothecary in her own right.

She moved into the house in Elbow Lane with Cook and Betty to look after her, although she did her fair share of the housework as Dorcas was now married to her Walter and living in a tiny terraced house in Plaistow. Moorcroft also moved in and Nettie visited as often as performances at the theatre allowed, although she refused to give up the new digs she had found closer to the theatre. Sarah suspected that this had something to do with Gaston, but refrained from comment as Nettie was adamant that her sole aim in life was to become the toast of London.

Although she had missed Dorcas's nuptials, Sarah was able to attend the wedding of Miss Parfitt and Franz Beckman. Mrs Arbuthnot travelled up to London for the occasion and Nettie managed to get to the ceremony. Even so Gaston had to whisk her away in his private chaise before the wedding breakfast in order to get to the theatre on time as she now had a speaking part. It was only a few lines but Nettie was confident that this was the start of a glittering career. Sarah could only hope that she was not deluding herself, and she could see similarities between Nettie and Elsie which made her fear for the future. They shared an intensity of purpose and a zest for life that could lead to huge success or dismal failure and self-destruction. But there was the strong possibility that Gaston, the pragmatic Frenchman, would keep Nettie from the excesses and dependence on opium that had almost inevitably led to her mother's tragic death.

Backed by Moorcroft, Sarah enrolled in the school of chemistry at Bart's and studied for the exam that would give her a professional qualification. She soon found that Elsie had taught her well, and that she had a natural aptitude for the subject. Miss Parfitt, now Mrs Beckman, was delighted to give her extra tuition in mathematics and Sarah spent many pleasant evenings in the Beckmans' comfortable home close to the sugar mill in St George's Place where Franz was the head sugar baker.

Whenever possible Sarah accompanied Moorcroft on his weekly visits to Blackwood House, and each time she was delighted to see the improvements that Mrs Arbuthnot had made. Moorcroft handled the business side of the estate and with Parker's help had hired gardeners and groundsmen. The rents from the farms and cottages were now collected by a bailiff who saw to it that the tenants were fairly treated and the money was used to improve the property and invest in new machinery for the home farm.

At the end of the autumn during one of their monthly

visits, the discussion after dinner turned to a new threshing machine that Moorcroft had bought for the home farm. Steam power was the coming thing, he stated with great enthusiasm. He admitted that he had invested a considerable amount of money in a company that manufactured these machines. 'There is no limit to what steam power can achieve,' he said proudly. 'In fact, I'm thinking of investing more money and building a manufactory for the sole purpose of making farm machinery. Inventors are coming up with new ideas all the time.' He danced Mrs Arbuthnot round the drawing room. 'And we must be married before the month is out, Sophia. I'm tired of waiting.' He glanced over his shoulder at Sarah who was openly enjoying the spectacle of two middle-aged people cavorting like children. 'Maybe I'll build a steam-powered vessel for you, Davey. You would be able to catch several times the amount of fish and you'd be set up for life. You could start with one such boat and when you made enough money you could buy another – soon you'd have a whole fleet.'

Davey slid his arm around Sarah, holding her close. 'What do you say to that, sweetheart? Would that bring our wedding day any closer?'

She rested her head on his shoulder. 'I'm taking my exam at the end of the year. Pearl thinks that I've a good chance of passing.'

'That's not an answer, my love.'

Moorcroft came to a halt in front of them. 'Put the poor boy out of his misery, Sarah. We all know that you'll qualify, and if you fail I'll go in person to the examination board and demand to know the reason why.'

Mrs Arbuthnot sat down, smiling breathlessly. 'I'll marry you when the harvest is in, Martin. I can't say fairer than that.' She turned to Sarah, raising an eyebrow. 'Martin is right, my dear. You'll pass with flying colours. I think it's high time you named the day.'

'I'm earning money,' Davey said firmly. 'And I'm repaying Martin.'

'But I'm still living in London.'

'I've put the house in Elbow Lane up for sale,' Moorcroft said, beaming. 'Don't look so alarmed, Sarah. It will take a few months to find a suitable buyer.'

She shook her head. 'But where would Davey and I live if we married so soon? We must find somewhere in the village so that I can set up a pharmacy. It will take money that we haven't got.'

'There is a sweet house on the edge of the village,' Mrs Arbuthnot said with a mischievous smile. 'I've had my eye on it for some time. The present tenant is an elderly lady who is too infirm to look after herself and is going to live with her daughter in Colchester. It would suit you down to the ground.'

'But there's still the matter of rent,' Davey said slowly. 'Do you know who the landlord is?'

Moorcroft chuckled and winked at his bride-to-be. 'It belongs to the Fitch estate. I'm sure that Nettie would not object to a peppercorn rent for the first year,

467

and after that it would be up to her land agent to make arrangements.'

'I didn't know she had a land agent,' Sarah said curiously. 'Who is he?'

'It's Parker, of course. He deserved recognition for his loyal service, and he's enjoying his new status.' Moorcroft rose to his feet. 'Come, Sophia. Let's leave the youngsters to talk this over. It's a fine evening and I could do with a breath of fresh air. We can discuss wedding plans as we walk.'

Davey waited until the door closed on them. 'Well, Sarah. Will you give me an answer now?'

The house was decorated with boughs of holly, and Parker had mischievously hung bunches of mistletoe at strategic points through the ground floor of Blackwood House. A huge pine tree filled the entrance hall with its spicy scent and Mary had decorated it with new glass baubles and red candles in metal holders clipped to the branches.

Sarah had dressed in her wedding finery with Mary's help, and she could hardly believe her eyes as she gazed at her reflection in the tall cheval mirror. The cream silk gown was lavishly trimmed with fringing and velvet bows. A pale pink satin sash encompassed her waist, which was laced in to measure a scant eighteen inches, and the full skirts were looped up to reveal an embroidered underskirt. The gown was a wedding gift from the newly-wed Mr and Mrs Martin Moorcroft, whose nuptials had been celebrated in late September.

For Sarah this was supposed to be a double

celebration, as before she left Elbow Lane for the last time she had received confirmation that she had passed her examination with honours, but that did not help when it came to pre-wedding nerves. Her knees were shaking as she left her room followed by Mary, who was resplendent in her finery as bridesmaid and taking very seriously the task of keeping the train and veil from trailing on the floor. Sarah paused halfway down the stairs as she prepared to descend to the entrance hall where she could hear the babble of voices. Pearl and Franz had come down from London, as had Bertram. Mrs Burgess and Betty were now resident at Blackwood House, but Dorcas was in an advanced stage of pregnancy and could not make the journey to Essex. The church would no doubt be packed and everyone in the village had been invited to the wedding breakfast after the ceremony.

There was only one person missing and that was Nettie, who had sent a message to say that she had an important engagement and might not be able to make it. This had hurt Sarah more than she cared to admit, but then Nettie was doing very well for herself on the London stage. She now had a small but quite important part in a pantomime at the Olympic theatre, which was where she had begun her career, and although Sarah knew how much it meant to her, she still wished that her oldest and best friend was here to see her married.

She took a deep breath and rounded the curve in the staircase. She hesitated as the assembled guests gave her an enthusiastic round of applause. This kind of attention was what Nettie craved but Sarah was finding it overwhelming. If only Davey were here to support her, but he would be waiting at the church with Parker, whom he had chosen to be his best man.

'Sarah, my dear, you look absolutely stunning.' Moorcroft stepped forward, holding out his hand. 'I know I'm not your father but I feel honoured to be giving you away.'

Sophia rushed forward, smiling through her tears. 'You are beautiful, my dear girl. Davey is a very lucky young man.'

A thunderous banging on the front door made everyone turn their heads to see who had come so late in the proceedings. Lemuel dashed to open it and on a gust of feathery snowflakes Nettie burst into the hall, looking magnificent in a russet velvet cape edged with fox fur and a pert little hat trimmed with bronze feathers secured by a diamond hatpin to a coronet of curls. She hurried forward waving a fur muff. 'We made it just in time then. Sarah, you look gorgeous.'

Sarah ran down the last few steps, holding out her arms. 'I thought you weren't coming.' She hugged Nettie, breathing in the scent of cold winter air mingled with expensive French perfume.

'I had my reasons.' Nettie drew away, turning her head to cast a brilliant smile at Gaston Fournier who stood in the doorway, brushing snow off his overcoat. 'And there he is.' She took her hand from her muff, flashing her rings under Sarah's nose. 'I had a rather important appearance to make at my own wedding. Gaston and I were married by special licence yesterday afternoon.'

There was a stunned silence as everyone waited for Moorcroft to say something. Sarah held her breath, hoping that he was not going to spoil everything by being angry, but to her surprise he smiled and hugged Nettie. 'You minx. You always get your own way.'

'I know, Pa. You do forgive me, don't you? My poor understudy had to step in at the last minute so we'll have to return to London tomorrow. Isn't that so, Gaston?'

He approached Moorcroft with an apologetic smile. 'I'm afraid I didn't have a chance to ask your permission, Martin.'

'If you make my girl happy I'll forgive you anything, Gaston.' Moorcroft shook his hand. 'But we're forgetting Sarah. This is her day and we should be heading for the church before the snow makes the road impassable.'

Sarah hugged Nettie. 'I'm so happy for you, and thank you for coming here today.'

'I wouldn't miss this for anything, nipper.' Nettie became suddenly businesslike and she clapped her hands. 'What are you waiting for? The carriages are outside and you should all be in the church, otherwise the poor sod will think she's jilted him at the altar.' She advanced on the surprised guests, shooing them out into the cold.

Gaston shook his head. 'She is wonderful, is she not?'

* * *

The church was, as Sarah had anticipated, filled to capacity. The warm bodies of the congregation had taken the chill off the ice-cold air and the smell of hot candle wax took Sarah back to the tiny church in the French village where she had sought help for Grey and Davey. She might have lost them both but for Gaston's help and now he was married to Nettie, who was her sister in all but name.

In a glow of happiness, Sarah walked down the aisle on the arm of the man whom she loved almost as much as her real father. She looked up and saw Davey gazing at her as if she were a miracle that had walked into his life. She knew then that she had come home at last. This was where her future lay and it would be theirs to face together, forever.

Getting to know

Dilly Court

Read on for an insight into *The Workhouse Girl*,
an interview with Dilly, plus an extract from
The Shopkeeper's Daughter by Lily Baxter

Dear Reader,

I hope you enjoyed reading *The Workhouse Girl*. I think that
Sarah Scrase must be one of my favourite heroines. The
hardships she endured as a young child helped to make her
into a strong and resourceful woman, and the friendship she
made with Nettie Bean in the harsh confines of the workhouse
was to last lifelong.

I had a soft spot for Nettie too, whose loyalty to Sarah was
never in doubt. Feisty, irrepressible and full of her own self-
importance Nettie managed to lurch from one difficult
situation to another, some of them of her own making, and yet
she always came through smiling. As the story unfolded all
the characters became real to me and by the end of the book
it was as if I had known them all my life. I missed them all,
even the villainous Triggs, when the tale was told and I was
very sad to say farewell to Tobias Grey, who was my personal
hero.

As with all my books I did a great deal of research. Studying
the conditions in the workhouses and reading about the lives
of workhouse inmates was revealing and shocking. It's hard to
believe that the human spirit can survive under such
conditions, and yet the institutions were meant to be humane
but never intended to be welcoming. They were a last resort
for the sick and destitute and the alternative for many would
have been dying of starvation in the gutter.

On a much happier note I was fascinated by the history of the
sugar bakers who set up their businesses in Whitechapel. The
sugar firms found it difficult to recruit labourers as the work
was hard and the conditions appalling. They offered unlimited
beer as a bribe to attract men, most of whom came from

Germany. Their life expectancy working in such grim conditions must have been relatively short, but I hope Franz Beckman and the lovely Miss Parfitt had a long and happy marriage.

When I'm writing I always pay particular attention to the location where the story takes place. I use old maps of London and real street names like Vinegar Yard and Hanging Sword Alley. I grew up in the suburbs of East London and I flat-shared in Chelsea and Hampstead when I worked in the City and the West End, so I'm very familiar with modern London. But due to the rebuilding after the war and the office blocks in glass and concrete that have sprung up since then there is very little left of the old City, and for that I have to rely on old photographs. My daughter gave me a marvellous book called *Panoramas of Lost London* by Philip Davies, and the photographs of streets and buildings long gone have been absolutely invaluable in helping me to recreate nineteenth century London in my stories.

I look forward to meeting you again in my next book, *A Loving Family*, which starts in Florence Nightingale's hospital at Scutari in the Crimean war when fourteen-year-old Jacinta Romero loses her father to the wounds he received in battle and her mother to the dreaded disease cholera.

With my very best wishes,

Dilly Court

Dilly Court grew up in the suburbs of north-east London. Her imaginary childhood friends soon became characters in stories that she made up to amuse her cousin, Clive. She wrote her first book aged nine, very much under the influence of Enid Blyton, and continued to scribble stories and plays all through her schooldays.

Her first job was with Associated Rediffusion, London's original commercial television company, where she began as a secretary and graduated to writing advertising copy. During her first marriage to a merchant navy officer, she lived in various parts of the country, giving up work to raise her son and daughter – who are now her best friends and have given her four beautiful grandchildren.

She now lives by the sea in Dorset, on the beautiful Jurassic coast with her most excellent husband, John. Her hobbies are gardening, cooking, oil painting and knitting things for her family.

1. What made you want to become a writer?
It's something I've done ever since I can remember. I was making up stories before I had learned to write.

2. Describe your routine for writing and where you like to write, including whether you have any little quirks or funny habits when you are writing.
I write every day, starting in the morning after getting my granddaughters off to school. I go into the engine room, as my husband calls my office (which is part toy cupboard, part working space) and I write until lunchtime. I'm very much a morning person.

3. What themes are you interested in when you're writing?
Relationships between the characters, and these change as I get to know each character a little better.

4. Where do you get your inspiration from?
That's a difficult one – I suppose from life and the places I have visited.

5. How do you manage to get inside the heads of your characters in order to portray them truthfully?

The moment a character appears they develop a life of their own. Of course it's in my imagination, but I see them and listen to them as they tell me their stories.

6. Do you base your characters on real people? And if not, where does the inspiration come from?

That would be very dangerous – I don't think my family or friends would speak to me again if I did.

7. What's the most extreme thing you've ever done to research your book?

I'd like to say bungee-jumping, but that wouldn't be true. I'm afraid it's much more boring than that – I have books on most subjects and I use Google.

8. What aspect of writing do you enjoy most? (i.e. plot, character development)

The plot develops as I get to know the characters.

9. What's the best thing about being an author?

Getting positive feedback from my readers.

10. What advice would you give aspiring writers?

Persevere. Write every day even if it's only a few lines and learn to take constructive criticism and turn it to your advantage.

11. What is your favourite book of all time and why?

That would have to be *Gone with the Wind*. I admire Scarlett's courage and determination and it's a real page turner from start to finish.

12. If you could be a character in a book, or live in the world of a book who or where would you be?

I think the character I would like to be is Jo in *Little Women* and the sequels *Good Wives* and *Jo's Boys*. She was an author too.

Dilly Court also writes under the name of Lily Baxter

**If you enjoyed *The Workhouse Girl*, why not read
Lily Baxter's wonderful new novel**

The Shopkeeper's Daughter

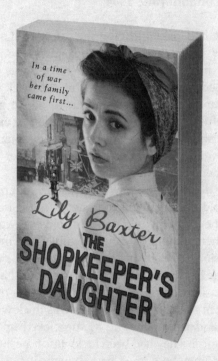

Available from all good bookshops 26 September 2013

Read on for an exclusive extract...

Chapter One

East London, June 1944

Ginnie had risked leaving the safety of the air raid shelter when Fred Chinashop suffered one of his funny turns. Despite her father's protests she had returned to the small office at the back of their furniture store, and was about to add a generous spoonful of her precious sugar ration to a cup of tea when she heard the dreaded rasping buzz of the doodlebug. The cup rattled on its saucer and the floor beneath her feet started to vibrate.

The deathly silence when its engine cut out made her hold her breath, closing her eyes as she prayed that the bomb would fall on fields or wasteland, anywhere but on the crowded suburban streets. The explosion when it came was too close for comfort, and she felt the repercussion of the blast shaking the foundations of the building. Large flakes of plaster fell from the ceiling and the air was thick with dust. Her hand was trembling as she picked up the cup and saucer. They had been lucky this time, but somebody somewhere must have bought it.

The all clear siren was blasting out its monotone

wail of relief as she let herself out into the back yard. Sidney Travis emerged from the Anderson shelter red-faced and bristling with anger. 'You stupid girl. You might have got yourself killed.'

'I'm all right, Dad. How's Fred?'

Her father shook his head. 'He'll live, but you could have been dead and buried under the rubble if there'd been a direct hit.' He gave her a clumsy hug. 'Give the silly old devil his tea. I'm going inside to see if there's any damage.' He hurried indoors and Ginnie could hear him exclaiming in annoyance, and cursing the Jerries. She hesitated, gazing anxiously at the surrounding buildings, and breathed a sigh of relief when she realised that the parade of shops in Collier Lane had escaped the worst of the blast.

Purpose-built before the war, the box-like units had been designed with living accommodation above and a functional but drab service road at the rear. The concept, Ginnie had always suspected, might have looked stylish and ultra-modern on the architect's plans, but surrounded by a hinterland of small factories and uniform streets of Edwardian terraced houses in one of the poorer suburbs of East London, the Utopian dream had rapidly deteriorated into a shabby mass of concrete and glass. Most of the windows were now criss-crossed with sticky tape and sandbagged, but Sidney had steadfastly refused to have his shop boarded up, declaring that it was bad for business, and Hitler and his Luftwaffe could take a long walk off a short pier for all he cared.

Ginnie knew that they had been lucky this time. They had survived, and she could only hope that no one had been killed when the bomb landed. She hurried into the shelter, wrinkling her nose at the pervasive smell of damp and sweaty bodies. Fred Chinashop was still sitting on the wooden bench looking pale and dazed. She gave him his tea. 'I hope it's sweet enough for you.'

He managed a wobbly smile. 'Ta, love.'

Ginnie glanced anxiously at the only other occupant of the shelter. Ida Richmond lived in a flat above the shop and had been administering her version of first aid to Fred, which consisted of making encouraging noises and fanning him with her handkerchief. 'Is he all right, Mrs Richmond?' Ginnie asked in a whisper.

Ida nodded vigorously, causing her hairnet to slip over one eye. She adjusted it with a practised tweak of her fingers. 'It'd take more than a Jerry bomb to finish our Fred Chinashop.'

Fred nodded in silent agreement and sipped his tea. His real name was Fred Brown but Ginnie's dad had a penchant for giving people nicknames. Fred Brown had become Fred Chinashop in order to distinguish him from Fred Harper, also known as Fred Woollies, the manager of the Woolworth's store situated a little further along the parade. 'I'm fine now, ducks.' Fred raised the cup in a toast. 'Sweety, weaky and milky – just how I like it.'

'He's all right now.' Ida picked up a willow pattern plate piled high with her latest attempt at baking.

'Nelson squares. Try one of these, Fred.' She wafted the cakes under his nose. 'You need building up, love. You're all skin and bone.'

'I won't say no.' He took one and bit into it. 'You're too good to me, Ida.'

'I was just using up the crusts of bread and some dried fruit that had been on the shelf since last Christmas. My hubby doesn't have a sweet tooth and I have to watch my figure.' She beamed at him through the thick lenses of her horn-rimmed spectacles. 'You bachelors don't know how to look after yourselves properly. I dunno why you never got married, Fred. You must have been quite a good-looking feller years ago, before you went bald and lost all your teeth.'

He swallowed the last morsel and took a mouthful of tea. 'I feel better now, Ida. Ta very much, but I'd best get back to my emporium and see if there's any damage. The blast might have shattered what little stock I've got left. It's hard to get hold of decent crockery these days.' He put his cup and saucer on the wooden bench and struggled to his feet, steadying himself with one hand on the wall. 'Thanks for the cuppa, Ginnie.'

'Any time, Fred.' She stood aside to let him pass as he made his way out of the shelter.

Ida rose to her feet. 'That man needs a wife. He lives on tea and toast. No wonder he hasn't got any stamina. My Norman is twice the man he is. He'll scoff this lot in one go.'

'It's very kind of you to share them with us, Mrs Richmond,' Ginnie said, smiling. She was fond of Ida, who had always taken a motherly interest in the Travis family. With no children of her own to care for and a husband who worked long hours on the railways, Ida had nothing to do other than clean her tiny apartment and she was always popping downstairs with samples of her cooking.

'But you haven't tried them yet, love. Norman won't miss one more.'

Ginnie shook her head. 'No thanks. They look lovely but it's nearly lunchtime and I'll be in trouble if I don't eat everything on my plate. Mum will have been slaving away all morning to make something tasty out of next to nothing.'

'You're a good girl, Ginnie. It's a pity your flighty sister isn't a bit more like you.'

'Shirley's all right, Mrs Richmond. She's just high-spirited, that's all.'

'And you're very loyal, ducks.' Ida stepped outside, squinting in the sunlight. 'Let's hope the war ends before you get called up or have to work in the munitions factory like your sister. How old are you now, dear? I lose track.'

'I'll be nineteen in August.'

'At least you've got another year before you're called up. The war might be over by then, God willing.'

'Let's hope so, Mrs Richmond.'

'Your dad would be lost without you, Ginnie.

5

I dunno how he'd manage the shop if you weren't there to give him a hand.'

'I enjoy it,' Ginnie said stoutly. 'Maybe it's not what I'd set my heart on when I was at school, but I've learned how to keep accounts and I know almost as much about carpets and furniture as my dad.'

Ida patted her on the shoulder. 'You're a treasure.' She ambled across the yard and let herself out into the service lane. 'TTFN, ducks.'

Ginnie collected a dustpan and brush from the outside lavatory and hurried into the partitioned off area at the back of the shop that served as an office. She had not been lying to Ida when she said she enjoyed working for her father, but there was a part of her that wished he would allow her to enlist in one of the women's services and do her bit for her country. In a year's time she would be conscripted anyway, or else she would have to do war work like Shirley, but she did not relish the idea of slaving away in the munitions factory or volunteering as an ARP warden.